Flight from Glastonbury

D H DAVIES

Copyright © 2015 D H DAVIES.

Front and Back Cover Illustrations by the author.
Map and Castle Plan by Jack Walsh

All rights reserved. No part of this book may be reproduced, stored, or transmitted by any means—whether auditory, graphic, mechanical, or electronic—without written permission of both publisher and author, except in the case of brief excerpts used in critical articles and reviews. Unauthorized reproduction of any part of this work is illegal and is punishable by law.

ISBN: 978-1-4834-3783-5 (sc)
ISBN: 978-1-4834-3782-8 (e)

Because of the dynamic nature of the Internet, any web addresses or links contained in this book may have changed since publication and may no longer be valid. The views expressed in this work are solely those of the author and do not necessarily reflect the views of the publisher, and the publisher hereby disclaims any responsibility for them.

Any people depicted in stock imagery provided by Thinkstock are models, and such images are being used for illustrative purposes only.
Certain stock imagery © Thinkstock.

Lulu Publishing Services rev. date: 10/13/2015

Acknowledgements

My interest in the Glastonbury-Nanteos Cup legend was rekindled when I moved to Somerset a few years ago, conveniently close to Glastonbury and its great ruined abbey. Then I read Janet Joel's most entertaining account of the history of the present Nanteos mansion and the Powell family (J.Joel: Nanteoa 1996, reprinted 2002, ISBN 0 9533044 0 X). In this she mentions a much earlier house on the site called Neuadd Llawdden, only its cellar still surviving directly underneath the present mansion. I chose to call that earlier house Neuadd Siriol. I now had entry at both ends of the trail my fugitives would take.

Since then various family members have, at different times, accompanied me on visits to the Somerset Levels; Llandeilo and Carreg Cennan Castle; Tregaron and the 'Red Bog', Strata Florida Abbey and to other places in between. I also received family support and encouragement – and some helpful criticism – during the writing phase. I am truly grateful to all concerned.

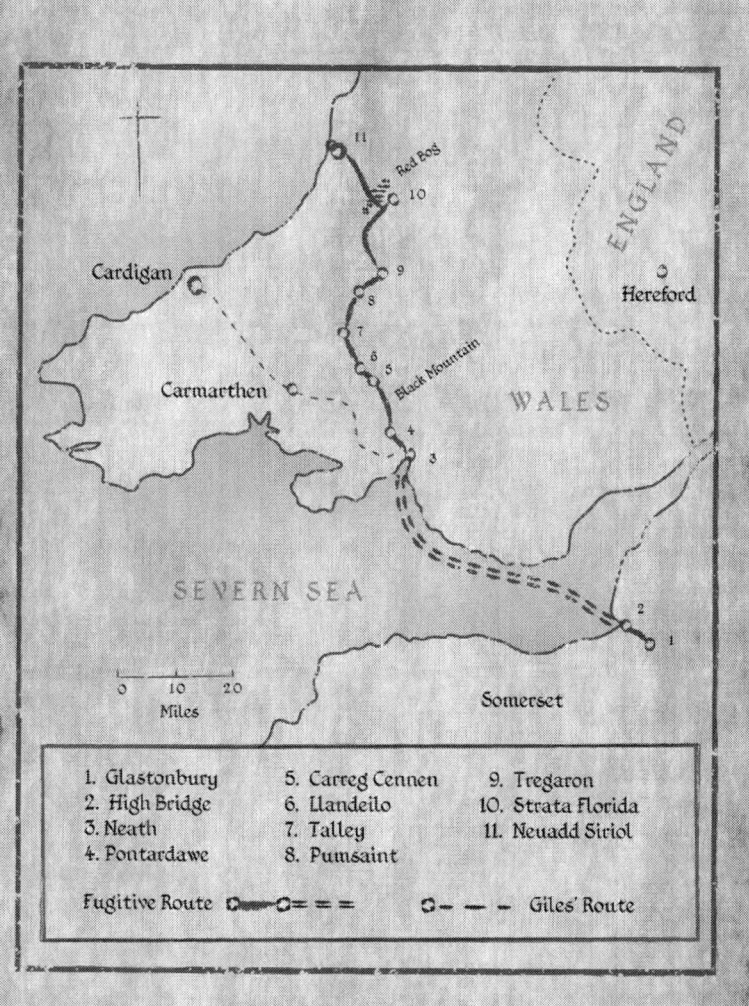

Outline Plan of
CARREG CANNEN
Castle

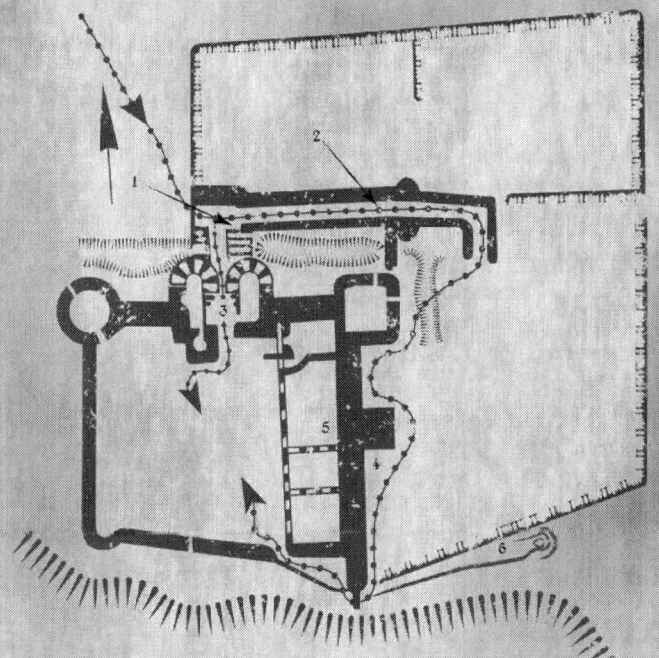

1. Middle Gate Tower (ruins)
2. Barbican (with pits)
3. Gatehouse
4. Chapel Tower
5. Domestic Range
6. Passage and Fissure leading to Cave

  Most Slighted Walls

Attack Routes

 Pits

CHAPTER 1

Glastonbury

Motionless, the man in the shadow of the porch watched as they rode away.

Out of his sight now the leading two men at arms would be turning their horses into the High Street bustle. Behind them the Bishop, soberly dressed for the road but handsomely mounted, had dimmed into the deep shade of the gatehouse. His body servant and a groom leading a laden packhorse rode a respectful distance behind - the bishop was not travelling light on his short journey. Still in the afternoon sunshine the other two men at arms brought up the rear, helmets glinting but lightly armed and relaxed in their saddles: the fifteen miles to Wells would be peaceful enough.

As the great oak doors of the gatehouse closed behind them the creak of harness and pad of hooves died away, the noise of the street hushed to a murmur. They were gone. This Lord Bishop of Bath and Wells might never have to make another such Episcopal Visitation but the watcher felt sure now that others would come in King Henry's name. One last time and all too soon. This monastic House, greatest in all England save only Westminster, was doomed.

Father Ralph Dawnay, Prior of the Benedictine Abbey of Glastonbury, turned abruptly into the abbey church, strode through the echoing nave jewelled with flecks of pure colour from the great windows and into the cloisters beyond. He must think.

Yes, he was certain now: time was fast running out. The smaller monastic houses had all surrendered and he discounted the bland assurances that the greater ones, fulsomely described in that Act of Dissolution as 'great solemn monasteries wherein thanks be to God religion is right well kept and observed', would be spared. That was Thomas Cromwell the jumped-up new Vicar-General, the King's hunting dog, lulling them into complacency, whatever his own abbot chose to believe. But Ralph's contacts at Court had warned him that the king was in desperate hurry to refill his depleted Treasury. He would soon pillage mighty Glastonbury, too. Why else had his Commissioners carried out that inventory of our relics and treasures? Ever since their second appalling visit, when they had accused the brothers of backsliding in religious observance and behaviour and the next moment had carrots of release from vows and life pensions dangled before them like so many donkeys, the message had been clear - we will return in the king's name, then surrender - or else! Not that all their charges against us lacked foundation: God knew how far this and other monastic communities had fallen from grace over the years. Yet nothing could justify this coming extinction.

And now this sleek bishop would hand Cromwell more arguments against them. There was a history of dispute between Wells and Glastonbury, cathedral against abbey, disputes over ecclesiastical authority and over land claims, which in the past had even led to violence, as when retainers from Wells had broken abbey sluices on the Levels. Yesterday the bishop had summoned them to the chapter house to score his own triumph. He had shown himself a subtle man, smilingly encouraging each monk to speak openly. And speak they had! It had been a litany of petty complaints - too many ceremonies, over-long services, denial of access to the library, the abbot's favour for senior monks at the general expense and much else. Even complaints about food, notwithstanding the rich bounty from the abbey's manors and fisheries - a far cry from the austerity of Saint Benedict. Was it to be wondered, the brothers had wailed, that they had been discovered playing at dice and cards? Ralph, became painfully aware of the hollowness of his own faith and the pull of the real world outside the cloister, could understand, even condone some of their grievances. But he despised the meanness of spirit behind it all and the want of intellect and learning among the monks, mostly low-born these days. The Order had been in decline for many generations and today the brothers were a puny lot. Only its spectacular material wealth spoke of the abbey's past glory, hardly a true measure for a house dedicated to serving God, not Mammon. It had been while listening to the bishop in the chapter house that Ralph had finally accepted he no longer belonged in this magnificent husk that was Glastonbury now. He could do more good in that world outside he had once spurned. Irony indeed that the King's greed might soon release him from the cloister!

Yesterday's outpouring of complaints had been disastrous for the abbey. The bishop would report them - not without satisfaction - to Canterbury, Cromwell would get to read it and would seize on it as strengthening his own case against them.

Yet at worst - no, at best - a few abbey treasures might be saved from the king's clutches in the hope of a return to better days. Only portable items of high value, of course, carefully selected. He himself had fallen from the spiritual to the material plane. So be it. It was Father Abbot who bore responsibility under God for the abbey's soul in these stormy days and he had obedientaries enough to support him. He could spare his prior for this humbler task of saving a little of its vast worldly wealth from the king's grasp, to be put to nobler use when - if - sanity returned to England. It would be a dangerous enterprise but one that might assuage his own guilt at his loss of faith - and renew his half-forgotten pleasure in secular and practical activity.

And so, little by little, in such privacy as could be found in a religious house, in snatched half hours in his cell between his duties and the daily Offices, by candlelight before a brief sleep to rise again before dawn for Lauds, he had made his preparations. Father Abbot had already approved this enterprise in principle but seeming abstracted, almost indifferent, requesting to be spared all details until it was time to turn plans into action - an event he seemed to think unlikely. Abbot Richard Whiting was sustained by the serenity of his sure faith, but in old age and sadly failing health he retained too little sense of the brutal reality of royal power.

Lost in thought Ralph realised that he had rounded the cloisters twice. He stopped: the time for action had come and for that he needed the abbot's final sanction. He headed for the Abbot's lodging.

Past the abbey smelting pit, amongst the workshops and stables, John Carpenter was teaching his apprentice. The afternoon was sunny and calm, wood dust barely stirring in the sunbeams slanting across the open front of his workshop. The lad's tousled fair head bent over the bench and he gnawed his lower lip as he concentrated on re-setting a crosscut saw.

'Good, Thomas lad, you've the hang of it.' The lad was deft with his hands and quick to learn: he would make a carpenter. The skinny half-starved waif had shot up these last years into a tall lithe youth, as yet seeming unaware, when errands sent him to the town, of the effect of his comeliness on the girls forever gossiping at the well.

He would make his way in the world well enough and carpentry was a respected trade. Had not our Lord himself worked with wood? An abandoned orphan, Thomas had been taken into the abbey's care eight years ago aged perhaps twelve - that could only be guessed at. The kindly monks had named him Thomas for no particular reason, taught him his letters but finding in him no aptitude for the tonsure, had assigned him to John to learn his trade. He was settled now, content and well-liked. In a year or two, armed with his new skills, he might set up his own shop in the town and settle down with one of those girls whose eyes followed him in the High Street.

'Well, Father Prior, what make you of our bishop's visitation?' The abbot's voice was cool: he had never warmed to his patrician prior. Slumped in his great chair before a fire lit even on this warm day, Richard Whiting looked frailer than ever. He's well over seventy and a sick man, Ralph thought, no longer up to this greatest crisis in our long history.

'He will write an adverse report, Father - which will soon reach Cromwell.'

'And then?'

'It will be the last nail in our coffin. Next time the commissioners descend upon us it will be to demand our immediate surrender. You know well that few monastic houses still survive here in the west country - or elsewhere.'

'But those that have surrendered - and so meekly! - lack our power and wealth.'

'Wealth that makes us the greater prize. King Henry must fill his treasury - where better to look?'

'But think on our prestige and influence in this realm…'

'Greatly diminished now, no longer strong enough to defy a king in a hurry, as once we did. And the gentry back him, for they covet our manors, while many common folk see us as little more than landlords. We stand alone, Father, and must surely fall.'

Whiting closed his eyes, loath to accept this hard truth. 'I have sent money and gifts to Cromwell. I have paid the First Fruits and Tenths. God forgive me, I have signed our consent to the Acts of Supremacy and Succession. What more can I do?' The old voice quavered.

'Nothing more, Father: that is my point. We face dissolution - and soon.'

'Yet even should you be proven right it must take them time - time enough for me to finish Abbot Bere's work on the Edgar chapel and our tidal works on the Levels.'

'The king demands and Cromwell provides with astonishing speed and purpose. That a common blacksmith's - or is it butcher's? - son can organise so well beggar's belief, yet it is so. Believe me, Father, we have no more time: our end comes within a year, likely before this year's end. All that is left us is to see to the well-being of the brothers and all our people, which is your charge before God, while mine is to save what little I can of our worldly treasures from the king's clutches. We have agreed on that and with your sanction I have made my plans. I come now to entreat you most urgently to grant me your authority to act on them without delay.'

Whiting gazed through his sunlit parlour window. It seemed an age before he spoke. 'Very well, Father Prior, if it must be so: choose what treasures you will and seek safe haven for them. You have my authority to act in this.' He groped for his stick.

'Have you no questions for me, Father?' But the old man's lack of interest in practical detail would give him a freer hand.

Whiting sighed. 'Well then, but briefly, for I must rest. When do you plan to leave?'

'At night during the September Fair when the town will be noisy with revellers but sober folk with clearer eyes remain indoors. Then we may slip out unnoticed by the water gate. That gives us five weeks to make all ready.'

'How many brothers will you take with you?'

'I have fixed on seven including myself as the best number for companionship and support on the road without attracting unwonted attention - but only five brothers and two of our laymen. All younger than myself and fit enough for an arduous journey.'

'You will travel deep into the west country, I suppose, where little remains to entice the commissioners.'

A practical thought from the old man but it would not do. 'No, Father, for commissioners already sniff to the west - the King means to net everything. Soon enough we will be pursued. Then the farther we travel west the more we risk being cornered between the widening Severn Sea and the Great Channel. No, we must go north where several ways lie open to us as opportunity arises.'

Now Whiting's face showed interest. 'I see. But if your urgency is justified - which you know I doubt - you must hasten to reach Bristol and then on to Gloucester in time to make your escape, for the commissioners will surely assemble in that area as they did when they came here before. Is that your plan?'

'I wish it could be for then we could cross the Severn dry shod by the bridge at Gloucester and make straight for the heart of England and then if need be go northward where the true faith remains strongest - if the king has not utterly cowed the folk there since their ill-fated uprising. But to make for Gloucester would take us towards, not away from the commissioners as they gather.'

'But - but where then is left to you?'

'Through Wales.'

Whiting, astonished, struggled to sit upright. 'Wales? Why Wales? Surely it is far off your track and it is said to be a wild land, the people there half savage.'

'I can believe it. Yet they are Christians, too. There are Cistercian houses there - if they have not yet all surrendered - who follow our Rule and will shelter us.'

'Men say Wales is a lawless land of brigands where the people speak no English!'

'Some must surely have some English - merchants and gentle folk - if there be such there. But amongst our brothers are two from Wales, who speak their tongue. Brother Hywel is too old to travel but I am minded to ask Brother Evan to come. I know little enough of him for he is a silent fellow, but he looks sturdy and must know his own country - and we must have a native speaker with us.'

'It seems you already have in mind who will accompany you!'

'I believe so, if they agree. There is ….'

Whiting raised a thin blue-veined hand. 'I leave all to you provided only that you leave me all obedienteries save yourself - treasurer, sacristan, almoner and others are needed here, for we still have our daily Offices and our manors to maintain. Do not forget that by far the larger part of our treasure, including our great library, is too bulky to be removed. If possible some of it should be secreted here - no small task for those you leave behind! And I alone must face Cromwell's men if they come again." An edge to that tired voice? Did the abbot think that he, Ralph, had chosen the lighter burden and left him the heavier? And sought to flee the coming storm? Not so. Whiting need only follow other abbots and sign the surrender, meekly but with some show of protest for the record. He would have no choice - and there was the promise of a life pension for all the brothers as compensation: as abbot he could hope for a handsome one. Whiting was truly pious and honourable and surrendering his abbey would cause him deep anguish. But the small band of men he himself would lead would have the more arduous task.

There was something else the abbot should know: 'Father, I have considered how best our party should appear to other travellers.' Ralph paused uncertainly.

But Whiting understood. 'You tell me you propose a pilgrimage?'

'Yes: or rather the semblance of one. In the guise of journeying to a shrine we can travel openly as monks, un-remarked and unmolested.'

Whiting frowned. 'You ask me to condone and bless such a deception on a mission that should be devout?'

'It is truly distasteful, Father, but these are desperate times. Where else could monks be going when monastic houses are closed everywhere? Even were we permitted to doff our habits for laymen's clothes and cease shaving our tonsures they would not quickly grow out. Could we then cover our heads at all hours? No, we are least conspicuous as what we truly are - monks. I see no other way.'

Whiting sighed. 'You argue well as ever, Father, but as ever with a worldly logic: I fear you would not have made abbot.' A shrewd thrust. 'Very well, if it must be so I agree to it. You have perhaps some shrine in mind?'

'Yes. There are several in Wales, but one is best placed for our purpose - that of the Blessed Virgin at a place they call Aber - Aberteifi - I think it is called Cardigan in English - on the west coast. Whiting's eyes brightened. 'I have heard of it. A statue of the Virgin marvellously carved in wood, found by a river bed. It draws many pilgrims. How I wish I could go with you!' He crossed himself.

He has no sense of what our journey will entail, Ralph thought: he could hardly survive crossing the Severn Sea. No matter though, for here the abbot must remain for he alone could surrender the abbey. 'We only seem to go, Father, for although at first our way points in Her direction that is indeed deception, for I plan to turn north where Brother Evan says there is high empty country where we may escape any pursuit. He hoped Whiting had not noticed that he had admitted questioning the Welshman before receiving final sanction for the enterprise, nor realised how little known was that land they must cross. He needed no misgivings from his abbot now.

But Whiting, although visibly tiring, was off on another tack. 'So be it. But, Father Prior, if you do not cross the Severn at Gloucester, how far upstream will you follow it before making your crossing?'

'Not upstream at all, for there lies Wells land, which I am loth to cross now we know its bishop's mind. No, from here we go direct across the Levels to the coast.'

'But then you cross the Severn Sea where it is wide? Surely there lies danger?'

'I acknowledge some hazard, Father, but it is our quickest and safest way into Wales before any pursuit can be organised. Once there we can choose among several ways back into England unnoticed. I shall arrange ship passage to the harbour and borough of Cast - Castell Nedd, as they call it' - again he stumbled over an unfamiliar name - 'where there is a Cistercian abbey, still not surrendered I have heard. There we may seek shelter while preparing to move on inland. I see no alternative.'

'All this because there is an abbey there?'

'There is more. You know it has a thriving sea trade: they own ships and trade regularly with our own wharf at High Bridge - one of their vessels can carry us. And the long estuary there will bear us far inland and well on our way. It all fits well.' Seeing Whiting look dubious Ralph unrolled the map he had brought from the library and weighted it down on the table by the abbot's great chair. 'See here, Father. Here are we and here High Bridge on the coast.' In truth the crackling parchment with its snakelike green squiggles for rivers and crudely sketched castles and towns seemed of little practical use, but the old man should know something of the route he proposed. Pray he did not notice that inland Wales showed largely blank, a terra incognita!

Whiting leaned forward to look. 'So from High Bridge you will sail direct to the coast of Wales - here, where it bulges towards us? That is your shortest crossing. What distance would that be?'

Showing him the map had been a mistake. 'Twenty miles or so direct - his long finger stabbed at the map. 'but ships sail in an arc up this coast and follow it to the river mouth.' Let him not mark that distance: it was nearer sixty miles!

But Whiting was exhausted now. He lay back with his eyes closed, his effort to concentrate painful to watch. When he spoke he was almost inaudible. 'You know your way to the coast over our own lands. I pray God will then see you safe over the water, which I think you do not know. But into Wales, Father Prior?' He shook his white head. 'Well, I must leave all in your hands for I have my own duties to attend to when I have rested.' He heaved a slow breath.' Just two matters more. First, what of daily Offices on your 'pilgrimage'?

'Indeed Father, I have need of your guidance and instruction on that....'

'I know no precedence for this - this adventure of yours - and so must place authority for everything in your hands as its leader. It follows that spiritual matters are also your grave responsibility. Therefore you must decide. Pray well on it, Father.'

Grave indeed in my unworthiness, Ralph thought. But Whiting had turned to practicalities again.

'Now my last comment. I also leave to your judgement which of our treasures you will carry away. As you have said, they must be small and light, yet of high value - some jewels, perhaps?'

'Yes, if well concealed, sewn into our clothing perhaps, for they could attract robbers. I must think further on that.'

'Take what you will: I shall inform Brother Treasurer you have my authority in this as in all matters concerning you enterprise. Arrange all with him and Brother Sacristan.' The old eyes turned with curious intensity to Ralph, then Whiting stood up slowly, grasped his stick and walked stiffly to a massive oak press opposite the window, unlocked it and fumbled inside. Another key scraped in a lock and he turned back to Ralph, holding a small plain wooden box. As he opened it he drew himself upright with sudden dignity.

'Whatever else you choose to take, Father, take what lies in this box. Keep it about your person at all times and guard it always with your life. Of all our treasures this relic, known only to successive abbots, is by far the greatest. You will have heard tell of it but until now you will not have seen it for each abbot has kept it a hidden secret. Reveal it to your companions only under dire necessity and fetch it from me only when you are ready to depart.'

The old man's rheumy eyes had sudden fire in them as he took out a small wooden bowl from the box. 'Father Prior, This will now be your sacred charge. This is the Sangraal, the Holy Grail itself!'

Brother John the Treasurer, Brother Roger the Sacristan and Father Ralph the Prior stood in the choir of the abbey church, notes in hand. For much of the day, whenever the church was empty between the Offices from which Whiting had exempted them, they had worked through the contents of each coffer and press in the treasury and sacristy, then toured the church from Lady Chapel and Galilee to East window, into the transepts and down to the undercroft. Even Ralph had been astounded by the accumulated wealth of relics and reliquaries, vessels and ornaments that had survived the great fire of 1184, or been replaced since. Here was a treasure trove of exquisite craftsmanship in gold and silver, of precious stones, of set and unset jewels and a wealth of coinage. And they had not even visited the great library where four hundred tomes in old script and the newer printing held even greater value, for they were impossible to carry away.

Sadly, the Sacristan eyed the paper in Ralph's hand. 'You are content, Father?'

'Hardly content, this list is pitifully short and to remove even these few items is a grievous business. Yet here is all we can hope to conceal while travelling on foot. Much the greater part must remain in your care, brothers, and you must consider what can be done to save the best of it, and our books too. Come, let us confirm what we have agreed and bring this melancholy task to an end. First in value is the peerless jewel from the altar stone brought by Saint David from the Holy Land, the gift of the Patriarch of Jerusalem.' Instinctively, they looked up where the splendid sapphire had once hung over the High Altar, recalling how it had sparkled in the light from the great east window. Once it had been hidden from marauding Danes, then lost, found again by Abbot Henry in the twelfth century, who reset it with gold and precious stones and consecrated it with chrism. With the first inkling of dissolution it had been taken down once more and hidden by the Treasurer.

'Master Aston shall sew it into his clothing - if its setting does not make it too bulky for even he to conceal. It has great spiritual as well as material value and will be safer with us.' Brother John nodded resignedly: what the abbot had endorsed he must accept, but he was unhappy at the removal of any treasure in his care and this was the greatest of them.

'Second, on a supposed pilgrimage we should carry a known relic. I have settled on one only, the phial of the Blessed Virgin's milk, which is tiny and easily concealed.' The others crossed themselves. They have more faith left than I have, Ralph thought. 'Third, the smaller of the two gold and emerald goblets, although I fear it is barely small enough. Fourth, Queen Philippa's rosary with the gold beads. Fifth, the ancient fragment of tunic woven with gold thread. It is fragile but of great value and weighs little - all other vestments are too heavy and would instantly be missed. Lastly we take as many of the best unset jewels and coins of value as we can carry about us. Should we check these again?' The others shook their heads: they were weary and sad and had already given their reluctant agreement.

'Then we are agreed. Brother John, you have noted the money Father Abbot has granted for the journey?' The treasurer nodded. 'Then that concludes our business for now. See that everything listed here is still in its place: we will speak again about handing over everything into my care - and the money, too - at the last moment before we leave. I need not repeat the need for absolute secrecy in this matter.'

As they left the church Ralph recalled that as Whiting had instructed he had neither listed nor mentioned the little wooden bowl, still with the abbot. What to make of it? There was a legend that the Grail had been brought to Glastonbury by Joseph of Arimathea, rumours much strengthened under Whiting's immediate predecessor Abbot Bere, who had revived the old Joseph cult, proposing his elevation to sainthood and even re-named the glorious Lady Chapel for him. Bere had died only thirteen years ago yet the legend was fading again. To his knowledge no brother had ever claimed to have set eyes on the vessel. Until now. Could it really be?

Had Joseph walked here in ancient Avalon, or was this another old canard to tempt pilgrims and their gifts? God knew there had been trickery in creating Glastonbury's wealth - the supposed presence here of those old Celtic saints Patrick and David and Briget; even the bones of King Arthur who, if he had ever existed, would likely have been some pagan warlord, notwithstanding his alleged remains being re-buried before the high altar in the presence of a king. Had the commissioners known about the bowl they would have reviled it as popery: as it lacked monetary value they would have burned it. He would keep his promise to Whiting and take it, but he could not believe in it.

Yet if the true Grail existed? Somewhere. Where might it have rested all these centuries? Why not Glastonbury? And what would it be? Some had believed that the jewelled silver chalice he had just seen in the Treasury - too large to be taken with them - had been the cup used by Our Lord at The Last Supper. He had heard of other claimants as splendid around Europe. But in all reason could a poor wandering teacher with nowhere to lay His head have used such a costly vessel? Or would He have used such a plain wooden bowl as this? Whiting, like Abbot Bere before him, clearly thought so, as must have previous abbots who had concealed it for generations. He remembered handling it very gently under Whiting's anxious eyes; a shallow wooden bowl barely a hand's breadth across, like an old mazer bowl but blackened and worn with age. Surely it was a more credible relic from that upper room in Jerusalem than a costly chalice better suited to Master Malory's romance! Unless, of course, it was the wealthy Joseph's room Christ and the disciples had used - and his cup? In which case?... No more of that: their departure drew near and practical matters demanded his attention. He could find comfort in that.

Sleep would not come to Brother Evan. He lay on his narrow cot, half-hearing the snoring and snuffling of his brother monks through the thin cell partitions, his eyes open but unseeing in a darkness hardly lightened by the tiny lamp at the head of the stairs leading down to the church, down which he would soon shiver in midnight chill to Lauds. Father Prior's offer of a place on his 'pilgrimage' had deeply unsettled him. He had a choice to make.

Six years ago, after weeks of wandering far from his home in the heart of Wales, he had sought shelter in the abbey. Sanctuary more than just shelter was the truth of it, although he soon realised he was neither pursued nor charged. He had offered himself as a man with a new-found zeal in his middle years to serve God by prayer and work - Ora et Labora, their Rule had it. That falsehood had imperilled his soul, for even then he knew he lacked true calling for cowl and tonsure. It was refuge he sought, a place to forget and be forgotten. He thought he had found it here. Since that desperate evening six years ago no-one had followed to accuse him. But, although still to take his final vows, he was now and forever exiled from his native Wales by his sin.

For Evan had sinned. He had killed a man. It had been an accident - a drunken lout reeling from an alehouse as Evan passed by, then viciously pawing a young girl come to her hut door to throw out slops; his own instinctive intervention; a clumsy struggle in the darkness as they wrestled across the road. The man had stumbled drunkenly, fallen heavily and broken his head on the low stone wall overlooking the river. Had the terrified girl seen something before she bolted her door? But in her distress and perhaps gratitude it was unlikely she had spoken of it to anyone, or he would have been pursued long since. Evan could still hear that sickening crack of head on stone, still make out in the darkness the black blood seeping onto the stones. He had panicked then and toppled the motionless body over the wall into the fast-flowing stream below. That terrible night he had fled his home for ever, a felon and a fugitive.

At heavy cost. He had abandoned his hill farm, small but freely held, where his years of toil were at last beginning to bear fruit. Far worse, he had striven to renounce his dream - his impossible dream - of someday winning the hand of Mistress Llwyd.

Eluned Llwyd, mature now but surely lovely still, had fathomless brown eyes, a sweet low voice and a stillness in repose that cried cartref - home - and pierced his heart. He had loved her and would always love her - but always from afar. She lived at Neuadd Siriol, her family home across the valley, mistress of the manor and carer of her ailing father. The name meant 'Pleasant Hall.' Pleasant it was indeed, a substantial homestead built onto an older hall, with grazing and timber on the slopes and arable land on the valley floor, for the family had connections and had become prosperous. She had seemed content with her lot. Was she? Evan had never revealed his feelings: he was never free with words and ever aware that she ranked above himself, whom the English might call a yeoman. Yet when by chance they met after church or at feast days or market she had smiled and spoken to him as to an equal and her father was ever courteous. He could neither reasonably hope nor shut hope out.

That dreadful night he had gathered a few possessions and fled without a word to anyone - what could a felon say? Since then, despite the rigours of monastic life, she was ever in his thoughts. But she was lost to him, surely married by now, perhaps blessed with children, and he must live out his life in an aching void which endless prayer and duty could never fill in the absence of the certain faith he could see in his fellow monks. Years of striving to resign himself to the cloister in lieu of life!

But now the king's assault on the monasteries, which was turning the realm on its head, had brought him the unexpected hope of freedom. If he understood aright - so much was yet unclear - when a monastic house was surrendered monks who had not taken their final irrevocable vows would be offered release from those already taken and be granted small pensions. He could be free of the abbey and its Rule, a freedom which with a sense of shame he knew he now longed for.

And now Father Prior had offered the means to leave and return to Wales at no cost to himself - as a monk he had no money - and with companions to ease the journey and provide some protection. He had never been able to bring himself to make confession of his sin as he should have, but surely to kill by accident while protecting another was no mortal sin. Could Father Prior's offer mean God's blessing was on him - in this at least! He could never return to his farm - what had happened to that? - for he could not bear to see her again, unattainable in this life and himself a stained killer. But at least he could end his days quietly somewhere else in Wales.

Yet King Henry's recent Acts of Union with Wales must have changed his native land. It had marked the end of such Welsh laws that had survived the English conquest centuries ago. Welsh law had been more benign than English, holding to compensation more than retribution. But now English law alone ruled Wales. Did that spell danger to him? Yet six years had passed since he had left: if he kept his head down he should be safe enough and might find work on a farm again, if never his own. And he had skill with leather, had worked with it at the abbey: leatherwork was always in demand. With hard work he might prosper, perhaps even find the means to compensate the family of that drunkard he had killed, if he had any.

He knew his mind now. Whatever the hazards of the journey no chance like this would come his way again. He must seize it. He would go with the prior. The burden of indecision lifted, he slept briefly until the tinkling little bell called him to Lauds.

His last full night at the abbey. Alone in the vast darkness Ralph Dawnay, Prior of Glastonbury Abbey, lay prostrate on the cold tiles before the high altar. Behind him the silent black cavern of the longest church in England stretched beyond the great arches of the crossing into seeming infinity. Between Compline and Lauds, all others abed, he was alone in its immensity. His candle shed its feeble glow to the base of the altar: above, Christ was lost in darkness. With their departure set for the following night, the die cast, Prior Ralph, a man known to all as devout and arrogantly firm of purpose, confronted once more the self doubt he hid from all but himself. Was this perilous journey he had planned justified before God, was he the man to lead it, would he be true to himself in so doing? Tonight he had prayed for reassurance but his prayers would not flow, were mere empty mumblings. He could not see Christ on His cross above. Could not reach him. He had received nothing, learned nothing.

No, not nothing! Once more he confronted the truth about himself. Chilled on the cold tiles like a medieval knight at vigil before a quest - odd to see himself again as a warrior like the fabled Arthur lying nearby - he knew at last with finality that the core of faith he once thought he possessed had vanished. Knew it with dismay, with guilt, but with certainty.

Well then. If unworthy of the cowl he would strive to be worthy of a place in the troubled world outside these walls. This coming journey would begin his new life. He would lead his small band as the good soldier he had once been rather than as false prior and priest - with fortitude, worldly resolution and firm discipline. A last chance to find meaning in his life.

He rose stiffly to his feet, picked up his candle and went to his final preparations.

Compline had past. It was a night of raw drizzle, a disheartening start for their journey. The September Fair was underway outside, drizzle or no drizzle, its noise not diminished enough by the abbey's thick walls. For the first time all seven of the travellers were gathered together in this one room, the abbot's private parlour that Whiting, surprisingly, had offered for their use because it was away from the ever-curious eyes of a closed community. Bread, meat and small beer were set out for their refreshment. Ill at ease, the abbot had welcomed them briefly, ordered them to obey Father Ralph in all things from now on and blessed their enterprise before departing shakily on his chaplain's arm to his bed. He no longer denies the impending disaster, Ralph thought, and has responded as best he can. Nowhere else could they have found this secrecy - and secrecy was vital tonight.

Only I have been in here before, Ralph realised. This sumptuous room was the abbot's private retreat, rarely admitting even dignitaries of his own lofty status, who were usually entertained in the abbot's hall below. It was familiar to him only because in his physical decline Whiting had become ever more reclusive, more and more leaving the day to day control of the abbey to his prior. He rarely left his lodgings now except to retreat to one of his manors. And because his great staircase had become a hazard for him it was here, rather than to the public offices below, that Ralph had come regularly to consult him.

The other six 'pilgrims' were sipping their ale, gazing wide-eyed at the rich furnishings, the glowing reds, blues and gold of the religious scenes painted on the walls, the velvet cushions, the silverware winking in the light of four-candle wall sconces, even a costly tapestry. Their faces showed amazement at the contrast between this opulence and the austerity of dortor and warming room - although monks now lived far more comfortably than Saint Benedict would have condoned - and the lodgings of lowly laymen like Thomas in musty nooks over barn or workshop.

One by one Ralph studied their faces. Had he made the best choices? Cloistered for years, could the four monks cope with the arduous road ahead? Sprawled in a chair by the fire as if by right was the one he had intended for his deputy yet now doubted the most.

Brother Giles Clifford, thin-faced and dark, was like himself a scion of a gentle family and like himself had learning and some years of soldiering behind him. His youthful experience of rough living in the field, beyond the imaginings of most monks, could have proved valuable, as could his lineage. The two had first met some fifteen years previously during the young King's rash intervention against France in the so-called Italian War and had become comrades in arms in the forces of the Duke of Suffolk and his Imperial allies in their sally from Calais into France. England had played only a small part in the war that had ranged across Europe, but their forces had advanced through Picardy, crossed the Somme and come within fifty miles of Paris before turning back for lack of support. Like Giles, he had been seeking youthful adventure and military honour before taking up his inheritance. Like him he had soon become disillusioned and then appalled at the filth, disease and drunkenness of the common soldiery, their looting and burning of harmless villages, rape of women and the wholesale slaughter of people and animals that had fouled their passage. They had shared a growing revulsion against the unexpected horror of war. Disgusted, on their return to England each had renounced the sword and gone his separate way. Ralph, no longer feeling close family attachments and with too little thought, had sought a new life in the abbey and for a time believed it enough. He had been delighted when Giles had arrived at the abbey declaring his wish to take the cowl. After his month as postulant Giles had been accepted. A monk's training was long and Giles had taken his solemn vows only a year ago, by which time Ralph was ordained a priest and newly installed as prior. Re-living their war experiences had re-kindled their comradeship. When Ralph had planned this enterprise he had seen Giles as his natural deputy and he was the first person he had asked to join him.

But now he had doubts. Giles had never spoken of his years between sword and cowl but Ralph suspected he had suffered in some hell of his own. For Giles had changed. Unlike himself, whose purpose he now knew had been driven not by true faith but by his need to escape a world become as repugnant to him as the battlefield, Giles' experiences, whatever they had been, had turned him fanatically to God. The undoubted faith he had brought to Glastonbury had warped into a religious zeal so avid, so obsessive that the two had found less and less in common. Had the monastic system survived Giles might - if he retained his sanity - have made abbot. Unlike himself - Whiting had the truth of it there! But was such zeal suited to this sham pilgrimage? Had he chosen the old Giles too hastily, given too much credence to their shared class with its assumption of born leadership? Had he landed himself with an unworldly unbalanced zealot? It was too late to change now yet he could not shrug off his misgivings.

At least he could feel sure of Robert Aston. One of the lay stewards, he sat comfortably in the other fireside chair, heavy set and putting on weight. He was a man who liked to dress well but Ralph was pleased to see that now his doublet was unadorned, the shirt showing through his sleeve slashes of plain material, the jerkin and the gown he had taken off in the warm room equally workaday and unobtrusive. Aston had the practical mind befitting his office and he knew the outside world and was comfortable in it. Ralph could rely on his good sense.

On a low stool, legs akimbo, sat Brother Evan, the dark sturdy Welshman. In Wales they would rely on his knowledge of the language and the country. He was a man of few words but seemed to possess some learning. But he was not English so could he be trusted? He should have found out more about him than just his knowledge of Welsh and Wales, but there had been no-one else he could have turned to for that.

The young novices Francis and Matthew, the one red haired, the other brown, sat on the floor against the far wall whispering together, inseparable as usual. He had chosen them for little more than their young limbs and cheerful energy, for they had been raised and schooled in the cloister and were woefully innocent of the world into which they must now be thrust. Being under twenty four years of age they had recently been declared free of their first vows, but might not yet realise that fact. Farthest from the fire the strapping young carpenter's apprentice Thomas stood respectfully; almost as innocent as the apprentices and with less book learning. Ralph had chosen him because John Carpenter had reported him strong, quick to learn and gifted with his hands. This journey might need brawn as much as brain and the lad was said to lack neither.

A mixed bunch indeed, five monks including himself and two laymen. Hardly ideal choices: that was all too obvious now! He had chosen them largely by default for after discounting the old, the frail, the utterly unpractical and the unavailable there had been few to choose from. Well, they must suffice. At least they had their health and he alone was over forty years old, although Aston and Brother Evan must come close.

During the last month Ralph had spoken to each of them privately - a privacy difficult to arrange. He had sworn them to secrecy, outlined his plan, assured them of the abbot's approval and finally invited them to join his enterprise - for in this he could not command. He had emphasised the dangers and invited questions, for he would not deceive them, and had insisted they think on the matter with care. He had been surprised but pleased when to a man they had agreed to come for, ever aloof, he had not realised the full extent of the rumours and unease now sweeping through the abbey. No doubt some of them were pushed as much as pulled. Only Brother Evan had asked a significant question - was it still true that when the abbey surrendered the brothers would be released from their vows and if so how would that be arranged - and when? He had replied that such was promised but as yet not explained: they must be content with that. Ralph wondered if any of them realised that as the only ordained priest amongst them he himself could never expect release. Or how he longed for it!

Weeks of secret preparation had followed, unavoidably involving a few persons outside the abbey. Aston's outside contacts had proved invaluable. Each monk now had a new travelling cloak, new shoes and pattens, large satchels and enough underclothing and utensils for the journey. Aston had provisioned himself and had found Thomas some basic needs. Meantime Aston had paid a widowed seamstress he trusted to sew pouches to be concealed inside clothing to hold money and jewels.

Then the problem of transport. The abbot had authorised use of his barge to the coast - if questioned he could claim it had been taken without his authority - but crossing the wide Severn Sea presented a problem. Ralph had taken a horse from the stables and ridden to the coast to negotiate with a shipmaster trading out of Castell Nedd who came regularly to High Bridge. He had enjoyed the rare feel of a horse under him but haggling over a price for carrying passengers on the ship's return voyage had not been to his fastidious taste. But in the end all was settled and he had given the mariner a sealed letter for the Cistercian abbot warning of their arrival and an approximate sailing date was agreed - cargoes and winds did not allow precision.

From then on he had timed each stage of his preparations backwards from that date. He hoped they would not be held up at High Bridge, which was overlooked by See of Wells land and where their monks' habits might arouse suspicion. He had arranged for food and shelter for his party before boarding ship. More than once Ralph had despaired of seeing an end to all these details. But the enterprise was his own idea and in truth he was finding pleasure in turning his hand to worldly matters again.

Money was not an immediate problem. Whiting had instructed Brother John to provide him with sufficient coinage, which was already distributed among them in their new pouches together with the smaller treasures. They should have enough money to buy food along the way and so would not need a pack animal - hardly seemly for a pilgrimage. But they must keep the money hidden from robbers and pickpockets. Especially in Wales! Too late, he was developing misgivings about passing through that obscure land.

He had told each of them to come tonight ready to leave and to make no farewells - let their absence be discovered after they were safe away. He was pleased to see they all wore their new shoes and their new satchels looked well filled.

Time for a few last words. Ralph rose to his feet.

※

It was dark: time to go. Will Ford the abbey boatman bolted his hut door, drew his hood over his head, hoisted a bulky sack on shoulders hunched against the thin drizzle drifting in across the Levels and headed for the river. A morose solitary man, he mumbled curses against his masters up at the abbey for ordering him out at this God-forsaken hour. What call did they have for a boat now? And why the abbot's barge, the biggest and clumsiest of them? He would have to take the steering oar all the way, leaving the rowing to useless monks, lubberly pen pushers all: it would be a long night. He hated them all, especially that pompous Prior who poked his long nose into everything and might endanger his profitable sideline selling the abbey's eels.

The Prior had ordered him to ready the barge to take a party of seven down the River Brue to the sea at High Bridge and bring it back empty. For his return passage he would be given money to hire oarsmen among the idlers always loitering at the quayside. He was given no reason for all this but there had been alehouse talk of a pilgrimage. They wanted to leave from the old town wharf at the little bay south of the town, a quarter mile from the abbey water gate. Before the abbey's dug channels had drained half the Levels there had been enough depth of water at that wharf. Now a man-made channel carried river craft to it.

Will walked up its towpath to look at the river. The winter rains had not begun in earnest and the black water flowed gently. But no-one knew better than he how quickly the river could change: even this drizzle might mean a hard pull back, although if the west wind held he could raise the sail re-crossing the Meare Pool.

The narrow twenty-five foot barge was in good order for it still carried goods if few people these days. He checked it over. Under the thwarts lay the steering oar, two poles, the four short rowing oars - long sweeps were useless on the narrow stream - and the stumpy mast. The single weathered brown sail lay on the deck amidships covering a pile of sacks. A small anchor and coils of rope were in place at the bow: astern lay his long wicker eel traps, other fishing tackle and two wooden balers. From his sack he took out the leather jacks of ale and the box of bread, cheeses and apples sent down from the abbey and wedged them firmly under the thwarts. They would not get far on such meagre provender and again he wondered where they were going. He knew of no shrine along the coast and anyway it was rumoured the king no longer approved of shrines. And why leave at this late hour?

Well, it was no concern of his. There was no more to do until they arrived. He had carried out the prior's orders - later he might hope for more profitable ones. Will curled up on the sacks and pulled the heavy sail over him. Presently he slept.

As Ralph stood up the murmuring died. His haughty mien had never inspired affection but his tall stately figure commanded respect, his rank no little awe. And had Father Abbot not enjoined them to obey him in all things on this enterprise?

The noise from the town was now intrusive. September fairs always turned unruly and Ralph had checked that the abbey gates were locked and the porters alert. Earlier he had climbed to the northwest corner of the walls to observe the market place below. This was the fair's main focus and from here he could view its extensions along the High Street and south into Magdalene Street. Already stalls selling food, all manner of craft goods, remedies for every ailment and much else plied a brisk trade. Crowds jostled around the booths, some folk were already drunk and more noisy, two groups jigged to ill-played pipes, a chained bear moped in a corner, an unruly line of youths pranced through the crowds bearing flaming torches, a fortune teller drew a crowd in one corner, a latter-day Lollard thundered at another. A group of men crouched around a lantern under the abbey wall throwing dice. From somewhere came the mournful lowing of penned cattle. The fair was said to be a shadow of its former self: to him it was still vulgar excess. But it would serve to cover their escape from the far side of the abbey.

Ralph raised his strong voice above the fair's hubbub. 'Brothers; all of you. Darkness has fallen and it is time for us to depart. You know our purpose and each of you has agreed to join me on this journey. Anyone wishing to withdraw may do so now without reproach although still bound to secrecy. We cannot know what may lie ahead and I want only willing companions. Are you all still with me?' There were nods and shuffling of feet: no-one withdrew.

'Good. Now to explain again briefly - we can speak more when safe away. First, you carry amongst you some of the abbey's richest small treasures that I seek to save from Cromwell's foul clutches.' There was a growl of approval. 'Speak of these treasures to no-one: I repeat, to no-one! If our secret leaks out before we are well away we fail and will be taken and punished. Be in no doubt what Cromwell will do.'

'Second, we aim to travel unnoticed, appearing to others as the monks and attendants we truly are, now on pilgrimage. We travel light taking little for our comfort. If provisions become meagre - as they well may - they will be shared equally amongst all.' Eyebrows were raised: that had not been the way of the abbey.

'Third, we avoid all king's men and especially his commissioners, some of whom I believe will return very soon with attendants to close down our abbey. Once they discover abbey treasures are missing we must expect pursuit - so be ever wary. I expect these enemies of the true faith to assemble and come down the old Roman way from the northeast.' There were puzzled looks from those who lacked any sense of direction and Ralph saw how lost they would be without his leadership. 'To avoid them we will take ship across the Severn Sea into Wales and then, when the way is clear, turn back into England to seek safe haven for the precious objects we carry - and for ourselves, God willing: as always the future lies in His hands. This night we cross the Levels to the coast, travelling not over land where some may still be abroad to report us, but by the abbot's barge on the River Brue. Except in high flood the river lies below the level of the land so we will be shielded from prying eyes by trees and reeds and can rest our legs, which will be tested soon enough.' He did not add that rowing would sorely test unaccustomed arms, even downstream. 'Our vessel awaits. I shall say a brief prayer, then gather your belongings and follow me quietly.'

The drizzle had eased into a thin mist as they came down the path from the water gate, the noise from the fair distant now. At their head Prior Ralph's flaming torch lit their way. Behind him the other monks fell by custom into pairs, Giles and Evan first, the novices behind, Giles held aloft the abbey's tall pilgrims' staff surmounted with its silver crucifix that they would bear on their journey. Then came Aston and lastly Thomas with a sack over his shoulder.

As they reached the moored barge they heard snoring. Unceremoniously Ralph awoke the boatman with river water scooped up with a bailer.

'I said keep watch, not sleep. Is all ready?' Spluttering, Will nodded surlily.

'Very well. You will take charge on the river.'

Swearing under his breath Will placed Evan and Thomas on the rear thwart, the novices forward of them, and showed them how to put oar to rowlock. Giles moved to the bow, raised the staff like a small mast and stared ahead. Momentarily the pale half moon appeared, coldly lighting its silver figure of Christ. In the instant before it was again masked by cloud Giles turned his face towards it and Ralph saw the whites of his upturned eyes: his lips were moving silently. His misgivings returned: Giles would need watching. Aston and Ralph sat on sacks near the stern, leaving room for the boatman to cast off and take the steering oar. Peering at Aston, Ralph was satisfied nothing showed of the bulbous little goblet under his incipient paunch. He himself had the wooden bowl strapped at his lower back, but it pressed hard as he leant against the side of the barge and he eased it to one side. At least the jewels and money were easier concealed amongst them. He dowsed his torch in the water, plunging them into near darkness as Will growled at his novice crew to row.

A sorry business they made of it at first, out of time and catching crabs, all but Thomas, who had evidently rowed before: apprentices were given many tasks. When Will instructed the others to take their time from him and Thomas to shorten his stroke to their poor abilities they began to make progress. Settling gradually into a passable rhythm they moved slowly downstream, aided by the gentle current.

Near the low Beckery mound the river turned north into a straight reach long since canalised by the abbey. Giles, emerging from an apparent trance, asked to stop and pray at the oratory of Saint Bridget.

Ralph shook his head. 'We have hardly started. We can stop for nothing now.'

'It is a holy place, Father, once the shrine of the Blessed Mary Magdalene ...'

'Thank you, brother, I am aware of it. But we must put distance between ourselves and the abbey while we have darkness.' Giles withdrew into himself again and they rowed on in a silence broken only by the creak and whump of oars and the splash and drip of their blades, occasionally the cry of a water bird, the startling splash of a fish. The silence of being on water at night was unfamiliar and eerie enough to stop the novices' chattering. They rowed on in near silence, Will feeling his way by experience in the gloom. He alone had much sense of where they were.

Presently the Brue became its natural self again, curving between the spectral silhouettes of alders and willows gliding past against the night sky above the level of their heads. Sometimes they heard the raucous croaking of frogs before silence returned.

Presently Will instructed the rowers: 'The stretch ahead is narrow for oars. 'Ship your oars - lift them into the boat. Careful you ....' he shouted above the clattering that followed: Francis had almost lost his oar. As they slowed Ralph noted that the boatman had not used the respectful 'Brother.' Respect was breaking down in these turbulent times and he must learn to accept it. But he was grateful for the skill and knowledge of the boatman: practical experience would be invaluable from now on. He wondered again about Giles.

Will growled orders. 'Turn to face the bow - yes, the front end. Right around. Pick up your oars and hold them short - not in the rowlock, you .....' Now paddle - dip your oar straight down and pull - gently!' As they picked up a little speed the loom of the banks closed in.

Gruffly, Will explained: 'Now comes a stretch where we had best pole. Then comes the Meare Pool and beyond that the river is wider and easier to the sea. But the poles are not easy to use. I will take one and young Thomas the other. Will you take the steering oar, Father, just keeping her in midstream?' Ralph nodded curtly: this was menial work but he must be seen to do his share.

Thomas managed the poling well, his natural dexterity almost matching that of the boatman. Soon they entered the broad pool and it was time to settle down to the oars again. The novices were tiring now - it was many years since choir monks had followed Benedict's strict Rule of Labora. But all the rowers had settled into a rhythm and Will decided to keep the same four across the pool.

Suddenly the half moon emerged again from behind a cloud, casting its pale light on the broad water. Ralph knew they must be careful here.

He whispered: 'Harken all! Keep silent across this open water, for on the far bank lie the water bailiff's house and the fish house with its keeper, although I hope they lie abed at this hour. But sound carries far over water and there are no banks here to hide us. Row softly and no talking.' He should have brought cloths to muffle the oars but one could not think of everything.

They moved quietly across the pool. Ralph sighed with relief when suddenly it clouded over again. Will, eyes straining for the gap in the low black smear of land ahead where they would re-enter the river, was becoming suspicious. What need for this silence? Why these precautions on a pilgrimage? Why did no-one show surprise at the prior's strange warning?

Once back in the river channel Ralph called a halt for rest, food and a change of rowers. Will tied up the barge by an over-hanging willow that gave some shelter from the rain spotting again. They climbed the steep little bank and scattered to relieve themselves, returning hungrily to their sparse fare.

Will grumbled: 'We could have cooked fish!'

'No time and no fire! Do as I say!' No fire? Again Will wondered at this caution. Presently they stretched stiffening limbs and set off again, Ralph, Aston and an abstracted Giles joining the tireless Thomas at the oars. The outflow from the pool made rowing a little easier. But most of their journey to the sea still lay ahead and the rowers bent their backs in silent resignation.

Slowly the night air cooled. Time crawled. Only one incident broke the monotony. In the darkness Will for once misjudged a bend in the river and the bow drove heavily into the soft bank, the stern swinging wide in the slow current. No damage was done to the stout barge but the abrupt stop threw all but Will at the steering oar onto their knees. As they scrambled to their feet a small shower of coins clattered around Giles' feet from his carelessly fastened pouch and those nearest stooped to retrieve them. Ralph frowned: he had no wish to draw Will's attention to their money. But even on pilgrimage the boatman would not expect them to travel entirely without funds. They carried on, the rowing ever more laborious, seeming endless.

Hours later, with a slow dawn breaking, they were exhausted when flickers of yellow light showed through the humped arch of a bridge ahead - torches along the High Bridge wharves. It was nearly daylight when they pulled wearily toward the low shore of a curving bay partly cut off from the sea by a spit of sand. Pale smoke marked small settlements around the edge of the bay, a larger one dimly visible to the south. Thankfully they tied up at the abbey wharf.

Along it, fronting a huddle of fishermen's shacks, stood a row of weathered timber buildings. Ralph led them to the largest one, a chandler's shop and warehouse. John Hamblin the wharf steward emerged to usher them up an outer staircase into a low attic above, where pallets of clean straw and blankets awaited them. Groaning with relief, monks and laymen alike fell onto them and at once lay dead to the world.

Ralph had made these arrangements on his first visit, judging the wharf steward trustworthy. Hamblin's family owed much to the abbey. It gave him steady work and granted his mother a small pension when his father, an abbey tenant, had died. With the money John sent her this enabled her to remain on their small holding, now farmed by her younger son Luke. It was useful to have a loyal and grateful man to keep an eye on events here and Ralph had told John his plan in confidence.

Hamblin, a faithful servant of the abbey, had approved and was prepared for them. 'As you ordered, Father, food and fire are ready. I can cook.'

The prior grunted. 'They need sleep more: they are not hardened to this. Let them lie while I find our ship.' There was no sleep for him yet for he must pay off the boatman and finalise arrangements with the ship's master - pray God it had arrived!

Will Ford was impatient for the money to hire rowers for the return journey. He hoped for something for himself - on top of what he intended keeping from the hiring money. But this was a sharp-eyed skinflint prior, so he was pleasantly surprised at the sum he counted out from the purses handed to him. No cause to haggle!

Knowing it a waste of time to tell this man to keep his mouth shut about their journey Ralph could only hope his pilgrim tale would pass muster. As ever his manner was peremptory. 'Go straight back - no dallying. I need not tell you to keep those purses hidden. Pay off your men only when you are safe back. Go now.' Will stuck out two fingers as Ralph turned back up the wharf. To his relief the ship was berthed there, its prow to the estuary mouth. 'Rhonwen' was crudely painted on the stern - whatever that meant. It was a crayer, a coastal cargo vessel. Twice as long as the barge and much wider with decking, it seemed ready for sea. His charges would welcome enough room to stretch out and its size would be some comfort on open water - which none save Giles and himself would have experienced before.

Ralph scanned the low-lying shore for the hides of land owned by the See of Wells. All seemed quiet there but he was anxious to get away.

'A girl's name, Father, like many ships.' The ship's master was at his elbow.

'What is, fellow?'

'My ship's name. Welsh - in English Rowena. High time it was changed to English.'

Ralph looked down his long nose at the squat seaman. 'You are English?' The man nodded. Ralph cared nothing for the vessel's name; only that it would sail soon.

'Are you ready to sail for Castell Nedd?' Again he hesitated over the name.

The seaman grinned. 'Most call it Neath now, Father, the Welsh tongue being out of favour since Union.' That was a relief anyway: he had no time for foreign babble. The man pointed to the gangplank, up which his crew were hefting bales and boxes. 'We are still loading, but if this wind holds we sail in two hours.'

This was better than Ralph had hoped. 'I shall have my people ready. How long across the Severn Sea?'

A shrug of the shoulders. 'Wind and sea attend no man. If both hold fair we should reach Neath before nightfall.' So it would be a long day, but hopefully a restful one.

As Ralph walked back to the chandler's shop he noticed a hill beyond the wharf buildings. Above its wooded slope a lone horseman stood motionless. Watching the wharf? He sought out Steward Hamblin.

'That little hill behind where you smoke your fish - whose land is that?'

'The hill is Brent Knoll, Father. I think it belongs to Wells. It is said there were once disputes with them over land.'

'Thank you. I know my abbey's history.' As he watched the rider turned his horse and trotted away.

Wells! Ralph recalled the bishop's frosty visitation. Was the horseman looking for them already? Would he report seeing black habits on the quay? If so, to whom? But what could he report? Their 'pilgrimage' was no secret - he had put that tale about himself - and what was suspicious about monks on their own land taking ship on pilgrimage? Ah, but it was said the king was beginning to close shrines, having apparently chosen to forget he had once gone barefoot to Walsingham, so his commissioners might want his party stopped. Yet it would take hours for a horseman to pick his way through the half-tamed, trackless maze of heath, summer grazing and dangerous marsh of the Levels to report to anyone: they should have time enough to get away. Yet should this fine weather break or they lost the tide or ….. Enough! They were in God's hands - how glib that too-ready phrase sounded on his tongue.

He found Giles snoring, his arms around the crucifix like a lover. It was time the zealot did something useful. Roughly Ralph shook him awake.

'Get the others up and ready: we leave as soon as we have breakfasted.' Downstairs he found the steward. 'Can you have breakfast for us within the hour?'

John did them proud. Washed and dressed, they came downstairs to a meal of fresh cooked fish, a sallet and bread, small beer, even a little watered wine. The novices' faces showed the resilience of youth while their elders looked a little rested. With more repose on the ship and, he hoped, some days of shelter at Neath Abbey, they should be fit for the strenuous walking to come in Wales. So far things went well.

Prior Ralph, bearing the pilgrims' staff high, led his small procession to the ship, the monks chanting softly. He hoped they looked like a pilgrimage, albeit a remarkably small one. Wharf idlers gathered curiously around them, rough-looking men but amiable enough at this sober hour. The novices looked apprehensive.

There was a promising south-westerly wind. Ralph was anxious to depart, but the last boxes and tackle were still being loaded. Thomas and the novices gazed open-mouthed at the unfamiliar broad waters of the bay. A few onlookers edged closer, grinning and chattering. Evan watched them silently; Aston sat relaxed on a bollard; Giles, who had retrieved what he seemed to regard as his personal staff, gazed vacantly out to sea; Ralph eyed the knoll but was reassured to see no-one there. At last they were motioned on board, the gangplank was raised, then the worn brown sail and they eased away from the wharf, the master and a crewman at the steering oar. The novices edged towards the bow, now uneasy and pale. Seasick already, Ralph wondered? Looking back, he thought he glimpsed the horseman on the hill again.

Will Ford watched the ship leave. He was in no hurry to return to Glastonbury but he was exceeding thirsty and his purses were heavy. He made for the only alehouse.

The water in the bay was calm but as they sailed between the tip of the sand spit and a tiny islet the wind freshened a little. Now came the first lift of waves. The novices squawked in alarm and clutched at their rosaries. But the waves were gentle, the sun shone and the travellers heard the reassuring chuckling of the little bow waves. Soon their spirits lifted in the pure pleasure of being at sea on a fine fresh day.

Except for the novices, at sea for the first time in their lives with nothing but open water ahead. Presently Brother Evan approached Ralph.

'The youngsters are sore afraid, Father.'

'The sea is strange to them, brother. But calm enough - they will soon feel better.'

'Not just the sea. Those idlers on the wharf have affrighted them with tales of the Great Wave. You have heard of it?' Ralph had not. The taciturn Welshman was actually talking.

'A giant wave high as a man, moving as fast as a galloping horse. It comes out of the west, tearing boats from their moorings and hurling them onto the land, drowning people and animals. The people here think the Devil rides it.'

Ralph peered westward at wavelets sparkling in the sunshine. He sniffed.

'Amazing indeed! Do you believe it real, Brother? Does it come every day?'

'It is real, Father, for many have witnessed it and felt its power. But they say it is seen far upstream from here, only a few times a year and at different times of day or night. I have not seen it myself and speak only of what I have heard.'

'Then it should not trouble us. Tell this to the novices and calm them.'

They sailed on over the gentle sea. All morning they saw only two other vessels, dark specks far to the east. Presently the low coast of Wales appeared and slowly grew larger. On the stern decking Aston was teaching Thomas some card game. Giles mumbled over his breviary, Evan kept an eye on the novices whispering together near the bow. Ralph had his breviary open but his mind was on the problem of how to keep the Offices on their journey. Unlike himself his charges were doubtless devout enough and the familiar routine of the Rule would sustain them, yet it would be impossible to keep to it on the endless walking that lay ahead and like Whiting he knew of no precedent on which to base a decision. He must decide on this, if not now at the latest before leaving Castell Nedd.

To his irritation Evan was at his elbow again. 'Father, I have told them why they should not fear the Great Wave. But they are still troubled.'

'Dear Lord, this world is not for such innocents! What ails them now?'

'More idlers' tales. They have told them Wales is a fearful place of madmen, bears and wolves and fiery dragons.'

Ralph snorted. 'Enough! They must learn some truth about the wider world, and quickly.' The land to starboard was closing. He called to the shipmaster and pointed. 'It looks close: how far now?'

'We are but halfway, Father. The mouth of Neath River lies behind that jut of land far ahead: you will not see it yet. Pray this wind holds.'

And to their relief it did hold, although slackening as they sailed northward close to the coast, to the reassurance of the novices. Stretches of clean sandy beach with dunes humped behind them had them chattering again. They sailed past the mouths of several small streams and glimpsed the squat towers of village churches inland. They passed the grey bulk of a much greater church or monastic house. To the west clouds were building sky castles but too distant to trouble them now. Twilight was upon them as the crayer entered a gap in the dunes, glided gently between low headlands into a large bay into which a river emptied between hills inland. Ralph thought the bay looked shallow: low tide would expose mud flats. They made out a stone quay on the west bank where a few sea-going vessels were tied up. To the east more quays and shipping and a mass of half-timbered houses and cottages marked the port and borough of Neath. Wherries plied between the banks and the novices pointed excitedly at tiny circular craft low in the water, each with its solitary fisherman. 'Coracles,' explained the shipmaster. There was bustle on the water and along the quays: this was a substantial port.

The novices spotted the imposing mass of Neath Abbey beyond the western quays and remarked on the familiarity of its architecture. In failing light the ship eased towards it and tied up at the quay. The abbey was set back from it on slightly higher and firmer ground: low reedy land stretched from it to the shore, a firmer path crossing it. It was larger than Ralph had expected. For all the Cistercians' vaunted austerity it was built in an elaborate style not unlike Glastonbury and not far short in grandeur. But its site, with that flat muddy ground in front, could not compare.

They disembarked and fell on their knees to give thanks for their safe passage in such fine weather. It seemed a good omen. They felt confident they were safely away.

Ralph ordered: 'All of you wait here a moment. Thomas, see we have left nothing of ours on the ship.' He turned to the ship master. 'You have brought us safe to land and we thank you: here is the agreed payment.' The shipmaster pocketed the purse unopened: it seemed monks were still trusted. 'You rest the night here, my man?'

'For some days Father, depending on cargo. My house is in the town. If I may leave you now I can take my ship across before both night and tide both fall. My crew are weary for their beds and we unload early tomorrow.'

'God be with you, my son.' 'And protect you all, Father, on your pilgrimage.' Turning away, Ralph saw that the abbey water gate had opened and pale habits were visible in the gathering gloom. One advanced up a narrow path towards them, waving. So his letter had arrived safely and they were expected! He could dismiss the fear he had kept to himself all day that they would find the abbey already surrendered and deserted. Now they could enjoy a brief respite before striking inland.

Will Ford had chosen his four rowers well. Strong young men in sore need of money, they were pulling well against the slow current. Soon they would reach the Meare Pool and pass the water bailiff's house.

Which meant he had a decision to make.

Last night, with money to burn, Will had drunk too deep and his head still throbbed. Today his late start had been made still later by his search for rowers. Still, he had found some handy lads. While waiting for them to arrive he had somewhat unsteadily swilled down the barge. It was then he had noticed something stuck in a crack between two foot boards. It was a coin - a groat - no doubt one of those dropped by that fool monk when they hit the bank, hardly worth the picking up for one with his heavy purses. But what if more coins had fallen through below? He had pulled up some of the loose boards and reached down into the scummy bilge water. His groping fingers had soon found three silver shillings. Just when he had decided to postpone further search - his hired men being overdue - he had seen something glint in the water and fished out a gold double royal - a whole pound! Now that was riches! Nor was that all. Near it lay a ring: a man's signet ring with a dark red jewel set in heavily chased gold. It looked old: it might have value above even the gold coin. He whistled. In his hand he could be holding the worth of years of his labour! It could mean security, too, if the abbey's rumoured closure left him homeless. And he might find more - when he had time to search thoroughly! Quickly he had pocketed his haul and replaced the boards as his new crew approached.

Now, with the Meare Pool ahead, he must decide. He could hide his loot, say nothing, wait for any hubbub to die down, then move well away somewhere where he could sell the ring and live in some comfort for years. Or, as he had done several times before, he could report his discovery to the man who spied on the abbey for the commissioners - Adam Bale the water bailiff. Of course he would then lose his findings and they had never paid him much for information - but he had had little to report until now. Telling all to Bale would be the safer course and should earn him the full confidence of the bailiff's paymasters. Then there might come richer rewards.

But had this information real worth? Steering by instinct born of experience Will considered this. He recalled the prior's strange caution on the journey. What call for it on pilgrimage? And they were carrying gold - likely he held only a part of it, for surely they would not have entrusted all to that half-crazed Brother Giles. The money would have been divided amongst them all, in which case they might carry a deal more of it! But should not pilgrims, especially monks, travel in poverty? The shillings signified nothing: some expense they must have and even a double royal might be explained. But the ring could not! No monk could wear it and it looked well beyond the means even of Steward Aston. Then who could? What did it all mean?

It dawned on him then. Only the Lord Abbot could wear it. In his possession he held abbey treasure! These so-called pilgrims were removing treasures before the king claimed them and they had no intention of returning! With all the monasteries being diss - what was the word? - closed anyway - there had been talk of such theft, although never at Glastonbury - yet. There would be the devil to pay if this came out - and he could be paid handsomely for this information. This knowledge had value. As they entered the pool he made his decision.

Play for safety and future profit, report and hand over his finds - not quite all of course. He steered for the north bank.

Leaving his crew on the barge grumbling at the delay Will drank the water bailiff's small beer and told his tale. He handed over one shilling, the groat and the ring. He hated parting with the ring but it was the one item that really supported his suspicions and would be difficult to dispose of anyway. The bailiff, who knew a little about jewellery and possessed a modest ring or two himself, held it up to the light.

He whistled. 'The chasing of the gold shows old work, perhaps a hundred years old, which gives it more value. The stone is surely a fair ruby.' He looked at Will. 'You are right: this could only have come from the abbey. Only the abbot could have worn it yet it would be nigh impossible to steal from some strong box in his lodging. No, this comes from the abbey treasury and could only have been taken by a senior official with his keys.' He unlocked a small coffer and handed Will a purse. 'You have done well, Master Ford. Speak to no-one of this, when you are alone search the barge thoroughly again and report to me at once if you find anything more or hear anything that might bear on this matter. For my part I shall get word to the commissioners' agent in Glastonbury. Not long ago they made an inventory at the abbey for the Valor Ecclesiasticus and should have a record of this ring. Action must surely follow. I shall commend you to them as a man of proven trust in the king's service. You may hope for further profitable employment!'

Will had made the right decision. And he still had the noble and two silver shillings.

'Sit, I would speak with you.' John Dawnay pointed to a stool. Geoffrey wondered what he had done this time. Lately down from Oxford and already bored with country life he had got into a few scrapes of late. Had his father heard something.

Apparently not. 'Son, the matter is delicate: it concerns your uncle. You have some memory of him I trust?'

Geoffrey had been a child when uncle Ralph had returned from the French wars. As the elder son, on Geoffrey's grandfather's death he had taken up his inheritance. Still unmarried, he had lived alone in this fine house. Geoffrey dimly recalled the aloof unsmiling man everyone said had so greatly changed, showing little interest in what was now his manor. But he remembered vividly the family tumult when a few years later Ralph had called to tell his father he meant to turn his back on the world and enter a monastery.

His father's chair creaked as he leant back and stretched his legs. 'You recall I summoned the family together to tell you this? That was at our old house, of course, before we moved here. Your mother - God rest her soul - was alive and well and you and your brother were still children at home. We were more modestly housed than here, but a family.' He gazed across the deer park to the wooded Gloucestershire hills. 'I told you then how brother Ralph had determined to take the cowl. He had been sickened in his soul, he said, by the horrors of war in France, more sickened now by the tawdry world he had found back in England - those were his very words. He had no more use for it or place in it. He was off to London to arrange with his lawyers to gift his inheritance to me. I was the family man, he said, with sons to carry on the line. Once all was signed and sealed he would take the cowl and we must forget him.'

Here was nothing new and Geoffrey wondered where all this was leading. This morning he had set eyes on the new dairymaid and …..

'And so it was. He returned from London saying the estate was now mine if not yet the full title - some legal flummery, still not resolved as you know. Then he ups and leaves and is now - so I hear, for he has not contacted me since he left - at Glastonbury Abbey. A gentleman turned soldier turned tonsured Benedictine, priest and now lately prior!' He shook his head. 'My brother was ever a strange man. So now I am master here and we live in more comfort than I ever expected as a younger son. And so all would continue until one day the estate would pass to you and then to your son when you get one.'

He saw Geoffrey fidgeting and his voice turned dry. 'To the matter then, while I still have your attention. In short, all this' - he waved at the pastoral scene outside - 'may be less secure than I thought.' Geoffrey stopped fidgeting. 'Even at Oxford you cannot have entirely escaped hearing something of the dissolution of the monasteries taking place around us.' Geoffrey nodded, all attention now.

'The question that now arises, son, is what will your uncle do when he is forced to leave the seclusion of his cloister, as soon he must?'

Some reply being expected Geoffrey racked his brains. 'It is said monks will get pensions, father: a prior should do well enough. And as ordained priest he can find himself a living somewhere.'

'Let us hope so. But unlike us he still clings to his popery - must do, to belong to the Benedictines. Remember that taking the cowl was his own choice. Can you see your fastidious uncle in some poor parish church, back in this rough world he turned his back on in such disgust, ministering to rude peasants with their miserable sins and troubles? The brother I knew was over-proud, a man of cold humour, looking down at everything and everyone with disdain. Turn country priest? No, I cannot see it!'

'But still free to serve his popish church and worship in the old way - his way.'

'But for how long, Geoffrey? We both know how this new thinking that floods in from abroad, spread so wide and fast by Caxton's presses, is changing this country. You and I are converts to that change and content with it. And many think that not only the monasteries must go but the church entire must change. Indeed it has begun.'

'It is true the king has made himself head of the church but he himself is said to remain a steadfast Catholic.'

'But Master Cromwell is not and it is he who presses for radical change and he has the king's ear. So do others of like mind with influence at court, some high within the church itself. Sweeping changes are coming soon. You and I can welcome them but not brother Ralph. So to my question, Geoffrey. What will he do then?'

'How does this concern us, father?' Geoffrey was becoming impatient.

'What if your uncle returns here?'

'You mean ….?'

'Yes son, return to reclaim his inheritance. Take back all this from me - and later deny it to you.' He waved a troubled hand.

'But he has gifted it to you! Can he now reclaim it in law?'

'I do not know, son but it sore troubles me. But I mean to find out. I must to London this week to seek answers.'

'You wish me to take charge here until you return?' With the run of the place he could hope for some fun.

A hope instantly dashed. 'No. Time for your brother to take some responsibility here. While I consult the lawyers I want you to seek out your uncle Ralph and find out all you can of his intentions - with the utmost discretion, of course. Is he still fervent for his church? Would he be content with a parish? In short, need I concern myself? I must know his mind in this.' His manner became business-like. 'I have a friend working with Cromwell's commissioners and he is arranging for you to take up employment with an agent of theirs in the south west charged to keep a watchful eye on Glastonbury Abbey until Cromwell's net is ready to close over it. He says he can use a trustworthy young gentleman assistant - one of reformist persuasion of course - with some learning and energy and a good horse to carry messages and generally make himself useful. By good fortune - for us anyway - he lacks such a person at present, his man having taken a bad fall from his horse and been sent home on the back of a cart. At least you possess the good horse. In this agent's service you will be well-placed to peer into the abbey and into Ralph's mind. Between us we may learn where we stand and what we can do.'

Geoffrey was dismayed. 'It will be far from easy, father'

'I know, but you must attempt this for the family. And Geoffrey - contacting me on this matter may prove difficult, even dangerous. Who can be trusted these days? You know my mind on this but you must act on your own initiative as need arises.'

'And if I find that uncle Ralph means to return here?' His father stood up and paced about the room. At last he stopped and turned. They looked at each other.

'In that case we must consider very carefully. Would you give all this up? But we will face that if and when we come to it. Glastonbury must surrender soon and you must attach yourself to the commissioners when they descend on it - there may lie your best chance to get to Ralph. But use your wits, son, and act as needs be. I shall write you a letter of introduction to my friend and another to the agent, whose name by the way is Knollys. And Geoffrey - arm yourself well. These are uncertain times.'

And so the new dairymaid must wait.

Geoffrey had found his way easily enough to Brindham, the hamlet close to Glastonbury where the agent lived, and had no call to question any over-curious locals. As he had been told, the agent kept livery stables and a smithy.

Knollys, a sturdy man who looked prosperous enough, was expecting him: his letter of introduction was read with a nod of approval. He was to have a room and board with all expenses paid.

'Not by me,' Knollys smiled thinly, 'I just carry out the commissioners' orders.' Middle-aged, with a watchful wife and silent daughter hovering in the background, he appeared of tradesman class: it would not sit easy to take orders from the fellow as he was instructed to do. But he seemed amiable enough and he must put up with it for now. When they had taken meat Knollys explained how well his establishment was placed for both his public and private business.

'I sit here at the north edge of town with horses to hire and stables to house them and attend to their needs after they have crossed the miry road from Wells - keeping my own feet dry. I keep a close eye on the abbey with the town between us for my own privacy and my livery business as cover, open for all to see.' His face showed he felt he might be saying too much. 'But of course you must not speak of these matters to anyone.'

Useful knowledge but the fellow's a talker, thought Geoffrey, perhaps less suited than his admirably placed house for his work for Cromwell. But he must learn more.

'Pray aquaint me with what is happening now at the abbey.'

'Nothing untoward. All seems quiet. But it is the quiet before the storm. Dr. Layton and the other commissioners - and this is privy for now, Master Dawnay - intend to force the abbey's surrender before year's end. Then there may be activity enough even for your young blood. Until then we wait, watch and report as needs be.'

'Are we to visit the abbey at all?'

'Not at present. We are to keep away until further orders or the commissioners themselves come, for they wish to lull the monks' fears as much as possible.'

'Surely the monks know full well what will befall them?'

'They can guess what but cannot know when. We suspect that if forewarned they will hide some of the renowned abbey treasures - they will know the king has his eye on them. The less urgent they think the matter the less they will hurry to do so and the less work for us later to find them, if we have to. So we keep away for now.'

This was disquieting: how speak to uncle Ralph now? 'Then my present duties?'

'A confidential report or two to carry but little else for now. Spend these days, Master Dawnay, in finding your way around our highways and byways so that when the time comes to bestir yourself you will not get lost. Begin with our drier country inland, which is easier. Towards the coast much of the land is low-lying, only part reclaimed from the sea, much of it swampy and in places dangerous. But there are tracks even there you must know. But begin inland. I have a horse for you while your good beast rests.'

His room was no worse than his dank Oxford lodgings had been, the weather stayed fine and the following days passed pleasantly enough. Geoffrey explored the town and rode placidly around the hinterland, which was hilly in places, well wooded and farmed with mine workings and quarries scattered around. The weather was fine, there were inns aplenty and the locals seemed amiable. He rode past the abbey walls at the heart of the town it had created and out in the countryside saw everywhere its mighty hand in its rich manors, watermills, mines and fishponds. Too heavy a hand, as throughout the realm! It was indeed time for England to take all this back from Rome. He looked forward to the commissioners' arrival and playing an active part in the surrender. His family would be proud of him.

One afternoon he sat his horse looking over the very different landscape stretching to the Severn Sea, the land the locals called The Levels. Cloud shadows skimmed over a patchwork of open water, dark peat and flashes of bright light where small streams meandered through what must be sea marsh to a dim distant shore. Here and there little steep-sided hills poked through the flat surface. Straight reaches of water and green late summer pastures showed where land had been reclaimed. Smudges of wood smoke disclosed a thin scatter of habitation. But for the most part this was empty land, confusing, even menacing. Easy to get lost and mired in it.

It was time to get to know these Levels: tomorrow he would make a start. As he urged his tired mount for Brindham his mind turned again to the problem of his uncle. If he was to keep clear of the abbey how and when could he get to see him, let alone learn his mind on his future? Almost he felt relief, for the task was daunting and he had no idea how to approach it. Well, he must bide his time for now.

Next morning Knollys and Geoffrey were finishing their breakfast when they heard a horseman dismount in the yard. It was Adam Bale the abbey water bailiff, who joined them at table and gratefully accepted bread and small beer. Setting down his drained pot he leant his elbows on the table and looked conspiratorial.

'News, Master Knollys.' He look sideways at Geoffrey.

The agent introduced them. 'You may speak freely, he is now one of us.'

The bailiff nodded. 'Yesterday I had a visit from Will Ford, the abbey boatman; a strange visit.' He gave an account of Ford's news; the night journey down the Brue, the monks' boarding the crayer at High

Bridge and his discovery of the coins. He fished under his jerkin and handed the coins and ring to Knollys.

Knollys examined them carefully then swore. 'We suspected they would hide treasures but not that they would flee the abbey with some of them, nor that they would act so quickly.' He thumped he solid table with his fist. 'So these birds have flown and for sure will have about them much more than a few coins and ring or two. They will have items small enough to carry yet of great value and so worth the risk - likely some of the abbey's famous jewels. It is fortunate we have them all listed so we can find out what has been taken. Gone aboard a ship to Wales, you say? Then where?' He asked Bale: 'Have you paid Ford for this news?'

The water bailiff nodded. 'And be sure the rascal kept some coins for his pains. Even so I said he would find favour for his news.'

'Good. I will give you more money for him: he must be kept sweet - and quiet - for now.' He fetched two purses from a strong box and handed them to the bailiff.

'You have done well. Give this smaller one to Ford and tell him if he keeps silent he may expect further reward. The other is for you with our thanks. Go home now before your absence raises questions.'

When Bale had ridden away Knollys sat at his desk and picked up a quill pen. After scribbling furiously he turned to Geoffrey. 'Matters have changed. Now we must hasten to the abbey with some force at our back to find out who and what are missing and how we may apprehend them. No time to lose. You ride to the town constable with this note: it warrants him to summon his guards and meet me at the market cross within the hour. Wait there with him. I will prepare the writs needed to set in motion hot pursuit of these renegade monks. And I shall summon another young gallant I have just put in place south of the town so we can search in two directions.'

By now Geoffrey knew where to go and lost no time. Soon the town guards were mustered at the market cross, where they were joined by Knollys accompanied by a young gentleman on a handsome grey.

Knollys introduced them. 'Geoffrey Dawnay - Robin Stukely,' It was clear that Knollys, Cromwell's man, had authority even over the town constable. 'While the constable and I question the monks, you two must pick up the trail of these renegades. Master Stukely, as you have yet to learn our local roads, you will take the high road to Bristol to cut them off should they take their ship up river for Gloucester. Master Dawnay, do you take horse to the abbey's wharf at High Bridge and follow their trail across the water and into Wales. We may yet trap them between the two of you. Here are the signed writs for each of you. They give you authority to raise posses, make arrests and bring them back. And here are purses to pay your way.'

Geoffrey was impressed by the man's authority, remarkable in one of tradesman class - but then, so was the all-powerful Thomas Cromwell. But he demurred.

'Master Knollys, I have yet to master these Levels of yours. I may lose my way. Perhaps a local rider who knows the paths....'

'And who it may be unwise to trust: the Benedictines still have friends hereabouts. What if he finds them only to warn them? No, needs must, sir. Hasten to High Bridge. If either of you picks up their trail follow hard and bring them back however far the pursuit takes you. Be assured you will find favour at court for it. Off with you now and remember, although he knows nothing of it yet, that in this you serve the king.' As they mounted their horses Knollys marched his armed men through a curious throng towards the abbey.

CHAPTER 2

Into Wales

The Abbot of Neath and the Prior of Glastonbury, cream white and rust black, were finishing a supper of sea salmon and venison washed down with a sound wine. His appetite sharpened by sea air and a day of meagre fare Ralph had done full justice to it. He had been pleasantly surprised by this abbot's table, for the white monks had been vegetarians and anyway this was not England. Replete, he looked around a well-proportioned room of goodly size but sparsely furnished, although what there was showed quality - but of course it could not compare with Whiting's luxurious lodging. He had almost forgotten that as prior he had slept in a cell, albeit a modestly comfortable one, and had rarely been invited to his abbot's table. Ralph, who blended naturally into surroundings that recalled his upbringing, felt himself well equal to his host. In his stiff manner he complimented him on his table.

Abbot Leyshon shrugged his shoulders. 'All home grown, Father. We have fishing rights on the Severn Sea and our deer park, although now our manors are leased out for income.' He stood up. 'Let us finish our wine by the fire.' Relaxing in its glow Ralph reflected that Abbot

Leyshon had been most hospitable. He had greeted each of them in person before the others were conducted to the guest quarters for ablutions, food and a much-needed night's rest. He had instructed they were to be made free of the precinct and might attend such Offices as they wished. They were welcome to stay until fully rested and ready to move on. It was all most satisfactory, especially for himself so comfortably lodged with the abbot himself.

Ralph looked at his host. Like his abbey he was more impressive than he had expected: a solidly built man of considerable years, he exuded a calm distinction befitting his rank. Of course he would be English and judging from his unusual name of Norman ancestry. Like himself.

The abbot stretched his legs to the fire. 'If you are not too tired, Father Prior, I am most interested to hear of your - may I say adventure?' Ralph pondered how much to reveal. Would Leyshon keep silence in these mistrustful times? Yet they shared the same vocation, followed the same Rule and were brothers in the present adversity and it was pleasant to converse again with a man of obvious learning and sophistication - and the wine was loosening his tongue. Deciding to speak freely he recounted the events of their journey and the preparations for it, not omitting its real purpose. But he did not itemise the treasures they carried, of which he was reminded by the hardness of the little wooden bowl ever pressing against his side.

Leyshon nodded. 'I commend your enterprise. We retain little portable wealth here or we might do well to follow your example.'

Ralph, feeling he had disclosed enough, changed the subject. 'I could get scant news of your abbey here and feared you might already have surrendered.'

'Indeed we were due for surrender two years ago.'

'Yet here you are and appear well settled. How can that be?'

'Leyshon smiled wryly. 'Still here, yes; settled, no. Like most religious houses we have long been in decline and are now reduced to only eight choir monks and barely more lay folk; not enough for our duties. Worse, we have lost most of our wealth.'

He saw that Ralph was puzzled. 'The one explains the other, Father. Foolishly I attempted to trade wealth for time. We are still here because I gifted moneys to Cromwell for an extension of time before surrender. So it was that much of our wealth was swallowed up. Now we can barely maintain these buildings even by selling off furnishing and plate. Look around you: these rooms were not always so bare. And yet Cromwell will close us whenever he chooses - I have heard he covets this property for himself, having some family connections hereabouts. What I did was in vain and foolish indeed.' Ralph sensed that the abbot welcomed an opportunity to unburden himself to someone in a position to understand.

Unusually for him he felt an upsurge of sympathy. He too doubted his own judgement. Was this journey wise or doomed to failure? We are brothers in crisis, he thought, both fearing we have made wrong decisions. He was warming to this abbot.

But he must seize this opportunity to learn more of this town of Neath and what dangers might lie ahead travelling among these Welsh, by repute a primitive and wild lot. 'What of your work here, Father? I see a town which seems to prosper.'

Leyshon nodded. 'The borough is well-placed with a safe harbour and sea trade across the Severn Sea and to Ireland and beyond. There is good fishing. The town has weekly markets and several fairs and the land around has good soil. As for our house, you have seen we have quays this side of the river and share in the trade, some goods carried in our own ships. We have sheep runs inland and traded wool before we leased our manors. We could never match the splendour of your famed abbey but we did well enough until this threat of dissolution - and my mistaken response to it. My concern now is for our religious duties and our pastoral work. There is little time left for them, I fear.' He sighed.

'As with us, alas. But tell me, Father, do you have much trouble with these Welsh?'

Leyshon stared into the fire, his mouth twitching slightly. 'Many along this coast are English and some have been here since the Normans came and took the best land. You will hear English spoken as much as Welsh, for the native tongue and culture are in decline since Union with England two years ago, which imposed English law on all Wales. The native Welsh are few in number. Most are scattered throughout the hill country inland, since the towns the English built were long denied them, although some have settled in them now. But both peoples live together peacefully enough these days. As monks you need fear no more danger on the road than in England, although sadly there are outlaws everywhere these days. No, Father, I have no trouble with the Welsh. But two centuries ago it was very different, when this house was sacked by native tribesmen.'

Ralph was outraged. 'Attack a peaceful monastic house! Utterly barbarous!'

'Indeed. Yet is that not what the king does now, with writs for weapons? Remember too it was French monks who created our houses with grants of land from Norman lords - who had seized it from the Welsh. They saw us as siding with their oppressors and whenever they rose up we were a convenient target. Mind you, that was not so at our smaller houses inland, which enjoyed the support of Welsh princes and lords and where generally there was harmony. But it was so here and at Margam Abbey down the coast. Well, all that lies in the past.'

Ralph was proud of his Norman lineage and Norman achievements, however distant. 'But we brought these poor creatures strong rule, civilisation and prosperity!'

'Among much else.' Suddenly Leyshon seemed to tire of the conversation and rose to his feet. 'You must excuse me Father. I must to my bed, for Lauds comes soon. You too must welcome sleep after your journey. You told me your abbot has excused you all Offices at your discretion while on your journey so I trust you will sleep late and wake refreshed: you will not be disturbed. Should you need anything call my servant, who sleeps within call. We shall speak again tomorrow.'

The wherry's bow bumped gently against the quay and Aston and Thomas stepped ashore. There was some high cloud but it was a dry and pleasant day for walking.

Prior Ralph had summoned them after breakfast. 'I have a task you should welcome. The brothers must remain within the abbey walls until we leave, for black habits would raise eyebrows and we dare not attract attention at the outset. Yet we must use this time to judge as best we can what lies ahead for us. You two can pass unnoticed in a crowd. Cross the harbour to Neath town and spend the day there with your eyes and ears open, talking to people and learning all you can. Watch for signs that Cromwell's men are about. Say nothing of our affairs, act as Englishmen passing through, which you truly are. Above all mark our best way west for Aberteifi before we turn north. You have money, Steward? Good; then away with you.'

They were delighted at the prospect of a day's freedom from clerical restraint and of a mild adventure. But Aston voiced concern. 'Father, we do not speak their language!'

'The abbot assures me English is much spoken here and English folk are everywhere. Speak with me when you return.'

They could cover more ground if separated. Aston gave Thomas a few coins and told him to make for the north end of the town and seek out their best route inland as instructed. Not over-fond of walking himself he confined himself to the waterfront, where there was activity enough to occupy him. He pointed to a nearby inn. 'Meet me there when the sun points to noon and we will eat.' He patted his stomach: no harm in a cooked meal.

Thomas' long legs took him quickly through narrow winding streets. He breathed the sea air, revelling in freedom from the constraints of the ship and the shuffling brothers. Overhung half-timbered houses soon gave way to low thatched cottages with small vegetable patches and then to an outer fringe of poor hovels: it all seemed much like Glastonbury, the only other town he knew. He was shy of speaking to anyone, especially obviously country folk talking rapidly in their strange tongue. They looked no different from the English but he wished he could understand what they were talking about - perhaps only the outrageous price of milled flour!

Soon he plucked up courage to approach overheard English speakers and was soon conversing freely, enjoying his foray into what in his innocence seemed an exciting place. A steep street led him downhill to the river again where a stone bridge crossed over and an old castle bulked on the near bank. On the far side a well-trodden footpath wound northward into the hills. Would that be their way? At ease now, he questioned two men approaching, realising too late they were speaking Welsh. One looked blank but the other, probably a townsman, replied in passable English, his accent instantly reminding him of Brother Evan.

'Aberteifi? A long way, boy. Over the bridge turn left and down the river bank then right onto the highway to Abertawe and Caerfyrddin - Swansea and Carmarthen in English. But if you travel on foot that track you see leading north from the bridge would save you some miles.'

'Is that way quiet and safe?' He knew the prior wished to avoid main roads.

'Yes indeed. Four miles over the hill brings you to great stones standing on edge - put there by the ancients, they do say - hard by a cluster of houses they call Rhos. From there you go down into another valley, then cross another river and - well, better ask again when you get there.' Thomas thanked him. He had done what was asked of him and could return at leisure to Aston and some welcome food. He had passed a few stalls and a carpenter's shop worth a closer look or he might find a different way back. He felt no regret at leaving Glastonbury: there was much of interest in this travelling, so much to learn. Despite what they had heard these Welsh seemed peaceable going about their business. If only he could understand them! He would ask Brother Evan to teach him a few words. He strode back to the quay, whistling blithely.

Before Thomas was due back Aston was comfortable on a bench outside the inn. He had walked and watched along the quay, ventured into a few streets and spoken to a few townsfolk. He felt he had earned the pot of ale before him on the table.

But learned little of note. Clearly the town was given over to sea trade and markets serving the surrounding countryside. The fishing boats and strange little coracles should land enough fish for local needs. There were workshops for the usual crafts. Nothing remarkable. His ears told him English and Welsh speakers were about in similar numbers; his eyes that they mixed peacefully although - perhaps - not easily.

The most profitable commerce seemed to be in English hands: certainly the better-dressed burghers were speaking English. He sensed that the native Welsh were an underclass who might resent their situation but must conceal it. He would have learned more had Brother Evan been here - he must speak to him. Would all this interest the prior?

Anyway, a personal matter concerned him more - his own future. He called for more ale to assist with the problem.

Had he made a grave error in joining this enterprise? Since the death of his wife and only child of a fever a dozen years back the abbey had provided him with a sound roof over his head and congenial employment without the monks' burden of unending religious observance. That comfortable life must end with the coming dissolution and there would be no pension for him. But local landowners were jostling for favour with Cromwell with an eye to cheap purchases or outright grants of abbey land and buildings - Glastonbury's manors were vast enough to satisfy the greed of a dozen of them. They would have no call to change the profitable but complex husbandry the abbey had developed over centuries and would need experienced stewards to manage them. Who better than himself who had already done so successfully? Should he have waited and offered to serve a new master and so retain his comfortable position?

The problem was that these gentry had their own stewards: he might well have been offered only a subsidiary position. Or, since he had worked for a religious order out of favour and by then dissolved, no position at all! On balance perhaps he had been right to seize this chance to leave.

The key was his elder brother who held a freehold in the fat farm lands in England between Hereford and Leominster. They had not met for years but had always got on well and kept some contact. Adam would take him in: he and his goodwife were ageing and their sons had long left home: they should welcome an experienced and still vigorous partner on the farm: after all he was family. The prior's intended return from Wales to England, however vague at present, might prove handy should they re-enter somewhere in Herefordshire, where he could leave his companions in good conscience. Well, it was done now. As he finished his ale the long shadow of Thomas crossed the table. They enjoyed a hearty meal together and made their leisurely way back to the abbey.

Prior Ralph had risen late and rested well. He had breakfasted alone, Abbot Leyshon being at Sext. Judging by the thin chanting of the handful of white monks in the church the service was nearly over. Ralph had visited his own charges and satisfied himself they were well settled.

It had been time to inform them of the decision he had finally reached. 'You know Father Abbot granted me full authority for everything on this journey. We are invited to join our Cistercian brothers at all services while under their roof. I urge you to do so but attendance will be voluntary. On the road ahead it will be impractical to hold our own Offices and I have decided we will confine ourselves to private prayer and our breviaries until, God willing, we find safe haven once more.' Hurrying on to avoid any disputation and aware of Giles' stare, he had ordered them to stay within the abbey and not show themselves at any gate.

Now, savouring some time alone, he was strolling around the great court examining the impressive buildings around him. Nearing the main gatehouse he saw Abbot Leyshon standing in its shadow talking to two workmen repairing one of its great open doors. His voice carried clearly and Ralph realised with surprise that he could not understand a word he said. Leyshon must be speaking Welsh and sounding fluent.

As the two men returned to their work the abbot saw Ralph and came towards him. White and black habits crossed the court together.

'You are well rested, Father Prior?'

'I am indeed, as are my charges. I thank you again for your hospitality.'

Leyshon shrugged. 'A pleasure. You would do as much for us.'

Ralph was curious. 'Father, just then you were, I think, speaking in Welsh?'

'Yes, for those two have no English.'

'It is admirable that with your many duties you have found time to master this native speech. It must have been difficult - and from the sound of its gabbling something of a penance!'

'Hardly difficult. It is a simple matter to learn a language at one's mother's knee.'

Ralph stopped in his tracks. 'Your mother was Welsh?'

The abbot's lips had developed a twitch again. 'My father, too. My family name is Thomas, a common name hereabouts. I was born and raised not far from here.'

Leyshon Thomas! This cultured man was not even English, let alone of Norman descent: the Christian name had deceived him. A native speaking good English without trace of accent and an abbot no less! Somehow it jarred. Embarrassed, Ralph wondered if he had said anything disparaging about these people the previous evening

'Forgive me, Father. I took Leyshon to be a Norman name.'

'Rightly so, but adapted from an old Welsh name - Lleision. Uncommon, though there are some around here. Perhaps we had pretensions to gentility,' he added dryly.

'But - if I may make bold to ask, Father - coming from Wales how did you come by your education?'

'I was always destined for Holy Orders, so after schooling locally - sound enough schooling too - I took myself to Oxford: being on the high road to London many Welsh further their learning there. I profited from my time at Oxford. But enough of myself. If you are still bent on your 'pilgrimage' to - or at least towards - Aberteifi we have an old map that may assist you. Come, we can visit the library before Vespers.'

Brother Giles came out of Nones, one black habit amongst a handful of white, and brooded towards the cloister. He alone from Glastonbury was now attending every Office, the others hardly one or two a day. It was true they were excused them but for now they were not on the road. It showed all too clearly how quickly they were abandoning their spiritual calling, forever chattering about Neath and the road ahead; always of worldly matters.

Giles too thought about the road ahead, or rather his destination. Thought about it more each day. He did not share the other's interests, had scant concern with their route, with places to shelter or even the rich treasures they carried. Nor with secrets and subterfuge and Ralph playing soldier on campaign again and turning ever more worldy. What mattered such mundanities?

For God would provide: not planning but faith would guide him to his destination. As his thoughts turned increasingly to that end this foreign abbey receded, his companions receded - never his true companions anyway. Always he was alone with his thoughts. Each day there shone more clearly before him the image of the Blessed Virgin, her manifestation as Our Lady of Cardigan! He had pored through chests of books and manuscripts in Glastonbury's great library and knew her proper name was not Mair as these crude Welsh had it, but Mary Herself. He had read how long ago her wooden image had been found on the riverbank, beautiful, wondrously carved and painted, untouched by weather. The Christ Child was cradled on her left arm, her right hand held a lighted taper that was never extinguished. How she had been moved to shelter several tines but had always miraculously found her way back to her riverbank, so that in the end a shrine had been built there to house her and how, at last content, she had made her abode there. At Cardigan she had worked her miracles and her shrine had become a great place of pilgrimage. It was to her he made his pilgrimage, his real pilgrimage. There she would grant him peace. He burned to be with her, to lose himself in her radiance.

The mewling of gulls circling over his head brought him back to dull earth and the question how and where to leave the others and turn his steps for Cardigan. Perhaps he might learn something from one of the Cistercian brothers.

Abbot Leyshon pushed aside the papers on his desk. It was almost time to join his guest for their meal before Compline, which the prior had said he would attend.

His thoughts turned to his visitors and their mock pilgrimage. An unpleasing deception, but he could condone it as a desperate act and none of his concern. Privately he would be glad to see them leave, for they almost matched his own few brothers in number and bore heavily on the straitened resources of his house. Still, they would soon be gone and he would have done his duty by them.

He regretted that he had not - Prior Ralph excepted - paid them enough attention, leaving their welfare in the ageing hands of Brother Peter, who combined the duties of bursar and hospitaller and was feeling the burden of so many visitors. Apart from the prior only Brother Giles had made much impression on him because he alone had attended every Office. No, there was more to it than that: the man struck him as an over-zealous fanatic, likely unstable. He had met the type before - they were not unknown in monastic life - and he knew how disruptive an influence they could be. Prior Ralph would need to keep a close eye on him on their journey.

But this stately prior was a man to keep a sharp eye on everyone. Here was a more complex individual, yet he felt he could read him too. Nature and experience had left him more secular than spiritual, arrogantly proud of his distant Norman blood, punctilious in organisation but overbearing in execution. A man of learning but lacking humour, too remote to be loved by his fellows. Yet his leadership seemed unquestioned, not only because his abbot had devolved absolute authority on him but because of his presence, his distinction. He commanded respect on his own account.

And yet - and yet! Something was missing there, something he could not put his finger on. Abbot Leyshon shook his head and stood up. People always interested him and this Benedictine prior intrigued him. But at the moment he cared more about his supper, for which his cook had promised capons and perhaps a duck. An hour at table with Prior Ralph might satisfy both interests.

In Glastonbury Luke Hamblin, his deliveries completed, enjoyed a pot of ale in the crowded market place before turning his cart back to the abbey kitchens, where he had left his mother overseeing delivery of more of their produce. He helped her up beside him, flicked his reins and old Jasper walked them sedately for home.

'I do not like that hubbub around the market cross, mother. Have you heard aught?'

'When is there not? Lasses fetching water, giggling and ogling every passing well-favoured lad - as I fancy you well know.' She looked at her younger son proudly.

'Mostly men there now though. The constable and his guards marching to the abbey, some official handing sealed scrolls to two horsemen who then rode off on the Wells road cantering faster than I'd care to on those cobbles.' His mother shrugged her plump shoulders.

'There is more, mother. At the alehouse they spoke of it. I listened. They ….'

'Son, I have told you before you are too young for alehouses and we are too poor.'

'I went to hear the news.' Which was at least partly true. 'Some were saying jewels have been stolen from the abbey and some monks have gone missing. The constable's men said they are the thieves and think they are heading for the coast. The two horsemen were off in hot pursuit.'

His mother looked askance at him. 'Monks steal? It cannot be! Which of the brothers they hear are missing?'

'They say the Prior himself and a Brother Giles, among others. They will be questioning everybody at the abbey. You saw naught amiss there?'

'Father Prior a thief? I do not believe it.' She hesitated. 'Yet something may be amiss, Luke. When I took our eggs into the monk's kitchen I heard some of them talking on their way to their refectory. They are never silent as they should be, but today they buzzed like an over-turned bee hive. I could not hear properly what they were saying, but if this tittle-tattle has any truth in it the missing monks may be in peril and not yet know it.' She crossed herself.

'What should we do, mother?'

'What can we do? Nothing. We little folk know only hearsay and it is none of our business.' She sighed. 'Yet I fear for these runaway monks, thieves or no. They must have reason to flee. The abbey has been good to us and I wish we could warn them.'

Suddenly she sat bolt upright on the gently swaying cart. 'Perhaps we can! We can send word to your brother John at High Bridge, for he stands well in the employ of the abbey and he knows the prior. He can find means to warn them.'

'If they went to High Bridge at all! We do not know that. The horsemen rode north for Wells and will likely go on to Bristol or even Gloucester!'

'Wherever they are going John will know best what to do. We must get word to him. Luke, take me home then ride Jasper to High Bridge and tell him everything!'

'There is much for me to do at home, mother. I must .....'

'This comes first and there is no time to lose. Luke love, we owe this to the abbey. Make haste to your brother.'

It was well that Luke knew his way across the half-tamed confusing Levels with their reed beds and marsh and the many drainage channels the locals called rhynes, for Jasper was heavy and no riding horse. It was near three hours before he walked into the wharf office at High Bridge. His brother, finishing his dinner, was surprised but pleased to see him. Luke mopped his brow, accepted some ale and told his tale.

John frowned. 'This is bad news. They hoped for more time before any pursuit. Someone has betrayed them.' Seeing Luke's puzzlement he went on: 'No harm in your knowing now, for they are away, if not yet safe.' Now it was his tale to tell.

When he had finished it Luke asked: 'If they are already over the Severn Sea need we warn them?'

'Yes, for now the hunt is up their pursuers will not stop at the shore but follow them into Wales. Father prior must be warned.' John paced about the room, considering. 'Yet no great haste. You say those two horsemen took the Wells road? My guess is they carry orders to the King's officers in Bristol to form a posse comitatus to ride around by Gloucester into Wales. That will take them time, as will finding remounts on their way. Even if they suspect our pilgrims intended taking ship here they must commandeer another vessel and follow and still find fresh horses in Wales. Whatever they do it will take them days - say three days - to reach that Castle - something - place. We have time enough. I shall write to warn Father Prior. The crayer Rhonwen that carried them is back here now with new cargo, but should have sailed for Neath again before the falling tide. I was about to take a look when you came. No matter: I will send my letter by the next vessel for Neath - they come and go almost daily at this season.' He stood up. 'Come lad, I'll get you some food and fodder for old Jasper.'

They were relaxing over bread and cheese when they heard the sound of an approaching horseman. John peered out over the narrow rhyne that emptied through a water gate into the bay near his window.

'Someone in a hurry, up to his boot tops in mud and his horse lathered. I'll wager he lost his way on the Levels and got into mires.'

Luke looked over his brother's shoulder. The rider was trotting upstream on the far bank obviously looking for a crossing point, for the water was too wide and the banks too insecure to attempt a jump even had his horse not been blown. Then they saw him turn to cast downstream again. As he came opposite their window Luke quickly drew back into shadow.

'That's one of the young bloods that officer handed the sealed papers to in Glastonbury. But I saw both of them take the Bristol road. So why is he here and without his companion?'

Suddenly John understood: 'Only one need ride to Bristol. I'll wager they have separated to cover more ground. The other one carries on north in case our pilgrims cut back east once in Wales. This one comes west over the Levels as you did - I fear they must already suspect our fugitives could have come this way. This fellow will take ship to Neath and raise a posse there. And so trap our monks between them.'

'How did he get behind me when he left before me on a better horse?'

'Because he does not know the Levels like you, Luke. Look at his muddied beast. You know how to thread your way through on drier ground: he did not and has been wandering in circles and into mires - which is why you did not see him.'

'Well, he's here now: I fear there is haste after all.'

'True. He may land in Wales and find our pilgrims at the abbey there preparing for their journey. He will carry writs to make town officers hold them until the other posse arrives, however long they take. We must warn the prior.'

'How?'

'Let me think.' John sat head in hand. 'The nearest crossing of this rhyne is a mile upstream: our horseman will turn back again and this time carry on until he finds it and soon be here. A second boat leaves the wharf on this tide, the Betsy - she should still be at her moorings for she draws less water than the Rhonwen. She is bound for Swansea, which is close to Neath. But who will carry my letter from there?'

The rider passed again, heading upstream. Luke said 'You have no time to pen a proper letter, John: he could be back here inside ten minutes, on this bank and looking for the wharf steward - you! And he has authority enough to make you find him passage!'

'You have the truth of it. Go outside - look along the wharf. If both ships have left he must wait as we must - at least we will have time to think.'

In no time Luke burst back into the room. 'John, both ships are still here.' They rushed outside. The Rhonwen and a smaller vessel were indeed moored at the wharf.

John saw a small opportunity but little time, for the horseman might have found the crossing by now. He called his servant, told him to lead Jasper to his stables, rub him down and if asked say he was

John's. Then he snatched up writing materials and the abbey seal from his desk and ran up the wharf, urging Luke along with him.

'You are right; no time for a proper letter. Luke, you must cross in the Rhonwen to Neath and warn Father Prior yourself. With the falling tide she has to sail soon - she is already very late. I cannot leave here and you have the whole tale now. Tell the prior everything and urge him to flee at once from Neath. I have only time to pen a short note explaining who you are, with my stamp and seal to ensure he accepts it.'

'But the farm ... mother ...'

'I will arrange all - a message to mother, return Jasper, some help on the farm until you return. Take the first ship back when you have delivered your message. You will need money.' He rummaged in a drawer for a purse. 'Take this. Tell the shipmaster as little of your business as possible, only that it is urgent.'

They raced up the gangplank, which a protesting deck hand was about to haul aboard. The shipmaster scowled at them. 'What means this? We are already late after re-packing from broken casks - he pointed at staves strewn about the deck - and risk grounding. No more delays!'

John drew him aside while Luke hid the purse, his mind in a whirl. Passage money changed hands and John was hurriedly writing, his desk an upturned chest, then fiddling with tinder, seal and wax. He came back to Luke, speaking softly.

'Lucky he knows me well: he will take you. I have paid your passage one way. But he is in black humour over the delay and wants me ashore. God speed you Luke: this is a good thing we do for the abbey.'

Luke pointed along the wharf to his brother's office, where the horseman was now dismounting. 'You think he will commandeer passage on the Betsy and follow?'

'Be sure of it - but I will delay him all I can. Brother, you must get to the Prior first. God speed you!' The shipmaster was bellowing angrily. John jumped ashore and waved as they eased from the wharf.

The previous evening Abbot Leyshon had enjoyed his capons but learnt little more about his principal guest. True, the reserved prior had relaxed a little, but he was a man who could only unbend so far and Leyshon had sensed a barrier he could not breach. The man seemed less sure of himself than his demeanour suggested but he could not fathom why, other than the strain of his responsibilities.

Uncertainty in leadership would serve them ill on their travels. The prior could ease his burden by commanding less and consulting more. As for the others the steward seemed a sensible fellow and the Welsh monk should know the country and language: both were mature men. How far did the prior confide in them or seek their advice? Although never the monastic style, primus inter pares would be the better policy for him now. That haughty mien of his must inhibit the comradeship they would need to see them through: a little humility would sit well. Last evening he had cautiously proffered that advice, clothed carefully in generalities - the problems of ruling a brotherhood, the importance of understanding and tact. He hoped it had had some effect. But now he must turn to his own problems.

For his guests it was a leisurely day for Ralph, confident they were clear away, had decided they would rest for two full days before leaving Neath. The brothers, although used to monastic confinement, envied the freedom enjoyed by Aston and Thomas to visit the town. Bored with inaction, their now voluntary Offices falling away, they were assisting their hard-pressed hosts with routine tasks, black habits mingling amicably with white with novel opportunity for whispered exchange of gossip. Only Francis, helping the almoner bring food to the poor at the town gate, had an opportunity to peer cautiously outside the walls: what little he could see from there looked much like parts of Glastonbury. Thomas, content with tools in his hands again, was mending a broken door hinge. Aston was in Neath buying supplies.

Only Giles had offered no help. He had been off on his own, which suited his companions, who were finding him increasingly strange. They were surprised when suddenly he appeared in a little herb garden in a sunny corner, kneeling to help an old Cistercian weed a border, whispering almost amiably with him.

No sooner had the Rhonwen left harbour than a stiff wind blew up from the west, where the sky had darkened ominously. Not wishing to risk being blown onto a lee shore the shipmaster headed her westward as close-hauled as the clumsy crayer could manage, making painfully slow progress in a roughening sea. Daylight was fading when at last they turned onto a northerly course. Then the wind strengthened to a half gale under a slate sky, rain fell heavily and the ship heeled steeply to starboard: it took three men at the steering oar to hold her course. 'We must ride this out,' the master shouted over the wind. They dropped sail and lowered the canvas sea anchor. His crew battened down the hatch, checked the deck cargo was secure and sheltered themselves from the rain under the lowered sail, securing it around their bodies. The master stumped over to Luke, who was hanging onto the mast vomiting, shivering and terrified.

'First time at sea, lad? Don't worry, I've seen worse and she's a stout tub. But this wind will not drop before morning. I'll be on deck all night, so you can shelter in my cabin.' He pointed to a tiny door under the slightly raised stern deck.' There is food in there if you want it.' Luke groaned and threw up again.

It was the worst night of his young life. The ship wallowed endlessly, woodwork creaked and groaned, spray hissed over the deck, the deckhands cursed under their sail, the air in the tiny low cabin became foetid. Night and his misery seemed endless. At long last came exhausted sleep.

When he woke up the ship's motion was gentler and he guessed they were under sail again. Bleary-eyed, he ducked through the doorway onto the deck. The sea was much calmer. Against a brightening sky he saw that the strips of material making up the sail were badly frayed, but the rigging seemed intact. Then to his delight he saw a jut of land to his left.

The master's horny hand clapped his shoulder. 'Swansea Bay,' he pointed. Not far now.' Mid-morning found them creeping into the Neath estuary and safety.

Shortly after Sext a damp and bone-weary Luke arrived at the abbey and was directed to Father Ralph, who was with the abbot. He handed the prior John's note and told his story, emphasising that the 'pilgrims' were thought to be in Wales, were suspected of major theft and must soon expect pursuit overland while another ship had following his bearing a writ of arrest.

Ralph was stunned. He had been wrong: they had not escaped unnoticed! Concealing his shock he extended his hand. 'Steward Hamblin's brother! I know your mother too, a worthy soul. I am grateful to all your family for this service. Please thank them when you return and inform Father Abbot - if you can do so discreetly.'

Leyshon, noting how the prior was attempting to soften his stiff manner and had gained by it, gripped the boy's shoulders warmly and called for a servant to attend him. 'You have done well, young man, but at much cost to yourself: you need rest and food - when you can stomach it.' As the door closed behind them he said: 'The lad needs sleep most: he is young and will prove as resilient as he has shown himself worthy. Your community inspires loyalty, Father.' Had Ralph been aware of that? 'When it is safe I shall arrange his return to his family and we shall pray that their part in this is not discovered. But, Father Prior, what will you do now?'

Ralph had already decided. 'We leave tonight as soon as it is dark. It seems our pursuers must come soon to arrest us. We must not be caught here to bring trouble to you after all your kindness.'

'Nothing is certain, Father, but I agree you cannot risk staying here another day.' He smiled. 'And do not concern yourself with us: should I be questioned I have your 'pilgrimage' tale to tell them in my innocence as, fortunately, has that lad's family. Make your preparations then, while I arrange food for your journey.'

That afternoon the little Betsy, battered, jury-rigged and under a torn scrap of sail, crept into the entrance to Swansea harbour half-swamped and in danger of sinking. As she was a hazard to other shipping willing hands fixed hemp cables to her and beached her. Her crew were brought ashore, two badly injured ones laid on cottage doors and all exhausted. Last to be helped ashore was the solitary passenger in the minute stern cabin with a cut on his head and bruises from falling out of a hammock. As his once-elegant dress indicated a gentleman, he and the two saddlebags that made up his baggage were taken to the town's best inn and a physician fetched. Pronounced to be suffering only minor injuries and exhaustion he was bathed and bandaged and put into the inn's best feather bed to sleep in peace.

Next morning young Geoffrey Dawnay awoke bruised and sore but rested. To his relief the sealed writ was safe in the lining of his jerkin. The contents of his purse and saddlebags were intact but his changes of clothing were as rumpled as the ones he had been wearing. Only his favourite bonnet with the cock pheasant feather and his fine riding gloves were lost.

After a hearty breakfast, energy and ambition restored, he left the inn to pursue his mission. The street outside jostled with dismounted horsemen clustered around some official: curious idlers were gathering. Geoffrey thrust his way through. 'Make way there: I am on a mission for the Lord Cromwell.' He waved his writ under the nose of the official, who was the town mayor. The leader of the horsemen, a burly middle-aged man, unceremoniously pulled him back. 'As are we, young sir. Await your turn.' He turned back to the flustered mayor. 'You say Cardigan is two day's ride away?'

'Nigh on eighty miles - and the road can be bad.' Geoffrey pricked up his ears: Cardigan was where his pilgrims were said to be heading - if pilgrims they truly were! He decided to listen before speaking again.

The burly man shrugged his shoulders. 'Well, we are in no hurry, for they cannot outrun us and the lady is unlikely to flee.' His companions chuckled, which puzzled Geoffrey. 'So we'll rest our tired beasts here, eat at this fine inn and be on our way this afternoon. Is there somewhere on our road where we may shelter tonight?'

'Carmarthen town lies halfway: after that nowhere of any size to Cardigan.'

'Then let us sleep in this Carmarthen tonight. But first rest, food and see our horses watered.' As his party drifted towards the inn door their leader turned to Geoffrey. 'Your turn, young sir. No doubt you overheard us, but there is no secret. I trust we have not delayed you unduly, but I too bear a writ.'

'Indeed not sir, but it seems we have something in common. I gather you are to arrest some lady. I know nothing of that, but are you by any chance also a posse comitatus sent to arrest thieving Glastonbury monks who also make for Cardigan?'

'We are, sir, but how do you know of us?'

'A gentleman named Robin Stukely may have reached you, for I left him at Glastonbury to ride …'

'So I did, and have joined them. Well met, sir!' That elegant youth came forward, pulling a face at Geoffrey's rumpled appearance then grinning broadly. The two young men greeted each other jovially then explained how they had travelled by different ways but with the same ends.

The posse leader smiled approvingly. 'That was well done. But now, sir, why not join us yourself? Another sword could be useful to us and since these runaway monks make for Cardigan let us arrest them together.'

'But what if they have got themselves behind us on the road?'

'Then we wait in Cardigan for them to fall into our arms. They cannot escape.'

Geoffrey nodded. But he was curious. 'You spoke of arresting a lady? Surely you have ample force for that purpose and to arrest some monks too without my help.'

The older man laughed. 'Indeed we have and neither she nor the monks will resist us. But your sword might come handy should the locals in Cardigan object to losing their lady and resist us.' He clapped Geoffrey on the back. 'I see I should explain. My party has two tasks. Arresting these thieving monks you know about. As to the second, having almost done with monastic houses the king's majesty has decreed that all papist shrines in the realm are to be destroyed - this is recent and you may not yet have heard of it. We are told there is such a shrine at Cardigan so we are to deal with it while we are there. The lady I spoke of is an effigy of the Virgin, the very one your monks may be seeking on pilgrimage, so Master Stukely tells me. We are charged to take it to London for public burning with other popery and raze its shrine to the ground as well as arrest your monks. Two birds with one stone.'

'Then I am honoured to ride with you.' Geoffrey held out his hand: 'I am Geoffrey Dawnay in the Commissioners' service in Somerset.' The older man shook it. 'And I am William Pentridge of Gloucester, knight: the rest you know. We are pleased to have you join us. Collect your baggage and join us at the inn.'

'Gladly. But if you can spare the time, Sir William, I must get me a horse and a new cap and gloves and other clothing to make myself presentable again - if such can be found here!'

'Well, we are in no haste for our monks cannot escape and the lady certainly cannot. Let us then stay the night here and make an early start tomorrow. This inn of yours looks comfortable: join us here when you have made your purchases.'

When Aston returned from the town Ralph called them all together and gave them Luke's news. A flurry of activity followed and by nightfall they were ready to leave. They left Luke to sleep undisturbed and thanked the abbot and his brothers warmly. A short prayer by the abbot, handshakes all round and an exchange of blessings, then Thomas led them along the footpath under the abbey walls to the western end of the stone bridge and the track leading north over the hills. Abbot

Leyshon had confirmed that this was their best route: 'Few live up there and it is quiet even by day. It is easy walking save where it descends to the Twyi valley. There lies a bridge over the river and beyond it the village of Pontardawe, where you should find rough shelter for the night. Six miles - three hours' walk in the dark.'

There was just enough light to see by as cautiously they climbed the stony track. The moon-blanched hills, eerily silent, were disturbing to brothers used to comforting confinement within stout walls at night: this was as foreign as their night journey down the Brue and their unease was almost palpable. Nervous sheep plunging out of their path startled them. There were stumbles on the uneven ground. Ralph determined that from now one they would travel by day wherever possible.

After an hour of uphill walking the track levelled onto higher treeless country. Suddenly, to their right, ancient stones reared up at them, huge and mysterious. The novices crossed themselves and all closed up and quickened their pace. Another half hour and the track turned left, dropping steeply to the valley below as Abbot Leyshon had described. Now they groped in inky darkness under trees that blocked out the night sky. At last they emerged into moonlight eerily pale on flat meadowland. They saw the hump of the river bridge and the loom of silent buildings beyond. As they approached the bridge Ralph whispered 'Quiet now lest we disturb dogs or geese and they arouse the village.' He turned to Evan. 'We must stop soon; a barn perhaps. Where best to look?'

'This side of the village, Father, for here are their meadows for grazing larger stock: the hills beyond will have only sheep and no shelter. But when we leave tomorrow we must pass through the village or go a long way round.'

'Then we start before dawn when even country folk should still be abed. Should we meet any they will see pilgrims and no threat to themselves. Let us look for a barn.'

They soon found one and managed to open its door noiselessly, the silence broken only by the mournful lowing of a cow somewhere nearby. 'They've taken its calf,' Aston whispered.

Thomas closed the barn door quietly as Ralph took out his tinderbox and lit a candle. Its feeble glow revealed stacked new hay but no livestock save for a dozen roosting hens that rustled indignant feathers but soon went back to sleep. It was warm and dry, with the sweet scent of the hay. 'This serves us well,' said Ralph. They lit two more candles, set all three on an old grindstone on the earth floor and clustered around it to eat the substantial cold supper Leyshon had provided. Most prayed briefly. Then they made individual nests in the straw, turning around like dogs before drawing habits and cloaks around them and hoods over their faces. The candles were pinched out. Soon the only sound was rustling as someone turned over. They slept.

All but Giles, who had been feigning sleep. He had learned from the old Cistercian that this was the best place to leave his companions and return to the main road for Cardigan. So far he had held his tongue but inwardly had come to despise their so-called 'pilgrimage' as sinful deceit. His would be real. Once satisfied all were asleep he rose stealthily and left a note previously written and some coins by Ralph's satchel. Then he took up the pilgrim staff and his own satchel and stole into the night.

With the strict discipline of daily Offices monks could wake up almost at will. Well before dawn Ralph opened his eyes to darkness. He had to rouse the two laymen.

'Time to leave. No candles. We break our fast later.'

Although clumsy with sleep and in darkness they were soon ready and gathering at the barn door when Francis whispered: Father, Brother Giles is not here!'

Ralph was unconcerned. 'Outside relieving himself: he will soon return.' But after perhaps a quarter hour there was still no sign of him. They were about to go in search when Thomas handed Ralph a scrap of paper and the coins he had found wrapped in a cloth. 'These lay where you slept, Father.' They risked lighting a candle, crowding close to shade its light as Ralph peered at it.

He looked up, grim-faced. 'Brother Giles has abandoned us. He has gone to the shrine at Cardigan - he writes that his, not ours, is the true pilgrimage. This money he leaves the farmer for his bed in the hay. One good thought at least. I suppose we should do likewise.'

A shocked Evan reverted briefly to Welsh. 'Mair o Aberteifi! Then in English: 'But he knew it was never our intention ....'

'It was always his intention, brother: I see it now.' He should have foreseen this!

Aston asked: 'What has he taken with him?'

'No great treasures: he carried none. But he had a quarter of our money on him.'

Thomas's voice whispered from beyond the candle glow: 'Your staff has gone, too.'

Aston was angry. 'He has betrayed us, shown no loyalty to our mission though he came of his own free will. We must pursue him and recover what he has taken!'

Ralph shook his head. 'No loyalty to us, true. He is consumed by a higher loyalty; credit him that at least. As to pursuit, all we would do in the dark is get lost and delay ourselves, perhaps fatally? No, we let him go and continue on our way.'

Aston objected. 'But Father, we put it abroad we were going to Cardigan and now he plans to go there. This makes his capture likely and if caught he may betray us and reveal that in truth our aim is to head north.'

'By which time we should be well away. Our best course is to keep to our original plan. Let him go his way and let us be on ours while we have this darkness.'

No cock crowed as they stole silently through the sleeping village. Then, guided by a chuckle of water to their left they felt their way up a path rising between the black loom of hills, edging past a few outlying silent cottages. Presently Evan, sharp-eared, said: 'water flowing the other way; downhill now' and the path began to descend. When at last the sun peeped over the eastern hills Ralph saw they were bearing north as planned. Appreciating its faint warmth they stopped to break their fast.

As the daylight strengthened they saw a larger valley ahead that crossed theirs at right angles: a wooden bridge spanned its river. Already thin blue wood smoke from early fires wreathed the valley sides. But their eyes were drawn to a grander sight beyond, where the ground rose in majestic swells to a high crest line. The lower slopes were a mix of woodland, rough meadow and grass where a few small shaggy ponies grazed among a scatter of sheep. Higher up the fresh green of cropped grass was dotted with more sheep. Nearer the skyline they saw a patchwork of yellow broom, mauve-tinged moor grass, scattered grey boulders and patches of orange-pink bracken, darker spots on them marking where fronds were dying back. To the novices, children of monastic confinement, this grand sweep of open land with its variegated colouring was entrancing. 'Mynydd Ddu - the Black Mountain,' Evan announced with some pride, as if inviting them into his home.

The novices and Thomas gazed in wonder. Ralph said 'black' seemed a misnomer and Evan replied that he should see it in winter when the low light cast deep shadows in its hollows. Aston asked dubiously: 'Must we climb up that?' All looked at Evan.

'Once over this mountain we descend to a valley that leads east to England, with towns and villages for shelter. But we should not turn east while on this high open ground for if our pursuers are already close we could be seen from miles around. It would be best if we keep straight ahead where I remember it is at its narrowest. With hard walking we can be across it and into the cover of the valley before nightfall. Or we can skirt west around it keeping to lower ground and around to the same valley, which would add miles to our journey but be safer.' But the morning was gloriously uplifting and they were beguiled by the view. It was decided to go straight for the crest. Only Evan seemed uneasy.

They followed a tiny tributary valley leading upward - drinking water to hand! But it proved hard going through its narrow strip of close set oak, ash and birch. Large birds circled lazily overhead which Evan said were kites and buzzards. Once onto open grassland the going became easier. But now a second crest line appeared ahead and they were tiring. They stopped for breath among outcrops of pale lichen-flecked rock breaking through short grass. Heather stretched away to their right. At their feet clumps of small yellow poppies waved in the light breeze. Butterflies danced, kestrels and falcons wheeled overhead, a glossy black raven strutted insolently nearby. Cloud shadows raced across the sunlit slopes, whose scalloped flanks were indeed in near-black shadow. Evan pointed to rocks piled in rough heaps. 'Man-made, they say - by the Ancients.' They were vaguely menacing.

Now the slope fell away to the head of a small valley, beyond it yet another and higher swell of land rose before them. They were near exhaustion now, not daring to linger in this exposed landscape yet doubting their strength to carry on. Presently, exhilaration gone, they slumped to the ground as one, indifferent to the grand view.

Which suddenly disappeared.

Instantly they found themselves enveloped in white oblivion, treacherous low cloud blanketing the mountain without warning. Their visible world was reduced to a few feet, to those nearest to them, to their own hands and feet. The voices of their companions were disembodied, coming from unexpected quarters: the air had turned cool and clammy. Without the sun only memory pointed their way: with no path to follow they knew themselves lost. They were fearful of the invisible slope ahead, the last thing they had seen - whichever way was ahead! Calling to one another they groped for the reassurance of human touch.

Again Ralph was assailed by self-doubt. He had led them into this. Should he have insisted they take the longer but safer way skirting the mountain? Long ago in Picardy he had known the fear of being lost at night in strange territory; never this white blindness. But he must sound confident.

'Close up or we will get separated. Keep moving - we cannot stay on this mountain all night. Hold onto another's girdle or belt and follow me in single file. We see nothing but we know our direction is down slope on grass then rising again, so we must feel our way with our feet. Slowly, now.' He beckoned Evan to fall in behind him: should the cloud lift even for a moment he might recognise some feature.

As they shuffled blindly forward they were startled by a loud clattering. 'Not the Ancients abroad,' Evan remarked dryly, 'just a sheep on those stones - even they cannot see in this.' He seemed composed, almost jocund, and Ralph sensed he was coming out of his shell. As they groped down slope drizzle began to fall and their white world darkened to dismal grey. This had become the worst journey of their lives. It was unnerving to follow the prior through this grey blanket, barely seeing the man in front though clutching his girdle or belt. The wet grass was slippery and there were tumbles and collisions and the danger of turned ankles.

Ralph tried to visualize this slope he had glimpsed before the cloud wiped it out. He thought it fell a hundred or more feet to the little valley floor below. The brook down there had emerged from what should be a spring hidden by a clump of bushes. If they crossed water it would mean they had drifted too far west.

It seemed an age to the valley floor. Their feet were bruised by rocks seen too late, hands sore when a slip had them grasping at sharp-edged grasses, ankles strained from turning on tussocks. But they could hear no running water and Ralph hoped they were still heading roughly north. Presently the drizzle stopped but the cloud showed no sign of lifting. They groped on over confusing minor rises and falls their eyes could not see, their feet not interpret. They heard sheep cropping nearby or stumbling away. Crossing a shallow depression Ralph heard rustling and looked down to see reeds brushing the skirts of his habit. His next step took him ankle deep into sticky mud and he stopped abruptly, Evan bumping into him. They lost time edging around to firmer ground. At last they felt they were climbing again.

While they took another brief rest Ralph whispered to Evan. 'I am utterly lost. We are still on this mountain and too exhausted to go much farther. What shall we do?'

'I am as lost as you, Father. From what we saw before the cloud came down we cannot hope to get clear of it this day for we move much too slowly.'

'Yet we cannot survive the night up here, even should the rain hold off.'

'I fear we must, Father.' Evan hesitated. 'Perhaps there is a way to survive it.' Ralph raised an eyebrow as Evan continued. 'We know we must go up-slope again to that last crest we saw - near half a mile away and as far as we can hope to carry on without sleep. Now from my childhood travels with drovers I remember - I think I remember - those higher slopes ahead have patches of bracken, which indeed we have already seen. The drovers avoided them because they believed something in the bracken makes sheep and cattle fall sick.' Sensing Ralph's impatience he hurried on. 'I think that if there is bracken on that slope we can rest the night there.'

'For sure it is as far as we can manage this day. But why not stop right here? Everywhere seems equally wretched.'

'The bracken, Father: it can shelter us. It grows four feet or more high and spreads its ferns into a canopy that will keep out any rain and leave the ground below fairly dry - and sheltered from wind if that comes. Now in September it drops its fronds on the ground to make a ready-made bed. If we can go on just a little we may survive the night in its shelter. By morning if this cloud lifts we can see again.'

Ralph had never heard Evan talk so much. But he was not convinced.

'If, Brother, always if! And if we do not find some of this bracken?'

'I confess it is guesswork.'

'Hmm. You say it can make animals sick? Can it then harm humans?'

'I have not heard so. But there will be ticks to trouble us, for sure.'

'We all know about ticks and must cover ourselves closely against them.' Ralph stared into the grey nothingness. 'You do more than guess, brother: you reason well from what you know. But is it enough? Yet it is our one hope - so let us then put it to the test.' They stumbled on with painful slowness, still climbing blind. After two thirds of an hour by Ralph's hour glass held close to his eyes their weary bodies were thrusting waist-high into a rustle of stiff bushes. There was bracken after all.

They burrowed under the thick canopy, wrapped themselves in their habits and cloaks, for a second night turned like dogs to make nests, drew their hoods closely over their faces and their sleeves over their hands against ticks and sank into exhausted sleep. Exhausted, Matthew was asleep before he had covered himself fully.

Thomas awoke to a sliver of sunlight through fronds close above his face. He backed stiffly out of his shelter, stood up and stretched himself. A skylark was singing high in a clear pale blue sky. The bracken was all around him, a few small birds scuffling in it. He spent several minutes carefully removing every tick from his outer clothing and body then gazed back down the slope they had groped up so fearfully the night before. How easy it looked in this clear morning air! Turning around, he saw they were almost at what must surely be a final crest. Leaving the others asleep he strolled up the last of the slope to look over the crest into the next valley.

His jaw dropped. On the far side a great castle reared on a mighty crag. He could see no smoke or movement up there. It looked derelict and inaccessible, its massive ramparts frowning menacingly over a great cliff. He hurried back to tell the others.

They sat along the crest eating their remaining food and gazing at the lonely fortress. With his old soldier's eye Ralph suspected it had suffered slighting in the past, although the great curtain wall immediately facing them looked virtually intact. The crisp morning sunshine and clear views for miles had raised their spirits and the food, although getting stale, strengthened them for more walking. Only Evan and Matthew were silent.

They descended slowly into the next valley. Evan was worried. 'If that is Carreg Cennen castle we have gone too far west in that cloud and will not join the Tywi Valley where I hoped to turn east. But we may as well keep straight ahead now.' They crossed a little stream dry shod over flat rocks. Now Evan felt dawning recognition. He said more confidently: 'we must move downstream now - westward: it should lead us to the River Tywi while skirting this higher ground.' Another mile brought them to a few hovels strung alongside a wide swathe of heavily trampled grass that crossed their path. A few ragged children peeped out to watch them.

Now Evan was certain where they were. 'This is a drovers' trail,' he said almost cheerfully. 'It leads to Llandeilo village four miles way. We should have been well east but this will do us. Once in the Tywi valley it will be easier walking.'

They followed the wide grassy trail through more yellow poppies. Bird cries were everywhere around them. At last the track dropped to a much larger valley with well-wooded flanks and flat floor where the river snaked through water meadows and small black cattle grazed. On the far bank a village was wreathed in wood smoke: west of it another old castle frowned on its crag. 'The River Tywi and Llandeilo, exclaimed Evan, certain now, 'and that is Dynefwr Castle, once the heart of a Welsh kingdom and granted to Sir Rhys ap Thomas for killing King Richard at Bosworth Field, some do say.' But nobody was listening as they trudged on stoically.

On the valley floor several tracks converged at a stone bridge which they crossed into the village. In its only street ill-dressed villagers stared at them 'Not much English from here on,' said Evan and went to seek food and lodging for the night.

By now even their pretence of pilgrimage was evaporating. The brothers' sense of vocation was fading fast: more and more they saw themselves as refugees, if still with a task to complete. Ralph realised that when - if - they found a haven for their treasures they would soon disperse into the worldly life around them. Under the new dispensation all but himself should be free to do so, for he alone had taken his final vows. With monasticism swept away and the invasive ideas of the renegade Luther spreading quickly only the firmest faith could survive unscathed. He must accept that Giles alone had really possessed that faith. Or had it possessed him? But Giles had gone to some mad apotheosis. Or were they the mad ones?

Evan found an inn that would lodge them. They were desperate for hot food and a night's rest under a roof. Like his regular drinkers who stared at them open-mouthed their portly host was perplexed by their sudden appearance, but business was slack and he had no mind to turn away even dishevelled monks in uncommon black habits. A meagre supper was brought to the two bedchambers they had engaged: crudely furnished and not over-clean they spelt luxury after a barn and a bare mountain.

Aston, his thoughts on his brother's farm, spoke to Evan. 'You say we are too far west. Is it not then high time we turned east for England?'

Evan had no intention of leaving Wales again but hoped to see them safe to the English border. He nodded and they approached Prior Ralph. While the younger men slept in the adjoining chamber the three talked quietly in the room they shared.

Ralph considered. 'I agree, Robert. I doubt we are still pursued and we must strike east sometime: let it be now while we still have strength to walk.' By now the others hardly noticed his use of Christian names and that he was beginning to consult rather than order. They were becoming easier with one another, even the youngsters.

Evan voiced a concern. 'Father, there are Cistercian houses here in Wales. If Cromwell has not yet closed them all we might run into commissioners on that sad business, if not after us.'

Aston nodded. 'True, and they would question our black habits here. Is it not time for you brothers to abandon them and dress as lay folk?'

But for Ralph that was a step too far. 'Only as a last resort. For now I see no cause, for our habits still protect us as pilgrims as we intended. Anyway we do not posses such clothing. Evan, how far to England from here?'

'I can only guess.' He counted on his fingers. 'Five miles back to Llangadog. From there to Llandyfri - a chartered town where we can buy all we need - is as far again. Say ten miles in all and more than enough for the day. From there to Brecon another day's march. From Brecon the road points to England.'

'Aston asked: 'Where in England?'

'I have heard the closest English town of size is Hereford.' Which left the steward more content.

Ralph asked:'But then how far from Brecon to Hereford?' Evan shrugged. 'I know not for I have never been there. But several days' walking for sure.'

Ralph frowned. 'So a full week's travelling lies ahead! That will test us sorely - but the sooner we start the better. Let us make for this - this - Llandyfri tomorrow.'

***

While they slept Giles also lay asleep in a small inn near Carmarthen. After abandoning the others, finding the main west road had proved a slow and tiring business but once on it he had been fortunate. He had chanced upon a carter in dusty doublet and hose stretching his legs while his horse grazed placidly at the roadside. His cart was barely half laden. Giles shunned human contact but he knew he had far to travel. He might spare his feet and he had enough money on him. He approached the man, hoping he spoke English.

'Good day to you. I am a pilgrim and my feet sore weary. Are you for Cardigan?'

The carter looked warily at the gaunt black figure with the burning eyes and black polished staff. He replied in slow English. 'Only as far as Carmarthen, Brother.'

'Will you take me there? I will pay you.'

'The carter was dubious: monks never had money. But his eyes widened when Giles held out silver coins.

'I stay with my brother at Pontarddulais this night and on to Carmarthen tomorrow.'

'Then I shall seek lodgings at that place. I will pay you half this now, the rest when we reach Carmarthen if you take me with you tomorrow.' And so it was agreed.

With Giles aloof again and the carter uneasy in his presence it was a silent journey and a slow one, for they travelled at walking pace. But the road was firm if dusty, not yet the quagmire of winter. They met travellers on foot and horseback, several carts and one lumbering wagon drawn by two white long horned oxen, the carter greeting all with a lift of his whip. Presently Giles, his thoughts on the shrine ahead and needing to be alone, pleaded weariness, inserted himself among the chests and boxes in the back of the cart and pulled empty sacks over himself against the dust of the road. It hid him from view and was not uncomfortable. Soon the rhythmic creaking and swaying and the soft thudding of the horse's hooves in the dust lulled him to sleep. He woke up when the cart stopped in a village at the head of a narrow estuary.

'Pontarddulais' said the carter and introduced the man emerging from a cottage as his brother. After some whispering in rapid Welsh

Giles was offered, for a price, a meagre supper and dubious cot in the attic.

Next morning a fresh horse was led from a stable behind the house - it seemed the brother provided a staging post, or perhaps the two were in business together. The weather had improved. It took an hour to clear the village, for goods were unloaded at two houses, a rope-bound chest was picked up at a third, all with time-consuming discussions and scrutiny of grubby tally sheets. At last they left the village behind.

'How far now to Carmarthen?'

'Fifteen miles.'

'Another five hours?'

'Longer: I have more goods to deliver. But we'll be there before dark.'

They climbed and descended and splashed through fords. Giles wondered if there was anywhere in Wales without hills and valleys and more sheep than humans. Everywhere scattered poor homesteads showed lazy plumes of smoke.

Six slow miles brought them to a hamlet where the carter delivered filled sacks to two cottages. Yet more slow miles, another river crossing: the journey seemed endless. Then yet another village. 'Pontyberem,' the carter announced. 'I rest the horse here.' An urchin appeared at an alehouse door to water it and the carter disappeared inside. Giles stretched his legs along the short dusty street, gnawing at a piece of stale bread which reminded him that soon he would reach his destination. From then on he must endure purification by fasting before he could approach the Virgin.

Curious onlookers stared at him. He drew his cowl across his face and stalked back to the cart, indifferent to them, indifferent to the world.

The last nine miles ended at a sizeable town. 'Carmarthen', said the carter. 'I told you we'd be here before dark.'

The previous night Giles had slept soundly in a hard flea-ridden cot. Now he tossed restlessly in a better bed in a clean inn. For he was nearing his goal - the innkeeper had told him Cardigan was twenty five miles away - and impatient to complete his pilgrimage. He would go afoot from now on, fast and drink only water, pray unceasingly. The last five miles he would go barefoot in the hair shirt he had brought with him. By God's grace he could be there by nightfall. He would see Her!

At dawn he rose and knelt to pray, including a prayer for forgiveness for taking money held in common and the pilgrim staff in Prior Ralph's care. He washed and dressed carefully, polished the silver crucifix atop the staff until it shone and filled his leather water bottle from a jug. He had paid for his lodging the night before. He shouldered his satchel and left, closing the inn door quietly behind him.

Giles' last and longest day began with a brief descent to reality. Aware of possible pursuit he avoided the highway, taking a hill path the innkeeper had pointed out. But once on it he was soon alone in his private exalted world, striding out unaware of his surroundings, of the brighter weather, of an occasional passer-by flinching from his wild eyes and gaunt black figure, of wearying legs and aching feet, of hunger, even of thirst. When he judged he was five miles from his goal he stripped naked on the lonely path, put on the hair shirt under his habit and threw away his underclothing and shoes to walk on bare feet, ignoring the hard stony path. As he neared his goal he felt growing exhilaration, not exhaustion, and his stride lengthened, not shortened. At last, in failing light, he saw below him a small settlement. Cardigan!

For a last moment he was again aware of his earthly surroundings. The road descended to the little port, beyond whose low buildings a long estuary snaked towards the sea, gleaming in the last of the sunlight. Torchlight moved and winked in the little town and he sensed ant-like human activity down there. He hurried on.

On a stream bank a crowd of people bearing horn lanterns and flickering torches milled around a small building with a thatched roof and walls part wattle and part stone with scaffolding around them. This then was journey's end. Here was Her shrine, for these people must be pilgrims like himself! They were many for such a small place and must include local folk. A festival, perhaps? A special Mass? As he hurried to join them he saw the small windows of the shrine suddenly glow golden, a glow quickly deepening and spreading into a wondrous red-gold radiance that lit the sky, the people around it become agitated silhouettes. He was not surprised. So it should be, so he had dreamt it, so he had prayed for it. Giles was gone from the world. In a dazzling, blanketing mist of ecstasy, he raised the pilgrim staff high, cried out in a great voice and broke into a stumbling run towards the radiance that was Her.

Pleased to be turning towards England - or in Evan's case keeping his distance from his old home - they were in better spirits next morning as they set off for Llandyfri. All but Matthew, now silent and walking behind alone. By now the others made their decisions together, even the youngsters joining in, for Ralph, still the acknowledged leader, was becoming a companion. After a mile they stopped an approaching carter to ask if they were on the right road. Evan spoke to him in Welsh.

The carter welcomed any break in his routine. 'Yes, brothers, this way leads you to Llandyfri. You will find the place a-bustle.'

'Market day?'

'That was yesterday. Today should be quiet - women clearing up and men nursing sore heads. But a party of horsemen - strangers they were - rode in this morning, official-looking gentlemen leading some soldiers and making a stir in the market place. Men and beasts looked travel-stained. But they were in no hurry, for as I left they were heading for the inn by the new town hall to eat their breakfast. I'd warrant they'll not hurry over it and their beasts need seeing to.'

Evan translated. He thought more might be learnt by affecting casual curiosity. 'Yes, such would indeed arouse interest. I wonder what might be their purpose? Could you hear their talk?'

'Only a little as they dismounted at the inn. I was fetching Dobbin here - he pointed to his horse - from his stable and overheard a few words. They spoke English so I could not understand much, but I think they spoke about what the road ahead might be like. Whatever it was, they seemed in ill humour.'

'So you learned nought of their business?'

'Nothing. And now, brothers, I must be on my way.' He saluted with his whip and horse and master continued their placid way.

Aston said: 'They are not our pursuers from Glastonbury, who cannot yet know we have left the west road. It is not us they seek. Indeed, they might not seek anyone.'

'True. But,' Ralph added thoughtfully, 'their business must be to uphold the law, serve a writ or make arrests. Why else bring soldiers?'

Francis suggested they might still be taking the surrender of monastic houses.

Ralph shook his head. 'Abbot Leyshon told me all smaller houses in Wales were closed by two years ago and there are no large ones here inland.'

Aston pondered: 'So they seek people, not monastic houses. Yet not us, it seems.'

Ralph nodded. 'But as we cannot be certain of their purpose it would be prudent to avoid them. Let us return to Llandeilo and hide under some roof until they are gone.'

'Have we time?' Thomas had grasped an essential point. 'Father, carters travel at walking pace and by Brother Evan's reckoning this one had come eleven miles and so left this Llandyfri place three hours ago or more. He told us these men were going to an inn for breakfast. However long that took them, travelling on horseback even at leisurely pace, they could already be almost upon us.'

Ralph patted him on the shoulder. 'Well reasoned, lad: we must find somewhere to hide at once.' They hurried back the way they had come. After an anxious ten minutes they came to a coppice where a large stack of firewood awaited collection on the roadside. Concealed in the trees behind it they waited anxiously.

Two foot travellers passed, a boy on a donkey, a wagon drawn by two heavy horses, its iron-shod wheels squealing. Then they heard horsemen approaching.

To their alarm they reined in directly in front of them, gesticulating and apparently arguing. Ralph motioned Thomas to crawl close behind the wood stack to hear what they said. He noted that the big youth moved with the stealth of a poacher.

At last the horsemen trotted on and Thomas returned. 'They spoke English and were in black humour. They have come from some place called Monmouth, are saddle sore, the inns were wretched, the natives surly and speaking no English, and so on and on.'

'Their business, boy?'

'Yes, I made something of that amidst their quarrelling. Their leader is indeed a Cromwell man. They have been to some priory called Llan - tony?'- he looked at Evan, who nodded - 'which had not yet - or not properly - signed the surrender. They were grumbling at their rough ride up some track to no purpose, for they found the priory already abandoned with nothing worth removing. Then they struck west over more rough country to another priory at a town called Brecon, which had surrendered, but there they had some dispute of law or something - that I did not understand. At Brecon they rejoined this road and are now to visit a third priory in Carmarthen. Then they would be free to go home, for from there to the western sea another of Cromwell's party would take over the work. They grumbled that tomorrow would be another wasted day. Some were for going home there and then but the leader ordered them to carry on. So then they left, still muttering. That was the whole if it, Father.'

Ralph frowned. 'So they are not after us but harassing humble priories: it seems nothing is to escape this king's net. Still, we had best stay out of their sight. Should they sleep in Llandeilo tonight we durst not do likewise and if they return this way tomorrow they must not find us on this open road.'

'Nor must we be forced even farther west.' Aston's mind was still on Hereford.

Ralph nodded. 'Indeed not. So we should skirt around this side of Llandeilo and head north again. Evan, what may we expect that way?'

'More of these hills and valleys you have all come to love so much. I remember a hill track we can take. After some miles it divides. We could take stock there and if all seems quiet take the more easterly way towards England again.'

There were nods of approval. Evan had more. 'Where the track divides there is a small monastic house, likely abandoned now and a possible shelter.'

Ralph said: 'Let us hope it is and of no concern of these iconoclasts. North then!'

By noon the monks were again concealed among trees awaiting the return of Aston and Thomas, who had gone openly into Llandeilo to buy food. Their lack of Welsh might draw attention but Evan's black habit would have attracted far more.

As soon as they returned with a sack of food they moved on. The constant walking was now as boring as it was tiring. Matthew lagged ever farther behind, Aston had developed a limp. Only Thomas maintained much curiosity, asking Evan the Welsh names for everything he saw. Evan approved, although the lad's accent had him smiling. They trudged on, heads down. They encountered only one person before the track divided, a shepherd coming down from hill pasture with a one-eyed dog at his heels. He was ready to talk when Evan questioned him about an old abbey ahead.

'Abaty Tal-y-Llychau.' They spoke in rapid Welsh then the shepherd tipped his cap and continued on his way.

'You heard he had much to say - no doubt better than talking to sheep all day. The name means the abbey at the head of two lakes: we should see them soon. The English just call it Talley.' Aston muttered something and Evan smiled tolerantly and continued. 'He says some "big men" came to close it two years ago but found only one ancient monk who was touched' - he tapped his temple - 'and they took him away. He says the place is neglected but the abbey church is sound and now serves as the parish church. He did not know who worships there - only that he does not except when his goodwife makes him!'

'Well then,' Ralph said, 'Let us rest and eat at this place and decide where we go next.' They carried on. The inevitable sheep dotted the hill slopes and higher up they saw a few crude wattle huts. 'Summer shelter for shepherds,' explained Evan, 'they bring the flocks down for winter.' They passed the two tiny lakes and then, as Evan had said, the track divided. Nearby stood the abbey.

Apart from its church, its doors firmly bolted and locked, it was indeed abandoned and already some outbuildings stood open to the sky. What had probably been the abbot's lodging, however, still had its roof intact and most of the glass in its windows. They made for it, entering the undercroft through an opening from which the door had been removed. Grass grew between the flagstones and there was a pungent smell of sheep. Thomas risked climbing the dangerously loose flags of a stone staircase to the upper floor to report that it was dry, still possessed some furniture and was dusty more than dirty. He guided them carefully up the stairs to a room where they found benches at a long table, fell upon their food and considered what to do next.

It was a damp dreary place and they felt its isolation keenly. Depressed, they had made up their minds to move on when suddenly everything outside was blanketed in low cloud and it began to rain. With their night on the Black Mountain fresh in their memories they saw no choice but to stay where they were. A scuffling noise came from below as sheep shouldered into the undercroft, their rank odour wafting up the staircase. There was no bedding so they settled down for another uncomfortable night stretched out on hard benches and table and the stone floor. At least they were dry.

It was late afternoon when Sir William Pentridge's party trotted into Cardigan. Geoffrey and Robin, more congenial travelling companions than his dour assistant and Reformists seeming as devout as himself, rode alongside him.

They roused the town mayor and Sir William waved his writ under the man's apprehensive nose. 'Read this, sir! We are charged by

Vicar-General Cromwell to destroy all papist shrines. You will take us to yours.'

The flustered mayor protested feebly. 'Sir, the Bless - as you see the shrine draws many pilgrims and is greatly revered: there may be trouble.' Indeed the little town seemed well peopled and folk were already gathering curiously around them.

'More than we can deal with, think you?' Sir William pointed to his grinning steel-helmeted men-at-arms. 'When you have shown us this shrine round up your town guards and any others you can trust and bring them here to support us if need be.' He left a soldier to guard their horses while they followed the mayor.

The shrine was a small building with scaffolding erected around it: piles of dressed stone lay around. Sir William pushed through the gathering crowd and kicked open its newly-hung door. The two officials and Geoffrey and Robin went in while the remaining soldiers stood guard outside. Inside, a man and three women knelt at a small candle-lit altar above which an effigy was set high on the rear wall. They were unceremoniously thrust outside and the intruders looked around them.

The one-roomed building was being rebuilt. Its timber-framed wattle and daub walls still stood, the daub cracked and missing in places, but solid masonry walls were rising outside them, already at waist height and higher at the corners, clearly the work of an able mason. Beyond the candle glow from the altar the interior was dimly lit and the walls bare save for some worn hanging cloths. The altar was a plain table covered with a rough blue cloth. On it stood two handsome silver candlesticks holding tall wax candles flanked by four small tallow candles in simple sconces. They opened a small chest against a side wall to find a chalice, paten and censer.

Sir William pursed his lips. 'I would aver that Low Masses could be said here when a priest visited. This building speaks to me of humble origin but a recently revived papist influence, enough to support this new building work and I dare say provide this plate. It is ripe for burning.' He and Geoffrey raised the large candlesticks high to throw light on the effigy. They were startled by what they saw. The wooden effigy of the Virgin, the Christ child in the crook of one arm and a lighted taper in the other hand, was more than life size, delicately carved and painted in glowing colours, gilt and red setting off the radiant blue of the gown. It was remarkably fine work for such a remote place. Despite their disdain of it they were privately impressed.

'Well, Master Crossley?' Sir William turned to his assistant, who was examining everything closely and making notes. Geoffrey realised that the man must be a valuer of goods for confiscation by the Court of Augmentations.

Crossley, now in his element, spoke with authority in a London accent. 'The altar and cloth, the chest, the small candles and sconces and the wall hangings have no value. The two larger candlesticks are silver, not silver-gilt, as are the Eucharist vessels in the chest: all these are costly and should be seized. The effigy shows fine craftsmanship - probably Flemish - and of course goes to London for public burning.'

Sir William nodded. 'You have a tally of the silverware?' Crossley nodded. 'Good. Have it wrapped carefully and distributed among the spare saddlebags.'

He drew Geoffrey and Robin aside. 'The man is a common clerk and a bore but he knows his business. We are ordered to take all effigies to London, but this one is too big and heavy for horseback: it would mean procuring a cart, which would greatly slow our return journey. My men are ill-pleased at being so long from their homes and would not take kindly to such delay. Nor for that matter would I. I fear the lady must meet with an accident!'

'You mean to burn her here with the rest, sir?'

'That would be convenient. I must convince Master Crossley, a punctilious fellow, but that should not be difficult - his concern is with valuables, not firewood.' He laughed. Crossley and a soldier wrapped the silverware in cloths and packed them into saddlebags while Sir William sent another soldier to find combustibles. The crowd at the door had trebled in size and had become ominously noisy: the two remaining soldiers had drawn their daggers. There was no sign of reinforcements.

'Well, let us to it.' They dragged the altar table against the rear wall, climbed on top of it and with difficulty took down the heavy effigy. When the soldier arrived pulling a hand cart filled with combustibles - tubs of tar, pitch and fish oil from the harbour, faggots, shavings from a carpenter's shop - a sizeable bonfire was expertly prepared in the centre of the room. The wall hangings were added, the altar table was smashed for its timber and piled on top and the tallow candles thrust in for good measure. Finally, the effigy was propped on top, upright in conscious mockery.

The crowd outside had grown even larger and sounded increasingly angry so Robin went to investigate. He reported that the mayor had just returned with three town guards armed with pikes, together with a few men carrying pitchforks and staves, presumably local reformists. They had joined the soldiers in a defensive arc around the doorway. The soldiers had primed their matchlocks.

Sir Williams was an old soldier and the situation appeared to give him grim pleasure. 'Right! Put the saddlebags by the door and be ready to fight your way through to the horses as soon as I have the place ablaze. Keep close. Soldiers to form the rearguard: shoot if you have to.' He fumbled with a tinderbox while the others waited at the doorway. After the usual repeated attempts the kindling at the base of the pyre caught fire, then the flames reached the oil and pitch-soaked cloths and flared into crackling light and heat, quickly engulfing the body of the Virgin and fingering up for her serene face. Satisfied it was well alight they grabbed the laden saddlebags and left the shrine: the armed men gathered around them as they pushed forward in a wedge through the angry crowd. Flames lit the windows behind them.

Suddenly the thatch of the roof caught alight and erupted in angry flames and the base of the low cloud above glowed orange. The angry crowd recoiled. At that moment a barely human scream was heard above the crowd's din. A flapping black apparition thrust savagely through them, leaving a man and two women sprawled on the ground behind him. It came on bare bleeding feet, knocking aside a slow-witted guard with its shining silver-tipped staff. Before they could react it had flung the scrawny Crossley to the ground and disappeared into the blazing shrine. They turned, aghast but helpless, then Robin and Geoffrey, with Sir William following, half-carried the dazed Crossley between them through the distracted crowd, now in chaotic retreat from the flames and searing heat.

Safely back on horseback they looked back. The fire, fanned by a light breeze, was roaring out of control. As they watched the blazing thatch and roof timbers collapsed in a shower of bright sparks and the red-orange inferno inside danced behind the silhouetted timbers and broken daub of the upper walls before they too fell inwards into the flames. A long shriek from inside sounded oddly triumphant.

The path descended to a small river that plunged between hills to their left but upstream meandered over a flat valley floor. Evan pointed upstream: 'This must be the River Cothi - our way to England lies there.'

Aston noted the weak morning sun. 'More north than east,' he grumbled: if he ever saw England again it would be far from Hereford. After following it for five or so miles, they came to more wretched hovels where a tributary entered. The hillside was pockmarked with curious holes.

Evan pointed to them. 'They say the Romans mined gold here. This is Pumsaint, meaning five saints - we have more saints than gold nuggets in Wales.' He went on hurriedly: 'Best keep to this path upstream for it leads east - well more or less.' He avoided Aston's eye.

Ralph nodded. 'But we'll rest here first.' Each day they tired earlier and the limping Aston and weakening Matthew lagged ever farther behind. All but the increasingly assured Evan and the ever-curious Thomas were withdrawn. It was nigh a week since they had left Neath and they knew they could not keep going without proper sleep and food. Yet they were no closer to England. Decisions must be made.

From Pumsaint the path Evan had pointed out followed the river towards an extension of the Black Mountain. Not wishing to alarm his companions Evan had not spoken of the dangers of this high moor country. In his youth it had been feared for harbouring robbers and outlaws: travellers had avoided it and drovers bringing their livestock down from summer pastures travelled in armed groups. Carreg Cennen castle had been a notorious stronghold of such robbers. From its protective walls they had swooped down on farms and villages stealing livestock, looting and, if they met resistance, burning houses and even killing. Punitive expeditions against them had failed, for they had defended themselves in the castle or scattered into caves known only to themselves, only to emerge and raid again. He had prayed those days were long past. But if there were still robbers about then this high moor so conveniently overlooking the rich farmland of the Teifi Valley was a likely place for them.

Evan questioned an ancient emerging from woodland bent almost double under a bundle of firewood. He was fearful of the unfamiliar black habits but reassured when Evan spoke to him in Welsh and offered him a coin.

'Robbers? Outlaws?' He sniffed. 'A few on the moor still, raiding the valleys. Not like when I was young, though.'

'We are pilgrims and must travel up the Cothi. How safe is it?'

The ancient's rheumy eyes studied the travel-worn habits. 'Poor brothers like you should be safe - they look for deeper purses. Mind you if pickings are poor and they are hungry even monks may be waylaid. But once through Mynydd Mallaen' - he pointed at the high moor - 'you should be safe enough.'

'This path goes through it?'

'Yes, up the Cothi then follow it towards the Tywi Valley. Years ago, when I still had my few acres as a tenant I sometimes had to take my cart that way: I feared that journey, brother, and always took a couple of stout lads along. But the lord took my land back and now we have nothing.' He spat and nodded at the wretched huts.

'How far through the Mynydd?'

'Maybe a dozen miles - I forget.'

Evan's heart sank: already it was well past midday. 'Could we find a night's shelter along the way?'

'One homestead halfway up there still lived in that I know of - where a smaller stream comes in from the north. Never raided they say - perhaps the folk there pay the outlaws to be left in peace.' With that he re-slung his bundle on his back and hobbled on his way.

Evan translated. Wondering what best to do they all looked at him.

He stroked his stubbled chin. 'I fear danger through that mountain. I think we should go up that tributary he spoke of. We may strike an ancient way called Sarn Helen, which should lead to the Teifi, where there will be towns and farms and safety.'

Aston's ankle was hurting. He exploded: 'Tuffy; Twitty!' Why do your rivers all sound the same and hardly human speech? Anyway, I say no. Are we forever to go north through this wilderness? Must we always be barred from England? I say let us carry on up this valley.'

'What of the outlaws and robbers he spoke of?'

'You said nothing about them when we were on the Black Mountain, Evan, nor have we seen any. Why believe that dodderer now?'

'He lives here and knows that road.'

'Knew it half his lifetime ago, not today. I say we go east.' There were nods: all were uncertain but eager to escape this forbidding country and turn east for England.

Evan persisted: 'Do not forget what we carry on us!'

Ralph interjected: 'Yet remember we still appear as travel-weary monks on pilgrimage - and looking the part all too well! Who would risk their souls to rob poor pilgrims?'

Evan's reservations overridden, they set off up the Cothi, Aston and Matthew lagging well behind. After passing two abandoned homesteads they reached the one the old man had described, where the tributary entered from the north. It was still farmed, for smoke curled from a stone chimney set against the end wall, itself evidence of modest affluence. There were several out-buildings. A few of the native black cattle grazed the narrow valley floor, two pigs snouted for acorns on the wooded lower slopes, a cockerel crowed on a dung heap, three mongrel dogs barked and ran towards them. Exhausted, they were desperate not to be turned away.

A glum-looking elderly man emerged from the house and called off the dogs, his stout wife watching from the doorway, an iron pot in her work-reddened hands. Evan told his pilgrim tale and asked for shelter, offering payment. To his surprise the man's face broke into a slow but welcoming smile. A modest payment was agreed and they were shown a small room in the house for Ralph and a large, tolerably clean and almost empty outbuilding for the others. But a changed Ralph opted to sleep with the others and soon straw pallets had been laid down with two thick woollen blankets on each. To Evan the couple seemed uncommonly well-supplied with bedding, but the woman explained that passing shepherds and tinkers sometimes sought shelter. 'We can use the little money they give us for lodging,' she said, smiling, 'and with that rough lot better here than in the house.' When they had washed at the trough in the yard the man returned with a large pot, his wife following with bowls, spoons, bread and mugs of small beer. 'Cawl,' she said, pointing to the steaming pot, 'you look as though you need something to warm you. Sleep well.' The smiling pair withdrew.

Evan translated. Ralph was impressed: I did not expect such hospitality in this poor place! Too long I have misjudged your country, Evan. Everywhere we find kindness.'

But Evan frowned. 'Something is amiss here! Hill folk should be more wary of strangers. And why so many bowls and brychans - blankets? Can so many passers-by need shelter? A shepherd or two perhaps, down from summer pasture - but where pen their flocks? And tinkers where they can expect little work? He shook his head.

The others were too busy with the nourishing broth to share his concerns. Ralph slapped Evan on the back. 'You are too suspicious, man! We have been truly fortunate and will travel refreshed tomorrow.' Evan dismissed his fears as groundless. Presently they slept.

Deep into the black night it was the lights that awoke them; a half circle of wavering yellow lights from horn lanterns held out at arm's length by dark shadowy shapes. Dazed with sleep and confused, they scrambled to get up.

'Lie still there!' The commanding voice, speaking confident English with an indeterminate accent, revealed a touch of learning. He murmured something which sounded like Welsh and the lanterns came closer and were raised high to reveal a dozen grinning ruffians with unkempt hair and beards in dirty hose and breeches and threadbare cloaks or short capes. The speaker wore a bonnet with a gay but broken feather and swirled a once-fine long cloak with some style. Francis whimpered, while Matthew, lying apart from the others, stared white-faced.

'Who are you? What do you want?' Ralph managed to keep his voice steady. He saw that the intruders were armed with an evil assortment of daggers, butchering knives and cudgels. A broken-nosed giant brandished an old halberd and the speaker flourished a naked rapier.

'I trust you have eaten your fill and slept well - until we disturbed you, for which I do apologise.' He doffed his bonnet and swept a deep mocking bow. 'Permit me to introduce myself. Folk hereabouts call me Diawl-y-Mynydd, meaning mountain devil, and these gentlemen are my companions. Not my real name of course nor my choice for I confess it is absurdly theatrical, but it serves to affright people. What do we want, you ask? In brief, Benedictines and pilgrims all, to relieve you of the weight of your valuables and so lighten your pilgrims' burden.'

These ruffians knew! Ralph sat up slowly and from the floor managed his most commanding voice. 'Robbers and outlaws too, no doubt. A disgrace to this country!

'Now which country would that be? Wales? Have you not heard that the king's majesty has abolished Wales two years ago? England then? England has outlawed us. We have no country.'

'Doubtless you have Welsh blood. Does that mean nothing?'

For some reason this annoyed the man. 'Blood? What are blood or country to us? We are Welsh and English and one Paddy and two Pembroke Flemings there by the door - better not call them Welsh to their faces. Some of us half English, half Welsh, half what you will, mongrels all and happy with it. We have no country, nor care. Do not speak to me of blood or country!'

'Outlaws, as I thought.' Ralph still contrived to sound his haughtiest. 'But you miss your mark with us, fellow. You see plain we are humble brothers and attendants and you yourself called us pilgrims, which indeed we are. We beg shelter and food on our way and possess nothing worth your taking.'

This seemed to restore the man's good humour although his smile did not reach his eyes. 'Nothing worth our taking? Unworldly souls without worldly goods? Admirable - but I fear untrue.'

Evan interjected: 'What have you done to that old couple?' He spoke English, trying to hide his accent: it might be useful to conceal his native Welsh.

'Safe and unharmed. Worry about yourselves.'

Aston, acutely aware of the great sapphire pressing into his side, strove to keep his voice steady. 'You said untrue? Do you dare doubt the word of these brothers in Christ? We are what you see; no more.'

The leader pointed to a gap-toothed ruffian. 'No more you say? This man has just returned from down south. Ifor, tell them what you learned there.'

The man stepped forward. 'Two of us took a pack horse to Llandeilo to collect supplies. Went through Talley.' His slight emphasis on 'collect' drew grins from the gang. 'We heard talk of a party of black monks passing through.'

'So we did! What of it?'

'There is more. Travellers from Swansea had brought news that king's men are pursuing black monks all across South Wales - they are accused of robbing their abbey in England of jewels. Posses hunt them in Carmarthen and beyond and many folk have been questioned, even the abbot at Neath where these monks are known to have lodged for some days. But he took them for mere pilgrims. Some think they fled north, which might well take them through Talley. I saw no posse myself but be sure they will come and travelling fast.'

Ralph's heart sank. Pursuers and so close! He saw consternation on the faces of his companions and knew he could not hoodwink these ruffians. Yet he must try. 'Some other pilgrims. Think you we are the only Benedictines in Wales?'

The leader abandoned his bantering tone. 'Yet we know your houses are closed or closing. Come, sir, you are fugitives and face arrest. Which means we have no time to waste or your pursuers may capture us too.' He turned to his men. 'Search their satchels!' Thomas's hand stole to his staff but Ralph caught his eye and gave a slight shake of his head: resistance would be useless against their numbers.

They watched glumly as the contents of each satchel were upended onto a filthy cloak spread out on the floor to reveal well-thumbed breviaries, shaving and washing articles and modest changes of underclothing; sad little possessions of scant value.

The leader grunted. For a moment they dared hope he might let them go.

But in vain. 'Ifor learned of jewellery stolen. As it happens we have some interest in jewellery.' The renewed mocking tone reminded Ralph of a cat playing with a mouse. 'I regret, gentlemen all, we must now search your persons.'

Ralph risked rising slowly to his imposing height. 'You have doubted the word of men of God - and I am ordained priest as well as monk - and now you will lay hands on our persons? This is more than theft, you ruffian. You imperil your souls!'

The leader was unmoved. 'Ah, but they were imperilled long ago.' He turned to his men. 'Get on with it. Start with their cloaks and habits. Feel every seam carefully for small jewels and coins. If need be strip them to their skins.'

How fitting, Ralph thought bitterly, that now they have turned us out of doors again it starts to rain. Are we doomed for eternity to trudge northward through these bleak hills, never to turn towards England? Aston, silent and sullen, limps badly and leans on Thomas. The novices are in distress, for their short lives have been too cloistered and I see - too late I see - how their slight young bodies have outgrown their strength. Gravest of all, Matthew sickens by the day with some ailment we do not understand. We are weary and woeful, for we have lost the abbey treasures - apart from the bowl - and with their loss this wretched journey ends in failure and shame! We have saved only our miserable lives and the blame is mine. I have failed utterly!

A grey dawn revealed the track along the tributary bank they had followed since their release. The hills were wreathed in low cloud and rain fell steadily. They trudged on heads down in the silence of despair. Evan was unsure where this path led: they could only hope he would recognise something to give him his bearings.

Ralph expressed concern for the old couple who had taken them in. Trudging alongside him Evan was dismissive. 'Have no fear for them, Father, for those two work with the gang. For sure the man was once one of their number and now they are old they earn their keep running that place. It gives those villains beds and hot food when all is quiet, while Carreg Cennen is their refuge when threatened.'

'That kindly old couple? I can scarce believe it!'

'Believe it. They saw advantage in our unexpected arrival and sent a message to the gang while we slept. We will not be the first so trapped nor the last.'

As they plodded on with heavy feet Ralph's mind returned to their confrontation with the robbers. Outnumbered and unarmed, they had not resisted the grinning men who surrounded them with drawn knives and to avoid rough handling had removed their clothing themselves. The wooden bowl at Ralph's back had been found immediately.

'What is this old thing?'

'You see for yourself - an old mazer bowl to eat and drink from.' The leader had turned it over in his hands. 'A poor thing even for a monk. Do you really live in such poverty these days? And why was it not in your satchel?'

'On pilgrimage we show poverty and humility so I have this as well as a better one in my satchel, which is too full to hold both.' It had sounded unconvincing but the leader did not question further. Ralph had been more anxious about questions about the shrine they claimed they were visiting, for as far as he knew they were nowhere near one. But the leader had tossed the bowl onto the cloak on the floor and ordered his men to put any small valuables they found into it. He had watched them closely as they opened pouches and unpicked or cut away linings.

To the robbers' delighted surprise the little vessel had soon overflowed. Coins, mostly gold and some foreign, had showered into it, together with enamelled hat brooches, neck chains, pendants and aiglettes, all modern but finely worked in gold. There were even a few strings of pearls for adorning women's hair. Most numerous were rings of all descriptions. Some were signet or posy rings of good quality, but the most valuable - Ralph had wondered if the gang realised it - were a dozen much older rings. Their gold settings were crudely wrought but they held precious stones that flashed their pure colours even in the weak lantern light - diamonds, emeralds and rubies among them. It had been the policy of successive abbots to turn much of the abbey's vast income into such portable wealth. Ralph recalled bitterly how carefully he had helped to select these from the Treasury: they were the best of their kind the abbey possessed. Here was treasure indeed. The robbers had gabbled excitedly: more wealth lay before them than they could have dreamt of.

As their grimy fingers continued probing even greater treasures had emerged. The fragment of ancient tunic puzzled them but was kept for its gold thread. The small jewelled goblet was gaped over and placed by the wooden bowl. The tiny phial found on a distraught Francis was sniffed at, judged to be a saleable relic of some sort and added to the pile. Last of all, under Aston's shirt they had found a velvet bag and drawn out the most costly prize of all, the ancient altar stone, Saint David's magnificent sapphire in its intricate gold setting. Ralph had closed his eyes.

The leader had whistled: 'a king's ransom!' The gang had been awed into silence. Even in the weak lantern light the great jewel had shone its glorious translucent blue.

'How turn that into money?' Aston had asked dryly. But his face was ashen.

'Let us worry about that. You worry whether we'll cut your throats.' There were cries of fear but at that moment, watching the leader's face, Ralph had felt sure they would be set free. The rogue enjoyed toying with them but would not kill without cause or suffer the constraint of keeping them prisoner. Perhaps mere practicality, perhaps some remnant of humanity remained in him, if not in all his followers.

He had been right in that, for when the last treasure was found they were told to dress and reclaim their personal possessions. As Ralph stooped to pick up the bowl he had glimpsed something glinting in the folds of the outlaw's cloak below. One of the valuable old rings! Barely hesitating, as he had grasped the little vessel he had picked the ring up and held it to the bowl's underside then slid it into the palm of his hand.

But the sharp-eyed leader had seen and instantly the point of his rapier was at Ralph's throat. 'Not so fast my arrogant priest: hand it back!' He pocketed the ring.

'I should slit your throat for this impertinence. Perhaps I will.' The sword point pricked at Ralph's throat, drawing a little blood.' Ralph's face was ashen, the others frozen in a shocked tableau. The outlaws watched in silence. After what seemed an interminable pause the leader relaxed, laughed and lowered his point. 'At least you show nerve: I like that.' He thought for a moment. 'Yet you must be punished - let me see now.' Then his eyes brightened: he was the cat again. 'I'll have that crucifix you've just put back around your neck. Hand it over!'

Ralph protested: unlike the plain ones worn by the others his was of ebony and silver and had long been in his family. 'You would deprive me even of my crucifix? I assure you it has scant monetary value.' He hated the pleading tone that had crept into his voice. But the outlaw, although smiling, was adamant. 'That may be. But you must be punished.' He raised his blade again and held out his left hand. His gang, amused, nudged one another. 'Your crucifix or your life, brother.' And Ralph had complied.

Afterwards they had been almost kindly treated. More cawl had been heated up and cold mutton and bread fetched: robbers and victims had shared the food together. They were given more food for the journey and the leader had even returned the commoner coins they had stolen, ignoring muttering from his gang.

'You have given us a rich haul, and will need this on your journey. You may go unharmed but do not take the path through the mountain for we do not want you at our back. Return the way you came or follow the tributary north as you choose - I will have a man following you and you will find me less amiable if you disobey me. I doubt you will speak to any king's men about us for you are fugitives yourselves - perhaps that is why I have gone soft on you! Speaking to anyone about us will do no good for no-one has ever caught us up here. Now go!' He had turned away abruptly, ordering his men to prepare to leave themselves.

So now his sorry band were plodding like sleepwalkers in the rain, heads down and silent with despair: the abbey treasures were lost and the purpose of their journey lost with them. Each had withdrawn into his own thoughts or the numbness of despair.

Ralph judged it was time to explain the old wooden bowl to the others, for now they had all seen it and at least it would provide some distraction from their misery. When next they stopped to rest he passed it around and told them of Abbot Whiting's belief that it was the Grail. 'He charged me to guard it with my life, keep it hidden even from you except under dire necessity and, God willing, bring it with the rest to safe haven until Mother Church can reclaim it.'

They stared at the little vessel with curiosity but little apparent wonder, almost it seemed with indifference. Ralph was little surprised: by now they were too dispirited to feel anything and he realised that their faith, like his own, was deeply undermined. The bowl had brought him only puzzlement: why should they be different? But looking closer he saw that Francis did show wonder, while the expression on Matthew's wasting face - ah, no doubt there! - was pale and intense, his pained young eyes glowing. Ralph was reminded of Giles and frowned.

Aston the layman asked bluntly: 'Do you believe in this relic, Father?'

Ralph, uneasy, answered question with question. 'Robert, do you believe Joseph of Arimathea once came to Glastonbury? Father Abbot believes it. So did Abbot Bere before him, who sought to canonize Joseph and even renamed our Lady Chapel for him. Abbots before them kept it safe over generations. Each of you must decide for himself, as I must.' For himself he thought: no, I do not believe in it: Glastonbury has profited mightily over the years from false relics. How is this poor thing different? Another thought struck him: a year ago could I have believed that I would tell these brothers in my care to decide for themselves? To think for themselves, not believe blindly? Where was the Rule now? Not only foundations of stone were falling.

Nobody seemed disposed to comment further and wearily they rose to go. As Ralph replaced the bowl he noticed that the cord tying its pouch at his back was badly frayed. He must remember to attend to it.

Another wearisome day and a half brought them to Tregaron. The streets of the small town were crowded with people and livestock but they managed to find food and beds at an inn. Despite their sadly depleted funds they decided to stay for two nights, for they were exhausted and footsore, needed fresh supplies, their shoes were now in sorry state and all were utterly despondent. The landlord made no demur at their bedraggled appearance.

That night only Matthew, weak and in increasing pain that he did not understand, failed to sleep as soon as he took to his cot. His mind kept turning to that little bowl. Prior Ralph had said each must decide for himself whether to believe its story. Think for themselves! The others did not believe it to be the true Grail: it was too insignificant an object and all knew about false relics. Yet their saintly abbot believed; previous abbots, too, all strong in faith. He could not dismiss it entirely, but …. at last he slept.

Next morning they felt a little refreshed. Evan explained the unusual bustle in the town. 'This is a gathering place for drovers driving animals over the mountains to markets in England - you have seen one of their trails. They ready them for the journey and crowd the inns for hot food and a last roof over their heads before nights of sleeping in the open. We were fortunate to find beds.'

Aston asked hopefully: 'Do they sell to the Hereford market?'

'I will ask. I should go out now to buy more supplies and someone to repair our poor shoes. There will be little English spoken here, but I can take Thomas - he can practise his Welsh! But repairing our sorry shoes may be a problem.'

Ralph said: 'A good plan. But what problem? Surely there are cobblers here?'

'Indeed, but they will be busy with sheep.' Smiling at their bewilderment Evan explained. 'Animals are shod for their journey - cattle and ponies with iron, sheep with leather, pigs with woollen socks with leather soles, even geese have their feet coated with tar and sand. Otherwise they could not be driven so far.'

When they returned Thomas was beaming, having ventured a few exchanges in halting Welsh with tradesmen and been rewarded with smiles for his attempts. Evan felt proud of him. They brought with them a cobbler with his bag of tools, persuaded by the offer of more money to turn his attention again to human feet. He raised an eyebrow at their wretched footwear and his price accordingly. Evan said a drover had told him they hoped to sell their herds at a border town named Kington but others favoured continuing to Leominster for better prices. Aston smiled: Leominster was close to his brother's holding. They agreed it best to follow the drovers.

Evan assured them there was no hurry. 'The drive will leave early in the morning. We can break our fast here in peace and follow them at our leisure for we will overtake them soon enough. I see only cattle and sheep here today, but even they cannot be driven more than a mile or so each hour for they graze as they go: even our sore feet will soon catch them.' He was getting too close to his old home for comfort and was considering where he could leave the others once safely on their road for England. It was fortunate they had arrived when a drive was setting out, or if they kept close to the drovers they would not lose their way and have some protection as many did. Not long now and he could leave them with a clear conscience.

That evening the innkeeper, obviously curious, joined them as they finished supper. He spoke to Evan in Welsh. Not much interested in shrines he accepted the pilgrim tale without question and had much to say himself. As with most elderly men it was mostly about his own youth.

'I was but a lad of sixteen when Henry Richmond passed nearby on his way to Bosworth field. People came from miles around to see him. A young man he was then, quite tall and lean. He had hundreds of armed men with him, some Welsh but most foreigners - French, people said. But not enough to challenge King Richard's host, so they were waving Cadwallader's banner and a fine dragon standard and urged us to join them. Earl Richmond spoke a few words in English which most of us could not understand but were translated for us by one of his officers, saying how his family the Tudors were Welsh like us and once he had taken the crown from the usurper Richard Crookback and his Sais those who joined him would be well rewarded. Then off they marched and we never saw him no more. Pity he couldn't speak Welsh, but fair play he'd been on the run most of his life and not lived in Wales if you don't count Pembroke which is English anyway. A few of us joined him here. They gave me an old halberd which was too heavy for me and then I got sick and after twenty miles turned back and never saw nothing.'

Evan translated and asked idly: 'What do folk here think of our Tudor rulers?'

The innkeeper pondered. 'I have heard Richmond - King Henry the Seventh, as he became - turned out not too bad. Stopped the old fighting and sorted out the money, like. They say he turned miser and he did nothing for us here, but they never do, do they? Anyway he was better than his son on the throne now. Pity his older boy Arthur died young! This one has taken away what was left of our laws and says there is no Wales no more and for a proper job you must speak English, so most folk can't get one! And another thing: they say he's spent all the money his father saved up, which is why he's kicking you monks out to get his hands on yours. I don't hold with that, neither, you didn't do nobody no harm.' Evan translated.

Curious, Ralph asked through Evan: 'But did the monasteries do any real good?'

The innkeeper seemed unconcerned at addressing monks: ask a question and get a straight answer. 'Not much. The white brothers were just landlords like the gentry but of course the abbeys went to pot long ago - a handful of monks left in places like Ystrad Fflur which was closed a year or two back. But not much harm neither. King Henry should have left you alone and not meddle with religion I say. Well, I'm for my bed.' Abruptly he stood up, unsurprisingly breathless, and bade them goodnight.

Evan translated again. Aston remarked dryly he had once thought the Welsh a dour silent people. 'Listening to that fellow has changed my mind and you yourself are not so quiet these days Evan! But has he said ought of use to us?'

Ralph said: 'At least that the king is not loved hereabouts. And save for those outlaws we have met with kindness from these people despite being strangers. If that is sympathy because of what has been done to monasteries it might serve us well. But what is that place he spoke of?'

Evan was yawning. 'Ystrad Fflur. A Cistercian abbey - Strata Florida in Latin, Vale of Flowers in English. A remote place with few monks left even when I knew it.' And with that they went to their beds.

The posse rode home from Cardigan by a different route inland, Sir William explaining it was a shorter way to their mustering point at Gloucester. At the small settlement of Llandeilo they put up at an inn for the night.

That evening as they drank their ale Geoffrey was so silent and withdrawn that Robin turned to Sir William for conversation. Geoffrey was unhappy. Sir William seemed to think that burning the shrine at Cardigan had completed his task. Surely not! That black-robed madman who had immolated himself there must have been one of the Glastonbury monks, for it was known they were going there. Then where were his companions? The posse had scoured Cardigan without sight of them and Sir William had promptly given up the search. But what if the rest of them had already fled north into the empty high country?

Sir William had confirmed they were now well north of the road by which they had ridden west. Which meant that if the fugitives had indeed turned north they could have been in this area very recently! Geoffrey went in search of the stout landlord.

'Funny you should ask, sir. Some monks and their retainers did spend a night here a few days' ago - I forget exactly when. Black habits are uncommon around here. I spoke with them. Pilgrims they said they were and for sure looked dog-weary and begrimed. No trouble, mind, quiet and paid their dues with no haggling.'

'Did you see which way they left?'

'Not I, but my tap boy saw them take the road east for Llandyfri.' So they were only a few days away and by now must be travelling slowly on sore feet! If Geoffrey could help catch them he would find favour at court; perhaps even fulfil his father's orders regarding uncle Ralph. Excited, he returned to question Sir William.

'Llandyfri? Yes, we pass that place tomorrow. Why?'

Geoffrey explained. 'Sir William, I have learned that the rest of those fugitive monks have but lately passed this way. They may still be within your grasp. If we ask around if any have seen black monks we can run them down and arrest them.'

Sir William grunted. 'Not so eager, sir. Burning the shrine is work enough for now. We are too long on the road as it is. Even should we find them it would be no simple matter if they have taken to the hills. I cannot spend more time chasing them there.'

'But we have a duty to try, sir, to pursue them until caught?'

Sir William scowled. 'Have a care young man. I decide the duties of this posse and I say it is useless to search any longer. You may do as you like.' Irritated, he got up and left. Robin, who had overheard, leaned over and whispered: 'He's right Geoff.: let them go. I am for Glastonbury tomorrow, for it is high time one of us reports back to Knollys. I'm sorry Geoff, but if you chase after them you go alone.'

Lying abed that night Geoffrey reflected that neither Robin nor Sir William knew about uncle Ralph and his father's instructions. He still carried Knollys's writ. Could he venture north after him on his own? Tomorrow he must decide.

But next morning his movements were decided for him. Robin had left at daybreak. As the others finished their breakfast a noisy half troop of mounted soldiers clattered into the inn yard and dismounted. A curiously mixed lot, some carried muskets, others longbows, halberds or swords. All but the leather-coated archers wore helmets and breastplates. Their young captain and his older sergeant fell into conversation with Sir William, who presently summoned his own men. They gathered around him, curious.

'These are county sheriff's men. Captain Harries here tells me they are here to clear out a nest of outlaws in some ruined castle in the hills near here, for the king has ordered an end to the banditry and vagrancy of recent years. He has this mixed force because he is unsure what he will find. But he has a problem. Local folk, who welcome them heartily, have warned that this outlaw band equals his men in number and has a fearsome reputation. They are well armed and protected by stone walls. The sheriff has spared him too few men for the task and he must bolster his numbers. I have agreed to support him.'

There was a chorus of protests. 'Agreed? You said we were going home now! Who is this captain to order us about? Can he do so? Why us?'

Sir William shrugged his shoulders. 'I know, lads: I am as eager for my own bed as you. But he can and has ordered us, for his sheriff's writ over-rides mine: anyway our task here is over' - he scowled at Geoffrey. 'It is a fair request he makes and should take us only today. Consider also that he answers directly to his sheriff, who represent the king here. Think carefully: Would you risk the royal displeasure for one days' extra work - with the promise of full pay?' The muttering subsided: they would not.

'Good. This being a military matter we now place ourselves under the command of captain Harries.' Who is half my age, he muttered into his beard: pray he knows his business. Geoffrey felt a degree of relief:

now he could postpone his decision whether to pursue his uncle and have a day's excitement instead.

Harries explained that a local man named Meurig who had known the castle in better times had talked long with him the previous evening: he would serve as their guide. He met them in woodland half-way to the castle, a weather- beaten former soldier with sufficient English. He said his own small holding had twice been ransacked by these outlaws: he sought revenge and an end to them, as did all hereabouts and made it his business to keep watch on them whenever he could. Two days ago, well concealed, he had seen them arrive at the castle. There were a dozen of them, one carrying a small sack - loot from their last raid he guessed and poor pickings by the look of it. A few more of them might already be inside, so he thought there were about fifteen in all. After such a raid they would likely rest at the castle for days, eating and drinking and sharing out their spoils. As to their arms, he had noted two muskets, several longbows, a sword and many daggers and knives, a halberd and even a pike. He did not expect them to be alert to danger for no-one had dared confront them in years. Yes, most would likely be drunk.

Meurig led them quietly to the wood's edge. Well hidden, they studied the castle carefully. Frowning atop its high ridge it looked more formidable than they had expected. It was supposedly a ruin, so slighted after the Cousins' Wars as to give easy entry for attackers. Certainly the facing curtain wall showed damage, much of the great gatehouse facing them had collapsed and the tumbled masonry of an approach tower was piled in front of it, only a stump of its masonry still thrusting up to the sky. Yet only the vestigal slighted walls of the outer ward presented no obstacle.

We have a problem here, Harries thought. The walls of the inner ward showed no real breach and the approach to them was over steeply sloping, rough and cruelly exposed ground, some of it bare rock. For his part Geoffrey wondered how their twenty men could force an entry and subdue desperate felons well sheltered inside. Surely the captain would need twice the force he commanded? Judging by their muttering some of the soldiers thought so, too.

But Geoffrey was no trained soldier and Captain Harries, who was, did not seem unduly concerned. 'A chain is as strong as its weakest link,' he remarked sententiously but with a boyish grin. 'I confess I hoped for an easy breach but I see none. Yet there must be a way in and we must find it. Unrolling and consulting a large scroll he had brought with him he found a stick and scratched a rough plan of the castle in the carpet of leaves on the wood's floor. Everyone gathered around.

'The outlaws will camp in the inner ward where they are safest,' he said, pointing his stick, 'and Meurig says that although much slighted the domestic buildings in there still gives them shelter of sorts. Now consider how we get in. It can only be through what was the middle gate tower - that stump and tumble of fallen stone nearest to us - and straight on through the slighted main gatehouse. From where we stand it all looks completely blocked with fallen stone but Meurig tells me the gang have cleared a narrow passage through - how else get in and out themselves? So we make straight for the gateway and hope they keep no watch - and are drunk!'

The sergeant interrupted. 'Captain, if they keep proper watch that narrow passage will be a death trap: their archers can shoot us down before we can deploy.'

Harries nodded. 'True. So we must creep up cautiously then deploy very fast.'

Pentridge asked: 'Is there no easier entrance on the far side?'

Harries smiled. 'Tell him, Meurig.' The guide explained that on that side the great curtain wall had been left un-slighted because it overlooked an impassable cliff.

'So no frontal attack that way,' Harris said. 'But I'll come back to that.'

'Can we then approach from west or east?'

'Too exposed atop that bare ridge. Nor any way through those curtain walls.'

Harries continued. 'So we must get through that main gateway. However, this old castle has an unusual feature to help us.' He drew again with his stick then pointed with it to the castle. 'You see that from the middle gate ruins a barbican extends to our left to defend the main gate. It has deep pits and ditches concealed behind it. Now mark this. Meurig thinks its parapet can still be crossed on foot and at its western end it slopes down to end on the outer ward on that side. He says the far wall of that outer ward is broken in one place. Through there we can pass around the corner tower of the inner curtain wall and into the inner ward by an old postern Meurig knows.'

They peered at his markings in the leaves and then up at the castle. A voice from the back asked nervously: 'Then if we get that far we are to pass between that wall and the top of a cliff you say is impassable? Is there room?'

Meurig said: 'Room enough in single file - it will only be for a dozen paces.'

Geoffrey broke the uneasy silence that followed: 'So which way do we go, captain, straight ahead through the gatehouse or left atop the barbican?'

Harries raised a condescending eyebrow. 'Both sir, of course. Both at once. We divide our force, take both routes and trap them between us.'

'Now to business.' Briskly he assigned his own men equally to each route, dividing Pentridge's less experienced ones to the rear of both. Each group had two musketeers and half the other soldiers. Harries himself would lead the barbican group, taking Meurig to guide them.

Geoffrey would go with them. Sergeant Woodman would lead the group to force the main entrance, Pentridge with them.

'Sergeant, have Brannigan and his infamous dagger deal with any sentry at the gate itself - in his usual quiet fashion!' A red-bearded soldier bared yellow teeth in a grin.

'Two things to remember if we are to surprise them' continued the captain, testing his sword edge with his thumb. 'First, we approach with great stealth, crawling on bellies and elbows and using such cover as we can find on that broken ground - I see rock outcrops for our purpose to your right so swing around that way. Breastplates and helmets to be left here and weapons slung on backs clear of the rocks - for we must make no noise.' For emphasis he snapped his dry stick against his knee and Geoffrey jumped. 'Second, both groups must charge into the inner ward together to divide and confuse them. To do that everyone must move at - and not a moment before - my signal, which will be a single caliver shot from my group. Any questions so far?' Woodman whispered to Geoffrey that calivers were the latest improved muskets - 'lighter, no need for forked stands which are the devil on ground like this.'

There being no questions Harries ordered them to check weapons. 'Musketeers load and prime when ready but no firing until the signal. Understood?'

He straightened up, fresh-faced and confident. 'Surprise is everything, lads. Silence and timing - wait for the shot, then all together - well, almost - my group will tarry a moment so that the outlaws will face the Sergeant's group and show us their backs.'

'One last thing.' Suddenly his young face looked older, grimmer. 'We deal here with outlaws - men already judged to be outside the law. So accept no surrender and take no prisoners. Kill them all! Ready? Now move off, my group first - and quietly!' Geoffrey swallowed.

As they crept on all fours up the steep rocky slope the castle looming over them lay silent as a grave. A weak sun came out to expose them cruelly and Harries cursed under his breath. Now Geoffrey saw the wisdom of leaving body armour behind: apart from the noise it would make scraping on bare rock it would reflect this sunshine.

The silence was unnerving. Impossible not to fear a trap; desperate musketeers and bowmen waiting behind the shelter of those grim stones. But they were committed now and after clambering up the near-vertical last few yards they reached the ruins of the middle gate without incident.

Here they stopped briefly, concealed in a narrow passage cleared through the fallen masonry. They saw that the main gatehouse had also been cleared of stones and rough planking placed over a deep ditch to reach it. Evidently the outlaws felt secure enough in their eyrie. After resting briefly Woodman's group waited quietly while Harries led his men cautiously along the top of the barbican. Grass had grown between its uneven and broken flagstones but it was still passable. Then, suddenly, they were confronted by a pit twenty feet deep with vertical walls lined with stone, too wide to jump over and impossible to clamber down into and up the other side. Between the barbican and the towering castle wall were more formidably deep pits.

Harries hissed at Meurig: 'You said we could pass over this barbican! Pray show me how!'

'I saw planks laid across these pits, sir, though some were rotten from the rain.'

'Pits you said? 'so there are others ahead?' Meurig held up two fingers to suppressed groans. Harries grunted. 'Damnation! It appears the outlaws have removed them for their own safety, leaving only one entrance.' The only way to pass the pit ahead was over the tops of the stone courses lining their sides, in places a mere foot wide. Nervously, they crept over them on hands and knees to stand on solid flags again, breathing heavily. One soldier had slipped but had been caught in time by the one following. Hands on knees and panting Geoffrey asked softly how the original garrison could have suffered using loose planking over the pits on their daily peacetime business.

Harries could guess: 'They would have movable wooden bridges on rollers, a sound device where ground like this does not permit a moat.' Nervously. they negotiated the remaining two pits safely and were mighty relieved when the barbican sloped gently downward and turned sharp right onto the outer ward with its vestigial remaining walls. Alarmingly exposed to view from the inner castle though this sloping greensward was, they had to rest for some minutes before regaining breath to move on, Geoffrey gazing sadly at the ruin of his elegant hose. But still they saw no sentry nor heard any alarm as they ran for the cover of a tall square tower jutting halfway along the high curtain wall to their right.

Meurig whispered: 'this was the chapel tower - but its postern is blocked with stones.' They crept on in the deep shadow of the high curtain. At its southern end, where the remnant of the outer ward wall met it at a near right angle they came to Meurig's promised small gap. Harries led through it then stopped dead, the others crowding into him. His young face suddenly pale, he recoiled into them.

One by one they crept to the gap to look down. What they saw was terrifying. At their feet the plunging cliff edge, almost vertical further down, seemed to draw them down to their deaths. They had no eyes for the stupendous view before them, mile upon mile of grass and woodland, the smoke of a scatter of hamlets and, rising behind, the majestic pink-brown slopes of the Black Mountain. They had eyes only for the pale grey cliff face plunging dizzyingly in the paler sunshine to the treetops three hundred feet below. They shrank back in terror, hands groping behind them for the comforting solidity of the castle wall. Geoffrey felt sick.

Recovering, Harries glared at Meurig again. 'You said we could pass around the end of this curtain, man. But it reaches to the very edge of this cliff. Are we then birds?'

'I'm sorry captain. I have not been in this corner of late: my memory was at fault. Abashed, he stared around then suddenly pointed: 'But not altogether so. See, the wall does stop short of the cliff edge. What bars us is this buttress, which slants down to the very edge. Its face is steep but broken. If we climb it we can reach the postern.'

Harries saw he was right. But the buttress's old weather-shattered stonework looked appallingly insecure, seeming to overhang the dizzying cliff. 'Climb over that? First you would have us turn ourselves into birds and now we are to become lizards?' He inspected the wall carefully then turned away. 'Well, needs must: Woodward's men will be wondering what has become of us. Let us to it!'

One by one, fearful but mercifully without accident, they clambered awkwardly over the buttress and dropped down on the other side gasping with relief. Ahead of them worn steps led steeply up to the promised postern opening, which had lost its door entirely. Cautiously they peered through the opening.

What they saw raised their spirits.

Over and around a low outcrop of bare rock they could see across most of the grassed inner ward. The gang were sprawled on the grass and on the outcrop itself, weapons scattered carelessly around them. They were eating and drinking in the sunshine, talking and laughing together, unaware of danger.

Meurig whispered. 'All there, captain. Fifteen - the three older ones were here already.' Another man appeared from a ruined building carrying a large platter of food and joined them. 'Sixteen. That should be the lot, sir.'

Harries was smiling: his risky plan had achieved total surprise. He nodded to a musketeer, who held his slow match ready. He applied it to his caliver's lock and fired into the sprawled figures. The phut of the explosion sounded appallingly loud as smoke wreathed into the air. The outlaws started to their feet, turning in all directions, confused by the echo of the shot chasing around the towering walls. As they groped for their weapons Woodville's men poured from the gateway beyond and deployed quickly right and left. Before the gang could react their two calivers had fired and their bowmen were shooting arrows into the outlaw's midst. Half the gang were down before the others gathered themselves to charge desperately at their attackers.

Harries' hand flashed down. His men rushed out and deployed, quickly, extending well left to avoid the rock outcrop. His remaining loaded caliver and his four longbows angled their shots into the backs of the charging gang while Woodville's bowmen kept shooting into their front, again and again.

It was over in minutes: Geoffrey had not even drawn his sword. Only one outlaw, the one brandishing a rapier, had reached Woodman's men before an arrow in the throat felled him. Most of the surviving outlaws sullenly accepted the fate they knew awaited them but two fell to their knees trying to surrender. It made no difference. Halberds and swords, hardly used so far, cut them down: daggers finished them off. Geoffrey felt sick again.

Woodville and Harries met at the bloody corpses.

'A fine day's work, captain.'

'Good enough. Casualties?'

'Nary a one.'

'Same with me. They never got in sword's length or got an aimed shot off.'

'You were right, sir: surprise was everything. You will find favour for this.'

'You, too. And Sir William's men - little to do but they stood up well for amateurs.'

'There was a sentry at the gatehouse after all, too drunk to stand. Brannigan dealt with him. Making seventeen in all. What shall we do with the bodies?'

'Stand the men down to rest and eat. Then pitch the corpses over the cliff.'

When all had finished their bread, cheese and small beer Meurig was thanked, paid off and told to spread the good news that these outlaws would trouble the area no more. The soldiers began lugging away the bodies. Harries, in high spirits, now proposed to inspect the castle, explaining to Sir William and Geoffrey: 'I am charged to report if further slighting is needed so that never again can this castle be used by felons of any persuasion. While my men and I attend to this small military matter would any of you gentlemen assist me further by making a tally of any loot these ruffians have not yet disposed of?'

But Sir William was anxious to leave while there was daylight and soon led his posse back to the inn and their horses. Geoffrey, still unsure whether to pursue the Glastonbury monks on his own, decided that after the exertions of the day he had earned another night at the inn to make up his mind in some comfort. He bad Sir William farewell, turned to Harries and expressed himself willing to assist.

He began his search in the range of domestic buildings against the east curtain. The slighting had left them in a sad state, the great hall and domestic chambers roofless and derelict, much of their roof and flooring fallen into the undercroft below. But one section of the undercroft was still roofed and roughly habitable and he began there. Evidently the gang had lived and slept here, for dirty straw bedding and blankets were strewn about and small personal possessions and stumps of tallow candles stood on upturned boxes. Unwashed platters and vessels lay around. But he saw nothing that looked stolen or of value.

At the north end of the domestic range the kitchens also had some roof left. In a sheltered corner he found a rough bed, a table and stool and a threadbare piece of tapestry hanging on one wall. The leader's private quarters, Geoffrey guessed. On the table an assortment of loot was piled, mostly used men's attire - doublets and hose, bonnets and caps, gowns and capes, shoes, belts, daggers and a tarnished rapier. A roughly made box contained meat knives and spoons, buttons and clasps and a few tawdry signet and posy rings and brooches.

It was a disappointing find, no doubt useful for the outlaws but nothing of real value. None of it could be clearly identified or was worth the tallying. Strange there were no coins! Had these been the dreaded robbers and outlaws? There had to be more to find.

But another hour of searching in the broken towers and finally along the remaining fighting platforms yielded nothing. Tired now, he descended worn steps to the inner ward. As he crossed it Harries emerged from the postern where his group had launched their attack. Oddly in the sunshine, he held a lit torch, its light hardly visible in the sunshine. Seeming indefatigable, he hailed Geoffrey jovially.

'Well sir! Have you found a treasure trove to dazzle me?' Geoffrey shook his head.

'Cheer up! Allow me to divert you with a curiosity.' He led towards the postern, where they heard grunts and thumps as the corpses were being hauled and pitched through an opening in the curtain wall and over the fearful cliff below. 'We must go back where we first entered but farther this time. Black as hell's gate down there. I have another torch. Light it from mine and watch your step for it is rough going.'

Geoffrey was wary. 'I'm not going over that buttress again!'

Harries thumped his shoulder cheerfully. 'No need for now we are going under it. Follow me.' They went down the uneven steps they had come up earlier. Almost at the point where they had scaled the buttress a low opening under it led down more steep steps to a narrow sloping passage. Light entered it through a row of small square openings on their right, revealing a well-made stone roof and floor. Then suddenly it was dark again and floor and roof became uneven rock. They groped forward into a cramped twisting passage, their flickering torchlight showing bare rock glistening with moisture. Geoffrey hear the drip of water and the air felt cold and damp.

'Are we in some natural cave?'

'More a great crack in the rock I think,' Harries replied. 'But you see where in places the sides have been cut back and smoothed with chisels. At first I thought it was a secret way into the castle but no light comes from the far end. So I went all the way to find out why. The entrance, which must lie east of the cliff edge we stood on, has been blocked with stones. Come, I'll show you. Mind where you step.'

Ten slow groping minutes brought them to the former opening. Its blocking stones were massive, the cracks between them jammed with smaller rocks and soil. Only chinks of light entered but they felt the breath of warmer fresh air from outside.

Geoffrey said: 'A curiosity indeed, captain. Think of the toil that went into placing these great stones. But is there anything of military import to concern you here?'

'Nothing I need report. But I thought it might interest you.'

'Indeed it does: I thank you for showing it to me.' They were turning back when Geoffrey saw something glint in a corner. He bent down, his torch lighting the floor.

'Look here!'

It was a small oak coffer bound with iron hoops, its heavy brass padlock weakly reflecting the torchlight. Harries whistled. 'Now how did I miss that? Let us take it outside for a closer look.' With much effort they carried its considerable weight to the top of the steps, where Harries peered out cautiously. 'Best not let my men see this.'

But the soldiers had finished their grisly task and disappeared through the main gatehouse, ready and eager to leave. They were unobserved as they carried the chest into the nearest roofed chamber of the domestic range. They forced the padlock with an old halberd blade lying nearby, lifted the lid and removed a filthy cloth cover.

The chest was two thirds full of coins. Most were common halfpennies, pennies, groats and half groats - but they saw the glint of some silver shillings.

'For sure no king's ransom' said Harries. But they must go to my sheriff.'

Geoffrey concurred. 'No doubt our Glastonbury thieves helped themselves to coins aplenty but I cannot identify any they stole amongst this lot, so they are for you to dispose of.' Idly he sifted through the coins with his fingers. 'What's this? He held up one with unfamiliar markings, then a second and third; all worn and surely old. From his jerkin he took out a creased sheet of paper and studied it. 'These few foreign coins are here in my inventory of stolen abbey treasures and I must return them. Here is proof positive these outlaws did indeed rob our fleeing monks - theft from thieves! But there should be many more of these coins.' He showed Harries his list. 'We must go through this carefully.'

Harries nodded. 'I agree, but in private, not here. Anyway I must get my lads back to camp.' He thought for a moment. 'I have an idea. Sergeant Woodman can take them back. I'll spend the night at your inn where in privacy and comfort we can check everything against your tally and make a list of what remains to go to my sheriff. I would welcome a comfortable night under a proper roof. How say you?'

'Capital! Sir William and I shared a bedchamber. You can have his bed.'

That evening after supping they retired to their chamber, bolted the door and set to work. The coins for Harries' disposal were stacked by denomination on a small table. There were fewer than they expected and only one or two were of silver or gold. Harries shrugged his shoulders: the total was of little concern to him and he would be glad to be rid of them. A tiny discoloured phial and a few other items on his Glastonbury inventory were placed on Geoffrey's lumpy bed together with an unlisted personal crucifix. By the time the chest was empty their fingers were grimy.

For Geoffrey this was more disappointment. He pointed at his bed. 'Look at them! A few of these foreign coins, rings and some minor bits of jewellery are on my list, but naught else is. The rogues must have sold off the best items before returning here.'

But Harries disagreed. 'This loot suggests to me they had not yet found time to divide it between them. This is very recent thieving. Also they would have found it hard to dispose of the items of real value. They could only safely dispose of such in London or a port town with backstreet dealers in stolen goods - all distant from here.'

'Anyway, we have found nothing of value.' Peevishly, Geoffrey overturned the empty chest and shook it over his bed. Nothing more fell out. As he righted it he saw a half groat wedged in the crack between the base and the rear side of the chest. Idly, he picked at it.

The base moved a fraction.

Pressing on it he felt a tiny movement. He held the chest to his eyes to compare its inner and the outer sides. 'A false bottom!' he cried. The thin inner base board was difficult to remove but eventually they prized it up with the blade of Harries' dagger.

And there lying on the true base was the remainder of the stolen Glastonbury treasure! For certain now the monks had been robbed of everything. And they had recovered it! For a moment they were speechless. Then, breathing hard, Geoffrey carefully began lifting out and checking each item against his inventory. There were gold and silver coins, finely worked gold rings and brooches, set and unset jewels in a glittering riot of colour. Tenderly he took out an exquisite little gold and emerald goblet.

Harries whistled softly at its beauty and then peered into the chest. 'That goblet was just too big for their false bottom. You can see it has been lifted and reset to make more space - but not well enough. Hence the crack and how you found it.'

'And why at first we found less coins than we expected.' Geoffrey looked at his list again. 'Only two more items still to tick off. First, the tunic fragment. I do not see it.'

Harries passed him the grimy cloth that had covered the hoard. 'This is it, I think. Under the dirt you can just see the gold thread.' Another tick.

'One thing more then and my list is complete - this velvet pouch, which should contain their greatest theft, the altar stone. Pray it does.' Geoffrey hesitated, then reverently lifted the pouch and drew out the priceless sapphire. Even in the feeble candlelight it glowed in its ornate gold setting. Geoffrey sat heavily on his bed, speechless. He had recovered everything.

Harries smiled and shook his hand. 'Well done sir: now we have both finished our business here.' Geoffrey nodded. He had forgotten about his uncle Ralph.

Harries picked up the now empty chest. 'I can carry my modest haul of coins in this.' It was sturdy and well made, a useful thing. He decided he deserved something for his efforts: his sheriff would get only its contents. 'But how will you carry all your great treasures back to Glastonbury?'

Geoffrey had regained his composure. 'Wrapped in linen bags in my saddle bags: I durst not attract attention with more robbers on the roads. 'There is a pile of such bags here, no doubt for carrying their looted coins: I'll do it now and be done.'

'You will need protection. Two of my men can escort you as far as Gloucester: we'll tell them it is only your valuable person they guard.'

'I would be truly grateful. Once there I shall come under the protection of the commissioners who sent me.' And who will be well pleased with me, he thought. He picked up some of the bags to begin filling them.

Harries was still peering at Geoffrey's remarkable hoard. 'Something puzzles me.'

'What?'

'The crucifix. A common enough thing. Why steal it?'

'Does it matter?'

'Is it on your list?'

'No, it seems it was not the abbey's. It was among the coins we took out first, before we found the false bottom. But surely it is not important.'

'I suppose not. Yet a personal crucifix sets me thinking about your monks. We know for sure now that these ruffians robbed them, but have you thought what they did with them afterwards?'

Uncle Ralph! In his excitement he had forgotten about him! Where was he now? But this did not concern Harries. To gain time to think he must keep him talking. 'What think you then, captain? Would they not rob them and then set them free?'

Harries pondered. 'Two things only the outlaws could do; set them free as you say or kill them. Now which?' A man who enjoyed puzzles, he paced the room stroking his chin. 'If they freed them they risked a hue and cry, for even today stealing from monks on pilgrimage would be something of an outrage and quickly reported. They would not risk that. I think it likely they killed them.'

Geoffrey's frowned. 'But what then? Bury them hurriedly leaving freshly dug graves for all to see or leave them unburied to be found even sooner? Surely outlaws do not look for such trouble?'

Harries stroked his chin. 'I agree they would not bury them down in the valley where there are people. Most likely they came upon them on this mountain, robbed and then killed them around here. You said yourself your fugitive monks would seek to avoid pursuit by keeping to the hills - these hills.' He waved a theatrical arm.

'But shepherds come up here: a few merchants and others must pass through sometimes. Even up here bodies or recent graves would be found in the end.'

Harries laughed: he felt sure now. 'You do not know this mountain. Nor did I, but Meurig told me much about it before our attack today. It is riddled with caves, some of which the outlaws must have known and used as hiding places or caches for loot - we are fortunate they had not yet hidden this coffer in one of those. Once placed in those caves your monks' bodies would never be found. That is what happened, man!'

'That is supposition, not proof.' Then a thought struck Geoffrey. 'Pass me that crucifix.' He turned it over in his hand. It was indeed of plain wood, unadorned save for its tiny gilt cross and figure of the crucified Christ, a commonplace personal thing. Yet the wood looked uncommonly dark. Carefully he rubbed the dirt off it with spittle and a cloth. Soon it shone black and fine-grained. He could not be sure but was this not ebony, an imported and expensive wood? He rubbed some more. Now he was sure: it was ebony and the tiny figure on its cross was surely not gilt but silver, most delicately crafted. This was far from commonplace and seemed vaguely familiar. No peasant could have owned it nor any poor monk. A Catholic gentleman might have, but papists were threatened these days and such a person would have kept it well hidden, not easily found by common thieves - or informers. More likely it had been worn by a senior churchman of the popish faith. A bishop perhaps, or an abbot.

Or a prior! Uncle Ralph was a prior! He rubbed again, peered closer and this time made out tiny lettering carefully scored into the back of the wood: 'Ora et Labora' - from the Rule of Saint Benedict. He had heard that most religious houses here in Wales were - had been - Cistercian, although following Benedict's rule. Yet this could have come from Benedictine Glastonbury! He held it up to the light. On the foot of the ebony cross minute initials were scratched which he made out with difficulty - RD. Ralph Dawnay! Suddenly he recognised it. This - or an identical one - had been in the family for as long as he could remember. And the initials were Uncle Ralph's.

Now he knew. Harries was right. Uncle Ralph was dead! All the fugitives from Glastonbury had been robbed and then slaughtered, their unshriven corpses were rotting in dark caves somewhere under this Black Mountain never to be found. Amongst them lay the uncle he had hardly known and could not in sincerity mourn. Like Harries he knew he had nothing more to do here. To complete his charge he would deliver the abbey treasures safely to the commissioners, make his report - and hope for some advancement to follow. Then he must ride for home to give his father the news that his brother Ralph was dead and he could rest certain now that the manor and estate were securely his. The manor that one day he, Geoffrey, would inherit. It had been a momentous day but a long one. And so to bed.

Early next morning, in pale sunshine, the 'pilgrims' watched as perhaps a hundred scrawny cattle and a few dozen sheep set off on the wide swathe of the drovers' track. Dogs barked and darted around the flanks as they set off, the lowing cattle in loose herds under different drovers, most on foot but some riding shaggy hill ponies. They travelled at a snail's pace grazing as they went but kept on their slow move by piercing whistles, excited dogs and the cracking of whips. Only Evan had seen such a sight before: for the others it was a welcome distraction.

As the last herd slowly disappeared under its cloud of pale dust they turned back to the inn for a leisurely breakfast. Ralph paid their due, saying nothing of their fast-dwindling funds. Evan urged waiting another hour before starting but Aston was impatient to leave and his plea won the day.

They set out on newly cobbled shoes, a small spring back in their steps, Aston limping with more vigour. But Matthew grew ever more withdrawn, lagging further behind and leaning heavily on his staff. Thomas now carried his satchel as well as his own. Their mission lay in ruins but at last they were heading towards England. Evan had judged well, however, for too soon they overtook the drive. They had to slow their pace for it was impossible to overtake the cattle grazing wide of the track while close to them the dust was choking. Herdsmen at the rear with cloths covering their noses recognised them from the inn and greeted them amiably, content to let them follow under their protection.

Aston, recalling Glastonbury's rich manors, sniffed: 'these are scrawny beasts.'

Evan nodded. 'You see how poor much of this grazing can be. These cattle will be fattened in England before sold on to market.'

They had paused to let the herds get well ahead again when up in front the entire drive came to a shambling halt. As the dust settled again they saw that the leading drovers were clustering around a small party of horsemen: the glint of steel showed soldiers amongst them. Soon a friendly drover spurred back on his pony. 'A posse up front asking about black monks: it seems you are pursued, brothers. We are keeping them talking as long as we can but cannot keep from them that you lay in Tregaron last night. Best you flee now and God speed you!' He raised his whip in salute and cantered back around the widespread herds.

For a long moment they were too stunned to move. This was disaster, their way east blocked again and their arrest imminent. They crouched behind the shifting screen of cattle ahead of them. They had reached the head of a small shallow valley whose trees had petered out into bare grassland. Only the thinning dust cloud and the small cattle screened them and they were spreading ever wider in their unconcerned search for grazing. They would be spotted at any moment.

With his old soldier's eye for country Ralph grasped the situation. 'Back down the valley, quickly. Crouch low.' As they stumbled back Francis panted: 'Tregaron is too for us far, Father, for those soldiers are mounted!'

'I know, and no refuge, lad, for we were seen there last night - someone will talk. We must find cover until they pass and then seek somewhere where horsemen cannot readily follow.' They reached the nearest trees and lay prone and breathless under them. Francis whispered that this was Llandeilo all over again, Ralph that at least the drover's friendly warning - and perhaps ingrained dislike of authority - had given them a chance. Aston, his hopes dashed again, was grimly silent.

Almost immediately the posse cantered past. Ralph warned everyone to remain concealed in case they should back-track. At last he rose to his feet, brushing down his habit. 'When they have searched the town they will return, so we must seek safety in the hills again. Which way, Evan?'

Evan was now on more familiar ground. 'One choice only, Father. Some of the posse are still ahead of the drive. Those who passed us have gone west but will return to rejoin them. That outlaw said they were looking for us to the south and I believe him. So east, west and south all spell danger. It must be north into the mountains again, I fear.'

'Is there any habitation that way? A chance of shelter?'

'There is a village called Pontrhydfendigaid - the bridge of the Blessed Ford - its name speaks of the abbey I know of in these parts.' Aston groaned at the outlandish name. 'It lies on the road north past the Cors Goch - a great bog stretching for miles. The village lies near its northern end.'

Ralph said: 'Then this bog further hems us in. If they take that road soon they could lie in wait for us! We cannot go to that village, Evan. So in all directions lie danger. Are we then trapped at last?'

Evan considered. 'Yet north is our only way. Strata Florida Abbey might shelter us. It is a mile or two from Pontrhydfendigaid, a day's march from here but I fear a hard one for we must leave this road and climb a hill track again.'

'Surely that abbey you speak of lies too close to Pont - what you called it?'

'Close yes, but as I recall separate from it. Anyway the posse may not go into the village and there is no refuge for us directly east, where the mountains are exceeding rough and barren - they have been called the backbone of Wales. Strata Florida is set apart as the Cistercians preferred and there should be no habitation nearer than the village. If we do not show ourselves in daylight we may shelter at the abbey.'

Aston grumbled: 'Will we never see England again? Why not follow the drovers again? We can soon catch them up.'

Ralph shook his head. 'Too risky! But this abbey of Evan's may serve us tonight. If only recently surrendered and remote it may stand empty but un-plundered. We have some food left and need only shelter. We are safer in the hills anyway. So let us make for this Strata Florida. At least 'Vale of Flowers' is an appealing name.'

Later Evan was to reckon it was less than ten miles to Strata Florida, but by now they were hardly aware of distance or time. Aston was supported by Thomas while Francis with ill grace shouldered Matthew's satchel. All felt near collapse.

At long last they stopped overlooking a little valley. Beyond the trees cloaking the slope below they saw it. 'Saint Mary's Abbey, Strata Florida,' said Evan in a toneless voice that concealed both his relief that he had brought them to some sort of shelter and his personal misgivings at drawing ever closer to his old home.

In the fading light they saw dignified grey buildings centred around church and cloister, small after Glastonbury and Neath but in the familiar monastic plan. The main buildings looked well-proportioned and undamaged. As they drew closer the deep-cut dogtooth carving of round-arched windows and doorways of the church reminded them of Glastonbury's Lady Chapel. Set among hills through which the upper Teifi flowed placidly, the place seemed isolated and peaceful with no sign of human occupation. Unusually there were no dwellings close to its walls.

Ralph felt more cheerful. 'As I hoped, deserted yet seeming intact - and no inquisitive locals to watch us. We can find a roof here and have a little food.'

But Evan was cautious. 'It may be the abbey can be seen from the village and the posse may have encamped there for the night. Best keep under these trees until dark.' They threaded through them to the edge of the abbey clearing to wait and doze.

When it was dark they passed through a gap in the abbey enclosing wall where some stones had already been filched and cautiously entered the precinct, the silence broken only by the raucous cawing of disturbed rooks. They found windows closed and doors locked except for one leading perhaps to the dortor which was missing altogether. Window glass appeared intact but woefully grimy. Everywhere the grass was tall and unkempt.

'No-one around' said Ralph. Let us find somewhere to sleep.' He sent Thomas to watch for soldiers in the village and see if the abbey was visible from there: 'your young eyes may spot something useful.'

They settled into the dortor, where they found enough abandoned cots for their use, even remnants of bedding. They were eating the last of their food as Thomas rejoined them.

'I kept well under the trees, Father. I saw no sign of life until I neared the edge of Pont - that village. It is closer than you said, Evan, barely a mile away. Then I looked back up the valley to see if they could see the abbey from there while I still had enough light.' Ralph nodded approvingly. 'But I could not be sure what they night see in daylight. The tower for sure but the other buildings might be hidden by trees.'

'You did what you could, lad. What of the village itself?'

'A few poor houses. Candles burning in a few and in one I heard men talking and jesting - in English. By the sound of them they were drinking - brought with them, for I saw no alehouse. I heard a clash as something metal fell to the floor - maybe a helmet - which raised a laugh. I durst not get close enough to look inside but they must have been soldiers of the posse, taken over the house for the night.'

Aston grunted. 'No doubt after turfing out its owner and his family. And their leaders, as befitting gentry, will be settled under a better roof nearby. Anything else?'

Thomas nodded. 'One thing more. I crept around the village looking for their horses. It was nearly dark but I found a barn. Inside a horse whinnied and then another as they heard me. I could smell them, too. Their beasts are stalled there for the night.'

Ralph nodded approvingly 'You did well. But your news is ill for it seems we have not escaped them. At daybreak they may see us, for they will surely take the trouble to walk a mere mile to search here. Let us sleep now, for by daybreak we must be into the trees again until they have gone - and leave no trace of our ever having been here.'

Soon after dawn they watched as two soldiers strolled up the valley, made a perfunctory search of the buildings and returned to the village. Thomas, who had followed them back, returned with the news that the entire party had mounted and were now riding unhurriedly back along the Tregaron road.

An argument followed about which way they should go themselves. As always Aston was for directly east for England.

'Would you have us die?' Unusually, Evan was short tempered. 'East is impassable for us. I have told you we would be crossing the backbone of Wales, rougher than anything you have endured so far, without habitation or even a clear track to guide us and at least two nights under the stars - or more likely cloud and rain. Would you repeat our misery on the Black Mountain?'

There was silence. Then Ralph asked: 'Then can we go north again, Evan?'

'We can, through Ysbyty Ystwyth, Pontrhydygroes and Pontarmynach. That way we can join a better way east to England. Shall I translate their names for you?' he asked dryly.

The response was a chorus of groans. Aston snorted at these ever more unpronounceable names and asked about distances. Evan admitted it would be a long way around. 'Our easiest way is indeed to follow the main road back to Tregaron - much better than the hill track we came by - and from there take the drovers' road east again. But if we do we would be following our pursuers, which could prove a dangerous irony.' He shrugged his shoulders. 'You must decide.'

Aston said: 'But by now the posse has given up searching and is far ahead of us and on horseback. I say we can safely take the main road east road again.'

Ralph pointed out that should the posse turn back they could be caught in the open.

'Why should they turn back? I tell you they have finished here.'

Evan said: 'They might think we plan to take the road west to Aberystwyth. There, not finding us, they could return and be behind us.'

'Or split their force and take both roads: they have numbers enough.' They knew they were arguing in circles. Knew they must come to a decision, for unless they found food soon would not get anywhere. Yet all the alternatives seemed hazardous.

In the end they settled for the main Tregaron road and set out. Moving cautiously, they reached it safely and found it straight and open enough to see well ahead. Nevertheless Ralph sent Thomas forward to warn them should any of the posse turn back. It was easy walking after the hill tracks and they met few travellers, but a lad riding a donkey told Evan he had passed gentlemen and soldiers walking their horses a mile or so ahead of them. Ralph called a halt, meaning to keep well behind them.

To their right, on both sides of a meandering river marked by a curve of willows, the wide valley floor was a reddish-brown colour in startling contrast to the green of the valley sides. Hawks, buzzards and fork-tailed red kites wheeled overhead. Ralph asked Evan if this was the great bog he had mentioned.

'Yes indeed, this is the Cors Goch, meaning the red bog. You can see why.'

'Indeed. Yet it looks too dry. Surely that is grass there?'

'Parts of it at this end, yes, although with wetter patches. But downstream it become a maze of reeds, large pools of open water, peat and marsh, unsafe in places.'

'Like our Glastonbury Levels then, yet this looks very different!'

'This is upland bog, Father, with different plants. But they are like enough for man's use - hard to tame, hard to cross and with danger of sinking in mud or drowning, yet rich in birds and fish to eat and peat to warm us.'

As they moved on they saw more clearly what Evan had described. Wild duck and other water birds rested on patches of open water. Some parts were dark with peat. Along the road verge stacks of peat turves awaited collection and there were more out on the bog. Aston, recalling his steward's days, asked if the abbey owned the peat.

'They owned almost everything hereabouts - granges, mills, a lead mine, most of this bog. They rented out land but kept most of the peat for their own use.'

'A smaller Glastonbury! I doubt it made them any more popular than we have become in Somerset.'

Evan answered. 'Yes and no. As landlords some thought them as grasping as the gentry and putting so much land to sheep cost local folk much of their food supplies. But the Cistercians also made roads where there were tracks and bridges where there were only fords. They built hospices for travellers. Once they supported and were supported by Welsh princes, for the most part a fruitful relationship - and memories are long here. Some of our princes are buried at Strata Florida. I have been away six years but I would hazard that folk accepted the monks more readily than they do the crown today - certainly since the Acts of Union. See how that drover warned us. At least the monks never threatened our language or what was left of our laws.' Evan talks more and more, Ralph thought. This journey is changing him. Changing us all?

They passed abandoned farm buildings on their left, where an overgrown track crossed the road and continued straight into the bog. Then came a little scarred hill. 'Old abbey lead mine,' Evan explained. Now the bog widened up to the road edge. He pointed across it to the distant far bank. 'Can you see that tongue of dry land reaching towards us? Beyond lies a well which had something to do with the abbey.'

'A holy well?' In the rear Matthew had heard: until now he had not spoken all day and his voice was weak as he struggled to catch up.' Evan did not know. Ralph noted how little interest the question aroused among all save Matthew: spiritual matters were fading fast. They plodded on.

Far ahead was the small figure of Thomas but no other traveller was in sight. Out on the bog bird cries broke the silence. Evan was uneasy. If the posse sent riders back for a last check they would be cruelly exposed on this open road. He saw Ralph looking at him and knew they had the same thought. The two fell back a little and talked quietly with heads down. Then Ralph nodded and they overtook the others.

As they did so Francis in the lead shouted: 'Father - it's Thomas!' The distant figure was running back towards them waving a bleached linen cloth, the agreed warning signal. Far behind him a small dust cloud rose into the air.

Aston cried: 'They are coming back! We must climb that hill!' But Ralph's commanding voice stopped him: 'No! They would see us at once and trap us on it.' The others hesitated then made to run back along the road they had just travelled. Again Ralph shouted. 'Stop! No escape on the road: they'd run us down in minutes.' Thomas was closer now, running fast, but the soldiers were in sight and closing at a sharp canter. 'Listen! We have one chance. But we must do exactly as Evan tells us.'

Evan cried: 'A small chance but all we have. Follow me in single file, keep close together and step only in my footprints.' With that he tucked up the skirts of his habit and ran towards the bog. The others followed uncertainly, Ralph at the rear urging them on and waving for Thomas to follow. The horsemen were close now.

Evan led at a fast walking pace into a mix of firm sandy soil and thin drier peat at the bog's edge. the others following gingerly on the uneven surface.

Aston protested. 'Why venture into this? We could have moved faster on that proper track we passed by that farm.'

'So could horsemen,' Evan explained over his shoulder: 'Father Prior and I have considered this. We must make for that tongue of firm ground beyond the river that leads to the well, which lessens our passage across the bog. To reach it we must ford the river, which swings towards that side. But on our way we cannot avoid all soft ground, so be wary. In places it will shake underfoot but mostly it should take our weight. There are danger spots, however, so step always in my footprints.'

Thomas, who had caught them up, panted: 'But they have seen us and will follow!' Evan turned around to look: although the mounted soldiers were very close now he seemed composed, a half smile on his face. 'Pray they do, Thomas, for then the bog and their heavy horses protects us. And hope they are spirited young idiots who see no quarry without a halloo and mad gallop after it, for then we may escape them. But if they have the sense to go around the bog by road we will be taken.' He saw that the civilian officials, slower but wiser men, had been left a hundred paces behind the others, their shouting to the soldiers to no avail. His smile widened grimly. 'It gets better. But we have no time to lose. Follow close.' Now they were on wet ground that quaked alarmingly underfoot. Although there was no wind clumps of reeds some distance away stirred from their weight. But Evan kept straight ahead and soon they reached a patch of firmer ground again. Then it was soft ground again, sucking alarmingly at their feet. Their footing became insecure and their progress slowed.

Now the horsemen were plunging into the bog's edge. A dozen strides they made at speed, enough to encourage their reckless stupidity, then came a greater trembling underfoot and they heard the thrashing of frightened beasts and the curses of riders fighting to control them. Turning, they saw that the leading horse was up to its hocks in the clinging mud, while those following were already fetlock deep. The two officers had reached the bank and were shouting angrily. Evan led on.

Now came stretches of difficulty and some danger; sodden peat that scarce bore their weight and their feet sinking ankle deep, reed-fringed patches of shallow water, soft marshy mud impossible to avoid. Evan led with care, trying to maintain an air of confidence. Twice someone almost come to grief. The heavy Aston, a foot astray from Evan's footprints, sank over his knees before being hauled clear of the sucking morass. Matthew, half oblivious in his sickness, stumbled into a reed bed and was soaked. For a while they were too concerned with their footing to think about their pursuers, but when they next stopped for breath they looked back anxiously.

What they saw through the tall spindly reeds reassured them: the horsemen were in dire straits. The leading animal was up to its belly in the sticky mud churned up by its frantic kicking: all but one of the others were in little better case and two riders had been thrown. Men were gathered around the terrified leading horse which was sinking. They appeared to be trying to fasten a contrivance of harness and clothing around it to pull it free. Others tried to calm the other animals and lead them back to firmer ground. 'They'll be busy awhile,' said Evan as he led on. The others followed him, concentrating on each step. Frogs croaked in wetter patches and Francis yelled as something furry shot over his foot. 'Just a water vole, lad,' Aston reassured him. When next they looked back the two officials had tethered their horses and were trying to take charge.

When at last they reached the line of willows that marked the riverbank the posse was out of sight behind thick reed beds. Again Ralph sent Thomas back to give warning should any of them get back to the road.

'Tread carefully and keep to our old tracks' Evan called after him, but knew he could trust the lad's common sense. He turned to the river. 'The Teifi again,' he said, 'swung back towards this bank now as I said.' The river was not wide but its bed was barely visible although the water was clear enough to see small fish swimming.

'You said we could ford it, but this is much too deep,' Aston exclaimed. 'Had you considered that?' Ralph raised an eyebrow at Evan.

Evan face showed his dismay. 'I had thought to wade across,' he admitted, 'There is much more water than I expected at this season. Can any of us not swim?' But he could guess the answer - Aston could not, Francis and Mathew had not even been into deep water and the score of strokes needed to reach the far bank might as well have been a mile. They gazed despairingly at the smoothly-flowing stream.

'Are there coracles about?' Ralph asked.

'Local folk might use them here but they carry only one man and anyway they have value so their owners take them home strapped to their backs.'

'Then we cannot escape.'

'We are not done for yet.' Evan was thinking fast. 'Search the bank for a boat.'

'But you said the coracles ....'

'Not a coracle, a longer craft.' He explained: 'If that well on the far bank was revered as holy then the brothers here would have cause to visit it in the past. They would come in procession. They could rest at their farm we passed and take that wider path we saw going straight into the bog and where it ends on this bank cross the water by boat. With a boat it would be much their easiest way.'

Ralph was struck anew by Evan's confidence but could not accept his reasoning. 'You speculate about a boat with no evidence of one and claim they would cross the bog, which we know to be hazardous. That path we saw may not even pass right through to this bank. Come, Evan, your argument is fanciful - and time is passing.'

'Not argument enough to search for a boat when most of us cannot swim?' Evan was assertive now. 'As for difficulty crossing the bog remember that unlike us the brothers knew their way. They may have used a safe path made by the monks or repaired by them from an older one. Not too difficult - we know the Ancients made them on land as wet as this on our Glastonbury Levels and made them to last. Such a pathway might have been used until the abbey surrendered and might still be used by local folk - as might a boat.'

Aston was dismissive. 'Then where is this path? We saw none.'

'We did not look. But a pathway leading to a ferry makes sense. Find such a path and it may point us to a boat.'

To Aston all this was idle fancy. 'No time for that - that posse will not be stuck in mud for ever.' Instinctively they looked for Thomas, but there was no sign of him.

But Ralph was thoughtful. 'A made path from the farm leading directly through the bog to that tongue of firm ground leading to the well? Evan may have the truth of it.'

Evan added: 'And it should reach the riverbank a little to our north. If there is a boat it should be near that spot. So let us look.'

They were moving off when Thomas panted out of the bog towards them. 'They have still not got all their horses clear and at least one is surely lost. But the officials have gone back to their own tethered mounts. The last I saw of them they were starting back up the road we came from Pont - Pont'

'Going around the bog to cut us off,' said Ralph. 'Only the two officials, you say?'

'Yes, but three other horses are almost freed and their riders will soon follow.'

'Then we must hasten.' They hurried up the river bank.

There was no mistaking the old pathway emerging from the bog. It was fashioned of large rough-hewn planks laid long-ways on supports of sharply angled branches driven deep where the surface was soft. In some places thin sticks of wood were laid crossways on top and fastened with strips of bark. The planks had sunk to ground and water level, some parts rotted. But judging by the ones they had seen on the Glastonbury Levels the path had been kept in good enough repair to be passable on foot.

Aston stared at it. 'If this abbey was in decline long before its surrender two years ago why still maintain this path?'

'As I said, local folk might keep it in repair for their own use.'

Ralph was abrupt: 'We waste precious time. Look for this boat - if it exists.'

With their staffs they beat about the tall reeds fringing the riverbank. As Ralph bent to search more closely the frayed cord supporting the bag under his habit gave way and the bowl fell onto the ground, rolled and wobbled into the reeds and splashed into the water. As he moved to pick it up Matthew said: 'Let me, Father, I am wet already.' He reached into the water and stooped to pick out the bowl. As he did so something caught his eye and he poked feebly into the reeds with his staff and struck something more solid. His thin cry brought the others running.

'The boat: this must be it.' They beat down the surrounding reeds to reveal a foot of its prow where it lay bottom up. Carefully they dragged it out of the water and turned it upright. Evan sighed with relief. It was a boat of sorts, twelve feet long with no keel, a framework of willow covered with stretched cowhide like a coracle. But it was in wretched state. There were neither paddles nor poles.

'No abbot's barge, for sure. Will it float?' Aston was anxious.

Ralph was listening for horsemen on the far bank. 'Let us find out. Get it in the water.' They carried its sodden weight easily enough but it sagged ominously. As the others stepped in gingerly Matthew remained on the bank staring at the bowl he still held in one hand: Ralph called sharply to him to get in. As they pushed off from the bank water immediately began to seep around them as they squatted on its floor. The flimsy craft rocked sluggishly.

'Sit still and paddle with your food bowls - anything. Hurry, they are almost upon us!' And we shall have sunk, Ralph thought. But struggling with satchel fastenings to take out bowls was taking too long and they paddled frantically with their bare hands. The leaking over-laden craft hardly moved towards the far bank a bare twenty yards away. Realising that he still held the wooden bowl in his hands Matthew scooped with it on one side and then the other while the two laymen used their bonnets. At once the sinking boat moved a little faster and they were able to reach the far bank sitting in inches of chilly water. As they scrambled ashore they heard the horsemen coming fast. 'No time to hide the boat.' They stumbled up the narrow tongue of dry land to a tiny stone building with a crude arch in front. 'The well,' Ralph panted, 'but holy or not it is no shelter for us.'

As they hurried behind the grotto-like structure they heard hooves pounding ever closer and broke into a desperate run over a narrow track and into the shelter of wild woodland where they lay panting behind a thick screen of bushes around some gnarled old oaks, desperately trying to lie quiet. Breathing heavily Ralph waved Thomas to watch their pursuers, who were galloping up and down the track searching for them.

After what seemed an age the horsemen withdrew and all was still. Francis slumped, head in hands. Ralph and Evan leant wearily against the trunk of the largest oak. Ralph pointed at Matthew and Aston, both face down in the leaves motionless as logs. 'We cannot carry on, Evan. Yet nor can we give ourselves up. Will we never find sanctuary?' They were now so close to Evan's old home as to bring a lump to his throat. He forced himself to think in practical terms.

'There are no other monastic houses hereabouts, so no sanctuary there. Homesteads are few and scattered and too poor to take us all in and we have little money left. Our only hope lies with the few manors that have the room and the means. I can think of four within our reach, but who knows where their loyalties lie these days? If, like so many gentry elsewhere, they have an eye to Strata Florida's granges they will seek to keep in favour with the King. Knock at their doors and we risk betrayal.'

Ralph sighed. 'Our case is hopeless. My foolish plan has failed you all!'

Evan felt a surge of sympathy for this burdened man, who in these few weeks on the road had changed from arrogant to almost humble and become companion as much as leader. It prompted him to reveal more than he had intended.

'Yet one manor nearby might serve us. Six years ago I knew its owner, Ioan Llywd, a man who had seen something of the world in his youth and a true gentleman of integrity and charity. His manor is called Neuadd Siriol. But it lies nigh on ten miles from here and he may not even be alive or living there anymore.' He wondered about that. Then what about her ….?

'You knew him, Evan?'

'Not well - he ranked above my station. But enough to know his worth.'

Ralph sat up stiffly. 'So they will remember you and more likely to take us in.'

Evan, fearing he had said too much, began a litany of difficulties. 'He was ageing then, likely dead now, had no son living, may not remember me. The house lies farther west again, only four miles from Aberystwyth town on the western shore. We have been forced ever westward. Can you hope to return to England from there?'

But Ralph, perversely, had turned optimistic. He slapped Evan's shoulder. 'Take heart man: this is not like you. Another ten miles? If they will shelter us for a week we can recover our strength enough and then - who knows? Even find a ship for England. We must attempt this, Evan.'

'Very well, Father, if that is your mind.' Evan could not deny his companions this slim hope and without his guidance they would be lost: he could not have that on his conscience. He would set them on the road to Neuadd Siriol and then must leave them, for never again could he cross the threshold of that house. From there they must find their own way to England. He himself would go far away.

A soft rustle of bushes startled them and Thomas was back, beckoning urgently.

'Three soldiers are with the officials now. They have all returned to the well to eat and rest - and argue! I am not sure what about. Will you take a look?'

Neither Ralph nor Evan possessed Thomas's ability to move silently but they reached the wood's edge without incident and peeped cautiously down at the well. The two officials and three soldiers were squatting around a fire grilling meat on sticks and swigging from bottles, the officers a little apart from the others. They were certainly arguing. Their horses grazed nearby, three of them woefully muddied and much the worse for wear.

Ralph whispered: 'Five only! Let us hope the bog still detains the rest.' Trying to ignore the hunger pangs aroused by the rich smell of grilling meat, they strained to hear what they were saying but could only catch the odd word. Yet they dared t creep closer. Ralph surmised that the soldiers were objecting to more searching. They would be saddle weary, homesick and loth to take more orders from civilians they probably hardly knew. This was not the first disaffection he had seen amongst those sent to capture them. There was no bond here between leaders and followers: this fell far short of military discipline. And were they not still concerned for companions and valuable horses still mired in the bog and perhaps dead?

Leaving Thomas on watch, Ralph and Evan crept back to the others. Ralph felt sure the posse would now abandon its pursuit. They must just wait for them to leave then make one more effort to reach this possible sanctuary.

Late the following afternoon Ralph and Evan stood on a wooden footbridge crossing a small river that Evan recalled was named the Ystwyth. The others were slumped by the wayside. As if fate still mocked them the previous night and morning had been as frustrating as any on their journey. Under steady rain they had waited under the oaks damp and hungry, unable to risk trying to light a fire. At long last, well after noon, the remaining posse had bestirred itself and left.

In the endless hours while the others shivered and dozed uneasily Matthew had been restless. He was feverish and weak and he was itching from loathsome ring-shaped swellings that had now appeared on his body. He had felt ashamed and loth to speak of them to the others: indeed he hardly spoke at all now. He knew he was desperately ill but knew not why.

Since leaving that red bog behind his mind had turned more and more to the bowl. Whatever the others chose to think he knew he had witnessed a small miracle. If the bowl had not fallen and rolled into the water they would not have found the boat and would not have escaped. The bowl had acted to reveal it to them. Then, crossing the stream, he had felt it tremble in his hands, demanding to be used and showing him how. Obediently, as he had thrust it through the water the sinking boat had moved forward, allowing them to escape. Abbot Whiting had the truth of it after all. This was indeed the Grail! He knew then that although the prior was its appointed guardian, should they survive this journey it would fall to him, its only true believer, to tell its story. If he lived long enough.

This wretched night Evan had seized this last opportunity to speak privately to Ralph. 'Tomorrow, Father, if all goes well I will put you on the road to Neudd Siriol. I pray you may find shelter here and that they will help you on the road to England. I am sorry it will now be a long journey. But tomorrow I must leave you.'

Ralph had half-expected it. 'I know you wish to return to your home, Evan. Of course you must go. But is it not nearby?'

Evan's voice was bleak: 'I have no home now. I shall seek shelter for a time with my brother Alun who runs a few sheep up in these hills - if he is still there.'

'And then take up farming again yourself?'

'I doubt I still own any land to farm. I may turn my hand to leatherworking again.'

'Will you not stay a few days more with us at this house you lead us to?

'No, Father, best I leave you before then.'

'We shall miss you greatly, Evan; not least young Thomas and your language lessons.' They smiled: the lad had endeared himself to all of them. 'You have guided us well and we should have been utterly lost without you. If you must go you do so with my regret but my blessing.'

'Guided you well? Hardly that, Father. We may still be in danger and you could not be farther from where you wished to be. I have failed you in that.'

'No fault of yours, Evan: you have been ever steadfast.' Suddenly Ralph thought of Giles, who had not: what had happened to him? 'The blame for our predicament is mine alone. I led us into this doomed enterprise where we have lost all we sought to save and should have saved.' Except the pathetic wooden bowl his abbot had valued so highly, now back in his keeping.

'No fault lies with you, Father: only you could have held us together these last weeks. You have shown true leadership. Do not scourge yourself with undeserved guilt.' He had never spoken so personally before: Father Prior might take offence. But Ralph laid a hand over his. Rarely had he known appreciation or understanding: he felt his eyes misting a little. This was a different Evan from the dour monk who had started out from Glastonbury. How this journey has changed them all! Perhaps for the better.

'Thank you my friend: you see how we shall miss you.'

Evan hesitated, but this was his chance. 'Father, if you think I have served you as best I could will you grant me one boon before I leave you?' He went on hurriedly. 'It is a small matter. When you get to Neuadd Siriol do not mention me by name or say you were guided by a Welsh monk who has now left you. Say only that you were on pilgrimage, became lost and arrived there by chance. And enjoin the others to say nothing more.' He lapsed into embarrassed silence.

'But Evan, it is your arrival with us - someone known to the household - that may gain us a welcome? And only you can speak Welsh.'

'You will be made welcome anyway: you may count on hospitality in this land save when politics or religion intervene, which I hope is not the case here. As to language, the old man has book learning and travelled much when younger, even serving a while at court in London. He speaks good English - Latin, too, should you wish it. I beg you Father, this is all I ask.'

So Evan has secrets, Ralph thought, perhaps his reason for seeking the cloister. Well, he was not alone in that. 'Very well. I shall not enquire why you ask this - but the others may well do so. What reason will you give them for leaving us tomorrow?'

'The truth. That I go to my brother and then try to make a new life for myself - as they all must do, for only yourself as a priest is committed to your life-long vocation.' Ralph winced at that reminder. Evan felt wretched: he had spoken truth but not the whole truth.

Now, on the bridge, Evan kept his voice firm and even. 'Cross over brothers and take that left-hand road. After a mile or two it fords a little stream where it joins a larger river, the Rheidol. Follow the same road keeping north of the river and after five miles you come to Neuadd Siriol manor set back in woodland to your right.'

Avoiding Thomas' hurt eyes, he told them he must now leave them and answered their questions as he had answered Ralph. In the silence that followed their exchange of blessings he shook each of them by the hand. 'God grant you sanctuary at Neuadd Siriol.' To Thomas he said, 'You should find opportunity there to practise your carpentry and your Welsh, lad. See that both improve.' Then he looked into Ralph's eyes, needing no more words.

He watched as they stumbled wearily down the valley. As he turned on his heel and walked away in the opposite direction the sky was darkening, a cold wind was rising and it started to rain again. He heard the distant rumble of thunder.

CHAPTER 3

Sanctuary

Already it was getting dark. Elurned put down her sewing and walked to her east-facing window. Seeing little through the small leaded panes she opened the casement to look out. Wind snatched a curl of hair from under her cap. In the gloom the boughs of the orchard trees, fruitless and losing their leaves, soughed restless in a rising gale. In summer she loved this hour when, her day's work done, she walked with her spaniel Geraint under those trees or in the little knot garden her mother had laid out.

But October had brought leaden skies and now the threat of a storm. As the first rain spattered the windows she shut the casement and turned to the comfort of her room. Her parlour, her precious retreat, was at the end of the family wing that Tad-cu - grandfather - had built. Tad-cu had prospered then and spared no expense on these private apartments. She had a wall fireplace of dressed stone, oak wainscoting and comfortable furnishing. Two Turkey rugs her father had brought home from his travels glowed red and blue on the stone floor - their warmth meant no need for rush matting, much harder to keep clean. With windows on two sides this was a sunny room - when there was sun.

But now it had turned gloomy and chill; time for a fire. The fire in her father's chamber was always alight while he kept abed, the one in the great parlour would not be needed until he came downstairs again and it was a long time since one was lit in the old hall. Only the kitchen fires were never out. Just her own to see to now.

To call a maid to bring a tinderbox and light the rush dips and candles around the house Eluned walked along the short corridor past the counting house to the family's private entrance, the stair well and the old hall. The corridor and the one upstairs were newer additions and truly astonishing: people came to marvel at them. Tada - father - had put them in after seeing one on some journey in an ambassador's retinue - he had never said where. It made the middle bed chambers upstairs smaller but enabled her to avoid walking through them when her brothers had slept in one: both were now guest chambers. Tada would do anything for his only daughter, people said. She walked through the gloomy old hall to the warm kitchen to prepare a posset for him. She would take it up to him herself. For two days day now he had kept to his bed and she was worried. Ioan Llwyd - since childhood she had called him Tada - was over seventy. A great age, yet she was convinced he was less frail than he seemed these days, sick more at heart than body - which was no less a worry. But lying abed feeling sorry for himself did no good: tomorrow she would get him dressed and downstairs, if only for an hour or two.

Later and alone - Catrin was away in Llanbadarn and not due back until the morrow - she finished the simple supper brought to her and sat by her fire: at her feet her solid little dog twitched in a dream. Candle glow and firelight were too dim for sewing or reading the heavy tome on the side table she was struggling with. Few fathers taught their daughters to read as hers had, but this English was a slow business. Nor did she feel like making music: running the household took up too much time and energy. But at this hour she could set its demands aside. Settling a cushion behind her head she stared into the fire. Outside the rising wind and rain battered the windows.

It threatened to be a bad storm but it came from the west so the house would be protected from its full fury by thick woodland. All seemed secure: she could relax and be comfortable with her thoughts, making shapes in the red glow between the logs.

Except that her thoughts were not comfortable. Buried during her busy days but when her work was done, body easy and mind not engaged, they surfaced and would not go away. Confront them again then? But to what purpose when nothing was ever resolved?

First there was Tada. She recalled the active man of her childhood, who for a time had held a minor appointment at the new Tudor court, the Tudors for whom as a youth of seventeen he had offered himself for battle at Bosworth Field before returning home to marry and take up his inheritance at Neuadd Siriol. They had been a happy family then but the death of her brothers - Ioan Fach in the new king's early wars in France and Dafydd of the sweating sickness at Oxford not yet twenty - had begun the slow decline in his spirit. Then her mother too, heartbroken by the loss of both her sons, had sickened and died quiet as a wounded bird. In their mutual grief her father had turned all his love and care on her, his only surviving child and now heiress. He had seen to her further education so that now, rare among women, she matched in learning and discourse most men of her station. Book learning only, she knew sadly, for in this remote household she was confined in a small enclosed world, seeing little of the increasingly turbulent one outside. And Tada depended on her for more than housekeeping. She was all his family now and he loved her dearly. As he grew ever more reclusive his daughter had become the core of his diminished life.

And so Neuadd Siriol had become her prison. She loved Tada, kindest of fathers. Loved this house where she had been born and lived all her life. But knowing man and household would wither without her she had resigned herself to their service. She was nearly thirty four now - middle-aged - and trapped in this gentle cage. Trapped most of all by her growing acceptance of it. Neither happy nor unhappy, grown apart from - feelings - suspended in limbo. Did she even want to break free anymore?

Free for what anyway? Daydreams rose wraithlike from fire glow in twilight, one more persistent than the others. Freedom for a woman meant marriage - if that were freedom - and she had turned her back on marriage when her mother died. Tada had needed her: this manor had needed her. Anyway there had been few possible suitors amongst the sparse local population and her father would not have thought any of them a suitable match for his daughter. One nobleman had an estate nearby but was always at court in London: she had never met him. Anyway an Earl, even one of the new jumped-up ones, would have been aiming too high for a daughter of what the Sais - the English - might dismiss as little more than yeoman stock, notwithstanding its ancient Welsh lineage. The others had been two tenant farmers, a third farmer with freehold title Tregaron way and a lawyer from Aberystwyth. The lawyer could talk and the others could dig and each had been eager enough for her hand - and her bed, for she knew she had been comely as well as a profitable match - but that had been nearly two decades ago! Tada would not have approved of any of them. Nor, for all his connections in those days, had he bestirred himself to seek a good match for her. With sadness she knew that had been largely self-interest: he needed her at home.

She poked at the logs. What did it matter now? The stirrings of youth had ever been frustrated and unfocussed, for not one of those men had truly awakened her interest. Now marriage had passed her by and her life was set on its uneventful course. If that course was too set and dull - well, the clumsy farmers and the mincing lawyer had been a dull lot, too. She smiled, imagining herself married to any of them. No regrets there. The small smile faded: did she still regret there had been no-one else? Could not have been?

Could have been? Sometimes even now she found herself thinking of another farmer living across the valley, never a prospective suitor. His small farm abutted two of Tada's tenancies. As a freeholder he had had no cause to come to Tada's counting room to pay his rent. Nor, unlike the tenants and their families, had he been invited to the Christmas feast in the Great Hall, the great event of the year. And so she had met him but rarely - at market in Aberystwyth, after church or out riding with Tada. A brief greeting and he was gone: she hardly knew him.

Yet his was the face that could still suddenly appear in the fire-glow, a strong grave face, almost handsome in its closed way. She remembered the softly vibrant voice he used so sparingly, like most folk seeming diffident before Tada the local landowner. For some reason she recalled his strong hands with their long sensitive fingers. Nearly always dressed in working clothes, he could be taken for one of Tada's tenants.

But Eluned knew better. Something about him, perhaps a sense of quiet assurance under his reserve, had intrigued her. Curious, she had made discreet enquiries and pored through a few local history pamphlets in Tada's book chest in the counting house, which served as their library. She had discovered that the man's family was as old as hers and esteemed enough for brief mention in a few of them. His name was Ieuan ap Howell, his family, like hers, a cadet branch of a once-leading one in mid-Wales. With too many Ieuans around he was always known by its English form Evan. It seemed he possessed fair learning and some love of books and music. But whereas her family had prospered steadily through effort and widening contacts his had fall foul of more powerful families in ways discreetly unrecorded. The head of her own family had been knighted but Evan's branch of his had lost most of their land and fallen on lean times. Their estate had been broken up before he had come to this valley to claim his share of what remained, by then reduced to his small hill farm. Tada would not have thought him suitable either.

Or might he? More than once he had commented that Evan ap Howell was proving himself a husbandman of ability and purpose and through hard work beginning to turn a profit. He had remarked that should either of his tenants on that side of the valley leave his farm he might offer to sell it outright to Evan, for he looked a man set to prosper and in these troubled times good neighbours were to be valued.

Respectable lineage then, book learning and culture, a freehold farm and unmarried! Tada might have accepted him. Evan was settled close at hand and perhaps, as Tada became too frail, could have helped him with Neuadd Siriol. He would have made a reliable steward to run the estate. She and Evan could have lived in the comfort of Neuadd Siriol, a late son for her father. And a husband for her.

Could have! Eluned sat up. She had trodden this whimsy road before and to the same dead end. Evan had shown no interest in her. And her own feelings? Could she have seen him as husband and lover? She simply did not know for she hardly knew him. Yet sometimes a sudden unwonted memory of him aroused those youthful stirrings she would rather thrust away.

But as always such reverie was futile. Six years ago Evan had vanished without word or trace. Briskly Eluned stood up, damped down her fire, listened to the moaning of the gale and went upstairs to her bedchamber. Weather permitting, young Catrin would be home tomorrow with the comfort of her chatter.

Sleep would not come to Ioan Llwyd. He lay within the heavy draperies of his great bed, eyes closed. Eluned had brought his supper which he had hardly touched, then helped him to the privy and afterwards sat on the bed and talked over the day with him as she always did. His fire was safely damped down. Now another black night would drag its way to another laggard dawn. He sighed, heard the rising wind and snuggled into the comfort of his goose-feather bed.

Comfort yet no sleep. His mind gnawed, a hound on a bone, at the tumultuous changes taking place in the country. So far Neuadd Siriol, managed now by Walter Beynon his new steward and with Eluned running his household, did well enough. Yet with money forever losing its value it did not prosper as in his father's day. When he was dead and gone, what then? Were there ever such uncertain times? In barely his own lifetime so much that was new was turning his ordered world upside down. Gutenberg and Caxton and their magical printing presses spreading knowledge even to common folk - where would that lead? Unsettling ideas from Italy. Luther and his reformists undermining the old church. And two years ago Cymru - which the English insultingly called Wales from the Saxon word for 'foreigner' although they were the newcomers - long subjugated and now without a by-your-leave 'united' with England, our surviving laws gone, our language banished from courts and public offices. And as in England the monastic houses being closed. And all at such frantic speed! Where would it all end? Was it for this he had followed Richmond to Bosworth, with his own eyes seen Crookback's fallen crown placed on his head as King Henry the Seventh. Part Welsh the new king had been, too, yet never set foot here afterwards. Now his spendthrift son on the throne was the cause of the present upheaval. Eluned would inherit what he possessed but he foresaw little but trouble coming with it. She deserved better.

Of course much of the change was to the good. Why should only priests and gentry like himself be taught to read and learn to reason? Reform to Mother Church was long overdue and much in this new thinking attracted him. Here in Cymru we had gained as well as lost: the discrimination that had made us second-class citizens in our own country was falling away and our horizons were widening - although the threat to our language was a heavy price to pay for the gain. If only change had come gradually with time for acceptance, not at this headlong pace. If only he could have lived out his few remaining days in peace. If only ….

Always in his thoughts was Eluned. He would carry to the grave his guilt that somehow he had ruined her life. She was middle-aged now, still unmarried and would never have children - or he a grandchild to carry on the family name. She loved Neuadd Siriol, her childhood and only home, but we are isolated and remote here. The few eligible young men at nearby manors had been drawn like moths to a flame to the royal court in London, the centre of affairs, and found wives there. Eluned's lot had been to take her dead mother's place and keep a home for him. Tied to him. And so she had never moved to court as her accomplishments entitled her - not to mention the beauty she had in her youth - still had. He should not have let it - no, caused it - to happen! Should have taken her to London while he still had contacts there, to the excitement and prospects of the Tudor court - keeping an eye on her for its dangers of course, or it was said to be very different from the one he had known under this king's father. Even that court life had finally palled on him, left him content to live quietly here at home, but Eluned had seen nothing of the wider world, met no eligible men. He had been selfish and wrong to keep her in this remote home - soon he would be judged for it. He turned restlessly on his pillow.

The storm had worsened. Even through the heavy bed hangings Ioan heard the moan of the rising wind. No raindrops pattered on the tester above him yet he feared for the roof thatch in this gale. He drew the hangings aside and lit a candle to see if rain was getting in anywhere. No, the floor looked dry. Suddenly the wind rose to a banshee howl. There was a loud crack, a thumping crash: that was a tree falling in the orchard. The un-curtained windows showed no lightning flashes: wind alone had brought it down and he feared worse before morning.

The crash of the falling tree woke Eluned and set Gelert barking. She lifted him onto her bed where they snuggled together in mutual comfort. Nothing could be done until morning when the storm had passed when there would be a deal of clearing up to do outside. She stroked the dog's silky ear and tried to compose herself to sleep again.

Now she thought she heard a hammering sound, faint through the wind. Imagination? A pause and then again, more insistent. It was real enough, coming from the servants' end of the house beyond the old hall. Something broken loose? She sighed, shrugged on her gown and crossed to the window overlooking the drive. The hammering continued but in the darkness she could make out nothing amiss.

Then, momentarily, the moon emerged from behind black clouds as the storm began to blow itself out. In its faint eerie light she glimpsed movement at the front porch. Someone was banging on the front door! She lit a candle, drew on her night gown and hurried down the stairs and across the hall, Gelert growling at her heels. Mair the cook and one of the maids were already in the cross passage looking nervously at the front door. Footsteps creaked on the servants' staircase and candlelight wavered as others crept down. The entire household was aroused!

Eluned signalled Mair to hold the barking dog and peered through the door's Judas hole. Dimly she made out a tall hooded figure and another slumped against the porch wall. The man at the door was shouting but she could not make out his words through the thick oak and howling wind. Dare she open the door? She looked around. Most of the women servants were now crowding the passage, chattering. But apart from the kitchen boys her father was the only male in the house at night, for the unmarried house grooms slept in quarters fifty yards away. She must chance it! Two of her women had armed themselves with heavy pokers from the kitchens and she beckoned them beside her. Then she drew back the heavy bolts and open the door.

A raw gust of wind clutched at her gown, rain spattered her face and the tall figure collapsed into the passage, almost knocking her down. He was soaking wet, his cloak, doublet and hose plastered with mud. His companion, in a monk's habit and as wet, lurched in after him and sank to the floor, still as death. Rainwater streamed off them onto the flagstones. Hurriedly closing and bolting the door the women looked askance as the first man rose with painful slowness to his feet, slumped heavily against the wall and pulled back his dripping hood.

Under the dirt and stubble his face was that of a young man. He was shivering and clearly exhausted. He mumbled something in English but Eluned's limited grasp of the language could make no sense of his slurred speech and strange burring accent.

They stared at each other without comprehension. Then with a huge effort the young man pulled himself upright.

'Colli!' he croaked in faltering Welsh. Lost! They had been lost in the storm. That was obvious now: no wonder they looked half dead! Eluned stood aside and pointed to the kitchens, where the main fire always burned. But the man's grimy finger pointed shakily outside. 'Arall,' he said. Others? There were others? She raised one finger: 'Un?' He shook his dripping head, finding the word but raising three fingers for emphasis: 'Tri.' There were three more out there! He swung a wavering arm in the direction of the Gors road, almost overbalancing in his weakness. The others were somewhere out on the road? Had they collapsed out there? This young sais might have even less Welsh than she had English but it was serving him well. Even so she would need her father to make true sense of this. But their urgent need now was shelter: simple hospitality needed no language.

Eluned took command. Willing hands supported the men to the damped-down main kitchen fire, which the fire boy was already reviving with his bellows. He was sent to start another fire in the great fireplace in the hall. A flustered maid brought the drenched men a pile of drying cloths. Mair, ever cheerful, peered into the pottage cauldron. Satisfied it held enough she lifted it onto its pulley and lowered it over the fire. 'Cawl,' she grinned, nudging the exhausted monk with a plump elbow without response. He had pulled his cowl back and Eluned saw that he, too, was young. Another maid brought ravelled bread from the bread box, all that was left until tomorrow's baking. Meanwhile Eluned had sent the spit boy to alert Steward Beynon at his cottage to arouse all the men servants and search for the missing men. Then she sent to the buttery for wine to warm the shivering wretches at the kitchen fire.

She had just returned to the darkened hall to call for more rush dips and tallow candles to be lit there when the youngest housemaid tugged at her sleeve and pointed. Her father was walking slowly across the hall with his stick, a spectral figure in long white nightshirt and sleeping cap, holding a flickering candle.

'Marged, run upstairs to his bedchamber and find him a robe before he catches his death.' She chided him: 'Go back to bed, Tada, it is too cold for you. I'm sorry you were disturbed.'

'I was not asleep, child. What is happening here?'

'I'll tell you tomorrow. Go back to bed now.'

'Tell me now, he said stubbornly. She was too busy for this but gave him the gist of what was happening.

He said firmly: 'Five in all you say? I see the hall fire is lit. Good! Now we must bring down truckle beds from upstairs - for tonight anyway. We have pallets enough somewhere.' She had not thought about beds for them and this was a good idea, for there were only two guest chambers and their beds were not aired nor their fires lit. When the grooms came in from their search she would see to it.

'I can help, you know. Tell me!' Her father seemed newly alert, even eager. She nodded. 'Tada, you are the only one here who can talk proper English and understand them. Go to the kitchen and find out what you can about them while I make ready for the others.' That would be useful and should not tax him too much. Obediently he left, shrugging on the robe Marged had brought him.

Eluned followed him to speak to Mair. 'Have we pottage enough for five?' Mair nodded: she had looked and anyway the cauldron was rarely empty. 'Give them only pottage and bread - not too much - and only a little wine or ale. They look half starved and too much food on an empty belly does more harm than good. We'll feed them up properly tomorrow.' Eluned hurried back to the hall where the fire was well alight and beginning to throw off heat: she was relieved to see it drawing well for the chimney had not been swept of late. She cautioned the fire boy to watch for sparks on the rushes. What next? They needed to wash before eating and sleeping, but the laver in the passage would hardly suffice for such dirty men. She hurried back to the kitchen and ordered water heated in the copper, water pots placed on the hearth, empty half tubs filled from the well and taken to the passage. From her still room she fetched bars of soap - it was fortunate she had made a new supply two days earlier.

Back in the hall she slumped onto a wall bench, suddenly weary. Presently her father came to sit beside her. 'I've spoken to that young layman. He says they are all from England. His name is Thomas - seems a pleasant lad. They're fleeing from Glastonbury Abbey in Somerset, been in some trouble - I haven't got the whole of it yet. They're in a bad way - well, you've seen for yourself. I'll tell you more later.' He saw how tired she was. 'Easy girl, you're doing the work of ten here. 'Look, the house grooms should be back soon, there are others to do the searching. When they return shall I get them to bring down truckle beds and pallets as we agreed?' He was asking, not telling her, content to follow her lead but remarkably sprightly. She nodded gratefully. 'They'll need brycans - blankets - too.'

At that moment the front door banged open and at once they heard and felt the wind. They reached the cross passage just as the two house grooms came in supporting a heavy-set man hopping on one foot and groaning mightily. Then came a tall monk leaning heavily on his staff. Last came another monk, his cowl thrown back to reveal an ugly bruise on one youthful but sadly wasted cheek, half-carried in the strong arms of Mostyn the blacksmith. All were drenched. Estate workers gathered curiously outside, their torches flaming in the wind. The new steward Beynon was not with them. 'That makes five in all,' said Eluned, 'all found and alive, thank God!'

To her astonishment her father took charge with much of his old authority. In short order the estate workers were thanked, promised some reward for their lost sleep and dismissed. The travellers were helped to join their companions around the kitchen fire. The house grooms were sent upstairs to fetch bedding. Eluned returned to her seat in the hall, tired but amazed at the change in Tada.

He was beside her again, pressing her hand. 'You've been splendid, daughter. Go to your bed now: I'll see to things here.'

'Thanks, Tada. I'll go when I've seen to that man's ankle and that young monk's face - how pale he is - and any other ailments they have. Oh!' She turned to face him. There are women everywhere - where can these men wash the filth off them?'

He laughed, something she had not heard in weeks. 'Leave them to me. I'll get the maid to set food out in the kitchen and fill the tubs in the passage and then I'll pack all the women off to their beds - they'll be glad enough to go. When they are all upstairs the house grooms can see our travellers washed, dried, fed and bedded here in the hall with no maidenly modesty offended.'

'In the morning - soon upon us - the maids must cross the hall to attend to us.'

'To find our travellers dead to the world with only their noses peeping out from their brycans.' He grinned. 'But I'll tell the maids to go out by the front door and in to us by our private porch. Will that satisfy your delicate feelings, daughter? Now see to your potions and then to bed with you and sleep your fill for I warrant our guests will sleep past noon.' Her father bright-eyed and teasing her again! They smiled at each other. Then each was checked by the same thought: 'But what can they wear tonight - and tomorrow?' They laughed. For a moment the father's face turned grave. 'I'll hunt out my boys' old nightshirts: not everything was given away when ….. Anyway, that must do them for tonight: tomorrow we'll find them day clothes and get their own washed.' He kissed her cheek. 'Now off with you, woman.'

Last night's storm had cleared into a fine brisk morning for riding but Catrin had to pick her way through fallen branches and arrived at a sedate walk instead of her usual carefree canter. She threw the reins to the stable hand who had escorted her and hurried through the open front door into the cross passage. She had much to tell Eluned. A delicious smell of baking bread came from the warm kitchen and she looked in hopefully, hungry after her ride.

'Not ready for an hour yet, missy: we're late this morning.' Mair knew all about sixteen-year-old appetites.

Catrin pulled a face. 'Where's the mistress?'

'Still abed.'

'At this hour?'

'Ask her about last night and you'll know why. No! - Catrin - don't wake her.' But the girl had already skipped into the hall.

Where she stopped dead in astonishment.

It was no longer empty. The embers of a fire glowed pink in a layer of white ash in the great hearth: grouped around it were five truckle beds occupied by bodies wrapped in brychans. Who? ... at this hour? One of the sleepers stirred briefly and muttered in sleep. A man's voice! The hall fire had last been lit at Christmas and she had never seen people sleeping in here, although she knew they had in the old days when the hall was the centre of household life. Puzzled, she tip-toed for the staircase and Eluned's bedchamber. As she opened its door Gelert's sharp bark was suddenly stifled and he hurled himself at her, the human who romped with him and whom he adored. He had made a puddle on the floorboards: he could not have been let out all morning. In the big four-poster bed Eluned stirred, mumbled and turned over.

'El, I've something to tell you.'

Slowly Eluned sat up, stretched her arms, yawned and opened reluctant eyes. The child's startling new beauty made her feel old. No child anymore, which was something to think about. Catrin had come to them nine years ago, the bastard of a kitchen maid at a nearby estate who had died of a fever. Lacking an heir and deep in debt the estate had been broken up and sold, its servants abandoned and left homeless with winter upon them. Eluned, hurrying to help with food and clothing, had been taken with the appealing waif and brought her home. Finding her quick and responsive she had trained her as her personal maid and taught her some letters. In her new security the child had blossomed quickly to become companion rather than servant to Eluned, almost a much younger sister, a family pet soon accepted by Tada, who soon succumbed to her vivacity and artless affection. Now she enjoyed the unheard-of luxury of her own tiny bedchamber, a closed-off section of the wondrous new corridor next to Eluned's own, and had only sporadic menial duties. As she never took advantage of her new position the servants accepted it readily enough. But what would be her future now she had suddenly grown up?

'Catrin fach. What time is it?' The angle of the pale sunlight slanting across the wall showed it must be late.

'Almost noon. There are men asleep in the hall. What's going on?' Eluned explained.

'And I missed it all! So what happens now?' Eluned shrugged: 'We'll let them sleep it off and then Tada will decide.'

'How is Tada; still sick abed?'

'Much brighter. Last night he came downstairs to help me with them. I must see how he is, set men looking for storm damage and attend to our visitors - some of them will not be up and about for days. Now let me dress and then you can help me. You said you had something to tell me'

'It can wait. You go down: I'll look in on Tada.'

Prior Ralph floated reluctantly up to consciousness and failed to open eyes gummed with sleep. Running a licked finger over his eyelashes he squinted up and saw beams and rafters high like a tithe barn's, beyond them the darkness of old thatch. Raising his head he saw that he lay abed in an old rush-floored hall, bare save for trestle tables and benches stacked on one side and four other truckle beds grouped with his own around the dying embers in a large fireplace. He fingered the clean linen sheets and woollen blankets covering him and the down pillow under his head. Two men in nightshirts sat whispering on the farthest bed and he recognised them as Thomas and Francis: Aston and Matthew must be in the other beds, neither stirring. So they were all together and seeming safe: this was Neua - something, the house to which Evan had directed them. The other two yawned and returned to their beds.

Now Ralph recalled the fury of the storm, their exhaustion and despair, Aston no longer able to walk unsupported, Matthew's strange weakness, their stumbling through that wild darkness. He remembered being helped into the house, his first sip of wine, the warmth of the kitchen fires, the greater warmth of being cared for. Overcome by a wondrous sensation of cleanliness and comfort he buried his face in his pillow, stretched his long legs luxuriously and fell deeply asleep again.

Ioan Fychan was up and about well before mid-morning. After looking into the hall - his guests were dead to the world and best left in peace - he breakfasted alone in the great parlour. By the time he had finished his pottage and small beer he had decided what to do about them.

First, they must be moved to more private accommodation for they needed peace and quiet to recover and by day the old hall was too much a crossroads. The two guest chambers upstairs must be made ready.

The prior and the older layman must have them - one in each, for the prior ranked too much the higher to share. Where to put the two young monks and the other lad? There were no more unoccupied bedchambers in the house. They would have to use the sleeping places in the loft in the main barn used by casual labour at harvest time and at present empty - first they must be swept and bedding found for them. All five men would need clothing while their own was washed and dried. He must make sure the cook had enough food on hand. So much to do! He would not disturb Eluned after her exertions but see to everything himself. Briskly he summoned grooms and maids to make a start.

Eluned had just finished dressing when her father sent up a note: 'Daughter, our visitors having departed to their bed chambers you may now with propriety set foot in the hall.' Tada in his old playful humour! Active too, for as she went down the upper corridor maids were already busy preparing the guest chambers. As she entered the hall she found Catrin there also looking for him. Ioan kissed them both warmly.

'Catrin fach welcome home: I trust you had a good visit.' He gave her no chance to reply. 'Eluned, you look rested.' He told her what had been done so far, adding with some pride that all would soon be ready for their uninvited guests. She nodded her agreement: his plans sounded sensible.

'Something more. I've been thinking. Five guests make a crowd to go on taking all our meals in the great parlour - how say you we bring the high table back here in the hall and eat our dinners with the household and workers in the old way as once we did?' Could we start tomorrow, think you? Ioan was positively beaming. The two women exchanged glances: how the coming of the visitors had enlivened him. Nevertheless Eluned insisted that there was more than enough work for her already and they would use the high table when she was ready. Ioan had to agree. While they discussed details Catrin looked around her.

The sleepers had gone, their beds replaced by the re-set trestle tables and stools for the usual staff dinner at noon.

Tada was still all enthusiasm. 'It will be like the old days and good to have new company, a prior with book learning and an abbey steward from vast abbey land holdings: I can discuss theology with one and farming with the other.' With a pang Eluned realised how far her father had lapsed into boredom and acceptance of old age. Whatever its problems this unexpected invasion was proving good for him. For herself, too, perhaps, despite the extra work. She nodded but had a question:

'All five of them to eat with us at high table or squashed into the parlour? Or only the prior and the steward?'

'All of them of course.' She had expected it and was pleased, but she persisted. 'They are English, Tada, with English ways: the two older men may not care for that, especially that prior.'

'Ah, you speak of class, daughter! They are our guests and this is our house so they must abide our rude ways. Have no fear. Were they ever of that mind then sleeping together in barns and worse - as I heard last night - should have knocked it out of them.'

'Are any of these men young?' Catrin asked. The tomboy was growing up: life would soon become dull for her here.

'Three are young,' said Ieuan, his eyes watchful, 'but two of those are novice monks and the third an apprentice or servant of sorts.' Catrin pulled a face and ran from the hall. 'Going to the stables,' she called over her shoulder.

'No more a child but a rare beauty with new thoughts and feelings stirring,' Ieuan said. 'Something for us to consider, daughter. But for the moment let us deal with these unexpected guests.'

'Where are they, anyway?'

'Conducted to their new lodgings, which should now be ready for them; the three youngsters in the sleeping places over the great barn, the older two upstairs in the guest chambers. They are all weak, girl, and need to stay in bed for days.'

Eluned nodded briskly 'I'll see to them now - that sick young monk's bruise first. I'll have their food taken to them for a few days while they rest quiet.' This invasion was invigorating herself as well as her father.

Later, Catrin tripped into Eluneds parlour without knocking and plumped onto the stool across the fire from her. Eluned put down her sewing. 'So what did you want to tell me, minx?'

Catrin poked at the logs, her astonishing blue-green eyes catching the glow. You know I've been visiting Sioned at Llanbadarn. Well, after breakfast she said - cool as you like - that we were invited over to that big house Plas Gogerddan for the day. Their son Harri - you met him once - is home for a week before he goes to Oxford. He has a friend staying with him and they pine to see someone their own age.'

'They said that?'

'Well - no - but that's what they meant.'

'And of course you went, the two of you unescorted.' Eluned heard herself sounding - oh God! - matronly.

'Of course not! Sioned's father and a groom rode over with us.'

'Good. So how did you find young Harri?'

Catrin pouted. 'Getting fat - and so full of himself these days! I don't like him much anymore, for all his family's grand house and airs.'

'And his friend?'

Catrin's eyes sparkled. 'Mmm! You should have seen him, Ell. His name is Gwilym ap Rhys and he's quite tall and dark with a curly beard and such an elegant leg in such fine hose and lovely brown eyes and he's one of that grand Rhys family and must be very rich and - and - I think he likes me,' she finished, blushing.

And so it begins, Eluned thought.

'What then?'

'Nothing then. We rode back to Llanbadarn - properly escorted - before dark and this morning I came home. I'll probably never see him - them - again.' She sighed mightily, pecked Eluned's cheek, tickled Geraint's chin and sped from the room.

But then again she might, Eluned thought. The Gogerddan family had money and influence and that other lad's family were still powers in the land. Could there be a match there? But what of her lowly origins? Could such as Catrin enter their wider world of consequence? Eluned too sighed as she picked up her sewing.

Two morning's later Thomas' strong young body was well on the way to recovery. After disposing heartily of the breakfast brought him by a supercilious house groom he put on the clean, slightly worn clothing laid by his bed. Having lost weight on the journey he was able to squeeze into them but the hose were too short and needed discreet adjustment under the doublet. Fortunately the scuffed shoes, slackened with age, were comfortable enough.

Apart from the shoes the clothes, although plain, were of finer quality than any he had worn in his young life - a linen shirt, a green doublet with slashed sleeves, a good leather jerkin and a fine bonnet with a jaunty feather. He wondered what Francis and Matthew would wear while their habits were being washed and ironed: were they permitted lay attire? A glance at their faces as they slept showed it would be days before that need concern them: Matthew in particular looked terrible.

He knew the journey had also taken a heavy toll on Father Prior and Steward Aston, particularly the steward, whose ankle might well be broken. For some days none of his companions would be company for him. That would feel strange after all their journeying together, but it would be pleasant to be on his own for a time with no-one needing his shoulder for support and slow him down.

Young Thomas craved fresh air and exercise. Since the storm there had been watery sunshine that might not last: he must make the best of it. He would venture out in his new finery and explore the estate of these kindly folk who had taken them in - his first sight of it in daylight. Perhaps he would meet the old head of the household who had spoken to him last night in fluent English. Would it be impertinent to thank him for his hospitality? Although clearly gentry he had seemed approachable. Perhaps he could practise his Welsh - and recalled Evan's abrupt departure with a stab of regret. But Thomas was never sad for long. Whistling gaily, he set off towards the house.

As he reached the point where the footpath opened onto the beaten earth of the forecourt two horsemen trotted in from the opposite side, dismounted and waited for a groom to take their glossy mounts. Curious, Thomas moved through a little knot garden and edged along another path alongside the house to watch, prepared to crouch in a pretence of weeding.

These were elegant young gentlemen, fine cambric bright around throats and wrists, gay plumes on bonnets, flashing gold chains and the wink of jewels on aigrettes and cap pins. The taller of the two cut a particularly fine figure, the sleeves of his rich blue doublet slashed to reveal what might be pale velvet beneath, his leather jerkin richly embossed like the wall hanging he had seen in the abbot's lodging at Glastonbury. Here was sophistication surpassing anything Neuadd

Siriol was likely to show. Such gallants must surely be English! He envied them and his new clothing no longer felt grand.

The porch door opened and the lady who had opened it to them in the storm came forward to greet the visitors, her slightly flushed face suggesting they were not expected. The men moved to the open door, their deep bows elegantly apologetic.

Suddenly a girl ran out, stopped abruptly then came forward into the sunshine with a coltish attempt at dignity. Against convention she was bare-headed, her black hair glossy in the sunlight. Her face lit with pleasure as she greeted their sweeping bows with a curtsy. Then they all entered the house.

Thomas leaned against the wall, of a sudden short of breath. Never in his young life had he seen such beauty. Her head would have reached just past his shoulder, her body slender but rounding into womanhood, her movements light and free. He had been too distant to see her face clearly, but he knew there would be perfect features framed by that raven's wing of hair - he was unused to seeing a woman bare-headed, to seeing a woman at all for that matter. He struggled with new and disturbing emotions. He would never forget this first sight of her. Was she a daughter of the house? Her bodice and gown were plain enough but their material looked too fine for a servant. Was she betrothed to one of those gallants? Furious at that thought Thomas stomped on his way. As he passed the porch he heard the girl's light voice, laughing gaily.

Ioan Llwyd gazed critically around his Great Hall. After several days of rest all his guests save Matthew had left their beds. Even Aston hobbled about with a crutch, for Eluned had found his ankle to be badly sprained but not broken. So this was the day Ioan would welcome them formally to his high table in the hall. It would be no feast - Eluned had said the coming Christmas feast would be trouble and cost enough, thank you - but she had promised a hearty dinner. While she bustled in the kitchen his task was to see that the hall was in good order.

It seemed to be. The rushes had been thrown out and the stone floor washed - Eluned had insisted it remained uncovered save for a scattering of dried lavender. The fire had been lit again. The dais had been scrubbed and its long table taken from store, cleaned and set on it with his great chair and enough stools for all. The servants' trestle tables and benches were set longwise down the hall as was usual. Candlelight from the wall sconces flickered on the old stone walls, which as always cried out for some wall painting or tapestries. Such extravagancies were costly but if the hall was to be put to proper use again he must think about that. At least the laver in the cross passage was freshly filled and the high table looked properly set.

What remained to do? He had warned his estate workers that the ladies of the household and his new guests would be taking meat with them from today: they were to be clean and mind their manners and language - he would be watching them. As reward there would be extra small beer and pickings from the high table. Was it his imagination or were they pleased to see more of him these last few days and feel his guiding hand again? Had his new steward not been doing his work properly? Something else to look into tomorrow. For now Ioan cold look around with satisfaction. He would play the host again. He went upstairs wondering what to wear.

'We are honoured to be invited to Master Llwyd's table - especially you.' Prompted by Ralph, Aston was instructing Thomas on deportment and making much of it. It was not seemly for the lowly Thomas to be present at all - but then these people were not English and evidently did not know better.

'All save yourself know how to behave at table, for even the novices dined with the senior monks at Glastonbury - not with Father Abbot, of course. But you, I think, did not. You must not disgrace us.' Thomas nodded: he accepted his lowly status lightly and was eager not to disgrace himself. She might be present.

Aston instructed: 'First there is the matter of dress. Our clothes have been washed and dried and the brothers will of course wear their habits, as will Father Prior.' He cleared his throat and continued:

'You and I, however, must dress the best we can. Even clean and darned and pressed my old clothes are no longer fit for high table and yours never were. So we must use what has been loaned to us. You will wash and shave thoroughly, put on the best shirt you have and make yourself tidy, which includes taming that thatch of hair you have grown - you really must crop it! Secondly - now mark me well - on entering the house it is proper to wash your hands at the laver and again when leaving: make sure you do so. At each place at table you may expect to find a napkin - these people are far from barbarous whatever we were told. Place it over your left shoulder to wipe your hands after picking up meat. It is bad manners to put elbows or clenched fists on the table, and then ...' It was some time before he left Thomas in peace.

Ioan took his great chair at the high table. The weather at noon was overcast enough to justify the lit candles. Past halfway down the long wall the fire blazed cheerfully. Candlelight, fire glow, hospitality: he gazed at the scene with satisfaction. He asked Prior Ralph to say grace. His workers at the long trestles below, who had been staring at the invasion of gentry, stood and bowed their heads, peeping from the corners of eyes at the imposing black-habited figure intoning his sonorous Latin.

Ioan sat back. Bench legs clattered as the company followed suit. He had seated Ralph at his right hand with Eluned beyond him: on his left sat Steward Aston next to an empty place with Francis beyond it: Thomas, feeling conspicuous, looked along the board from one end while Matthew was at the other end. Ioan cut a dignified figure in almost unadorned black, Eluned was quietly elegant in a deep green gown, a single small jewel at her throat. Aston and Thomas were respectable in their borrowed clothing; the monks' habits were clean but sadly worn.

Serving maids brought dishes of venison and mutton to the tables. While the workers ate heartily the guests helped themselves from bowls of sallet and manchet bread, ale appeared with wine on the high table, where conversation began to stumble against the barrier of language, for only Ioan was fluent in English and Welsh. Under its generalities all had their private thoughts. Ioan felt his decision to use the hall again fully justified but he intended scolding young Catrin for being late at table. Eluned suspected the girl's absence was because young ap Rhys had called again earlier but only to say a brief farewell before leaving to visit his parents before going on to Oxford. She had moped ever since. Eluned was also worried her own gown was too grand for the occasion, but she had determined to show support for Tada's initiative: he was enjoying himself so much.

Looking about him Prior Ralph found the hall rather small and somewhat threadbare. There were no wall hangings, insufficient napery at table and maid servants, not men, served the food. He had had to wash his hands at the common laver by the door. But he conceded a degree of gentility and genuine hospitality. Aston's thoughts turned to Hereford and under his breath he cursed his sprained ankle. Francis, round-eyed, plied his knife with gusto, his world expanding rapidly in unwonted comfort. Matthew, who had been assisted to get dressed and attend, toyed with his food and struggled to conceal his illness.

And Thomas? His mind veered between Aston's lecture on table manners and that unoccupied stool. Was it for her? Then where was she? And for that matter who was she, for he had not seen her since that first day? He shook his head and turned his attention to the delightful task of heaping his platter. When next he looked up - there she sat on the vacant stool between Aston and an embarrassed Francis! She seemed to him a vision of loveliness in a cream-coloured gown, her hair now properly covered. Close to, the small regular features and clear complexion were all he had imagined. His knife clattered to the floorboards and he bent to retrieve it, blushing in confusion under the accusing eye of Aston and wishing himself a hundred miles away yet not wishing it at all.

The falling knife had attracted little attention in the general chatter but a silent and withdrawn Catrin, trapped between a fat old man and a freckled young monk, neither able to converse in Welsh, heard the sound, leaned forward and observed Thomas for the first time. Their eyes met briefly, looked away, locked together for a moment, then she pouted prettily and turned to try out her few words of English on Aston. She felt herself flush: the hall was getting too warm.

Presently there was another scrape of bench legs on stone as the workers, after a nod from Ioan, bowed to the high table and returned to their duties. Little work will get done this afternoon, Ioan thought, but it had been worthwhile. Bowls of the season's apples and pears and a fine cheese appeared at the high table.

Father Ralph's hand was on his sleeve: 'Master Ll-llwyd' - he could not get his tongue around the double 'll' sound.

Ioan smiled. 'My given name "Ioan," is plain John in English. I was John at Oxford and Court, so call me John.' We will all be using English names soon, he thought.

No doubting that the prior was mellowing. 'I shall - John. And as I no longer deserve the title "Father" please call me Ralph - Ralph Dawnay as I once was.' Ioan raised an eyebrow but bowed his agreement.

'John, we are deep in your debt. I would speak to you about our leaving and ask your advice about - other things.'

'So you shall, but here is no place to talk. There is no hurry, surely: wait until you are all fully recovered and had time to consider your position. Come, Let us finish our wine now and speak of lighter matters.'

'But five of us - five strangers - have descended on you uninvited: we must not burden you much longer. We should leave before your winter snows arrive: having crossed your high country. I can guess what it will be like then.' He shuddered.

Ioan nodded, 'Impassable for weeks. Believe me you are no burden and I welcome your company - my daughter knows how much - and your steward has agreed to advise me on some matters of farming, my own man proving a sore disappointment. And your young Thomas has asked if he may assist my carpenter. I welcome it for Emrys is old and heavy work with timber is needed on out-buildings before winter.'

He slapped the prior's shoulder. 'Do not doubt your welcome here, Ralph. Stay as long as you wish. Now help me finish this wine, then I'll to my bed for an hour.'

Later that evening Catrin was in Eluned's parlour again, fondling Geraint's long ears and elaborately casual.

'That big young man with the ill-fitting doublet sitting at the end of the table: who is he?' Eluned, relaxing after her busy day, opened one eye.

'From mooning over a fashionable young gallant to eyeing a mere apprentice in a few days? Come, minx, as ever you move too fast in all directions at once.' She had noticed the boy was comely. So, evidently, had Catrin.

Catrin stamped a dainty foot. 'I did not say I was interested in him - great clumsy English lump. Just curious - because we were never introduced.'

'If you had come to table on time you would have been: Tada is ill-pleased with you. The lad's name is Thomas - an abandoned waif taken in by the abbey and some sort of apprentice there. He did not want him left out of our company when he has endured as much as the others. Nor did I. But if you aim too high with young Rhys then equally this lad sits too low for you. Forget him.'

'I said I'm not interested - just curious!' Catrin flounced from the room.

Eluned gazed into the fire. Low? Too low for her? She had forgotten that this pert young lady was a maidservant's bastard and once an abandoned waif.

Two weeks had passed peacefully since their arrival and the fugitives, well rested and hopeful that pursuit had finally been abandoned, could turn their thoughts to their own affairs. Aston, his ankle almost healed thanks to Eluned's salves, pondered how to get to Herefordshire. For all the hospitality here he wanted to get 'home'- as he now thought of his brother's farm. Their kind host showed no sign of wishing them gone but his burden would surely be eased with one less mouth to feed.

Aston's purpose was clear but how achieve it? With winter almost on them and snow already mantling higher ground, crossing the mountains even on horseback would soon become nigh impossible for weeks on end, for snow would lie deepest in January and February. By sea perhaps? That would mean sailing south to the Severn Sea and then up past Bristol. Too close to Glastonbury and even now courting danger. Worth the risk? Were ships available? One day he had borrowed one of Ioan's horses and ridden the four miles west to the port of Aberystwyth to find out. He had enjoyed the short ride, but the harbour master there had dashed his hopes, explainig in halting English that in winter almost all coastal traffic shut down because of storms and lack of cargo. Aston had jogged home no nearer to solving his problem.

Matthew had begged writing materials from Ioan, explaining he wished to take notes from some of the books he was borrowing and reading. Too weak to be of help around the house he spent most days hunched over Ioan's desk in the counting house, quill to paper, attempting to record their arduous flight from Glastonbury. He deeply regretted it had been impossible to take notes along the way for now he could not remember many details. But mother church - if it survived - should know the truth of that journey. Know their struggles and final abject failure with the loss of the abbey treasures in their care. He would set down as faithful a record as he could. But he knew he was sickening by the day and fretted that he would not live to finish it. His quill scratched in into the night.

Caitlin turned Myrddin onto the bridle path through the wood, walking him gently over the rutted surface where they had been dragging down logs for winter repairs. Close ahead was the clearing where in summer she often sat munching an apple or pear, enjoying the view over the little valley. She would not stop today, for despite the wan sunshine it was cold, her horse's breath visible with every snort.

She did not miss her usual gallop: the cold was invigorating enough and she was content to jog along. She was thinking about that tall English lad - again. She saw him regularly at dinner now, for Tada was persisting with his new arrangement, but she had pointedly ignored him as beneath her interest. So why think of him at all?

His name was Thomas. A common name. That odious Cromwell's name. An apostle. She smiled: this Thomas was not her idea of an apostle. She kept comparing him with Gwilym ap Rhys, whose regular features and neatly trimmed beard were so much more refined and handsome than Thomas' open face - a Saxon face, Tada had called it, intending no disparagement. And there was no comparison in deportment. Yet Gwilym's was the face fast fading from her memory.

As she passed the clearing Myrddin whinnied and tossed his head: another horse answered from behind some bushes. As she reined in a man stepped into view and bowed. 'Mistress', he said, straightening up and grasping her rein. Bow and voice had mockery in them. He was Beynon the new steward.

She had been repelled by what little she had seen of him so far; close to even more so. He smelled of ale and seemed half-drunk. A squat ugly man in his thirties with an ugly scar down one side of his face, a bad complexion and an insolent eye, she recalled Tada's complaining that he had taken advantage of his own days lying abed to shirk his work and had better watch his step. Eluned, too, had mentioned a complaint of his harassing one of the house maids. It was unlikely this man would keep his job.

'What do you want?' Her voice was cold.

'I see you ride alone, little Catrin. Is that wise? Shall I escort you?' His speech suggested a touch of learning but he was clearly no gentleman.

'Do not speak to me in that manner!' She urged Myrddin forward but Beynon's hand was firm on the rein. The horse, uneasy, pawed the ground.

'A lady we are now, is it? Too high and mighty to ride with the likes of me.'

'Get out of my way.' She moved to raise her whip but in a flash he snatched it from her hand. His face darkened with sudden anger.

'Don't play the fine lady with me. I know where you come from. Heard about your mother and know you for a bastard.' Catrin went pale. The Llwyd family, her family now, knew more about her than she cared to remember herself, but they would never have spoken of it. Yet this man knew.

With an effort she kept her voice steady. 'I asked what do you want?'

Again he swept a mocking bow. 'What do I want? Let me see now. A little kindness to a poor man not fallen into the butter like you? A little money to keep your secret - or would you fancy old Llwyd's house grooms smirking your story about, I wonder? Or if, being such a lady these days that you carry no money about you, perhaps a little payment in kind - on account?' He came closer, leering. His teeth were stained, some missing altogether.

Desperately Catrin put spurs to Myrddin. Startled, the horse suddenly reared. She fell, to be caught in Beynon's arms. She felt his sour breath on her face as he bent to paw her.

As she let Gelert out of the front door Eluned saw Thomas striding towards the west wood. When not busying himself in the carpenter's shop the indefatigable youth explored the estate, usually alone since no-one could keep up with him.

She looked at him approvingly. He must have charmed a seamstress to improve his borrowed attire, for it fitted much better now, lending a new grace to his vigorous frame. He was indeed a comely young man. On reflection, why should he not make a match for Catrin should she want him? They would make a handsome pair, the black and gold heads together. Their lowly backgrounds were similar. But had Thomas the wit and spirit to match Catrin's or even her learning, such as it was? How much schooling had he received at his abbey? Old Emrys had told Tada of his promise at carpentry and alone amongst the visitors he was steadily improving his spoken Welsh by practising it willy-nilly on everyone he came across. That showed an active mind and no small assurance - something he would need if he tied himself to Catrin! Both were innocents hardly aware of their charm yet well nigh ripe for marriage and he looked fit to father sturdy sons. He was English, of course! Tada had said grimly we would all be turned into Sais under the new laws. Yet their English guests were pleasant enough and grateful, too. Need that be so bad? But should they marry Thomas would spirit her away to his England and she would lose her for ever? Could she bear that loss? Yet Thomas, a penniless fugitive, was in no position to take a wife for years. Nor did she know their feelings for each other - if any! Yet her instincts told her …..Eluned turned into the house, sighing. She could only wait and watch. And suppress a stab of envy.

Thomas was not exploring: he had work to do. Emrys needed two more trees felled - twelve foot logs, he said - to replace two seasoned ones just taken from the drying shed for repair work on the great barn. He had sent Thomas to pick out and mark them for felling. He was proud of the confidence the old carpenter had shown in him and he liked nothing better than a walk in the woods. Much more important, he knew she often rode on the bridle path: perhaps he would catch a glimpse of her. He strode on, a small axe for marking the trees under his belt, swinging a six foot measuring staff and whistling softly.

Reaching the bridle path he turned onto it and strode down towards the valley, meaning to search for suitable trees near the road where the wagon could be brought close for loading. With no need to start looking yet he kept up his usual swinging pace. Suddenly somewhere ahead he heard a woman scream. He broke into a run. To his horror Catrin's gelding stood by the path, reins hanging loose. Another scream came from the clearing to his left, instantly smothered. Bursting through undergrowth he saw her struggling in the arms of a man. Her riding cloak, hat and undercap lay on the ground and her black hair streamed loose. He saw the man's hands on her body.

With an animal growl Thomas rammed the end of his staff into the small of the man's back. The vicious kidney blow sent him sprawling in agony. Thomas swung the staff, catching him across his scarred face and felling him to the ground screaming in pain. Catrin had slumped to the ground, dishevelled and sobbing. He spread her riding cloak on the sward next to a nearby fallen tree trunk, carefully lifted her light weight and gently set her down on it with her back against the trunk.

His mind seethed, a maelstrom of rage contended with sudden acute awareness of the supple body he had held in his arms. He looked at her. Her sobbing had ceased but her eyes were closed and her pale cheek and throat already showed signs of bruising. Her square-cut bodice was torn and …. Thomas looked away while he covered her with his jerkin. He picked up her undercap, thinking to wipe her face with it, but there was no water at hand. Then Catrin opened unfocussed eyes and with a painful effort croaked 'ceffyl!' Horse! It was one of the first words Evan had taught him and he ran to Myrddin still pawing uneasily nearby, tethered him and searched the saddlebags. There was no water bottle but he found a small flask of mead. Running back he put the flask to her lips and she sipped a little, then gulped more, wincing at the soreness of her throat. Slowly her eyes opened and focussed. She smiled wanly.

Then, instantly, her eyes opened wide and flashed a warning. 'Look out!' The Welsh words were unfamiliar but their meaning clear. Thomas turned swift as a big cat: Beynon, blood dripping from his face and hunting knife in hand, was almost upon him. Thomas stuck out a long leg and tripped him, sprang up and kicked the knife from his hand. As Beynon staggered to his feet Thomas punched him on his bearded jaw and he fell on his back. Thomas pounced, knelt on his arms and drew the sharp little axe from his belt. His face a frozen mask he raised it above his head.

'No, Thomas, don't - you'll kill him!' Catrin's voice was a croak as she struggled to get up. He hesitated an endless moment, then slowly lowered the axe and turned his face towards her. His eyes were blank.

'He - dared to - to touch you - he tried ……' His face was white with cold fury and for a moment she was afraid of him, then afraid for him. But she willed herself calm as she staggered towards them, trying to reach behind his empty eyes.

'Thomas please: no blood on your hands! Don't spoil it!' He stared at her, unseeing, unmoving. Very gently she took the axe from his hands and flung it behind her. She hesitated, then stooped and softly kissed his cheek. Slowly he rose to his feet, trembling, become human again. But as never before.

Reaction set in then and as he raised her up she too was trembling and then her head was burrowing into his shoulder as gradually she recovered her composure. Thomas was awhirl in ecstatic confusion. She had spoken his name, she had kissed him, was in his arms. Very gently he tilted her chin up. 'That brute; did he….? His Welsh was not up to this. She shook her head and to his delight found painful words in equally hesitant English. 'You came in time. Thank you.' She stood back and looked up at him through her long eyelashes. The faintest of smiles touched her pale lips, lit her eyes. There was a long moment of silence before he spoke.

'Catrin' - now he had spoken her name! 'What did you mean by "don't spoil it"?'

She was recovering: a glint of mischief in her eyes. 'Well …. You have proved yourself my gentle parfit knight. Parfit gentle knights must behave - perfectly.' She looked at the prostrate Beynon. 'Perhaps not gentle. What about him?'

'He'll live. I'll send someone back for him. Now I'll get you home - I'll fetch your horse.' As he walked away he turned back, puzzled: 'Knight? I am no knight!'

She smiled. As a child Tada and Eluned had read her Malory's tales of the great King Arthur and his court, They were cherished stories. 'You are my rescuer, my knight in shining armour - which must never be tarnished.' Her words meant nothing to Thomas.

'You meant nothing more?'

Her smile softened. 'Take me home now - Thomas.'

Ioan and Ralph had become companionable. Now they sat in the great parlour drinking wine together.

'As I have said, John, for all your kindness we cannot burden you indefinitely.'

'And as I have said, Ralph, you are no burden but a pleasure. Leave it at that.' He paused. 'But can you tell me what have you in mind for the future?'

'You know we were to return to England and find a haven for our treasures.'

'So you told me. And now that all are lost?'

Ralph sighed: all but one was lost: true to his abbot's command he had not told Ioan about the wooden bowl. 'So our purpose is lost with them and my companions have only their miserable selves to dispose of, each as he chooses for all are now free of monasticism. The situation of our laymen is clear enough. Aston means to live with his brother in Hereford, his problem only how to get there without money and in winter, so he believes. Young Thomas knew no home but the abbey until he came here. He has his life before him, the abbey gave him a little learning and skill and he has uncommon character: he could settle wherever he chose, perhaps even here.' He did not mention the lad's evident attachment to Catrin: Ioan might not be aware of it.

Ioan was well aware of it but said nothing on the subject. He said: 'Then he, like Aston, need not concern you further. I can provide mounts for them to ride for England and a man servant to guide them and bring the beasts back. But for their own safety I am loth to do so until the snows are over. You need feel no more responsibility for them, Ralph.'

'But I do, John and cannot pretend otherwise. I have led all of them to failure, penury, and homelessness.'

'Your feelings do your credit, Ralph. But with all abbeys doomed your monks and lay folk would soon be homeless anyway. Their problems are merely practical and I may have the means to tide them over until they can depart safely. Consider Aston. His ankle is weakened and he cannot safely leave until the snows are over.' He raised his hand. 'You say none of you should burden me for so long. But Aston is no burden. He has managed your abbey lands - vastly greater than mine - and occupies himself learning our farming ways here. He has knowledge of new husbandry I lack and has already given me much sound advice. I am minded to dismiss my new steward, who has proved worthless, but I am now too old to manage the estate alone. Who better than Aston to act as my steward until he is ready to leave? He can have the steward's cottage and earn wages to save for his journey in spring, giving me time to find someone permanent.' He leaned forward. 'Ralph, this would help me as much as it would him. What say you? Shall I ask him?'

Ralph warmed to the old man: he was all that Evan had claimed. 'It is not for me to advise you, John. But he would be foolish indeed to decline and it would be one less worry for me. I thank you.'

Ioan brushed his thanks aside. 'I also have a proposal regarding Thomas. The lad is a promising wood-worker and strong and willing. My good old Emrys is ageing: I can no longer in good conscience let him do the heavier work, especially the coming winter repairs to my barns. Thomas already helps him, for the lad is never idle. I can pay him a little as apprentice carpenter, he can learn more of his valuable trade under Emrys and leave whenever he chooses with some silver to smooth his way. How say you?' Ralph could only nod agreement. Eluned had told him how her father's wellbeing had been transformed by their arrival: his clarity of mind and practicality were remarkable for a man his age. Perhaps that was something they had been able to repay.

'That leaves your novices. Am I right in thinking them your greatest concern?'

Ralph nodded. 'Yes indeed. You see clear, John. You remind me of the good Abbot Leyshon in Neath. Forgive me my folly but I confess that in my ignorance I did not expect to find such understanding here in Wales. I have learned better now.'

And gained some humility that becomes you well, Ioan thought. He laughed. 'Do not over-praise us. I could show you as much folly here as elsewhere. We are wise and foolish, good and bad, like you English. But regarding your novices, they need not be a pressing worry. They are ill equipped to leave in the depths of winter and must remain under my roof at least until spring. Meantime we can find something to keep them occupied and content, perhaps even useful. So you can set their problems aside for now.' Ralph nodded, grateful for the further easing of his burden.

Ioan poured them more wine and carefully phrased his next question. 'So much for your companions. That leaves you, Ralph. Let me venture to ask you about yourself. Can you tell me what concerns you most now - you yourself?'

Ralph hesitated: not ready for this, he sought avoidance in a real but lesser concern.

'Matthew is too sick to do anything but you have shown me that the others can be of some use to you, even Francis. And they will welcome the opportunity to repay a little of your goodness to us. But my poor self does nothing of use here and it shames me to the point of leaving. But what can a dismissed cleric offer you?'

Ioan noted the bitterness in his voice: Ralph needed some occupation. He had given some thought to this.

'If you permit me I can suggest something.'

'Please do so.'

'You may know I try to get some learning into Catrin's pretty head but the child is no Eluned. She lacks enough English for reading or instruction in your language although of late she is learning quickly.' He thought of Thomas and frowned. 'As she improves could you help her in her reading and general education? I lack the time.'

'Gladly. But not quite yet, you imply? You have nothing for me now?'

'There is something. You have seen we lack a family chapel, a proper building large enough for the household servants to join in our worship, our parlour being too small. It was said work began on one long ago but I have never discovered even foundations. Would you look into this and perhaps sketch me a plan?

'I am no master mason, John.'

'Nor I, nor anyone here. But you know best what is needful and seemly for a family chapel and can make a start. I have been greatly remiss in this matter and would be grateful for your help.' Again Ralph nodded, his face brighter.

Ioan hesitated, then leant forward to grasp Ralph's hand. 'My friend, I think much more concerns you than useful employment. Will you not confide in me?'

Suddenly Ralph desperately wanted to unburden himself. Hesitatingly at first, with none of his usual fluency, he struggled to explain Whiting's charge on him, his mission, his failure to lead it to a successful conclusion, his loss of self-belief, his worry about the future of the innocent novices who had followed him so blindly. But John already knew all that: he must go on. Above all - now his words poured out as he felt the release of full admission - above all there was his loss of faith. He saw John struggling to understand his raw emotions.

Now Ralph became acutely aware of an absurdity. Here was an anointed priest confessing - in a sense - to a layman, one he suspected of reformist leanings to boot. And feeling the blessed easement he had seen confession bring to others. Absurd yet real. A reflection of a world turned absurd! He fell silent.

Ioan pursed his lips. 'These are deep waters, Ralph: I doubt we can go further into them today. I think you have still to confront your demons head on: only then can you explain them fully. Yet you need to unburden yourself fully to someone. If you feel able to do so to me I shall deem it an honour - and be assured all will be in total confidence. Or, if I might suggest, write everything down - I find writing best imposes order on the mind. When I have read it you can burn it. Meantime think about my chapel.'

It was sound advice and he would take it. Ralph was taking his leave when there was a bang on the door and a house groom rushed in.

'Master - an accident - Mistress Catrin. Come quickly!'

Eluned and a maid were already outside as they hurried out onto the drive. Thomas was lifting the dishevelled girl from her horse while a groom ran up to take its reins and lead it to the stables. Thomas carried her in his arms towards the porch. He alone heard her murmur into his shoulder: 'I can walk, you know!' or sensed her secret smile when he merely tightened his grip and walked on.

'How is it with her? What has happened?'

'I trust not much amiss, Mistress; a bad fright and sore bruising. She will tell you herself.' Thomas, suddenly commanding, did not check his stride.

But once inside Eluned took charge. She kissed Catrin and examined her bruises carefully. Thankfully, whatever had happened - which she meant to find out - she could find no serious injury.

'Take her to my parlour and settle her by the fire. Tada, go with them.' She ran to the kitchen calling for warm water, fishing in her pocket for the heavy key to her still room - her sanctum, where no-one entered except under her supervision. There she collected soap, salves and dressings of her own making and hurried back to Catrin. The girl lay back in the fireside chair, her bruises turning angry, Tada holding her hand. Thomas, an outsider again, had left reluctantly for the carpenter's shop to explain why the trees were not yet marked.

Catrin, in pain but relaxing, told her story in a strained voice. Eluned, dabbing salve on her neck, saw her eyes brighten as she described Thomas's part in it. 'Ell, you should have seen him.... he ....'

'It seems the lad did well. Did that man ...?' Catrin shook her head. 'No, nothing ...Thomas came before ....' Eluned was shaken: what if chance had not brought him there at that moment? She had called him a lad. Lad? She had seen his demeanour as he carried her into the house. A lad no longer nor Catrin a child. She rose to her feet. 'There! No more talk. To bed and stay there. I will prepare a potion to help you sleep.'

When a maid had helped Catrin upstairs Eluned turned to her father. 'No great harm done, thanks to Thomas: she should soon recover. But think what might have been!'

'I am thinking on it. Fortunate indeed he was to hand. What of the marks on her pretty face and neck?'

'Those on her face will soon fade. Those on her neck where that man's foul hands pressed will take longer, but they too will go. Have no fear, she should heal completely.'

'I thank God for it. But I blame myself for letting her ride around the estate alone. That must stop. But now I must attend to Beynon.' He spoke quietly but as he turned on his heel and called for a groom his anger was palpable.

Evan sat on the narrow cot watching his brother die. Only two years older than himself, Alun was sadly aged by the wasting sickness, his face whiter than his coarse pillow and skeletal under the dark stubble. He could no longer speak and his sour breath was faint and irregular. Evan had sent for the priest but the farm was remote, the weather wintry, the priest indolent. Alun might lie unshriven in the hard ground.

When Evan had arrived exhausted that stormy night five - six? - weeks ago Alun had taken him in, but morosely, seeming to welcome his help with the farm more than himself He was ever the dour and solitary hill farmer and since childhood they had seen little of each other. He had shown scant surprise at his lost brother's sudden appearance in sodden habit and cowl. Nothing surprised Alun, nothing aroused his interest. He endured but did not live. His only affection, and that fickle, was for his dog. And Evan had seen with pain that his brother was mortally sick.

Evan looked around at the crumbling daub of the dirty walls, the sagging thatch, the crude furnishings knocked up from boxes and tubs, the cracked horn panes in the tiny window, the one tallow candle with its smoke and smell. No woman's hand had ever been here. This was a hovel. The farm was a failure, the few outbuildings half derelict, the small herd of sheep sheltering against the lee wall wretched. Like Evan's it had been inherited freehold but unlike his had failed, been sold and rented back again but Alun could no longer pay the rent. So much for his share of their inheritance!

After his arrival Evan had rested for two days and then, discarding his habit - keenly aware of the symbolism - for one of his brother's ragged smocks he had thrown himself into a determined attempt to save the farm; Alun listlessly accepting and helping where he could. In the early winter chill, from dawn until darkness drove him indoors to sit by the smoking peat fire with his silent brother, he had toiled. He had tended the sheep, repaired the shed roof and a wall of the sheep pen, made a start on the cottage walls. He had mended a cracked water trough, cleaned the cottage top to bottom and painstakingly acquainted himself with the local fairs and sheep marts. His hands had hardened again and his arms and back had strengthened. In toil he had found peace of sorts, too weary each night to brood over the collapse of his monastic life and his faith. But he could never forget the woman perhaps still living a dozen miles away. Too close! When he had left his charges at Neuadd Siriol that wild night he had meant to stay only briefly. Then he had seen death in his brother's face and could not bring himself to leave him. Doggedly, drawing on all his strength and former experience, he had begun to claw back the shortfall in rent, to repay what Alun owed market stall-holders. The brothers had drawn a little closer to each other.

But it could not last. Prices of needed goods were rising by the week: landlords, the lesser ones themselves feeling the pinch, squeezed higher rents from struggling tenants. For Alun it was the end. He took to his bed, turned his face to the wall and abandoned his problems to Evan. With no other family and in a sad gesture of ratitude he insisted on making a will leaving his few paltry possessions to him, calling a reluctant neighbour from miles away as witness. In truth he has left me only debt, Evan thought, however much I have reduced it by my own labours. As a displaced monk I came here with nothing. I shall leave with less than nothing and the landlord will soon turn me out.

The priest did come in time to shrive Alun and bury him in the parish churchyard in pouring rain. Only Evan and the silent neighbour attended, the uneasy dog watching head on paws from the shelter of a yew tree. There was no money for a wake. That night Evan sat alone in the cottage trying to decide what to do. Although saddened by his brother's death he was unable to grieve deeply for a man hardly known since childhood. He knew he must be practical about his own future. But always he was tormented by his own loss of faith and hope. And always by thoughts of her.

Late that night he came to his decision. He would ask the bailiff to let him stay until all the debt was paid off - it would be in the man's interest. With luck he might manage that by year's end - not that he believed in luck. Then he would sell the pitiful livestock and furnishing and begin again with his life somewhere. He would have no more to do with the church - not being an ordained priest there was no living for him there anyway. He would survive with his leatherwork: perhaps in time save enough to work and live on a farm again, if only as someone's tenant.

His decision reached, he went to his cot. The last thing that crossed his mind before drifting into restless sleep was that his branch of the family would end with himself.

Almost the entire male workforce was turned out to hunt for Beynon that afternoon and for most of the following day. But he was not found. Somehow he had slipped behind his pursuers, for when his cottage was searched all his possessions had gone together with a few small items that were not his.

It was thought he might make for Aberystwyth, the nearest town, and somewhere in the dark alleys around the old castle try to sell his paltry loot. But Ioan decided against further action. 'I would have him punished for what he did to Caitlin. But by God's grace she has not come to great harm and he stole so little of mine that neither the mayor nor the constable in Aber will bestir themselves to catch him, nor can I expect them to. If he is off in some other direction and keeps his head down we will never catch him. And I can spare no man myself for further search at this time. I shall report him, of course, and he can suffer a long cold winter as a declared outlaw and fugitive. But he durst not show his face here again. Let it rest now.'

He was adamant that Catrin might no longer ride alone. She had recovered well with only the fading bruises on her neck as reminder of her ordeal and was impatient to be in the saddle again.

Eluned approached her father. 'She should ride again Tada and soon or she may lose her nerve and with it that bright spirit of hers.'

'I agree, daughter, but not alone, even on our land. No, never again alone. Someone must always accompany her.'

They looked at each other. Ioan shrugged his shoulders: 'All my trustworthy men have their work. Even the stable hands are needed to help with the repairs on the great barn before the snows come. So it will have to be one of our guests. I doubt the novices can sit a horse and they would be poor protection and worse company for her. Aston has his work and although Ralph might enjoy riding now and again he will hardly see himself as regular escort to a chit of a girl and I am loth to trouble him with it. That leaves only Thomas. I am considering offering to apprentice him to Emrys while he remains here. But for now he has the time.'

And doubtless the inclination, Eluned thought dryly. 'Can he ride?'

'Surely he can sit a horse after a fashion, what young man can not? Anyway, we can find out.'

'Tada, is this wise?'

'He has proved himself trustworthy and honourable with her and possesses a strong right arm.'

'You know that's not what I meant!'

'Yes. But Catrin is old enough to know her own mind - or think she knows it. In the end she will follow her heart whatever we say or do. Nor would I willingly dim that bright spirit you spoke of.'

As your needs dimmed mine! She covered a stab of guilt at the thought with a hurried objection. 'No duenna for her then? You trust them?'

'Ah! We are to speak Spanish now? You mean when not out riding. Eluned, I trust the lad. We can contrive not to leave them totally unattended when not on horseback - discreetly of course. Ralph can help us there. And I shall speak frankly to Thomas and put him on his honour while you tell Catrin she may not be alone with him except when riding.'

'Very well, that should serve - for now. But you speak of Thomas's honour, Tada? Is he then gently born?'

'Fie, girl: you speak like a stiff-backed Sais! I judge him an honourable young man whatever his birth.' With which she could only agree. Yet every objection must be raised: 'She's only sixteen!'

'Only? A marriageable age!' And I am more than twice that, Eluned thought. But he's right. Whatever convention said - and convention could still speak gently in Wales - it is right that Catrin makes her own choice if the time comes. They could do no more for now.

They sent for her and told her that from now on she could only ride with an escort. She pouted prettily. 'But I always did before on our own land. I like riding alone. I don't want some dullard always with me. There is no longer any danger, surely?' She gave Ioan her most bewitching smile. 'Please Tada!'

He appeared unmoved. 'We have thought carefully on this, child: it is for your own safety. Unfortunately all my most trusted men will be too busy to accompany you.' He paused, his face expressionless. 'I can think of only young Thomas who might be spared for a time. Would you object very much to having him as your escort? If his dullard company offends you can order him to ride some paces behind. What say you? Shall I ask him?' Catrin's eyes shone and for a moment she seemed about to choke. Then she heaved an elaborate sigh. 'Oh! If I must. He would be better than nothing I suppose.' Eluned turned away to hide her smile but Ioan kept his straight face.

'Very well. Of course as a guest I cannot command him. He may not wish to ride around aimlessly with a silly chit of a girl.' But Catrin had caught the glint in his eye and grinned. 'You're teasing me again, just like you used to.' She flung her arms round his neck.

Winter descended on Neuadd Siriol with cold and frost and blustering wind. Trees became bare of leaves, animals were penned and slaughtered for salting and eating, repair work was finished just in time and the household awaited the heavy snows. The days passed quietly with no sign of pursuit to threaten the guests. Ioan retained his restored vigour. Catrin seemed to enjoy her riding more than ever and in all weathers until Ioan had to limit her to milder days. Thomas, now happily dividing his time between carpentry and escorting Catrin, proved inexperienced and clumsy on horseback but soon improved enough to be secure if never graceful in the saddle, occasioning much mirth from the accomplished young horsewoman he escorted.

Increasingly he impressed Eluned, despite a new-found tendency to stare vacantly into space. When he was not at his carpentry or they were out riding the youngsters, aware of discreet scrutiny and with their growing feelings for each other confusing and as yet undisclosed, spent much of their time in the old hall, which was so much a passageway as to meet Ioan's ban on their being alone. Here the fire was now lit for them every day. Here they bent their heads together over Ioan's books and lessons for Catrin. With Ioan's agreement they became students together, for Thomas was ever keen to learn and now desperate to keep up with her, while his natural application disciplined her often wayward mind. Here, too, they taught each other Welsh or English with much giggling at each other's accents, growing ever closer. And here Ralph sometimes passed them on his absorbing searches around the estate for signs of the old chapel, always with a greeting and often stopping to assist with difficult passage they were studying. Their bright youth and evident affection for each other warmed his heart yet at night disturbed him anew with regrets for his own lost youth, his missed chances and ever-present lack of freedom.

As always Eluned appeared her competent and enclosed self. Aston, who had gladly accepted Ioan's offer to act as temporary bailiff, buckled down to his duties, counted his wages and awaited spring. But by now the two novice monks, once inseparable, had drifted far apart. They barely spoke to each other, Francis choosing to spend his days outdoors as Aston's assistant and Matthew ever more reclusive.

With her much enlarged household settled in good order it was to them that Eluned's thoughts turned. She had observed how Francis, although naïve and lacking practical skills, clearly enjoyed his active outdoor life while Matthew was for ever in the counting house reading and writing. He was increasingly frail, silent and solitary. To her dismay Eluned's potions seemed to have done little for him and she was increasingly worried about him. One afternoon she overcame her diffidence in the presence of the austere prior and went to speak to him about the novice. With all these Sais about the house her English had improved enough for her purpose.

She found Ralph reading in the great parlour. As he put down his book and rose courteously she was struck, not for the first time, by his fine bearing. Unsettled but as ever concealing it she sat primly on a stool and came abruptly to the point.

'Father Prior, I am concerned about your novice Matthew. He sickens more each day and nothing I do seems to help him. I confess I do not understand his condition. He needs a proper physician but there is none within reach. Also he seems unhappy and I fear we have not made him feel welcome. What can you advise?'

Ralph looked into her concerned brown eyes. Women had played no part in his life since his callow youth but Mistress Llwyd increasingly disturbed him. Not just her mature beauty that were arousing feelings he thought he had thrust from him for ever, but the deep well of womanly compassion he sensed in her. He recalled how John seemed to treat her as an equal even in men's affairs. Certainly she possessed unusual breadth of learning for a woman. He had been astonished when John had explained that women had enjoyed near-equality under the remaining old Welsh laws and customs under which she had been brought up. Yet he felt sure that her standing came more from within herself. She was a remarkable woman. He was becoming accustomed to speaking to her as to a man but at this moment he was acutely aware of her as a woman. He resisted an alarming urge to lay his hand on hers as they lay folded and composed on her lap.

'You perceive him truly, Mistress. His sickness is a mystery to us all and I know you have done all you can. It is true he is unhappy and his mind has drifted far from us all. But that has nought to do with you or your father, who have been kindness itself. No, apart from his grievously sick body his problem lies in his upbringing and now in the fall of the monasteries.' He explained how younger children like Matthew, some from good families, were offered to religious houses to be educated for the cowl. Virtually abandoned by their kinsfolk they had grown up confined by high walls, never able to leave without their abbot's permission, seeing almost nothing of the wider world outside. Matthew and Francis had learnt the discipline of monastic life but not the self-discipline of fending for themselves in a harsh world.

'And so beyond the abbey walls they are lost. We so circumscribed their young lives that now they cannot stand alone. Soon they must do just that but they cannot comprehend such a future and it troubles them greatly.'

'Yet they survived that terrible journey of yours, Father.'

'True, and proved equal to its hardships and so full of wonder at the wide world in which they found themselves as to gladden my heart. But they had only to follow my lead and that of ....' He hesitated, for he had almost mentioned Evan .... 'the others. God forgive me, they trusted me implicitly. But our mission has ended in failure and soon each of us must go his own way. Then those two innocents must learn to think for themselves, learn to survive and live their lives - whatever they can find to do without worldly skills except for clerking.'

'But especially hard for Matthew, Father, for he is so weak now. Rest and food and physic do not rally him: you see how he worsens by the day. Was he always frail?

'No, indeed, or I would not have brought him. He seemed in good health when we left but he weakened strangely during those last days before we came to your door - far beyond the exhaustion all of us suffered. I know of no reason for his condition and it concerns me as it does you. I should have paid him more attention.'

'Tada - my father - told me you had proposed finding the novices some light work with us, for their sake as much as ours.'

'That is so, so that time would lie less heavily on them and they might be of some help to you. Francis assists Steward Aston and has taken readily to open air life. I doubt he is much help but at least the two have become companionable. I have no immediate concern for him. But Matthew?' He shrugged his shoulders.

'He spends so much of his time in the counting house reading and writing.'

'Yes. We wished him to rest his frail body yet keep his mind exercised, so John set him to check his ledgers.' He grimaced. 'I think you know the results - he showed no head for figures and John had to take him off the work before he turned his accounts into chaos. Then Matthew asked for paper, quills and ink and the use of your father's desk. Now he scribbles there most of each day and your kind father leaves him in peace for it keeps him occupied. Thankfully monks can write - whatever he writes.'

'Indeed. Whenever I pass the counting house door I hear his quill scratching away.'

'Well, we shall not enquire what he writes for it will be innocent - no- one is more innocent than Matthew. But it is not his mind but his body that concerns me as it does you, lady. If only we knew what ails him!'

'I will keep an eye on him Father and still seek some cause for his condition.' She saw an opportunity to learn more about Thomas and how he might stand with Catlin. 'But young Thomas has settled well.'

'He has indeed. But as a layman his case is different. He came to us a waif of byways and alleys who from early childhood had to survive by his wits. Save for shelter all we gave him was a little book learning and an apprenticeship in carpentry. But he would survive anywhere, for he is truly a remarkable young man. I came to rely greatly on him on our travels. But I was wrong to bring the novices, especially Matthew.' Ralph shook his head sadly.

Here was nothing wholly new but suddenly she sensed the bitterness of the prior's self-reproach and, to her surprise, a vulnerability in him. It made him less austere and remote, more human. For the first time she really looked at him as a man. Sitting down he was less intimidating. The fine-boned face was tired and strained but refined and - yes - handsome too. Nor as old as she had assumed. Not too old. One did not think of priests in that way and hurriedly she directed her thoughts back to the novices.

Her voice was even as ever. 'Thank you, Father: you make all clear to me. Tell me what more I can do for the youngsters.'

She saw him smile then, a rare attractive smile that curled his long lip and lit eyes as deep and brown as her own: she felt their sudden warmth deep within her and felt herself flushing. 'Lady, you do so much for everyone: you cannot take the world's woes on your shoulders. The novices remain my responsibility. I have been too little concerned for them and you do well to remind me of it.'

As she rose to leave his hand moved as of its own volition to touch her firm shoulder. 'Thank you for speaking thus with me, mistress. I pray we may do so again.'

One dull afternoon in mid-December a laden wagon was driven through the double doors of the great barn, the great carthorses steaming in the cold air. Ioan, Ralph and Aston watched boxes and casks being unloaded. Ioan's face was unusually grave.

'I thought you might like to see this, Ralph,' he said quietly. 'This wagon comes from Abertawe - Swansea. It brings us our last certain load of provisions before the heavy snows, when at best a few pack animals may get through. But with this and ample firewood already stacked and drying we shall be snug until Spring.' He turned to Aston. "Robert, the wagoner and his guard warm themselves at the kitchen fire. Will you check their tallies against these goods, for not everything you see here is meant for us? Then see ours safely stored, their horses stabled and tell Mair to get them fed and cots ready for them in the loft.' He explained to Ralph. 'The wagoners stay the night here.' Ralph, who was feeling relief that he too was beginning to earn his keep remarked on the large quantity of goods being unloaded.

Ioan nodded. 'We have many workers and their families to feed and clothe and physic. When winter cuts us off we become a little world of our own and all we need should be at hand.' Leaving Aston to his work they turned into the house.

When they were comfortable before the parlour fire Ioan appeared uneasy. After a long silence he said: 'I have heard something that should interest you, Ralph.' He explained that the wagoner was a valuable source of news from outside. 'He delights in spreading his gossip at the kitchen fire, the women agog around him. But I pay him a little to ferret out more serious matter for I like to keep an eye on the world as best I can.'

'So you have spoken to him already! Is his news to be relied upon?'

'I have always found it so and I believe him now. He has interesting news today. He tells me that it is rumoured - judge for yourself how much to believe - that King Henry's court in London is in turmoil, as is the realm entire. This I believe and think myself well out of that place. It beggars belief how much havoc this king has wrought - you know I say this in confidence, Ralph. Consider the facts: he divorces and is excommunicated for it, makes himself supreme head of our church, remarries and sires a daughter, executes the mother, marries again and has a son born last year. Makes Thomas Cromwell his chief adviser, virtually abolishes what was left of my country, deceives and then stamps cruelly on the leaders of the Pilgrimage of Grace up north - hundreds hanged, they say - and allows our coinage to lose its value by the day. His thrifty father must turn in his grave! For three years now he has been closing monastic houses - some say eight hundred so far - so that but a handful remain, including your own great house. And all this in a few short years! Our world is turned on its head!' He shook his head. 'Forgive me, Ralph, in my choler I digress: all this you known only too well.'

Ralph nodded. 'Indeed I do and melancholy knowledge it is. I was aware the world outside my cloister was turning as topsy turvy as that inside, but never felt it so keenly until now.' He sighed.' But enough of that. John, has your wagoner brought you more recent news?'

Ioan nodded grimly. 'He has indeed. He tells me that our king, having destroyed the monasteries, has turned Cromwell loose on friaries while holy shrines are being closed and their images carted to

London for public burning. It is said even Becket's shrine at Canterbury and that at Walsingham are despoiled.'

'So that rumour is true! Dear God! And this across the realm?'

'It appears so. In Swansea he learned that the Shrine to Mair - Our Lady, that is - at Cardigan on our west coast is burned to the ground and her wondrous effigy with it. It was believed by many to possess great power of healing.'

Cardigan! Whence Giles had taken his lonely exalted road. Had he got there before these despoilers or found only ashes? 'If it was so wondrous did no-one protect it?' But did we monks protect our monasteries, Ralph thought bitterly?

'He heard that an angry crowd gathered but could not withstand armed men. Then all were driven back for their lives when the place was put to the torch. Then came a strange thing. A wild man clad all in black - surely a monk - wielding a great pilgrim's staff ran into the shrine shrieking like a madman as the burning roof fell on him. The fire roasted him: only his bones were found.'

So Giles had completed his pilgrimage! A terrible end yet somehow fitting for him. Ralph caught Ioan's eye and nodded grimly. 'Yes, that must have been our Brother Giles. It was the pilgrim staff in my care he wielded. God rest his tortured soul.'

When Ioan broke another long silence his voice was strangely muted. 'There is also news of your abbey in Glastonbury. Ralph, it was closed nigh a month back. This is sad news for you my friend and I am sorry for it.'

Ralph pursed his lips and stared into the fire. Then he sighed and shrugged his shoulders. 'Sad indeed: I shall make it known to the others. But we knew full well it would come: indeed I had expected it sooner. We were the last religious house to stand in the west country. At least our demise would have been peaceful. As elsewhere the abbot will have signed the surrender document and the brothers will draw their pensions - it seems Cromwell is meticulous about that.'

Ioan leaned forward to lay a hand on his shoulder, his face grave. 'My friend - it grieves me to have to tell you this - but Glastonbury's end was not peaceful.' Ralph looked up, startled. Ieuan continued hurriedly: 'by all accounts your abbot defied them. He refused to sign the surrender document.'

Aghast, Ralph was on his feet. 'Refused? Father Abbot Whiting refused to sign? Defiance from that frail old man? But he made no protest before.' He paced the room distraught then swung round. 'This will have cost him his pension!'

'It cost him more, Ralph; much much more. It seems he was then arrested, sent to the Tower on a charge of treason - some say interrogated there by Cromwell himself. But they wrung no confession from him and could not find him guilty of any treason. So then they took him to Wells and tried him in the great hall of the Bishop's Palace there for theft from the abbey, and your Sacristan and Treasurer with him....'

'Brother John and Brother Roger too? For theft? Theft from their own abbey?' Ralph sat down heavily, his face buried in his hands, his voice muffled. 'My God! Theft of the treasures I carried away, albeit with his sanction.' Treasures I soon lost, he thought bitterly. 'Removing them was my idea and Father Abbot was loth to agree to it, but I pressed him so hard! John! I have betrayed him, betrayed them all!'

'Not so, man! The charge was not only the theft of the treasures you removed. The commissioners had come with the inventory you told me about. Armed with this they ransacked everything they found of value, including your great library. It was then they discovered that many listed treasures were missing - not just the few you had carried away. They ferreted around and found most of them secreted about the abbey: it is said some even mured within the walls - if you believe that.' Ralph did believe it. Before leaving he had discussed with Brother John and Brother Roger what might be done with treasures too bulky for him to remove. He had left the decision to them. Yet the guilt lay also with himself.

He tried to pull himself together. 'And the outcome of this so-called trial?'

'All three were found guilty.'

'Guilty of theft? Monstrous! Well at least Whiting is too old and far too frail for prison, nor are the other two men young.'

'Ralph ...' Ioan's face revealed his distress. 'The verdict was guilty of treason after all - I know not how they came back again to that first charge. But you know that treason carries a mandatory death sentence. So it was death for all three of them - by hanging, drawing and quartering as is the custom.' He heard Ralph gasp and hurried on, desperate to finish. 'The sentence was carried out with brutal haste the very next day - atop your Glastonbury Tor.'

His head still in his hands, Ralph's voice broke into a sob. 'That saintly old man defied them in face of that horrible death - while I ran away and still live!'

'Their deaths are no fault of yours, my friend, you must believe that. I doubt it was even a legal verdict. Why the charge of treason again and not just theft? And as a member of the House of Lords should not your abbot have been attainted by Parliament, a process that would have taken weeks or months? This was a trumped-up charge, Ralph, its verdict decreed in advance and executed in shameful haste - its purpose to send a stark message to any who would defy the king.'

Presently Ralph composed himself enough to ask: 'So now with our abbot and our treasures gone what of our glorious abbey buildings?'

'I think you can guess the answer. As elsewhere it was despoliation. Ransacking of your remaining treasures and books. Lead is already being stripped off the roofs and smelters are set up in your great court to receive it. The weather will do the rest.'

'So now everything is lost! Everything! I cannot bear it!' Slowly Ralph raised his head and looked around the pleasant room almost resentfully. 'Be thankful, my friend, that you live secure here and have a wonderful loving child to comfort you.' There were tears in his eyes now.

'I account nothing for security anywhere in the realm any more, not even here.' Then Ioan's voice fell to a whisper: 'Nor do I deserve my remaining child's love.'

But he could offer Ralph a crumb of comfort. 'At least the wagoner bring one piece of news you can welcome. You know all too well how travellers are preyed upon by robbers these days. Well, it seems that sheriff's men are at last bestirring themselves far and wide, hunting them down and hanging them. They cornered one such gang at an abandoned old castle south of here. It seems they fought like trapped rats but all were killed on the spot, being without the law.'

'Carreg Cennen castle!' In his mind's eye Ralph saw that great slighted fortress.

'Yes, the very outlaws who robbed you: it must be. Rough justice for them but I hope some peace for travellers in those parts - for a time at least. Even better, when the soldiers searched the castle they recovered all your stolen Glastonbury treasures.'

'Better? So now they are in the king's treasury from which we sought to save them. We have achieved nothing. Nothing at all!' A last bitter pill to swallow.

'They were lost to you anyway, man. But there is yet more. It seems the treasures have been verified as the very ones you carried away with you. It is believed that for them the outlaws must have murdered you all and buried your bodies in caves where they will never be found.

Not that any will bestir themselves to look for them - now they have the treasure they care little for your fate. As they believe you all dead they should not trouble you again - if you but keep your heads down a little longer. At least you are free of that worry,'

'Yet believed dead.'

'Which matters only if you have kin or friends to mourn you. Which of you has?'

'None of any account save Aston, for we turned our backs on the world or were never truly in it. Should any still remember us they will think us dead already.'

'So Aston alone hopes to find a home when he leaves here?' Ralph nodded bleakly.

The burden of delivering his appalling tidings behind him, Ieuan's voice was brisker. 'Which brings me to you, Ralph. I thank you for what you wrote down for me. I have read it with care.' He handed the papers back to him.

'My "confession"!'

Ioan acknowledged the irony. 'I know. An ordained priest with doubts "confessing" to a layman with doubts! Uncertainty and reversal, a wry reflection of our world now. But perhaps these days we are learning to reason and to question: let us hope that in that will lie progress, if not in our lifetimes.'

He picked up a poker and stirred the logs in the fire. Flickers of light picked out bright pinpoints around the darkening room. 'Ralph, what you have written has helped me understand a little of your mind. Now I put the obvious question to you - what will you do when you leave here?'

Ralph shrugged defeated shoulders. 'Can you help me answer that?'

'Your abbey is lost to you. Is there nowhere else you wish to go, no-one you wish to see again, nothing you should be doing?'

'Nowhere, no-one, nothing.'

'Not return to your family home?'

'No.'

'Then stay here.'

Ralph stared at him. 'I can no longer …..'

'No longer as my guest but as my chaplain.' Ioan hurried on before Ralph could reply. 'Did I tell you my old chaplain died two years ago? I have been slow to replace him. Why? Partly sloth, the inertia of age. But more because I could not foretell how the wind would blow in religious matters and because of my grave doubts about my own faith. I have developed reformist leanings if not yet certainties, John: I think you have guessed as much. But my workers and servants who keep to the old faith still need a priest, for our parish church is miles away and they must travel far on their day of rest because of my neglect. Their faith deserves better of me and it troubles me. I planned to build a family chapel and chaplain's lodging here years ago or restore that old one you have been searching for - if it were ever found. But I have dallied shamefully. I would begin the work even now if I had a chaplain to oversee everything as part of his duties. And there is so much pastoral work for a priest here. Will you undertake it Ralph?' You have lost your cloister and can never truly replace that loss outside it. You left this sad world for its sanctuary but in the end found none. You re-entered the world but you will find no true refuge in it either. You fled from uncertainty to uncertainty: if you leave here that will ever be your fate.'

He leaned forward, his voice urgent now. 'I know we are part of this sorry world and even here you cannot escape it entirely. Yet this is a peaceful backwater sheltered by our remoteness and our insignificance. When I left court I never wished to leave here again. Nothing lasts for ever: only change itself does not change. Yet it may come more slowly and more gently in quiet places like this. Here you may find shelter and relative peace for the score or more years you can hope to be granted.

Could this not be the retreat I feel in my bones you seek and need? And for what it is worth you will have my friendship for what time remains me. And we can still dispute together over our wine'- he smiled - 'we have still to dispute where Erasmus stands on Luther, among much else.'

Ralph's voice was as expressionless as his face. Then he frowned. 'You would appoint a chaplain you know full well has lost his faith?'

'But one who confronts honest doubts with courage, as I try to. Faith may return when order returns to this country, perhaps in different form. Who knows? But you have true humanity in you if you would but recognise it, perhaps the greatest quality for ministering to a flock lost and troubled in this woeful time of change - no, of revolution. Why not be my chaplain, Ralph? Other priests must be riven by doubts today, yet they carry on their ministry, knowing its worth in serving others. Such work can be balm to you too, man. And you must know by now how I have come to value your companionship. Could we not, two comfortable dialogists, sup our wine of an evening while we argue how to put this foolish world to rights?' He smiled. 'I am being selfish, you see.'

'I do not speak Welsh.'

Ioan snorted. 'Think you we hold our services in Welsh? There is no prayer book or bible yet printed in my language, nor would our English masters permit its use if there were - for that matter even Caxton's English Testament is not yet allowed in your churches, although I hope someday it may be, and the bible translated into Welsh for us, too. But for now our worship is in Latin, which the common people neither understand nor expect to. They find their comfort in its familiar sound and ritual. Is that any different from England?' Anyway, you can pick up some Welsh - see how young Thomas has progressed, although lacking your learning.' With a raven-haired beauty for incentive, Ioan thought wryly.

Ralph, still stunned by the news of Whiting and only half-listening, could find only objections. 'What of sermons?'

'One thing at a time, man. Until it is clear what new services the law will allow you need only say Mass and hear confessions. Perhaps share duties with our parish priest, who becomes feeble and would welcome any lightening of his load. New forms of service may be imposed on us soon, but if you have truly lost your faith you cannot argue they would be impossible to swallow. But above all else I would value your pastoral work, for my people need care only a priest can give in these times.'

Ralph stared bleakly out of the window. Then he turned to Ioan. 'I shall give my companions the good news that we should no longer be hunted. But I wish to keep our abbot's terrible death from them until your Christmas Feast is over. They are looking forward to it greatly and deserve the good cheer you promise after what they have been through. So let me break it to them afterwards. As for your offer to be your chaplain, John, I thank you most sincerely for it and will think carefully on it. Now if you will excuse me I must visit poor Brother Matthew.'

But even as he turned to leave it was clear to Ralph that he could not stay in this household, close to Eluned but barred by God from her and living a lie as faithless priest. John, kindly John, meant well but there was no lasting sanctuary for him in this place. Neuadd Siriol could not be his permanent retreat, nowhere could, for he could never retreat from himself. In a flash came to him a realization overwhelming yet appalling. The only true sanctuary he could ever know in this life was Eluned, whom he knew now he loved. But that could not be.

Ieuan watched the retreating upright figure with compassion. In his heart he knew that Ralph would reject his offer. The prior carried his burdens within him: it mattered little where he laid his head or found a stout door in hope of keeping the world out. The strangest thought came to him then. In utterly different circumstances Ralph and Eluned would have been well matched. But that could not be.

With painful slowness Matthew cut himself a new quill. He pressed trembling fingers to his red-rimmed eyes, pulled his worn habit around his thin shoulders and drew his candle closer. He had determined to write an account of the flight from Glastonbury. Holy church must learn how hard they had tried yet failed to safeguard its treasures. It had been God's judgement on their backsliding and forever their shame. He regretted it had been impossible to make proper notes on that arduous journey for he could not remember many details and knew his account would be incomplete and disjointed. But at least he now had most of it set down in writing - the barge down the Brue, crossing the Severn Sea, endless weary walking and pursuit over wild hills, the terrifying outlaws and the robbery, that dreadful bog, the storm and their exhausted arrival at this house. He had intended a straightforward record of their flight and of the good people who had given them sanctuary. But now he was so weak he could barely put pen to paper to finish the task or even marshal his thoughts clearly. He had managed little more than disjointed jottings about their time at Neuadd Siriol. Now Christmas Day and its Great Feast was almost upon them and common courtesy demanded he attend, at least briefly. It would be an ordeal for him but if he could sleep a little tonight he might survive and even manage a brief mention of it.

But now he must turn his mind and his pen to the wooden bowl that filled his thoughts: all else must be set aside until that was done. When Prior Ralph had revealed the bowl to them he had been filled with wonder. That such a puny object might be the Sangraal itself! Clearly his companions had not believed in it, but then they hardly believed in anything anymore. He himself had neither dismissed nor accepted it. Only wondered.

Crossing that dreadful bog had changed everything. He remembered it vividly. Father Prior had dropped the bowl and it had rolled into the river's edge. Already wet from falling into the mire he had retrieved it for him. He had groped for it in that cold water. As his fingers had closed on it he had felt it quiver under his trembling fingers - he was sure of it - and so it had pointed him unerringly to the hidden boat, the boat without which they could not have escaped their pursuers. That was not chance! Then, in that wretched foundering boat it was his use of the bowl that had driven them forward across the stream to escape their pursuers. Mere chance again?

Not so! He had witnessed two small miracles. Not human hands had saved them. And as it could perform such miracles then that plain little bowl was indeed the true Grail as previous abbots had believed!

And both times it had saved them he had been holding it in his own hands! It had come to him then as in a blinding light. Himself, a sick unworthy novice, had been chosen to be the next guardian and protector of the Grail! The prior had guarded it until then, but like all the others - except the lost Giles - even he had so lapsed from faith as to be unworthy. He himself, poor novice Matthew, had been chosen.

So now, knowing death beckoned, he must set all else aside and finish the Grail's story, must summon the last of his strength to reveal its powers to others. Then, before dying, somehow he must find the means to pass it on to … whom? And how? But first to write down its story! If he had strength enough he would mention the coming

Feast - he could leave a little space for that. But first the Grail. So little time! Dipping his quill in the inkwell he began to write again.

Evan could not avoid it. Next market day he must go to Aberystwyth - and hope Eluned would not be there and see him. Working himself to the bone he had finally paid off all his brother's debts only for the landlord's bailiff to order him off the land by Christmas, which was almost upon him. He had expected ejection, but so soon? He had sold the few sheep to a neighbouring tenant - the moping dog included in the poor price. All that remained were the wretched house furnishings, some farm tools and the horse and cart. They would fetch little at the small local market - if he could sell them at all. But Aberystwyth town with its shops and a sizeable market before Christmas promised better sales.

On the day he set off early. Everything for sale was stacked on the cart, including Alun's battered chest packed with Alun's old clothing - all he was not wearing himself -and, he knew not why - his monk's habit. His few other personal possessions were thrown on top. He was homeless and almost penniless, hoping to make enough money in Aber to see him well away from this place for good. Then what? His future was a blank. Uppermost in his mind was fear of meeting Eluned - a fear painfully at odds with his longing.

He wrapped Alun's tattered cloak tighter around him against the penetrating old. He had a dozen miles to travel on the road overlooking the Rheidol Valley - the shorter way through the hamlet of Gors passed too close to Neuadd Siriol. If the road was not too mired he should reach Aber well before noon, in time to catch some buyers before their money ran out. He jogged along, the horse's breath steaming in the cold air.

Aber market was bustling, with festive as well as regular wares for sale. Fortune tellers, jugglers and street players amused the crowds. It was difficult to drive his cart into Great Dark Gate Street and impossible into the narrow alleys around the castle and he lost time finding a corner to set up his cart as a makeshift stall. Throughout the day he kept scanning the crowds. But she was not there.

By dusk he had sold everything although too much at a poor price. Tired and hungry, he sat by the horse trough at the top of the street watching his last sale, the horse and cart, being led away. He took off his bonnet, looked around furtively and counted his last takings tucked inside it before stowing them away with the rest of his money in the purse sewn inside his jerkin. It was little enough but all he possessed and there would be pickpockets about and, as always after fairs, robbers would lurk on the road home. Home? He had only an empty hovel and that for only a few days.

He was getting to his feet when a hand fell on his shoulder. He looked around, startled, and recognised a hale and well dressed Aston.

'Evan, so it is you! I looked twice since you do not wear habit and cowl. Man, you look thin. Are you not well?'

Startled, Evan made as if to run then shrugged his shoulders in resignation. 'Well enough; not as well as you, by the look of you. How did you know me in these clothes?'

'Something about the way you always sat; very still. I remembered. But I was unsure until you doffed your bonnet and I saw the short hairs on your crown. A tonsure growing out, I thought: then it is Evan. You do not prosper, by your dress.'

'But you surely do. Did they shelter you at Neuadd Sirioil? Are you still there?'

'I am, for they are as hospitable as you promised. I am here to buy a few last things for the household before Christmas.' Aston was concerned at Evan's appearance - and curious. The man looked worn out and in need of a good meal and there would be news to exchange. 'But come, let us find ourselves food and drink and talk awhile.'

'I must find me a bed for the night before dark.'

But Aston was insistent. 'No hurry! Eat with me first: I am famished and it is over an hour to home.'

'Home?'

'Neuadd Siriol. For pity's sake let us eat then I'll explain.'

'Will you be there by dark? What of robbers? You know how they prey on fairs.'

'Robbers favour the south road and I have two stout lads with cudgels guarding my wagon. Come!'

Almost two hours passed before Aston found his stout lads in another alehouse: like himself they were a little drunk as they clambered heavily onto the laden wagon.

Aston leaned over to Evan standing sober alongside. 'Will you not change your mind and come with us?' When Evan shook his head he went on: 'I come to market most weeks. Let us meet again at the same place for I would welcome more talk with you.' He flicked the reins and the wagon lumbered away.

Evan turned back to the first alehouse where he had found a bed of sorts. He had revealed little of himself to Aston beyond the bare facts of Alun's farm and his death, but had listened intently to the steward's news. So Eluned was alive and well, still mistress of the household! Had she changed in six years? Had he? Ioan alive and seeming recovered from whatever ailment had befallen him. And hospitable as ever since all the 'pilgrims' were still snug under his roof. The girl Catrin he remembered vaguely as a scrawny child: it had been typical of them to take her in. And Aston now acting steward until he left in the spring. So Ralph and Ioan had become companionable - of course their book learning would have brought them together, to the benefit of both. Young Thomas settled well and improving his Welsh - no surprise there: the lad would always get on. Aston had not mentioned the novices, but they had always kept to themselves. And the lost treasure found and back in the king's grasp! That was sad, but with its recovery the hunt for them must surely be abandoned and his old companions would lie safe and snug through the winter. Then not only Aston but likely all of them would leave for England. He was glad for their good fortune.

Evan spent a restless night with this news. Eluned still unmarried! She ranked above him still, yet still she haunted his dreams. But he had killed a man, was irrevocably stained by it and so doubly denied her. He had to get away - somewhere, anywhere, quickly. Slip away quietly - best he did not meet Aston again. He would travel north and try to eke out his life with his leather working.

When the first snows threatened Neuadd Siriol thoughts turned towards Christmas and the Great Feast, the most important event of the year, to which all the house servants and estate workers and their families were invited. Eluned decided that this year the presence of guests and Ioan's renewed spirits merited extra effort. The hall floor was again cleared of rushes and washed and sprinkled with dried lavender. The massive yule log, drying for months in the barn, was borne to the hearth and embers kept alight all year from its predecessor brought in with ceremony to light a new fire and so bring continuing good fortune for the New Year. Holly symbolising eternal life, mistletoe to ward off evil and masses of evergreen foliage adorned the window ledges. The festive boards must make their bravest show so a boar hunt was organised and poultry killed and hung - not too many for in winter they were precious for their eggs. Pipes, lutes and drums were dusted off and tuned; men chosen for their voices practised traditional songs and the newly popular carols; Ioan's elderly harpist blew on stiff fingers and tuned his instrument. Everyone down to the fire boys worked to a cacophony of musical instruments blowing and scraping. All worked cheerfully, for Ioan kept to the tradition of twelve days' rest over Christmas, symbolised by threading dried flowers around the spinning wheels to still them. All looked forward to food and drink aplenty followed by days of well-earned ease. In the kitchens Eluned and Mair sorted out vessels and utensils, gathered raw materials for the feast and set a maid to begin the taffy making. Eluned herself would portion out the costly sugar from her still room and prepare the marchpane.

Ioan had striven hard to lift Ralph's spirits and slowly the prior seemed to be coming to terms with the tragedy at Glastonbury Abbey. Now, redundant to the final preparations scurrying around them the two surveyed the hall from a doorway.

'I remember Christmases as a child. I am wondering how yours differ in Wales?' Not such grand affairs as ours were, Ralph felt sure.

'The same worship, of course. As for our feast, we shall have a wassail bowl - now there's a Saxon word for you - and much the same food I knew in England although,' he added dryly, 'you will doubtless find us more rustic. Some music will be familiar but you may not know the triple harp old Ianto will play for us - if sober enough - and there will be Welsh songs. In the days following I hope the weather will permit us falconry and hunting, our archery contest and all the old games our people enjoy so much, some of which will carry on until the first footing and New Year. All in all not much different from England.'

'I look forward to it.' At least I must put a good face on it, Ralph thought.

'One or two of our traditions may differ. I shall keep them as a surprise.

Evan had checked over his preparations three times, finally realising that his fussing signified only his reluctance to leave, this time for good. Yet it must be so. It was late on Christmas morning when he finally left Alun's farm, aware of irony in stealing away alone on this day of family gathering and faith. It was later in the month and in the hour than he had intended. With scant food in his belly he set off on the road to Machynlleth and the north, his worldly goods strapped on his back and too few coins in his purse. Frost had hardened the mire of the road and the going was firm but rutted. It was another clear day but very cold and he strode out briskly to get warm, his breath visible before him.

Presently he came to cottages huddled around an inn near a small fast-flowing stream, a place he remembered was called Talybont. The brisk walking, the cold and a rich smell of cooked meat as he passed its inn door brought sharp hunger pangs and he realised he needed hot food inside him before continuing, whatever the cost. He pushed open the stout inn door and entered the grateful warmth of a dark little taproom. He called out and the owner emerged from a back room wiping his hands.

'God's day, friend. Have you food for a cold and hungry traveller?'

'It's Christmas Day man: we are closed.' Yet the man seemed amiable enough.

'So it is, but I have far to travel and smell your excellent roast meat.'

'For our family dinner. We have just eaten it.'

'Have you no cawl at least?'

'There is always cawl.'

'And bread and ale and, I'll warrant, some scraps of meat or a pie left over from your dinner. Come sir, I beg your Christmas charity for a hungry traveller and can pay.' Evan held out a precious coin. Business was business and soon he was seated away from any draught with a steaming bowl of the rich broth and a hunk of pie before him, trying not to worry about the cost.

Presently, warmed and replete, he sat back and looked about the room and for the first time noticed another occupant, a shadowy figure silent in a dark inner corner. Presently the man rose to leave. As he passed Evan he lurched clumsily against Evan's trestle, spilling his ale, but walked on without a glance or word of apology. Evan half-rose angrily, then sat back stunned as the outer door slammed behind the departing man.

No mistaking that ugly face, even though an old scar had faded and there were fresh bruises over it! Six years had not wiped out the image: that was the lout who had molested the girl, the man he had fought in the darkness and pitched over a wall into a stream and to his death.

As he struggled to comprehend his discovery the innkeeper returned. 'My goodwife sleeps off her dinner and my daughter busies herself in the kitchen. Best leave them to it.' In good humour, he drew two horn mugs of ale from a cask in the corner.

'Christmas Day to you, friend: this ale's on the house - a new broach I'm minded to try. He sat down heavily opposite Evan, relaxed and ready for male company.

Here was an opportunity to find out about the man who had just left. 'Thank you, friend and to you too. An excellent meal! Good health to your family. I see you served another customer.'

'Ale only. I durst not refuse him - he can make trouble, that one.'

'Indeed, he looked something of a ruffian. A troublemaker?'

The innkeeper sniffed. 'Name of Iolo Beynon. A bad lot: poacher and thief and worse. Needed his neck stretching years ago if you ask me. I can do without his custom at any time but as long as he pays what can I do?'

'A vagabond?'

'Not always. He was steward over at Neuadd Siriol manor some months back but didn't last long. Got himself sacked for molesting a lady there. Somebody gave him a sound beating for it - you saw his face and he limps a bit now. He can't have been much of a steward!'

Evan was on his feet. 'What lady?'

'I don't know. They say the pretty young one.'

Young? Not Eluned, then: Evan heaved a sigh of relief. Then it must have been that young Catrin, still almost a child. Molested? He felt his anger grow again.

The innkeeper was warming to his tale. 'Seems no real harm done - well, you know - but he's an animal, that one. Not the first time neither. Old Llwyd got him declared outlaw for it but he ran off before they could catch him. Lives rough around here now with a couple of other louts he's ganged up with. They make trouble with their brawling and pilfering. They comes in here now and then for their drink.'

'And he's still on the loose? You did not report him?'

'And have them smash this place up? No thank you! It's little enough but all I have. Where have you been these last years, man? The law does not stretch its arm much beyond Aberystwyth town these days. Anyway it's none of my business - and I have a young daughter, too.' He drew them more ale.

'An outlaw you say! I wonder he didn't move farther away for his own safety.'

'The innkeeper belched contentedly: his new cask had passed muster. I told you - he's safe enough here. And it's handy for his unfinished business with old Llwyd.'

'Unfinished business? What business could he still have up at the big house?'

The innkeeper hesitated. 'Just something he said in here one evening. I don't want to go into that: don't want no trouble, see.'

But an alarmed Evan was insistent. Another precious coin changed hands. The innkeeper lowered more ale, wiped his mouth with the back of his hand and leant forward. 'A fair brew. You never heard this from me, mind. About two weeks' ago the gang were here drinking late and deep. Beynon's tongue was loosened with it - I couldn't help but overhear,' he added unconvincingly. 'He was going on about how he hated them all at Neuadd Siriol - that girl he got a beating over, the brute who re-arranged his face but most of all old Llwyd himself for sacking him and getting him outlawed. And more gripes against what sounded like half the estate staff who had worked under him and must have loathed him - no doubt with good cause! He said he was going to do for the lot of them once and for all. "Do for the lot of them once and for all" - those were his exact words. I never saw no-one bear grudges like him. You should have seen his ugly face when he said that. Gave me the creeps.'

'Did he say what he meant to do?'

'No. His two cronies asked him about that and said they'd help - they were always up for mischief and no doubt fancied pickings in it for them. But he said he was going to do this alone and the less they knew the better. It was personal and there was no money in it. At that they lost interest.'

'Did he say when, then?'

'Just that in two weeks' time they had best make themselves scarce as he was going to himself, because his revenge on that accursed household would be the talk of the shire, enough to bring the law out in force he said - which would take some doing these days! Posses would be hunting him, he said, and any vagabonds picked up would be tortured for information and likely hanged. He was well in his cups and bragging, like.'

'Two weeks' time? That's now!' But Evan was finding all this hard to swallow. 'Do for the lot of them once and for all? How? One after the other while everyone there stood by? The man must be possessed. Even so he could be dangerous on the loose.'

Suddenly it dawned on Evan. The Great Feast in the old hall was today, starting around noon - it must be well past that already - and the carousing that followed would continue well into the night. Nearly everyone on the estate would be in the old hall, including women folk and even some older children, all oblivious to any danger. Not 'do for them' one by one but all together. Whatever Beynon had planned was to be done at the feast. And he must be heading there now!

He must warn the household! But what if he were wrong? What if he barged in on the feast only to find nothing amiss? He would make an utter fool of himself - and in front of Eluned, whom he could not hope to avoid! Anyway was he not on the road away from that household for good? Yet if he was right? Could he risk ignoring this?

Evan made up his mind. He must warn them. Abruptly, with a word of thanks but none of explanation he paid his dues, slung his pack on his back and hurried back the way he had come. To prevent whatever evil this brute intended he must get here before him. But Beynon had a half hour start and darkness would fall early, when finding him would be almost impossible. His only chance was to find a short cut, a more direct way through the thick woodland. Coming north he had noticed a foresters' track wide enough for a horse and cart striking off the road in the direction he wanted.

Only as he turned onto it did it strike him. He was no murderer after all!

Christmas morning had dawned ice cold, the frost-hardened ground almost clear of snow save in shadowed corners. Ralph was woken early by men singing outside in a strange blending of sounds. Later Eluned would explain that this tradition, known as Plygain, meaning dawn or cockcrow, had replaced early mass. Now at midday, seated at high table at Ioan's right hand, he watched the feast getting into full swing. He had regained his outward composure but was still stunned and sickened by Whiting's martyrdom and in no humour for this festivity. But courtesy required he attend and to keep news of it from the others until afterwards he must dissemble now.

He gazed at the familiar scene, with a kindlier eye now, even in his grief recognising a profound change, a mellowing in the way he saw it. He felt the warmth from the great yule log, from the candles in their wall sconces and on the tables and from the fifty or more bodies packed around the lengthened rows of trestle tables, men and women seated together with a few older children on best behaviour. All wore what looked like their Sunday best while the busy serving maids had places kept for them while they brought the food from the kitchens. Each laden board had its bowl of punch of hot ale, spices and mashed apples and a Christmas pie stood ready - a goose stuffed with a chicken stuffed with a partridge stuffed with a pigeon, all encased in a pastry coffin. Down the tables large platters were heaped with vegetable sallets, sausage-shaped puddings of spiced meat and oatmeal, crib-shaped pies of mince meat and bowls of fruits and nuts brought out from some dark storeroom. The air was heavy with the aroma of rich food and the smell of candle wax and tallow. Scattered between the dishes on the high table stood curious little figures he had never seen before, an apple stuck with almonds and topped with evergreen sprays, each standing on three little twig legs. 'They are called Calenig, Ioan said, 'but don't ask me to explain: we have always had them.'

Now punch was ladled out from great bowls. Before they were half empty the clatter of wooden trenchers on tables and the chatter and laughter had drowned out the delicate sound of Ianto's harp. He was applauded and took his place at table, to be replaced by minstrels playing a viol, an hautboy and pipes and tabors. Soon even they struggled to be heard.

At the high table Aston and Thomas had been found more borrowed attire, the former in russet and Thomas, by now quite at ease in these surroundings, in plain dark grey. Ralph and the novices were sombre in their dark habits, Matthew haggard and red-eyed after writing late into the night. Their host was dignified in a fine black jerkin with a trimmed fur collar, the slashed sleeves of his grey doublet showing rich red cloth beneath A simple gold chain hung around his neck and he wore a jewelled brooch on his cap. The men's dark attire set off the bejewelled glow of the women's gowns, Eluned in rich ruby red and Catrin radiant in blue. Both wore the fashionable French hood, their dark hair uncovered at the front. Two beautiful women, one mature and one young, they were the cynosure of many eyes. The high table before them winked with pewter and greenish glassware but the main courses were the same as those on the trestles below.

Now came the sound of pipe and tabor and servers - men this time - emerged from the cross passage and processed up the centre aisle. Two bore platters of marchpane and other sweetmeats. Two more followed bearing aloft a great trencher on which a noble boar's head rested on a bed of bay leaves, rosemary, dates and apricots, an apple in its indifferent mouth. Then came the musicians and lastly men capering and singing a rousing tune. With evident pride the serving men placed their dishes on the high table, bowed and withdrew, to return with more dishes for the long trestles.

Ralph exclaimed: 'Surely that is The Boar's Head Carol they sing! I remember both tune and words - Let us serve with a song." That is an English carol!' He recognised a little animation in his own voice.

'Those were indeed the words you heard, Ralph, translated by me into Welsh,' Ioan replied. 'I took a liking to it at Court and brought it home with me when I left: it was new then.' He asked Ralph to say grace and then the assembly fell on the food with gusto, the noise level dropping immediately. All too soon Matthew, who had only pecked at his platter, mumbled his apologies and withdrew. White-faced, he staggered as he rose and it was Ralph who helped him to his bed, returning to table afterwards.

After almost two hours of feasting Ioan stood up and the assembly, at last replete, hushed respectfully. He spoke in Welsh but his meaning was clear to Ralph - the master thanking them for their year's labour and hoping they had feasted well - enthusiastic clapping - before relative quiet returned. Then Ioan leaned across him to whisper to Eluned. He must have invited her to sing, for a stool was brought to the front of the dais. After the customary show of reluctance she seated herself gracefully on it and her lute was fetched. Her deep red gown was trimmed with velvet; from under the crescent hood her dark hair, entwined with a single string of small pearls, gleamed in the candle light. Ralph caught his breath at her mature beauty and poise. Everything in his life was now cold and dead, but she - she alone - seemed to him warmth and life itself. He struggled to keep his feelings from his face.

The hall fell silent: a child was shushed. She sang to her lute in a soft sweet alto, a plaintive Welsh air totally foreign yet beguiling to Ralph's ears. When she finished there was an appreciative hush, then loud applause. Ralph clapped heartily as she returned to her stool beside him: 'Mistress, that was delightful; most excellently sung and played' and was rewarded by her ever-composed smile. Such beauty still and such accomplishment! How had this woman remained unmarried? What ailed the men in these parts? Never so acutely as now he regretted his drab habit - symbol of his solemn vow of chastity and of a solitude turned to loneliness.

Ioan leant toward him: 'My daughter begins the entertainment on a seemly note, but we can never be quite sure what may follow.' The minstrels played several pieces, a young man sang to a strange bowed instrument that Ioan called a crwth, the men singers sang a Welsh carol in their strangely blending voices. Although becoming noisy the entertainment had not turned unseemly, unlike some Ralph had watched wide-eyed through the bannisters as a child so long ago. Should dancing follow, though …? But that could not be for him. He would seek his bed.

John had used the word 'rustic.' He suspected irony in that word now but in truth this hall could not begin to compare with his old family home, nor this Christmas revelry with that he remembered in his youth.. In his mind's eye he saw its gleaming linen fold panelling, the two great fireplaces, the blaze of candles of finest wax, soft winter light from the two great mullioned windows, the family escutcheon bright on the back wall, liveried men servants - never women bearing bowls of perfumed water to table for individual washing of hands before eating. He saw the costly imported delicacies on a festive board crowned with a great stuffed swan; once even the glorious intact plumage of a peacock to delight the eye, its cooked flesh concealed beneath it in a vast pie. There had been noble and distinguished guests: liveried minstrels playing in their gallery. And then the dancing. With his younger brother he had watched from a doorway until their nurse had taken them off to bed, where the drunken revelling had kept them awake half the night. Next day had begun the round of deer hunts, bear-baiting and cock-fighting; in the evenings card games and gambling and more dancing. And always the whispering and giggling in dark corners that he had not understood.

But here is a smaller, plainer hall with mostly women servants in attendance in no sort of uniform and few with a word of English. And nary a guest save their poor lost selves. Yet the food has been good and plentiful and well enough served. There is an unforced gaiety here, an ease and warmth my aristocratic parents somehow never conjured up. Simple goodness underlies this unstinting cheer. Not so simple either, nor so rustic. Perhaps Ioan, a commoner if a gentleman, is not entitled to that fine fur at his collar, but there is no doubting restrained elegance in his attire and in that of his ladies - from his rare attendances when his abbot had entertained distinguished guests he recognised the hoods introduced by the tragic Queen Anne herself. He had come to respect Ioan's learning and his knowledge of the world. And never before had he met a woman like Eluned. He hardly dared to look at her for what his face might betray.

As the last entertainer sat down to applause an apparition appeared from the cross passage. It was a terrifying horse's skull gleaming white in the candlelight, carried high on a pole by someone concealed beneath a long white garment that fell to the floor. The skull had long pointed cloth ears and huge glaring glass eyes. Its jaws with their great yellow teeth opened and closed as it capered into the hall, its mane of coloured ribbons and tinkling bells tossing wildly. A few children buried their faces in their mothers' skirts, the adults rose to their feet clapping and cheering as it ran amongst them, tossing its grotesque head and lunging as if to bite. The guests at the high table sat in amazed silence.

Ioan had to raise his voice over the din: 'I promised you a surprise, Ralph: Eluned will explain.' He rose to his feet, rounded the high table and walked slowly down the centre of the hall where the creature, suddenly still, awaited him. They bowed gravely to each other and then began to speak in Welsh, each in turn in the cadences of verse. Quiet at first, their voices gradually became louder and they began to make threatening gestures at each other.

In the body of the hall all were on their feet laughing and clapping at what were evidently verbal sallies, but at the high table the guests were mystified. Ralph stirred uneasily, but Eluned shook her head, smiling as she laid cool reassuring fingers on the back of his hand - and for a long moment he forgot the strange spectacle.

She explained: 'This is a tradition called Mari Llwyd, or Grey Mare. Don't ask me why it is white not grey for I have no idea, unless it is because white horses are called greys. At Christmas she - really a he as you can hear - goes around the homes and confronts each host. Strictly speaking he should not be allowed indoors before this confrontation, but my father prefers to face him inside where all may enjoy the performance in comfort. They are now exchanging witticisms and insults, each trying to best the other with words. The assembly plays the judge and decides on the winner by acclamation. If they choose the Grey Mare the host must offer 'her' refreshment.' The combatants' exchanges became vehement, the excitement and applause louder. Eluned had to lean towards Ralph to be heard, her mouth at his ear: instantly he was aware of her perfume, the woman's warmth of her. 'I do not know its origins, but it is old. They must end up sounding angry but these days it has become an amicable ritual, although they do try to outwit each other and the word play can be clever, with rhyming, punning and alliteration I cannot explain in my poor English. These days the Grey Mare is expected to win, but win or lose he will not lack refreshment.'

Suddenly the raised voices fell silent, the antagonists bowed to each other again then a hand emerged from the white covering and shook Ioan's. Someone called for a show of hands and the Grey Mare was declared the winner by a comfortable margin. Ioan, flushed, was smiling as he ushered his weird antagonist to the high table.

Ralph whispered to Eluned: 'Will he show us his face?'

'No: we are not supposed to know who he is.' Somehow the man had dropped the mare's lower jaw right down, enabling him with obvious difficulty to drink deep of the proffered punch. Then he bowed elaborately to the company and capered down the hall and into the night to more applause. All sat down again in a buzz of voices.

Ioan, his voice a little hoarse, said there would be much disputation about the performances of the Grey Mare and himself: 'No doubt they will find us wanting compared with previous years, for the past is always better - never more so than now! My people love a good contest, be it song, poetry or wrestling. There was a time when we Welsh sat down together to poetry and music competitions that brought renown to the winners. But not much these days.' And doubtless even less in future, he thought.

There was indeed to be dancing: with much clattering trestles and benches were cleared to one side of the hall and presently the musicians struck up again.

Ioan leaned towards Ralph: 'This is not for me these days nor, I am sure, for yourself as a man of the cloth. No gay galliards or peacock pavanes here, just the energetic rounds and sets of the old country dances my people love so much.'

The company at the high table stood to take their leave, except for Catrin who would lead the procession of the first Christmas carol-dance with the head house groom and Thomas, who lingered hoping his turn might come.

Ralph turned to Eluned: 'You do not dance, mistress?' He imagined the two of them dancing together, himself elegant again in remembered finery, a gallant figure. They were bowing and curtsying, hands touching, eyes meeting, turning away, turning back. He knew he loved this woman, this ever-composed, unreachable woman. Knew himself for ever barred from declaring it by this drab monk's attire. He felt short of breath and his hands clenched into fists.

'I always used to lead the first dance but now Catrin is old enough to take my place.' She smiled, but he thought a shadow in her eyes spoke for her - 'and now I am too old.'

They were standing very close together on the crowded dais and the room had become over-heated. Ralph sensed the sweet warmth of her body. He felt himself losing control. Almost roughly he grasped for her hand and whispered a hoarse reply to what she had nor said: 'Far from old, Eluned. You are ....' John was approaching.

'Come Ralph, let us leave these revels to younger and nimbler limbs and finish that excellent wine we left in the parlour. You will join us, my dear?'

Gazing wide-eyed at Ralph Eluned was slow to reply. 'Thank you Tada, but I'll to my bed: it has been a long day.' She felt breathless. As the two men walked away her eyes followed the tall erect figure in the drab worn habit. She stood still and silent but an inner voice spoke: Dear God, let me not feel desire now.

CHAPTER 4

....

Dissolution

I t was almost dark, a ghost of a wind, a rising half moon, frost and bitter cold under a star-pricked sky with a few streaks of clouds. From the hall the sounds of revelry carried clear to Beynon crouched at the edge of the dark wood. Soft yellow light spilled from the slit windows and shone from the porch doorways where the doors were wide open to let night air into the over-heated room. Beyond the hall the silent darkened household wing showed a flicker of light as a candle was carried past a window; a member of the household heading for bed?

All was well: in his satisfaction Beynon barely felt the chill. One last time he cast his mind over the preparations he had made over the preceding nights so that all was ready for him now. Kindling and wood faggots soaked in oils and fat had been laboriously prepared and carefully concealed until last night - how fortunate the early snow had been replaced by dry cold so the faggots and the roofing thatch should be dry enough. It had taken him nights of stealthy labour but it had proved easy enough to avoid being seen, for he had learned the routine of the traditional feast. All but the most essential work had just ceased for the twelve days and most estate workers would stay in their cottages except today when they had come with their families to the hall. The old and infirm and the younger children staying at home would be huddled around their cottage fires or abed. The over-alert geese who had survived the feast were safely penned and the nervous horses were stabled, all well away from the house. Ieuan's mastiffs were locked in a shed so as not to disturb the revellers.

Last night's final preparations had been the most arduous. One by one he had concealed his prepared bundles of faggots close around the base of the timbered house. Most difficult had been to thrust others under the roofing thatch of house and hall and soak their surrounds with more oil. It had been exhausting work with only one ladder tall enough, but the greatest problem had been to work in silence with the hounds still about - fortunately they knew him and the cold had kept them in their kennels. He smiled to himself at the memory of his stealth: he had not been a poacher for nothing. He was bone weary from all that effort, but at last everything was ready; the ladder in place in the deep shadow behind the house, torches and tinder hidden at its foot. A pity there was so little wind but what there was came from the right direction and anyway the under thatch should be dry enough. He should have time to shift the ladder to fire the hall roof, perhaps in more than one place before the alarm was raised. But he must not delay too long! The dancing would not go on for ever whatever the noise from the hall suggested. Timing was everything. He would wait a little longer: he could be a patient man. He drew his hood closer around his face against the cold.

Thomas hovered around the fringe of the energetic dancers, watching Catrin's small tapping feet and graceful body. She had hardly spoken to him all evening. She was smiling up at her momentary partner, a young stable hand, as they touched hands passing each other in the lively dance. Her hood was slipping and her glossy hair shone blue-black in the candlelight.

Thomas scowled. The youth was handsome, damn him, but as lowborn as himself and worse dressed. What business had he touching her hand, talking to her? Why could these people not keep seemly social barriers? He was light of foot, too, and Thomas knew he would look clumsy in comparison. Still, most of the men danced no better than himself and at least the round they were performing must be an English one, for he knew it. He must take the floor. Taking a deep breath he edged closer.

Time to move. Beynon left the cover of the trees and ran silently across the deserted forecourt, making for the deep shadow of the house. He edged through the little knot garden and around behind the building. The sound of music and laughter was fainter here but he could have done with more light as he took out his tinder box and checked that his ladder was firmly grounded. A darker shape in the dark shadow, he climbed it silently.

Evan swore, so far gone from the cloister now as to feel no guilt for it. The trail had divided. It had begun well enough. The broad cart track had been firm going and he had set a brisk pace with little concern where to put his feet, his mind elsewhere and in a whirl. Was there truly danger for Eluned's household? If so could he get there in time? Could he bear coming face to face with her again, as now he must? And through all this his mind struggled to assimilate the astonishing news that he had not killed the man he was now trying to overtake. What might that mean for him?

But as the wan daylight faded his troubles had begun. The cart track veered from the direction he wanted, leaving him only a narrow and evidently little-used footpath to follow straight ahead. It was so overgrown that in trying to maintain his pace he stumbled twice, risking a sprained ankle. He had no choice but to slow down.

Soon so little daylight reached the narrow path between the looming tall trees that once he fell flat over a fallen branch. Picking himself up scratched and breathless, he saw that just ahead this path also divided, the two branches diverging so little that he did not know which to take. He cursed himself for not sticking to the road like Beynon. No hope of overtaking him now. But he must get there!

Which path? He might have tossed a coin but in the gloom could not have seen which side fell uppermost. He hesitated, then took the right-hand one and carried on.

It was getting dark and he was feeling his years when at last the path descended towards Neuadd Siriol and he knew he had chosen correctly. A patch of clear sky ahead marked the edge of the wood flanking the house. Would he be in time? As he quickened his step moonlight picked out the tall chimneys of the house and the hall.

Something was wrong! Overhead the rising moon shone cold and the stars were remote as ever but ahead the chimneys showed a wavering pinkish glow. Emerging from the trees he saw that the thatched roof of the hall was wreathed in heavy oily smoke and in several places bright flames licked in his direction. Smoke was spewing from the roof of the timbered house too and in it he saw more flames. Fire! At once he knew that here was no accident. Fires could not have started in so many places at once nor be spreading so quickly without human hands at work. This was arson! So this was Beynon's revenge - on a household at play and suspecting nothing, for music and laughter sounded merrily from the hall while the house itself lay dark in sleep.

Breathing hard Evan plunged recklessly down the short grassy slope towards the forecourt, then hesitated. His mind was racing. Where go first to warn them, hall or house? It must be the house. The old hall was crowded with people and there might be panic but at least everyone there was wide awake and the cross passage doors stood wide open. The thick old beams supported on massive stone walls should resist the fire long enough for people to escape before the burning thatch fell on them. The dancers stood a chance. But the newer house wing had half-timbered walls and the plaster between their uprights sheathed bone dry combustibles: the house would go up like so much tinder. Worse, those inside would be up a flight of stairs, in darkness, drugged from sleep and slow to react. Was one of them Eluned? As he raced towards the house he thought he saw a dark shadow flitting away from it. Beynon? But no time for him now.

Thomas had joined in the dance and for a passing moment Catrin was his partner. She had lost her hood altogether, her hair was loose, she was flushed and she was beautiful. Both knew men's eyes followed her. She smiled up at him and as always he caught his breath, tongue-tied and awkward and feeling over-large.

She was excited and in teasing mood. 'Master Thomas! Not still propping up the wall? So you can dance in England.' They whirled around and as she moved away her light voice floated back: 'Well, more or less' as she spun away in another man's arms.

But Thomas was growing up. That particular smile was for him alone. When the round ended he caught her wrist and drew her to a table near the open cross passage door where punch and small beer were served and there was fresh air. 'You look heated mistress: stop your whirling awhile for a drink.' She obeyed, her manner teasingly demure but not entirely so: sometimes he could be masterful and it excited her. She recalled that horrid Beynon and how....

The crowd around the laden table pressed them close together and he felt the warmth of her. His heart lurched. This was not the place or time. It was too public, too crowded, too hot, too stifling. But suddenly he could not help himself.

'Catrin ...'

She looked up at him, not smiling now.

'Catrin ... cariad ....' He stopped, looked away, speechless. Catrin caught her breath. His Welsh was coming on so well: he must know that word was not used lightly. Cariad meant much more than the shallower English 'love' or 'dear': it meant 'beloved.' Nothing less - and there could be nothing more. Was this it then - here, now? She looked at the floor.

Thomas felt himself sweating. 'Catrin. 'I! You must know I ....'

Deep in the hall a woman screamed.

She was pointing at the roof. Everyone looked up. Brown oily smoke was wreathing down towards the dancers and parts of the thatch began to glow a malevolent orange. The music faltered and died away. In the sudden silence they heard crackling. Now live yellow flames were licking at the old thatch.

A man's voice shouted 'the roof's afire' and pandemonium reigned; screaming and shouting, the wail of frightened children and a stampede for the cross passage with its open doors at each end, a few slower or weaker revellers thrust aside.

But Thomas was first. Fast of thought if slow with words, he grabbed Catrin's hand and pulled her into the passage and out of the front door, the crowd at his heels. Outside they ran up the grass slope to the edge of the trees and stood looking back at the house, panting in the cold air.

They saw disaster. Half the hall roof was now alight, the roar of the flames as loud as the music had been, burning thatch already tumbling into the hall, sparks flying. People were spilling out from the front passage door and they knew others would be escaping by the back one. But the great oak beams seemed still in place, holding up most of the burning thatch. Pray they might last long enough for everyone to escape.

'Poor old hall!' Catrin's voice was dull with shock. Then she looked beyond it. The roof of the family wing, her home now, her family, was ablaze and fire licked down its walls. Orange light danced behind the windows and in a few places glowed through the walls themselves where plaster and filling were burning through.

'My God! Thomas, they're asleep in there - Eluned, Tada, the others, little Gelert.' She started forward but Thomas caught her. She struggled frantically in his arms.

'No Catrin, no! You can't do anything: in that gown you'd be a torch, woman. I love you! I'll go. Look, all the outhouses are well clear of the fire. You go to the back hall door where people will be gathering outside. See them all safe away then get some of them fetching water.' And much good that would do, he thought as she obeyed. But it would keep her safe and give the women something to do except scream.

In the courtyard he overtook a man also running to the house; someone utterly astonishing in rough lay clothing. 'Evan! What ....?' But no time now for questions.

'Thomas, lad!' Evan had already sized up the situation. I'll find the Mistress - and her father and any others. Do Prior Ralph and Steward Aston sleep in the house?' Thomas nodded. 'Then they can help me. You go back to the hall and help out any still inside - some may be hurt in the rush, there will be affrighted children. Go man!' He pushed him away.

The horse trough in the forecourt was nearly full. Evan broke the thin film of ice, tore off his cloak and soaked it then put it back on again, gasping at the sudden wet aching cold. Then he was pounding at the heavy oak side door.

It was bolted on the inside.

Ioan had retired for the night tired but well content. Today had been the best Christmas Feast he could remember. Eluned and all the servants had excelled themselves, his guests had praised his meat and drink and entertainment. The music and the dancing he could hear from the hall would go on for hours yet, as it should do for those young and energetic enough on this especial night. Today had been a great success and tomorrow would bring days of quiet and rest in which his old bones could recover. Smiling, he plumped up his pillow and was soon fast asleep.

Aston also slept soundly. The night before he had tossed and turned, trying to decide if he should use this break in the bad weather to leave at once for Hereford. He had Ioan's promise of a horse and guide. But if the snows returned soon he might be caught in the open in that dreadful high country and he knew he could not survive that. Anyway his brother, by now shut down snug for the winter, would not need his help until spring and he would be only an extra mouth to feed. He was enjoying his work here as acting bailiff; was comfortable and saving a little money. In the small hours he had finally decided to stay awhile longer and with his mind at rest had snatched a little sleep. This morning he had woken up looking forward to the feast, where he had enjoyed himself eating too much and drinking too deep. He slept and snored.

In the next chamber Ralph lay sleepless. Most long nights he wrestled with the guilt of his loss of faith and what it would mean for him in the years to come. Would this new dispensation one day allow him to renounce his solemn vows? But his vows had not been to King Henry, the self-appointed new head of the church. They were to God. For all his life until death released him they bound him as priest if no longer as monk. But what kind of a priest performed his duties without true faith? Oh, he had heard of others who had done so, but in all conscience could he live such a sham? And if not then how could he accept John's offer of his chaplaincy? His talk with John had brought to the forefront of his mind all these problems he was no closer to resolving. Yet they had tormented him long before his arrival here and he was learning to control them by forcing his mind elsewhere, tonight even managing to push away the horror of Whiting's death for a while.

Yet sleep would not come and he knew why. Eluned! That moment of closeness in the hall had been a culmination of ....? Tossing restlessly, his mind took him back. It had begun so gradually, his growing admiration for her - her calm command during the upset of their arrival, her constant care for their needs, her cool efficiency in her household. Such excellent womanly qualities! Even more remarkable was her intelligence and learning. Of late, when others had been about their business and she had an hour free of her responsibilities, they had taken to sharing the parlour fire, she usually with her needlework, he with a book, in a silence that had become companionable. Gradually they had begun to talk, really talk, sometimes even in Latin until her English flowed more readily. He had come to realise the breadth of her knowledge and interests. Of course she knew little of rhetoric and less of science. But in other respects her knowledge matched his own and that of her father, although she had made plain it all came from Ioan's tutoring and from his books, for she had never been anywhere, done anything. Unmistakable regret there! Unlike most of the few women he could recall she spoke little of the domestic matters she managed so efficiently. Their talk had ranged so widely during these weeks - from the vagaries of trade with the Low Countries to the development of the modern lute she played so well, to this new influence of Italy on English art and taste, recent trends in tapestry design and so much else. They had discussed the state of the realm in this time of turmoil and what the future might hold. From her he learned about native Welsh customs and why the recent Acts of Union troubled her people so. He had tried to explain the political complexities that lay behind the on-going dissolution of the monasteries. Of course he heard her father's voice, her mentor, in hers, but she had her own opinions too, her own excellent mind.

Gradually they had become less formal with each other; drawn closer. He began to call her by her given name and after diffidence on her part and his gentle insistence, he had become plain Ralph. Each had become aware - if as yet but dimly - of the other's troubled mind behind the rigid outward control: somehow it drew them closer still. He still enjoyed his scholarly talks with Ioan but now he looked forward more eagerly to sitting quietly with her by the fire. He hoped that she did too and sensed that perhaps she might, although she never revealed as much. To him it had become a true meeting of minds.

But now, especially this night, so much more! Now he was acutely aware of her as a woman, shapely and graceful, still beautiful, with that stillness in repose that turned his heart over. Her fathomless brown eyes turned on him, that low voice with its lilting accent - speaking in English, for while her command of it was fast improving he to his shame still had few words of Welsh - unsettled him. He had known no woman since the soldiering days of his youth, when the crudity of the encounters among the rough camp followers had turned his fastidious nature towards celibacy long before habit and cowl had required it of him. Then he had turned to his faith but he saw now that if he had ever had true faith it had been briefly indeed: long since he had dropped the anchor of his well-being in thought and reason. Now this sudden up-welling of emotion confused and alarmed him. It was absurd in a cleric approaching old age: it threatened the stability and repose he needed above all else.

He had tried to put Eluned - Eluned the woman - out of his thoughts. But he could not. It was disturbing to meet her gaze, a thrill to brush her hand with his. This was no return of youthful feelings, which he remembered with distaste as callow and gross: this was a new awakening, profound, overwhelming, as in a young unsullied man. He loved this woman and wanted her, mind and body as a man wants a woman. But always came the thought: what good such love to a priest chained for ever to celibacy? And even if by some miracle she could return his feelings - and he did not know what might lie behind that impenetrable composure of hers - what could it bring either of them but misery? She could never be his. How then could he remain at Neuadd Siriol as chaplain, unfulfilled as celibate priest yet seeing her every day, ever unattainable? Yet how bear to leave this quiet place and never see her again? With a groan he raised his head and pummelled his pillow.

In her cool bedchamber at the end of the corridor Eluned had at last fallen asleep. She lay quietly, the smooth contours of her face serene as ever but her fingers twitching slightly on the bed linen. She was dreaming again. This was a new dream, strange as dreams always are yet unusually clear. From an infinitely benign velvet darkness a hand was reaching slowly towards her into the soft light, a man's strong brown hand with long, clean, sensitive fingers. Very slowly it came closer. Now the searching fingers touched her face, moth light in their caress yet utterly assured. She was trembling. She was young and mam and her brothers were alive. Slowly, so slowly, he drew closer until she could feel his hard shadowed body press against hers on the bed. Now his arm was around her, infinitely gentle yet not to be withstood. She knew he would not be withstood, accepted it, welcomed it. Her eyes must be closed: she could not see his face. Why could she not see his face? Yet she knew he was not Evan: the vanished Evan's face no longer appeared in dreams or fire glow. But now as the man drew her close and his firm lips sought hers she knew the face she would see when she opened her eyes. And now she did see it, saw clearly the lean, worn, still handsome face above her. She could not see into his still-shadowed eyes but she felt their burning intensity. Ralph! Dear God it was him! She knew then it had always been Ralph, long before she had met him! Deep in her dream she sighed as she opened her arms and her mouth and her body to him. And there was no sin.

 Still pounding his pillow Ralph became aware of something amiss. A smell of smoke, a faint wavering glow, a crackling sound, smoke drifting into the darkened room. Fire! Quickly Ralph found his habit and was out in the passage pulling it on over his night clothes. The smoke was thickening fast here and small flames flickered above his head. He must wake the others! Which way? To Eluned of course, but what of Ioan? He thumped on Aston's door, got no reply, rushed in, flung open the bed hangings and roughly shook him awake. Aston sat up blearily. 'Fire! Get up! Quick, man! Get John safe outside: I'm going for the mistress.' Ralph stumbled down the dark corridor. The crackling overhead was louder now, the under-thatch shedding an evil orange glow: the fire was spreading fast.

 As he reached Eluned's bed chamber he heard her dog barking and scrabbling at the stout door. Pray God it was not bolted! Mercifully it was not. As he flung it open the little animal shot past him, turned and whined. Inside the room acrid smoke was billowing down. Coughing now, he edged inside, the glow from the roof thatch enough for him to make out her pale night shift as she sat up in the bed, its hangings open. Her head was bent forward and she too was coughing painfully. Sparks were falling around her and the roar of flames was terrifying.

Still half in her dream Eluned was not fully awake to the danger. As he reached her she looked up, saw the face in her dream bending anxiously over her. Smiling, expecting him, she reached out her arms. 'Ralph! Cariad!' Then she was coughing again. Ralph lifted her in his arms, wrapped a blanket around them and snatched up drying cloths to cover their mouths. Then he carried her out into the corridor, his eyes watering, her face buried into his shoulder, her little dog at his heels. She heard its frantic barking and reached down feebly but Ralph did not stop.

'Leave him! He's well under the smoke and can run faster than us.' The fire was spreading fast now, licking down the walls, stinging smoke everywhere, roaring and crackling ever louder. It had become unbearably hot. But Ralph saw that the stair head was not yet touched by the fire. He was going to get them both out, he would save her! He held her more tightly. Overwhelmed by that unmistakably welcoming smile and accepting arms as he had picked her up from her bed he was wondrously aware of her warm supple body and under the smell of smoke the faintest scent of rosewater in her hair. At that moment he knew with astonishment yet with certainty that she loved him too, knew too that he would save them both. Above all else he knew that then he would declare his love, shout it aloud and the devil take this sorry world. She would have him and they would be together. He laughed aloud in his joy, coughed again because of it then shook his head: first he must get them out of here, get down those awkward stairs without falling. She was still racked by painful coughing: could she manage it on her own feet if he held onto her?

Then, beyond the stair head outside Ioan's bedchamber door he saw that a main beam had fallen. Smouldering and shooting off sparks it lay half across something bulky on the floor. It was Aston, unmoving with one leg trapped underneath. So the steward had not reached John, who must still be inside. Mercifully, with her head buried into his shoulder Eluned had seen nothing. He could do nothing for the other men yet: first he must get her out. Tightening his hold on her and even in that moment aware of delight in the feel of her, he eased them both cautiously down the stairs to the side door, reached out a hand to unbolt it and flung it open to the sweet cold air.

Evan was kicking frantically at the heavy door when suddenly it opened inward. Acrid smoke billowed out, a little dog shot past him and then Ralph stumbled out carrying someone in his arms, both of them coughing painfully. For a moment Ralph was startled in recognition, then, gulping in fresh air, he unceremoniously thrust Eluned into Evan's arms.

'Evan! What are you ….? Here, take the lady. Ioan and Aston are trapped upstairs. I'm going back for them.'

With a shock Evan realised who he was holding. But the fire's blazing insistence blotted out all emotion but fear. He said: 'I'll come back to help you,' then carried Eluned a safe distance away, laid her gently on the ground and ran back. As he reached the open door Ralph, already at the foot of the stairs, shouted. No! Go back to her! She is overcome by the smoke and will die of cold. Look to the lady Evan! She is precious, Evan; so precious! He sounded near hysterical, almost exalted.

Evan was at his shoulder now. 'Calm yourself, man: she is safe enough for now and others are arriving to help. Where are the master and Aston?' Both men were spluttering between coughs.

Ralph turned for the stairs. 'Oh, very well! John must still lie abed: I'll go for him. Aston is on the landing felled by a roof beam: you get him out.' And with that Ralph was scrambling up the staircase, which was now alight. Evan, appalled at the dancing flames and heat, hesitated and then followed, dodging through the licking flames. He heard Ralph shouting and putting his shoulder repeatedly to Ioan's door, which must be locked or jammed, then he himself was heaving a heavy smouldering beam off Aston's leg, protecting his hands with the skirt of his wet cloak, then slowly pulling him free. Aston was barely conscious but managed to stand on his good leg with Evan's support. The staircase was well alight as they half stepped, half fell down it to fresh air and safety.

Eluned was still coughing and retching as they reached her, being lifted to her feet by two men: others were hurrying towards them. Evan's voice brooked no disobedience. 'Give her to me! Get this man to the great barn - he's heavy but go gently - his leg may be broken.' Then he was coughing again.

Recovering, he carried Eluned to the great barn, which was well clear of the fire and fast becoming a general shelter. The forecourt was a hellscape of baleful light, smoke, noise, ant-like activity. Men had formed a chain to carry water in pails from the duck pond to the burning hall roof, but their efforts were clearly futile as the shallow pond quickly emptied. Outraged ducks quacked and waddled underfoot. Other men were gathering around the blazing house. With more purpose a group of women, marshalled by Mair, beat with brooms at wisps of burning thatch falling too close to the nearest outbuildings. Some folk milled around aimlessly: others stood dazed, staring blankly. In the barn Gelert had found Catrin sitting on a hay bale and was being furiously hugged amidst a crowd of distraught women, children and old men. A few injured folk were being tended in one corner.

Eluned, half-conscious, had not recognised the man who had carried her and whom she had not set eyes on for six years. When he laid her down gently she fell into Catrin's arms, Gelert nosing between them whimpering and wagging his tail furiously.

Seeing they were safe for the present Evan ran back to the burning house, calling for men to help him, racking his brains what more he could do. He must help Ralph.

But in the few minutes he had been away the timbered house had become a roaring inferno, ablaze from roof to floor, the heat from it overpowering, wood sparks spitting everywhere. Surely now impossible to go inside! But Ioan and Ralph were in there and he must not give up. There was still some water in the horse trough and he wet his cloak again, shrugged it back on and willed himself through the dancing red hell of the open doorway.

And at once saw it was hopeless. The searing heat drove him back, foul billowing smoke had him spluttering again, flames fingered down the collapsed staircase towards him, burning timbers crashed around him. There was nothing he could do, nothing anyone could do. A falling beam just missed him as he staggered back out retching.

In the hall the revellers were more fortunate. Everyone had been merrily awake, the stone walls would not burn and open doorways were at hand. Thomas and several other men had just time to help out the slowest of them before the central beams gave way and the main mass of roof thatch crashed down. The fire, fed anew on trestles and stools and fat-smeared platters, flared up again. A few of the revellers nursed minor burns and bruises but none seemed serious and, God be praised, there were no dead. Thomas was the last to leave after ensuring no-one remained inside.

In the forecourt eyes turned towards the blazing timbered house. Surely nothing could save it now but Thomas meant to try and ran towards it, other men following his lead. As they reached it the appalling heat felt solid as a wall.

Evan emerged through the smoke gasping and coughing. 'Lads, no more can be done here tonight - believe me, I have tried. Go back and comfort your womenfolk.' To Thomas he said quietly: 'I have got Aston safe out but I fear old Llwyd and the prior must be dead.'

'My God! What of the mistress?'

'Safe in the barn. Overcome by the smoke but not injured, but I fear in deep shock. What of the old hall?'

'The roof has fallen in but all are out safely, a few with burns and knocks.'

'Then we too should return to the women awhile. Nothing can be saved here tonight - if ever. It will be bitter cold away from the fire and we must make sure all the household people have some shelter and if possible food. All others should return to their cottages. We shall have much to do when morning comes!'

As they turned away Thomas stopped abruptly and pointed at the wood beyond the forecourt.

'Evan, look there!' Beyond the fire-lit figures milling around on the forecourt a shadowy figure stood motionless at the dark edge of the trees. But for the flickering firelight it would have been invisible. Thomas exclaimed: 'That's Beynon.'

Evan was unsure but trusted Thomas' young eyes. 'Come back to gloat, has he? Put your arm down and keep still: he mustn't notice us.' He looked at Thomas. 'Believe me when I tell you I know he did this: I'll explain later. So shall we take him?' Thomas nodded grimly. 'Then let us thread our way quietly through all these people and get behind him to block his escape into the trees. The forecourt is so well lit by the fire that he will not escape your long legs this way.' All these years I have lived with the guilt of killing that wretch, he thought. What will I do if we catch him now?

Beynon had been clear away into the trees when he gave way to an overpowering urge to gaze one last time at his handiwork. He turned back: there was little danger if he did not linger too long. From the wood's edge he could see everything on the forecourt, where people were ushing around like headless chickens. What a fire he had created! Far grander than he had dared hope, for what he saw before him looked like total destruction. Tomorrow old Llwyd and his accursed household would have not a stick to call their own, some of them perhaps not even their lives. He hoped Llwyd in particular would be a roasted corpse when found. This was revenge indeed! This was triumph! Utterly absorbed, he edged forward a few paces. Just a few minutes more to savour it all before making good his escape. He licked his lips and a dribble of spittle rolled down his beard.

Behind him a dry stick snapped underfoot.

He whirled around. Against the greater darkness of the wood behind him two dark figures stepped into the firelight, their hooded faces in deep shadow. One was tall, his lithe form suggesting youth, the other stockier; both broad of shoulder, both motionless. Beynon gasped. He did not recognise them but he recognised danger.

The shorter man's finger reached out for him and beckoned. 'Come, Beynon, it is over for you.'

But Beynon had a poacher's wits and his reaction was cat quick. Seeing no way past them he turned and ran a few steps towards the forecourt and then stopped. Lurid orange light played on its milling figures. Could he escape by dodging in amongst them? But either left or right he knew he could not outrun that younger man.

There must be another way! In the angle where the house joined the old hall stood the small private porch and doorway used by the family: the brighter blaze there showed that its door stood open or had burnt away. As steward he had used that entrance when reporting to Llwyd in his counting house and knew it led to the hall. If somehow he could get through the hall he could escape through the back door of the cross passage and into the woods beyond, the woods he knew like the back of his hand where no-one could match him in stealth. But could he get through that porch doorway? Dare he attempt it? The porch was aflame and most of the hall hatch seemed to have collapsed so its floor would be strewn with burning timbers and thatch. Could he get through all that alive?

Above the crackling and roar of the fire he heard the two men coming for him: they were close now. That terrifying doorway was his only chance. He took a few more steps forward, stopped and let his shoulders sag in feigned defeat. Then, catching them off guard, he was racing for the forecourt, turning right as though making for the drive and the road beyond. When he heard their shoes crunch on the forecourt behind him he slanted sharp left again and reached the doorway before they had time to react, desperately willing himself into the fire.

Evan and Thomas could not prevent his reaching it. They watched in horror as he disappeared into the little porch, his body momentarily silhouetted against the flames before he dodged out of sight. Then another crackling roar, a great shower of sparks and part of the upper wall of the house fell full onto the porch. An appalling scream and then a dancing black silhouette re-appeared. A blazing torch, it reeled out of the holocaust and collapsed shrieking and twitching on the ground,. Flames and oily smoke rose from the hideous thing. The screaming seemed to last a long time.

'He's lit his last fire' Evan said, surprised at his own detachment. He hadn't killed the man this time, either. He wondered if he would have if he had caught him. In truth perhaps he had.

They made their way to the barn wondering how to tell the women that Ioan and the prior were surely dead. They found Eluned, eyes open but unmoving, lying as in a trance. A small burn on one forearm had turned angry red. Catrin sat beside her holding her limp hand: Geraint crouched on the straw, soft eyes pained and watchful.

'Her coughing has eased and that burn on her arm is not serious.' Catrin said too calmly, 'I would put a salve on it - she has taught me a few of her skills - but I have none here. A bandage alone would do no good.' Abruptly she stood up and buried her head in Thomas's shoulder as his arms went around her. Her voice shook. 'I am so worried about her. She seems - seems no longer with us. Dear God, I don't know what to do!'

Evan watched. So that's how the land lies with those two: Ioan would not have approved! But small wonder Thomas looked so smitten, for dishevelled and distraught though she was the scrawny child he vaguely recalled had grown into a rare beauty. He knew then that Thomas must be the one to break the hard news to Catrin.

Evan turned and bent over the unblemished face he had seen for so long in his dreams. Eluned's breathing was too light but sounded regular enough, her eyes open yet unseeing. He longed to hold her in his arms again but instead straightened up: no-one must know what it cost him to see her like this, to keep his voice steady. Somehow he managed to sound composed. 'No more we can do for the mistress or anyone tonight. Think of the ordeal she suffered trapped upstairs in the house: small wonder it has taken its toll. We can be thankful she lives. Catrin, get some men to help you and move her up to one of the cots in the loft. Keep her warm and comfortable there and stay with her until her mind returns to us, as it surely will.' He must sound reassuring. 'I have seen something like this happen in men much older and feebler than she is and they recovered fully. And get some rest yourself, girl.'

It dawned on him that the girl he was ordering about would not remember him, would see him as a stranger. With a warning look at Thomas he introduced himself awkwardly as that farmer across the valley who had left years ago and had just returned: 'Family matters, much too prolonged,' he explained lamely!' The absurdity in the circumstances of their instinctive small bow and curtsy brought a fleeting smile to Catrin's face.

'I remember hearing of a farmer who disappeared - not from El though: I was a child then.' She smiled again, accepting him, and he realised that these youngsters - yes even Thomas - needed someone to take control in this crisis. Given a lead they would give him admirable support.

Well then, he would accept the charge. Turning his back on the motionless figure on the straw he spoke with a brisk confidence he did not feel. 'First let us see how matters stand here in the barn.' They saw that the household servants were making themselves bedding for the night in the straw. Pitchers of drinking water had been brought from the well. Well and good. But some fool had lit tallow candles, some stuck insecurely in the earthen floor with loose dry straw lying everywhere. 'Do you wish for another fire tonight?' he shouted angrily and ordered all but four candles to be put out and those left alight to be placed in containers filled with water. Stunned by the disaster no-one demurred at taking orders from this ill-dressed stranger and he saw they would accept his leadership for now.

Turning to Catrin and Thomas he said: 'We should manage well enough for what little remains of this night. But grave problems follow.

Three matters we must consider now. First, we must put out every trace of fire and make sure it cannot flare up again to threaten the outbuildings. If the wind does not get up there should be no problem, for by morning there will be little left to burn. Second comes shelter for all those who slept in the main house and hall. This barn serves them for a few days so we can set that problem aside for now - although not for long! That leaves our most urgent problem - food! We can start by counting heads to find out how much we will need.'

Thomas interjected: 'Count in the household grooms and men workers. They have their cottages but have been taking their dinners in the hall of late. Some are married but there will be less food laid on for them at their homes.'

Evan nodded. 'You make a tally, Thomas. Now let us consider what food we can lay our hands on.'

Thomas thought. 'There is salt meat and fish stored in an outhouse and grain in the granary, perhaps a little still on the threshing floor. All safe from the fire and ready for winter. Enough for now.'

Catrin added: 'There are roots and fruit in store, too.'

'Where kept?'

'In the cellar below the kitchens with the milled flour and fats and other things. Her hand flew to her breast. Oh! They will be lost in the fire!'

Evan held up his hand. 'Perhaps not. We must find out tomorrow. And we need many things from those kitchens if we are to cook - and your salves from the still room, too, lady. But can we cook without use of the ovens? Could the kitchens have survived the fire? Is the flooring above them of wood or stone?' They were unsure.

'This we must know. Catrin: you know the cook. Will you find her and bring her here?' When she had left he added: 'those kitchens are the key for us.'

Thomas agreed. 'Well reasoned, Evan, but even if they can be used there will be a deal of burnt timber to remove before we can get into them.'

'True. That must be our first task when daylight comes and for that we must round up every available helper. Some rain but no wind tonight would be a blessing. And Thomas - I am sorry for it but it must fall to you to break the news of Ioan's death to Catrin as soon as you can get her alone and can comfort her - as I see now you are best able to do. But neither of you must tell Mistress Eluned until she is fit to hear it - then I will undertake that task. Ah! Here is Catrin with the cook.'

He asked Mair what was needed to feed everyone for the first few days. Glad to have something to think about except the destruction around her, she thought for a moment. 'Sir, we can fetch salted meat from its store shed and spit it on fires outside - if the rain holds off. But we lack all seasoning. There are live geese and fowl kept back from the feast for their eggs - although we cannot have both. We need stew pots for cooking scraps and making cawl. We can still mill flour and try to bake bread - of a sort. But everything will take so long and people will be hungry.'

At least unlike me you all ate your fill last night at the feast, Evan thought wryly. He was desperately hungry himself. He asked: 'Mair, can we feed everybody if the kitchens and everything in them have been destroyed?'

'Only poorly as I have said, sir, and not for long. We need pots and vessels, knives and spoons, cooking fats, spices and much else from the kitchens. Most of all we need use of the ovens.' She shook her head as the extent of the problem dawned on her.

Evan was consoling. 'Take heart: we are not beaten yet. Now Mair, heed me for this is important. Tell me how the lower end of the hall - the kitchen end - is built.'

'On two floors, sir, our sleeping chamber above and the kitchens and still room on the ground floor. And there is the cellar below them where we store beer, ale, flour, salt, all the things we may need daily - and need now. Odds and ends, too.'

'Now think carefully for this is very important. Has the kitchen ceiling - that is the floor of your sleeping place - a wooden or a stone floor?'

'Stone, sir, stone floors and walls to roof level and down to the cellar floor. All the same as the old hall, all that same thick old stone. Hundreds of years old, they say.'

'Stone staircases, too?' She nodded. Evan heaved a sigh of relief. The servants' lodgings would have been ruined when the roof collapsed on them but kitchens and cellar should have survived. Tomorrow would tell if they could get into them.

Light rain had fallen during what remained of the night and was only now, at mid-morning, easing off. There was no wind. Smoke wisped straight up from the blackened pyre of Neuadd Siriol and the sour stink of wet ash pervaded everything. But no trace of fire could be seen although men and women searched carefully everywhere. At the hall men with pitchforks, billhooks and bare cloth-covered hands had cleared the doorways and cross passage and were pulling away still smouldering timbers from the servants' staircase. Francis was among them, undistinguishable now in his lay clothing. Men were working their way up to the tangled mass of burnt roof and furniture on the stone ceiling of the kitchens. Evan called from below: 'don't waste time clearing upstairs - just enough to make safe passage into the kitchens.' With their prospect of cooked food depending on it the men were working with a will and making good progress. 'We shall soon be into the kitchens,' Thomas judged.

'Let us hope those stone floors have saved everything below' Evan replied. He was desperately hungry and felt faint, not having eaten for a full and arduous day. He sent Thomas to fetch Mair again and with her any kitchen maids she could find.

It took a while to find her and when she and Thomas arrived with two maids Catrin was with them. Evan saw that Thomas had told her about Ioan for she was red-eyed from weeping. Careless of appearances Thomas had his arm around her shoulders. 'Eluned is unchanged,' Catrin said, her voice flat. 'I can do nothing until - until she comes back to us - so - so - I've left Marged watching over her. I came to help here.' Then she burst out: 'I had to get away, just for a while!'

The youngsters need to be together, Evan thought, and as much alone as can be in this chaos. He turned to them briskly: 'You two are not needed here now but there is much to do elsewhere. See there is enough drinking water in the great barn, that a few geese and fowl are killed and plucked and hung for cooking - but spare enough for their eggs. And see enough of the stored grain is milled. Come, you know well what is needed.' He pushed them away.

A worker called him from the hall porch, thumb raised. Turning to Mair Evan said. 'Wait here while I see if it is safe for you to go inside.' He joined the man at the porch and the two disappeared inside.

He was soon back.'Good news. The kitchens seem little harmed although black with soot. But they are still a deal too warm underfoot, so tie cloths around your feet, then it is safe enough. Mair, you are in charge here now. Find what you need in kitchens and cellar and get their fires started and the ovens heated - you know best what to do. I have something else to attend to for an hour or so. When I return we will speak further on how we stand for food and cooking until better arrangements can be made.' He smiled encouragingly at her. 'Can you do all that, Mair?' She nodded.

But Evan had nothing else to attend to for an hour or so. He had done all he could for the present. He had stirred up a hive of purposeful activity around him where everyone knew what to do. The kitchens would be put to use again and they could all survive for a week or two. Now he desperately needed to be alone, to rest for an hour. Weak from hunger and strain he walked unsteadily up the grassy slope into the privacy of the wood and fell face down on the cold leaves. He had earned a brief sleep.

It did not come. Overwrought, his thoughts wandered past the coming week to the months and years ahead. Which was right enough, for immediate concerns could now be left to others. He must think of the future, at least until Eluned had recovered her old competence. Then he could leave - or stay to help her should she wish it. If Ioan's lawyers had done their work she would surely inherit Neuadd Siriol and keep it - unless she married. Don't think of that! But inherit what? A ruin beyond repair and beyond her means to rebuild even should she wish to now her father was dead.

What means - what income - would she have? She would need a new bailiff - in his mind's eye he saw Beynon's corpse smouldering on the forecourt and then Ioan and Ralph lying dead in the house and as hideously burnt. He had not thought about recovering their bodies! But that must be later: the ruined house was too hot still. Then he must see to their burial! Dear God! He could not think of everything at once!

Now came a grim thought. The house, the only home Eluned had known, the core of her too-sheltered life, has gone. Where will she live - and young Catrin too? Then a more terrible thought: I have still to tell her that her father is dead!

It was too much. Exhausted and at last alone Evan broke down. He lay on the cold leaves wracked by dry sobs. In his agony he knew no-one would hear him; no-one must hear him. And he must pick himself up and carry on.

Men were hard at work clearing away the debris around the house. Amongst them Thomas, sweating and grimy, became aware he had not seen Evan for some time. Instantly he felt the absence of his guiding hand in this chaos. Where was he? Lying injured somewhere? He must find him.

Then to his relief he saw Evan's dishevelled figure crossing the forecourt. Pale streaks ran down his begrimed face and he staggered slightly. For all his youthful strength Thomas instantly recognised the exhaustion Evan was feeling.

'Where were you, Evan? I missed you!'

'Taking a breather: I'm not twenty like you.' Evan's voice was determinedly brisk but devoid of its usual timbre. He looked at Thomas. He had developed deep affection for this youngster almost as a father. There was no call to explain himself further. But suddenly he needed to.

'- and readying myself to face Eluned! About her father' he added weakly.

'You've not told her yet?'

'She was asleep - not asleep - shocked - not thinking straight - you know ....'

'Well she's awake and thinking now: Catrin told me.' He looked keenly at Evan. 'I know too well how hard it will be. But get it over with, man.'

'I'm just going.' Yet Evan lingered, gazing at the smouldering ruins. 'When can we get in there and get them - the bodies - out of there?'

'We can get into the edges now and into the heart of it within the hour if we tread carefully. Evan: are you going to tell her or not?'

'I'm going. You begin the search. I'll be back as soon as ....'

Save for a few injured folk in one corner the barn was almost deserted; everyone who could was helping outside and others had returned to their cottages: Evan was grateful for some privacy. Eluned had been moved to Thomas's cot in the loft. Wearily Evan climbed its ladder. She was propped up on a makeshift pillow of straw and sacking, her face drawn and pale. Catrin sat beside her, strained but composed:her dog, who would not leave her and had whined until he had been carried up the ladder, lay heavily across her knees. As he reached them Catrin stood up, looked meaningfully at him and went down the ladder without a word. So he was to break the news alone. He must summon all his remaining control.

At last he could look closely at Eluned's face, into her eyes. A little expression had returned to them and she managed a wan smile of recognition. But her voice was weak. 'Evan! It is you - after all these years! Catrin told me you had come back – what? – why? - I don't understand. But we can talk properly later when I'm better. She said it was you saved me from that dreadful fire. And I was too faint to recognise you! How can I ever thank you?'

Evan kept his voice steady. 'You were overcome by the smoke, mistress. But it was not I but Father Prior who bought you down those burning stairs and safe outside: I only carried you here.'

'Call me Eluned, please. It was Ralph who saved me? Dear Ralph!' Her eyes brightened then widened in sudden alarm. 'Ralph - and Tada! What of them? Are they safe? Evan, where are they?'

He couldn't do this. He hesitated; drew back. 'They're both - still at the fire. Everyone is helping there. I must go back there soon to help.' Take it slow for her sake. And mine. One thing at a time. A minute more before ….

He took a deep breath. 'Mistress - Eluned. Listen. I must tell you Neuadd Siriol has gone - destroyed - burnt to the ground. I'm so sorry.' This was bad: this had been her home. And so much worse was coming.

'Our house all gone? Nothing left standing?' Nothing saved?

'Only the blackened walls of the old hall. I'm so sorry!'

'Oh God!' She leaned forward, buried her face in her hands, became utterly still. There were five grey strands in the crown of her dark hair. Her silence was unbearable: he must say something into it. 'But only the house has gone. You still have your estate.' Her hand crept out timidly and he dared to take it in both of his. It was ice cold.

Do it now. Tell her now: get it over with now. Again he hesitated; took another deep breath. Now! 'Eluned, I have worse, far worse, to tell you.' He paused for another moment and then spoke quickly, the words tumbling out. 'You were always the strong one: you must bear this. I'm so sorry, but your father is dead. So very sorry. He tightened his grip on her limp hand.

Very slowly she raised her head, looked blankly at him. 'Dead? Tada dead? He nodded slowly, needing more words. 'The fire spread so fast. We couldn't get to him. We tried - God we tried! It was all so fast, can you remember how fast? I'm so sorry.'

Her body sagged forward again. A slow tear fell and glistened on the back of his hand covering hers, then another. He took her in his arms then and her living hair brushed his cheek. Her tears were flowing silently now and he rocked her slowly to and fro, to and fro like a little child. Neither spoke but he felt the relieving tears and the gentle rocking drawing them closer, uniting them. He was holding her, comforting her. He had never known such closeness, felt such love.

Holding her in the quiet barn Evan's mind turned again to the future. Her future: he had forgotten his. He had thought about this in the wood. Think it through now! Her life need not be over. Parents die and Ioan had been very old. She would grieve but in time come to terms with it: everyone must lose parents. What was left of the estate was still hers, the home farm would still pay its way, her tenants must still pay their rent. She would have enough to live on and more. And Ioan must hold money in a stout locked coffer somewhere: that might have survived. He must find it for her before someone else did! She could bear this: she was ever courageous, ever mistress of her situation. Eluned would survive.

But crucially she lacked a steward. She had managed her household splendidly but never the entire estate. She could master its money matters and oversee everything but no woman could handle the complex routines of a large estate - nor would she have the time. Aston would soon be gone - Thomas had told him that he planned to leave once his leg was mended enough to sit a horse. She must never be landed with another Beynon - again Evan pictured that smoking thing on the forecourt. Her father had shown poor judgement there or, more likely, no-one better could be found. But he must find her someone capable, someone to be trusted with a woman on her own. But who in this sparsely peopled land where Ioan, for all his connections, had failed?

The inevitable answer still surprised him. Himself! It was so obvious now. He knew farming hereabouts, knew this valley and its people, knew from last night that people would follow his lead. This then was how he could serve her! As for himself he needed to come home and stay home, to farm again, to have a proper roof over his head - the steward's cottage would be luxury after his monk's cell and his recent experiences. This could work so well for both of them - if she would agree!

And why should she not? She must know from her father what he had achieved years ago in his farm across the valley, must know he would make a worthy steward. In the wood an hour ago such thoughts of the future had overwhelmed him into despair. Now they uplifted him. Working with her to save this place would be a glorious challenge. He had seen how vulnerable she was now, but with his support she would become her calm strong self again. He could give her that support and at last find his contentment in it. Never had he felt such clarity of purpose, felt so strong as now with his arms around her, rocking her gently! They would be mistress and steward together; mistress and faithful servant, for she would always rank above him even though the gap between them had narrowed with the loss of her home and his new and wondrous freedom from the guilt and shame of felony. He would ask only to serve her and he could do so now with head held high.

She had fallen half asleep half swoon in his arms. Very gently he laid her back on the straw and covered her with her brychan. He looked down at her, marvelling at their closeness. Her eyes were closed, a bluish tinge on the skin below. She looked so fragile, so different from her old self. He could stay a few more minutes looking at her, cherishing her.

But now another thought plunged him back into despair. She had nowhere to live - with winter upon them! The steward's cottage was probably the only unoccupied dwelling left intact and he would be living there himself as steward if …. But of course she must have it: he would make shift in the barn. But could the mistress of a manor raised in hall and parlour and surrounded by servants live in a cottage? Could she even oversee her estate from it? Impossible! She would need a secure counting house, a still room for her physicking and much else. And where would her women servants live should they remain? Even for the most basic of her needs and duties the steward's cottage would have to be greatly enlarged and improved. And there was Catrin, too! He smiled briefly. That problem at least he might hope to dismiss. Thomas, that admirable youth thrust so quickly into manhood, would care for Catrin - let no-one dare stop him. They were made for each other.

Eluned stirred but did not awaken. He laid his hand gently on her forehead and presently she lay still again, her breathing more regular.

But as steward neither could he manage the estate from a cot in the barn: there would be records to keep and he must have security for them and for money, too. They would need another cottage for himself and his work. Two building projects at the same time! What would that cost? How much labour that should be at work on the land? Was there enough seasoned timber in store to make a start - an immediate start if they were to survive this winter? He closed his eyes. It could not be done. He had been day-dreaming.

Unless! If she would marry him their immediate need would be a single dwelling. For now they could just enlarge the steward's cottage, a far more manageable project. But with the thought of marriage to her his practical thoughts became trivia: longing for her welled up to sweep them away. Could it be possible after all? He knew he would be released from the lesser vows he had taken - something, of course, she as yet knew nothing about - and be free to marry. And knew himself a new man now, a stronger man reconciling to his loss of faith, freed from his earlier guilt for Beynon's death, confidently come to terms with his re-entry into this world outside the cloister and seeing a place for him in it. His family was as old as hers and he had learning if no match for hers. Eluned was alone and vulnerable now and a husband was far better protection than a mere steward. He could be both. He could do this!

Again a wild swing from hope to despair. Six years ago she had shown no personal interest in him: why accept him now? He was almost forty, a penniless man who had disappeared for six years and as suddenly re-appeared. Hardly an augury for stability let alone for love!

She would see him as a man after her wealth - whatever was left of it - for as her husband it would become his in law. And that must never be!

Then what? Then it must be the stewardship only. He would ask her to consider that. Or marriage in form only so that at least he could protect her, look after her. He would ask nothing more, somehow keep his longing for her to himself.

Eluned gave a soft cry and stirred. Her long eyelashes flickered and her deep brown eyes opened. Slowly recognised him. Did not smile.

She seemed confused. 'I must have slept again. I …. can't remember. I ….' He saw her flinch. He saw that she had she recalled that her father was dead. Her voice faltered.

But the new Evan's voice was firm, persuasive. 'Eluned. You know the worst now. Believe me, you will get over this. While you slept I could not help but think about your future. Forgive my boldness but I know we can help each other, you and I. May I tell you….?' She stared at him blankly as he told her his thoughts, fluent in his new confidence. When at last he had finished there was long silence.

'Well?'

'What?'

'I have been telling you about ….'

'Becoming my steward? I remember …. I can't think about that now.' Her eyes were looking past him but surely they were brighter?

'Of course not. I'm sorry. It's too soon and I should not have troubled you now. Forgive me. But Eluned, we have so little time for repairs and rebuilding before the big snows come and then we must prepare for the spring planting. Will you think about what I have said soon - as soon as you feel up to it?' She nodded abstractedly. She was staring past his shoulder.

Evan ploughed on: 'I have been thinking where you can live in the meantime. Could you endure living in the steward's cottage for a while? I know it's not good enough for you, but just until I can build you something better?'

She looked at him then. 'Live there with my new steward?' The ghost of a smile crossed her pale face. Evan was embarrassed yet pleased. She was coming back.

'No, no, I didn't mean … of course not! I would stay here in the barn.'

She was still with him. 'No need for that, you could have your old house back.' Seeing his bewilderment she struggled to sit up and explain, her voice a little stronger. 'After you'd been gone all those years, Evan, your pastures between our tenancies across the valley were sore neglected, little but thistles. In the end we decided you had gone for ever. So Tada bought your farm - such legal wrangling with no proven seller - and joined your land to one of his adjoining farms. But your house stayed empty and still is, much neglected now. You could return to live there. And Tada held your money from the sale, not knowing how to pay it. That is yours, too.'

She sank back weak from talking. But it's done her good to think of practical matters, Evan thought. She's going to be alright. And his old house back: even some money! It would be a bit far from his work as steward but worth the extra walking - he was hardened to that. Perhaps he could buy a horse! He felt excitement mounting, a foretaste of joy. This is going to work!

Carried away by his new hope the old taciturn Evan could not check his torrent of words, was hardly aware of them. He talked about his plans for the stewardship, detail on detail. Then, abruptly, he fell silent. His love for this woman, so long suppressed, and his vision of being close to her overwhelmed him. He forgot his plans. His words tumbled out again. 'Eluned - cariad. I love you - always have, always will. Will you marry me? I'm not good enough and I know you can't love me like - but I won't ask to - to share your bed. Only to live and work by your side. We can make a good team, you and I. Together we can rebuild your home. Be companions, grow old together instead of lonely apart. I would never ask more. I ….'

She wasn't listening. She wasn't looking at him. She was bolt upright now, hand over mouth, staring past his shoulder again. Her eyes were shockingly bright, wild as he had never seen them. When she spoke her ever-beguiling voice had turned harsh.

'Ralph! I knew there was something! How could I have forgotten him? Forgotten Ralph! But you would go on talking and talking, you kept talking on and on and on. I couldn't think. What of Ralph?'

'What ….?'

'Ralph. Is he safe? Evan, where is Ralph?'

Ralph? She must mean Father Ralph. Why was she using Father Prior's given name all the time? Of course, he hadn't got around yet to telling her he too was dead. More pain for her, yet not to be compared with that of losing her father, which she had borne. She could bear the prior's death well enough.

Evan sounded almost casual. 'You mean the prior, Father Ralph? I didn't finish telling you. After he carried you out of the house he went back into that fire for your father. It was a brave thing he did, Eluned, but quite hopeless. He …..'

'Where is Ralph?'

'Still in the house. He couldn't get your father out - nobody could have saved him: I know, I went back there to help. But by then it was hopeless. He couldn't get himself out either. Father Prior is dead, too, I'm sorry for it. They are searching for the bodies now and I must go to help them. Eluned, about the stewardship ….'

Eluned stared blindly past him then suddenly fell back on the cot, hands over face, her fingernails clawing. A tiny trickle of bright blood emerged between two finger tips. There she lay rigid as death in a silence that seemed endless. When at last it came her long wavering shriek was heard on the forecourt. Then the barn was silent and still again.

Matthew groped for his staff and raised himself painfully from his straw bed. He thought he could hear a man who sounded like Evan - surely not - and the mistress talking up in the loft. But the almost empty barn was quiet enough for him to hear the activity outside.

Last night he had followed the others to help fight the fire but in his weakness had fallen twice and returned abjectly to the barn, feeling useless. He had prayed for all the household, that all would be safe. Then he had slept a little.

Now, leaning against the barn door, he saw for the first time in daylight the full horror of the smoking ruin that yesterday had been a home and his refuge. Men were busy clearing away debris. He must try once more to help them: there must be something he could do. Leaning on his staff he hobbled to the ruin. Among the workers there he saw Francis in his lay clothing. As he went to speak to him a single terrible scream came from the barn behind him. A woman's voice. The mistress? One of the injured? But whoever it was up there would see to it.

Francis, tugging at a charred piece of crossbeam, had no time for his once inseparable friend. No more time for church or abbey either, unlike Matthew who seemed to have time for naught else and had withdrawn from everyone in sullen silence. His voice was cold: 'You ask what you can do to help here? You, Matthew? Nothing!'

'Francis, there are injured folk in the barn. Are any more hurt? I have prayed no-one would die and no more suffer.'

'Then your prayers go unanswered. The old master and Father Prior are in here somewhere burnt to death. Would you like to help carry their corpses out? To grossly physical for you? Then go and pray for their souls and do it somewhere else and not under my feet.' Francis turned his back and bent again to the heavy timber.

Two men dead! Their kindly old host and Father Prior! Francis had turned cruel as well as worldly but he spoke hard truth: in his weakness all Matthew could do for them was pray. As he turned away despondently he saw Evan emerge from the barn and stumble towards them. So it was Evan come back to them in grimed lay clothing. His face ashen under its dirt and stubble he was staring blankly as if struck blind. Matthew saw him shake his head violently and then in a toneless voice he called some of the men around him. They fetched two hurdles and cautiously began searching in the still warm ruins. Others joined them, poking with sticks into the thick blanket of ash, looking for the bodies and anything else to recover.

Standing uselessly by watching them work Matthew remembered the bowl. Except for a few minutes in that dreadful bog Father Prior had kept his promise to Abbot Whiting never to let it out of his keeping. It must have been with him in his bedchamber in the house and so must now lie near his body - if not burnt to ashes! But Matthew had witnessed the bowl's miracles. The vessel used by Christ at the Last Supper could not burn in mortal fire. It was in there somewhere waiting to be found by one of those men poking around with their sticks. If and when they found it what would happen to it now that Father Prior was dead and could no longer guard it?

Not long ago that little bowl he had been holding in his hands had guided him to the old boat that had saved them all. But could it - would it - save itself? In a flash of revelation he knew it now fell to him to save it. To find it, hide it, guard it and then make known its story, the story he had already written down. Urgent but unsteady he clambered over the warm wreckage and joined the others, thrusting feebly at the thick ash with his staff.

It did not take long for Evan's men to find the blackened gristly lumps that had once been men. Trying to conceal their repugnance they lifted them gently onto the hurdles, covered them with cloaks and carried them across the forecourt, Evan leading and four men bearing each hurdle. Folk stood aside silent, genuflected. Heads were bared and bowed as they were taken to a small storeroom to await burial.

The short daylight was fading fast. In ones and twos workers drifted wearily back to the barn bringing pathetic small objects recovered from the fire - pewter plates, knives and spoons, fire irons - before returning silently to their cottages. Soon only Matthew was left searching. He concentrated on the area near the collapsed staircase above which the prior's bedchamber had been, his staff turning over each little mound in the thick grey-white ash. He found nothing. He was tiring quickly now, leaning on his staff more and more and stopping often to regain his breath. But he would not give up. At last only one mound nearby remained unexamined, half hidden under a jagged section of burnt oak wainscot. With an effort he dragged the broken wood away and poked underneath.

He heard a sound, muffled by the ash but faintly hollow. Painfully he kicked away the ash to reveal the corner of a small wooden object. Using the sharp edge of the broken wainscot he dug around it until he could pull it out. Gasping for breath he knelt to clean its surface with the hem of his habit too reveal a small sturdy oak box, perhaps a trinket box. It was heavily charred. He could not open its locked lid but one corner and part of the adjacent side had burnt right through. On his knees he carefully inserted his trembling hand into the small gap. His groping fingers found a bundle of oiled cloths wrapped around something solid. It was too big to pull through the hole but with the end of his staff he broke away charred edges of woodwork until he could draw it out. The covering cloths were burned in patches. Carefully he unwrapped it.

And drew out the wooden bowl!

He had found it! The prior must have begged this box from Master Llywd for it had not been with him on their journey. The bowl was blacker than ever and newly charred around its lip but otherwise undamaged, having been protected by wainscot, box and wrappings. Matthew was transfixed by what he held once more in his hands. Not long ago it had saved them all: now it had protected itself, saved itself. His head bowed and his lips moved in silent prayer.

'What have you there?' Evan stood behind him, his face like stone. But his toneless voice had an edge to it.

Reverently Matthew held up the bowl. 'See, Evan! The Grail!'

Evan made no attempt to hold it. 'How did it survive the fire?' Silently Matthew pointed to its coverings. Expressionless, Evan thrust his hand into the hole in the coffer and felt around the inside.

'There was nothing else in here? You are sure?' But the small part of Evan's mind that still functioned was reassured: this was far too small to be Ioan's strong box. There might still be enough daylight left for him to find that. But he must be alone with no prying eyes watching him. He must get rid of Matthew, who looked about to collapse.

'You have done well - Brother.' A title he had not used in weeks, but the novice still held to his faith, and still wore his habit and cowl: it would please him. He stared at the haggard youth and suddenly understood.

'Now that Father Prior is dead you want to take the bowl into your keeping.' It was a statement.

Matthew clasped the bowl to his thin chest. 'It has been given into my charge now, for only I amongst you all have kept the faith.' His weak voice carried utter conviction, his look contempt and challenge. Dulled though his mind was Evan winced, for this stricken boy had the truth of that. He nodded; what matter now?

'Very well, Matthew: take it. But never forget our abbot's charge that it be kept secret and handed on only when …. when you know the time is right.' He could not bring himself to say 'when death comes for you', for the wasted young face told him that must be soon. Matthew nodded indifferently, needing no human instruction.

Evan asked: 'Where will you conceal it? … No, don't tell me. Don't tell anyone. You are its guardian now, Matthew. Hide it under your habit while you think on that. Go now, seek rest in the barn before you collapse. You need food as we all do. I hope Mair will have something for us tonight.'

No doubting that Matthew stood at death's door. Nothing could save him for no-one knew what had struck him down. Evan felt dimly that he should have supported him back to the poor comfort of the barn. But he watched dead-eyed as Matthew hobbled away, leaving him alone in the ruins. He had scant concern for Matthew and less for the bowl. Should he even trouble himself to look for Ioan's strong box?

For Eluned was lost to him. Lost to the world and her home lost with her and destined for oblivion. After that one appalling shriek she had fallen silent, pale and still as death except that her eyelashes twitched and she still breathed. Her body lived but her eyes were dead. He had known then that something had broken: that her mind had gone. Through his grief and exhaustion he had been bewildered, had not understood. He had watched her begin to return to life, to come to terms with Ioan's death. That strong controlled mind of hers had surely been coming back to the world, beginning to consider what he had blurted out about the future - their future. If she could bear her beloved father's dreadful death why this sudden utter collapse on hearing of Father Ralph's? Was that the last straw that had broken her?

But he knew the answer - the appalling answer - to his own question. She had loved the prior. Loved that lofty, remote, admirable man he himself had guided to her. Loved an ordained priest! She had not even heard his own misplaced, stupid declaration of love or, if she heard, had instantly dismissed it. She had only wanted to know about Prior Ralph and when he had told her he had watched helpless as she fell to pieces before his eyes. Ralph's words at the house door came back to him: 'She is precious, Evan, so precious.' So he had loved her too! But Ralph had died trying to save her father. Ralph's death had destroyed her. And her destruction had now destroyed himself.

He had sent for Catrin to watch over Eluned and then left the barn. As in a trance he had seen to the finding and removal of the bodies. Now he would look for Ioan's strongbox and see it safe for Catrin - and Thomas.

But why trouble himself with that - or with anything else in this place? Yet he knew he must. Because so many had depended on Ioan the good master - young Catrin, the household servants, the estate workers and their families, too. Who would see to their needs through the winter now Eluned was gone from them, too? Ioan's money was needed for all of them. He must find that strongbox and give it to Catrin to keep and use as Eluned would have done. It would fall to young Thomas to comfort a grieving Catrin, to see to all who depended on Neuadd Siriol, as far as possible even into an unimaginable future. Young Thomas and Catrin must now grow up too quickly, but they had each other. He himself, who had nothing, would be finished here.

Matthew lay on his straw bed barely breathing. He was dimly aware of people returning heavy footed to the barn, of the murmur of bone-weary voices. He thought that was Mistress Catrin crying up in the loft - he had heard her light step run past him but had not seen her because his sight seemed to be failing him. There was something he should have done. What? He must think! With great effort he remembered. Before he died he must pass both the bowl and its story into other hands for safekeeping - even though none about him were worthy to receive it. Already it might be too late and he might fail in that charge! He struggled to sit up, clutching for the bowl and the crumpled roll of shaky writing that bulked under his habit. Tried to speak.

Someone else was hurrying past now. Matthew's voice croaked and the person stopped, looming over him. In his darkening vision he just made out Thomas, who was looking for Catrin. Thomas could barely hear the novice's feeble words and stooped closer. At once he sensed that Matthew was now close to death. Despite their arduous journey together he had little in common with the novice but he felt a pang of grief for one dying so young - no older than himself.

Thomas! No more a true believer than the others but young as himself and still untainted by the sordid world. His transparent wholesomeness were not wholly unworthy - and his own time had run out. 'Thomas! Thank God you have come! Take these!' Matthew's skeletal fingers clawed at his habit. Curiously reluctant, Thomas helped Matthew draw out that old bowl and a crumpled roll of papers. Matthew sank back gasping with the effort. When he spoke again Thomas bent still closer to hear.

'…… the True Grail: here it is. It has passed into my keeping …. too little time God granted me …. now I cannot ….. cannot ….. Thomas, you must guard it now, preserve it from harm, keep its secret and return it to Mother Church when you judge it safe. Here - look - I have written its story, told of its power. Mother Church must know of this. So take these papers. Guard them also and preserve them and pass them on with the bowl, if need be to Rome itself.' His voice faded into silence.

For a moment his weak grip on Thomas's hand tightened. 'Thomas. You must do this for me! For Holy Church. I have your solemn promise?' Thomas hardly comprehended what he was hearing. He hesitated.

'Protect your Grail? This poor broken thing? Mathew, how can I? Reformists meddle everywhere and I have no home now, no stout door to lock. How preserve it, for years, perhaps all my life? And how can I hope to return it to the True Church?

'I found it in a little box, charred but sturdy enough if repaired. Evan knows where. Mend that with your skill with wood and it will serve.' Thomas saw that Matthew clung fervently to that old legend and his intensity frightened him. He was deeply reluctant. But he could not deny the dying youth. He promised.

Matthew spoke once more. 'I'm sorry I could not write a better account of our journey together and our refuge here. I began some sentences on the feast - although I did not care for such merriment. But I had no time left so I set that aside. My mind was filled with the Grail. But God did not grant me the strength to finish its story.'

After a pain-racked pause he continued, his voice ever fainter. 'Thomas, my death matters nothing. Only the Grail and its miracles matters and that Holy Church shall learn of it through my poor words. For all the doubts I know you harbour this is now for you to undertake. You have promised. So take the Grail and these poor scribblings. God speed you good Thomas - doubting Thomas!' There was the faintest of smiles on his lips as he died. Very gently Thomas closed Matthew's eyes, picked up the little wooden bowl and the crumpled roll of papers, thrust them under his jerkin and made for the loft and Catrin's tears.

Ioan was laid to rest at the local parish church Aston, Francis, Catrin and Thomas arranged everything with no help from a numbed and distant Evan. News of the fire and Ioan's death had spread and neighbours filled the small building, some bearing gifts of food and clothing. Eluned was not there: still as death in her makeshift cot in the barn loft, stone eyes open but unseeing, she was unaware of it. She was not anywhere. Ioan was interred in the family plot with his wife and sons. There was no wake and the visitors were quick to leave for their scattered homes before darkness fell.

There was anxious discussion about burying the two monks, friar and novice. They had been brothers of a now abolished order. They had been fugitives accused of serious crime and no-one could be certain their pursuit had been officially abandoned - or their presence at Neuadd Siriol never betrayed. Harbouring them even in death might still be dangerous and their sojourn for months in the household was unlikely to have remained a secret. Ioan's people were surely loyal to him yet someone might have talked, perhaps inadvertently.

In the end it was decided to bury them secretly. The old parish priest, enjoined to secrecy but fearful, would conduct the last rites. To their dismay the servants and estate workers were told that only the family and the remaining guests might attend the burial. Because the ruined hall was abandoned and unlikely to be rebuilt its sturdy remnant, the cellar, would be used for the internment. Total secrecy was unlikely but they hoped for the best. They could do no more.

In the dark cellar where the two bodies lay in the coffins Thomas had knocked up in haste - hating his enforced poor workmanship - he and Francis set up torches and swept the floor clean. Then with cold chisels and mallets they prised up enough of the massive old flagstones to dig two graves side by side in the dry packed earth below. As the graves would be protected from the weather by the replaced flagstones and by the stone ceiling above they were dug shallower than usual. They would be unmarked.

Thomas said he would finish up while Francis went to call the priest and the others to the burial. Left alone he gazed at the two graves with their mounds of freshly turned earth and the raised flagstones stacked alongside. He was deeply troubled by Matthew's dying request. He had promised to safeguard the bowl. Now it lay in its little box in a sack in the corner - with utter indifference Evan had fetched it to him and he had mended it roughly and nailed the bowl in its wrappings inside.

Only Matthew had believed it was the Grail. He would honour his promise to guard it - but from what? And return it to Mother Church - 'when you judge it safe' Matthew had said. When would that be? Years? Never? Matthew had been right to call him Doubting Thomas for he could not believe the legend. So did all this matter?

The answer he could not avoid was yes! Yes because it had mattered so desperately to Matthew, who had died un-shriven yet comforted - he must believe that - by his promise given, a promise he would keep. In his own way.

For Thomas knew now what he must do. He was indeed unworthy of the charge laid upon him. It had been mere chance that he had passed by a dying man who had no-one else to turn to. As Matthew himself was the only one of them worthy of the charge he must take the bowl with him in death. It was his by right to guard and his alone, even in eternity. If someday on this earth, somehow, it was to be handed on then Matthew, who had kept his faith and believed he had witnessed its miracles must by some new miracle find the means to do so. Or, if he had been right about the bowl's sanctity it would find its own means. Picking up his spade he dug deeper into the darkest corner of Matthew's open grave and placed the box into the small deeper hole he had made.

From his jerkin he drew out the roll of crumpled paper. He did not unroll it for he read slowly and the light was poor: anyway Matthew had told him what he had set down there. Nor had he the time, for the others would be on their way. He hesitated. If he placed the unprotected scroll in the hole alongside the bowl then time and decay would soon destroy it. He should have wrapped it in the box with the bowl. Now he had nothing on him that would protect it and already he heard slow footsteps above as the others approached the top of the cellar stairs. Quickly Thomas covered the bowl with soil and smoothed the earth on the floor of the open grave until it was even all over. The papers he stuffed back under his shirt to be dealt with later.

In the cellar under the flickering torchlight they buried a prior and a novice monk of the old faith, doubter and believer. The bodies lay in their crude coffins, which still smelled sourly of the charred house timbers from which they were made. For this secret interment some ritual was omitted; some could not be. The old parish priest still possessed a vibrant singer's voice but, distressed and confused, his Latin stumbled. Catrin, Thomas, Francis and Aston gathered around him, the torchlight wavering on their bowed heads and dancing across the rough cellar walls.

Evan stood apart from the others, deep in shadow against the back wall. He had not found Ioan's strongbox but the head groom had stumbled upon it. An honest man who had revered his master, he had brought it to Evan still locked and intact. Evan had passed it to Catrin. At her request Thomas had forced the stout lock and she had showed them the money inside it. It was less than Evan had hoped for them but would give the youngsters the means to find some shelter and care for Eluned through the winter, if not for long beyond that. It would rest with them alone what would happen afterwards for Aston and

Francis were leaving immediately for Hereford. Their burden seemed an impossible one but they were young, had their lives to pick up from the ashes and live again. Above all they had each other. He had nothing; no-one. Any future that could be snatched from this desolation would be for them. He was done with this place. Taking no part in the brief service Evan saw only the flickering shadows, heard little and felt less. The priest's familiar words washed over him: in their hypnotic sonority his numbed mind drifted to Glastonbury. The abbey would be surrendered soon, perhaps had been by now - there had been no news. The last abbey standing in the west country and the greatest, it would have ended its days like every other monastic house. In his mind's eye he could see Abbot Whiting, frail but dignified, signing the document of surrender at a cold formal ceremony in the great octagonal chapter house, then handing over the abbey keys - there would be some such ceremony. Then the monks shuffling up one by one to sign for their pensions. The name given to this madness was 'Dissolution.' Dissolution - disintegration, decomposition - a good enough name. The end of an era. End of a world.

Dimly Evan recalled Ioan's funeral yesterday, where again he had stood apart from the others at the back of the parish church. Now in this cold cellar he watched as Ralph and Matthew were lowered into unmarked graves under a ruined house that he felt sure would never be rebuilt. Despite everything he had been brought up to believe, he knew now that life went its own uncontrollable indifferent way. Here at Neuadd Siriol he was witnessing a parallel dissolution to that at Glastonbury. Here too only oblivion lay ahead. He did not care. He was not here. For she was forever absent.

Slowly, silently, they trailed up the stone staircase and gathered outside on the cleared space that had been the cross passage, Evan as always well behind. The wooden screen between passage and hall had burnt away and they gazed directly at the lumpy blackened wreckage stretching across the hall floor wide open to the sky. At last that sky showed small patches of blue, pale but slowly widening. In silence they saw weak sunlight shimmering in the last of the rising warmth from the dead fire. They gazed at it silent and mesmerised.

Then, in the silence, they heard the bird singing. A whistling warbling call followed by a sharper tic, tic, tic. A little bird. They could not see it in the heat-shimmering light over the wreckage of Neuadd Siriol. Then their eyes were following Catrin's outstretched arm, her finger pointing. Momentarily the bird appeared to flutter up in the heart of the shimmering shaft of heated air rising above the wreckage; tiny, cheeky, gaily orange-breasted against the patched blue of the sky.

Evan saw that this was illusion. The little bird was flying upwards well behind the rising column of air, returning to its perch high on the heat-cracked and blackened wall of the ruined hall. A common robin about its common tiny business.

Without a word he turned away, his heavy footsteps breaking the spell. He was going north again and this time there would be no turning back. Then Aston and Francis turned to leave together for Hereford.

Catrin and Thomas, her dark head on his shoulder, were left alone together. Utterly still they watched the bright bird rising into the blue sky.

Daylight was fading when they made out the true land ahead. Since leaving their ship they had rowed and poled the small boat, sometimes helped by a fitful breeze disturbing the single limp sail. The ten younger men taking turns at oars and poles were exhausted now, the middle-aged man at the steering oar and the bent old man seated beside him giving directions in no better state. All the long day they had driven the boat through the calm shallows, following an intricate route between reed beds and mud islets that stood mere feet above the sullen still water. They had avoided larger islands crowded with the rude huts of fishing settlements where cooking fires flickered behind rough timber palisades, where children and women waiting for their men to come home with their catches watched as they passed by. They saw no other boat. The silence of their passage was broken by the rhythmic creak of the oars, the drip of poles, the cries of water birds; rarely by their own tired voices.

At last they closed the true land, a long steep-sided hill of rough grass and thicket and clumps of trees, its greenness faded to dull grey in the gathering twilight. The keel grated on a tiny gravel beach as they hauled the boat ashore. Landfall! The younger men looked wearily around and then at one another but did not speak.

The old man, their leader, was helped ashore. He gazed impassively up the slope and then, grasping his staff, began very slowly to climb the hill on the arm of the helmsman, who was his son. The son carried the old man's baggage as well as his own, except for one small cloth bag the old man clutched to his chest. The others secured the boat, shouldered their scant belongings and followed in silence. Higher up the hill a dog fox watched them from under a bush.

At the highest point on the long hill the old man stopped and looked around him, breathing heavily. In full daylight this would be a commanding view point. Even now he could make out the flat sombre marsh and stretches of open water they had left behind them and, turning around, low hills receding inland. One hill close by stood isolated, steep-sided, curiously prominent.

The old man nodded. 'Here,' he said, and drove his staff deep into a cony hole. Exhaustion overcame him then and for a long minute he rested his head on his gnarled hands folded over its crook. At last with a sigh he straightened up slowly, releasing the staff which stood upright.

'I am weary all,' the old man said. The dog fox watched.

Author's Note

This novel is based on the legend of a mysterious old wooden bowl known as the Nanteos Cup, allegedly brought to Strata Florida near Aberystwyth in Wales in 1539 by monks fleeing the dissolution of Glastonbury Abbey and much later appearing at the nearby Nanteos mansion. Information about this little artefact can be accessed on the internet, including photographs and accounts of its reputed healing powers. I first heard its story as a child and later saw it for myself, but with no thought of following it up. But when reminded of it a few years ago I thought it posed some intriguing questions. Trying to answer them provided the impetus for this book.

Accepting for my purpose that the legend has some factual basis the first question was how might those monks have travelled from Glastonbury to Nanteos, presumably on foot and possibly pursued? I pored over Ordnance Survey maps and worked out a feasible route that would suit my purpose.

Secondly, why would they have ended up at Nanteos, on the face of it an unlikely choice of destination? What decisions did they take - or were forced on them by circumstances - that led them from the great English abbey to the remote Tudor manor – a manor that in my story would have preceded by two centuries the present eighteenth century mansion on this site?

Working out a route and plausible reasons for taking it led me to the third question, the characters of those fugitive men and their leader, their prior. What kind of men might they have been? What were their feelings as they stole away from their abbey, abandoning sheltered and severely ordered lives to venture into a strange and surely threatening world? How would they have coped with the loss of familiar context, of every touchstone in their lives as the entire realm must have seemed to be spiralling into chaos about them? How might the physical hardships, uncertainties and hazards of their journey have affected these hitherto cloistered men; how changed them as it progressed? Would their faith have remained resolute in such adversity? And as individuals as well as members of a community how might their reactions have differed one from another? Could character differences have created tensions between them? (I replaced two of the monks with abbey laymen in order to increase the possibility of this).

The legend has it that at least some of the monks found lasting shelter at Nanteos where they became variedly employed and in some fashion absorbed permanently into the household. When they died they left behind the enigmatic little Cup. It was destined to be long forgotten but to achieve remarkably sudden fame again almost four centuries later for its healing powers and was believed by some to be the true Grail itself. This linked it back to the legend that Joseph of Arimathea had brought it to Glastonbury.

There are obvious difficulties here and my final question was how, given the sketchiness of the legend, might all this have worked itself out? In particular how might these fugitives have interacted with my Tudor household?

As usual and proper with legends there is a dearth of facts and surfeit of speculation but I am solely responsible for any 'factual' errors. To anyone familiar with the legend it will be evident that my version ends differently from what might be termed the 'orthodox' one: but this is fiction after all. I accept that corridors did not exist in Britain until the Seventeenth Century. But I could not have my ladies barging into guest chambers occupied by strange male intruders, so corridors they have. The affliction that eventually killed Matthew was Lyme disease. I hope it existed in the Sixteenth Century: if it did it would certainly not have been understood.

And so my story grew as one version of the legend. But I also claim a small family interest in the Cup, which helped sustain my interest. The last direct head of the Powell family that had occupied Nanteos since the eighteenth century (his only son was killed in France in 1918, a few days before the Armistice) instructed his estate carpenter to make a box or case to house the Cup, perhaps anticipation of its future wanderings. And wander it did, after his death it seems to have sojourned in several bank vaults before finding a new home with a family in Herefordshire.

That carpenter was my grandfather, much later allowing my irreverent teen-age self to claim 'My Grandad made a box for the Holy Grail! Wow!' Good for a family smile or two. I hope I have shown more respect now.

But the Nanteos Cup itself deserves the last (latest?) word. In July 2014 it was reported on the television news to have been stolen from a house in Herefordshire where it was on loan to a sick lady – evidently still at its healing work! It seems the thief took only that one old, blackened, tired and broken little mazer bowl, by now broken and held together with wire. Nothing else. And then a year later (2015) it was reported that it had been as suddenly returned. What can one make of that?

About the Author

D.H. Davies is a former academic now living in retirement in Somerset.